MAKING HER MARK

MAKING HER MARK

P.D. WORKMAN

ISBN: 9781988390680 (IS Hardcover)

ISBN: 9781988390673 (IS Paperback)

ISBN: 9781988390635 (KDP Paperback)

ISBN: 9781988390642 (Kindle)

ISBN: 9781988390659 (ePub)

ALSO BY P.D. WORKMAN

YOUNG ADULT FICTION:

Between the Cracks:

Ruby

June and Justin

Michelle

Chloe

Ronnie

June, Into the Light

Tamara's Teardrops:

Tattooed Teardrops

Two Teardrops

Tortured Teardrops

Vanishing Teardrops

Medical Kidnap Files:

Mito

EDS

Proxy

Toxo

Pain

Breaking the Pattern:

Deviation

Diversion

By-Pass

Stand Alone YA novels

Stand Alone

Don't Forget Steven

Those Who Believe

Cynthia has a Secret

Questing for a Dream

Darkness before the Dream (prequel story)

Once Brothers

Intersexion

Making Her Mark

Endless Change

Gem, Himself, Alone

MYSTERY/SUSPENSE:

Parks Pat Mysteries

Out with the Sunset

Long Climb to the Top

Dark Water Under the Bridge

Immersed in the View (Coming Soon)

Skimming Over the Lake (Coming Soon)

Hazard of the Hills (Coming Soon)

AND MORE AT PDWORKMAN.COM

To all of those trying to make their mark on the world

CHAPTER 1

Kelli scanned the area around her. Her heart thumped hard and fast, but she forced herself to slow down and carefully consider her surroundings. It was three against one and she wasn't going to come out on top unless she used all of her resources. Sensei always told her she was too rash. She rushed into things. Rushed her attack when she should be making a plan and sizing up her opponent. But in the dojo, she knew all her opponents. She had fought them all before and knew their strengths and weaknesses. This was different.

Two boys and a girl. Clark was taller and probably had thirty pounds on her. Michael was closer to her size. Then there was Lizzie, shorter than Kelli but clearly heavier, a chunky, smiley girl who was as mean as a snake. She was a blond now, but Kelli could remember when her hair had been mouse brown, like Kelli's, when they were in the younger grades.

At first, Kelli hadn't been paying attention. She had just been walking through the park on her way home, like she did every other day. But something hadn't felt right. Her subconscious mind must have picked up on her pursuers. Starting to get jumpy, she had looked around and realized she was being tailed.

It would have been one thing if they had stayed together, laughing at her and catcalling like the gruesome threesome was wont to do. They were bullies, but usually they just kept each other entertained with verbal abuse.

Lizzie was still behind Kelli. Walking steadily, keeping an even distance.

Clark and Michael were flanking her. Even though Kelli picked up her pace, they were still moving faster than she was, pincering her between them, blocking her in. When Kelli looked around for help, there was no one nearby who was likely to be of any service to her. Little kids playing cops and bangers. Older men at the chess tables on the north end. Occasional teens like herself, on their own, headed for home. Loners, keeping their eyes averted and hoping to avoid trouble.

Kelli could hear Lizzie closer behind her and glanced over her shoulder. The girl was definitely closing in. She gave Kelli a brilliant smile, like a shark might give to its dinner.

"Something wrong, Smelly Kelli? Wait up, I want to talk."

"I'm not talking to you," Kelli asserted. Though obviously, she was. She knew she was surrounded. Talking was a stall. She was trying to work out what she was going to do, evaluating the strengths and weaknesses of the three players.

"Don't you want to talk about your *boyfriend?*" Lizzie taunted. "I just wanted to make sure he was okay. He didn't get his feelings hurt, did he?"

Kelli swore in answer. It would have been nice if Les had walked home with her. He wasn't her boyfriend, but at least she would have had better numbers on her side. Les wasn't a fighter, but he would split their attention.

"He's not my boyfriend," Kelli snapped.

"Oh, that's right. He doesn't like girls, does he? Is that why the two of you hang out together? He loves dogs?"

"Why don't you and your friends go bug someone else," Kelli suggested. Brilliant. That little jab was sure to convince them to leave her alone.

Michael was moving in the fastest, just two paces from her. Kelli made her decision and drove toward him. *Go on the offensive. Don't wait for him to make the first move.* He actually stepped back, making eye contact with the two others, not sure of what to do with Kelli.

She didn't give him any longer to think, but went straight for his eyes. She wasn't going to have much time to deal with any of the three. Her goal had to be to disable them as quickly as she could. Even with one of them down, that still left two, one to hold her down while the other used her as a punching bag. Michael jumped back, but was too slow to avoid Kelli's clawed fingers. He howled, bringing his hands up to his face to protect his eyes too late. Kelli slammed a palm into his nose and he doubled over, giving a shriek.

Clark and Lizzie attacked together, leaving nothing to chance. Both came at her swinging, trying to get her down before she was able to defend herself. But Kelli had practiced two-on-one attacks endlessly. Her training kicked in and she was a whirl of arms and feet, hitting, kicking, clawing, grappling, whatever it took to keep an edge on the attackers. There were shouts as people saw what was going on, but no one was brave enough to jump into the fight to stop them or to try to even the odds.

Almost too late, she realized Michael was back in the fight. Scratches on his face and blood streaming from his nose weren't enough to stop him. Kelli aimed a head-butt at him. He was a nice height. Just right for the top of her head to hit his nose. No matter that it was already bleeding, she went for it again, hoping to hear it break this time. Maybe that would keep him down for longer.

But it was Clark who went down next. Kelli got a lucky jab to his solar plexus, and while he was sucking wind, a high kick to the chin caught him off guard and he went down like a log. Lizzie was the only one left fighting. Michael wasn't out, but he was staggering around with his hands over his face, and Kelli wasn't sure whether he would recover well enough to reenter the fight. She wasn't about to wait around and see.

Lizzie was a force to be reckoned with. Despite her flabby figure, she was strong. Kelli warded off Lizzie's attack, letting her wear herself down while Kelli waited for the right opportunity to disable her. Lizzie was a street fighter with no apparent training that Kelli could spot. She might be able to defeat others with brute force and some dirty moves, but Kelli was careful, and sooner or later Lizzie was going to open herself up. Kelli couldn't keep an eye out to be sure the three fighters weren't joined by anyone else. They had other friends and followers at school. If one or two of them spotted the fight in the park and decided to lend a hand, Kelli was going to be in trouble. Three of them were bad enough. Even Lizzie by herself was formidable. Kelli didn't want to be fighting the entire posse.

She didn't have long to wait before Lizzie dropped her left. Kelli drove straight in, punching Lizzie square in the jaw. Everything slowed down, just like in the movies, and Kelli saw Lizzie's face ripple with the force of the strike, saw her head whiplash back, and saw her eyes roll up for an instant. Lizzie stayed on her feet, not toppling over like Kelli had hoped. Lizzie took a step backward to steady herself and Kelli punched again, hitting her in the chest, then tried to sweep her legs to get her down on the ground. Lizzie was like a rock, her legs supporting her like two pillars. She didn't go down. But she did turn her head away, and Kelli realized in a second why she had. A siren. Michael, both hands still over his nose, gave a shout of warning and tried to stumble away. But he was too groggy, and when Kelli threw a kick into his hip, he went down.

She turned back to Lizzie. Lizzie was hurt. A little stunned, one hand wanting to reach toward her jaw to make sure it was still properly attached. Kelli tried again, kicking her behind one knee. Lizzie went down with a satisfying crash.

With all three of them on the retreat, Kelli scanned the park to make sure she had a clear path home and none of Lizzie's other goons were around.

Hard, strong hands grabbed Kelli from behind. She went limp, falling to the ground as if in a dead faint, with the full intention of sweeping the latest attacker and meeting him on the ground. She was good at close work. She did some of her best work on the floor.

But the split-second before she swept the legs out from under the new attacker, Kelli saw his uniform and stiffened, forcing herself to stop before she could be accused of resisting arrest or assaulting a cop.

"Stop! You're under arrest!" the cop shouted at her, pointing at her as if his finger was a weapon and he would deploy it if she didn't obey.

Kelli held her hands up. "Stopping, stopping," she agreed, showing him her empty palms. She stayed there, frozen, watching for the others. Until they had all been handcuffed, she couldn't let her guard down. Just because there was a cop there, that wouldn't necessarily stop any of them from hitting or kicking her while she was on the ground holding her hands up in surrender.

The cop yelled into his radio, trying to keep eyes on all four of them. Another man, either a plainclothes cop or a brave bystander, grabbed staggering Michael and took him to the ground. They were all down and Kelli gave a sigh of relief, letting her eyes close for a minute while chaos swirled around her. She tried to get centered and tried to relax her body again. She didn't open her eyes when the cop reached down and turned her over onto her belly. He gave her a swift pat-down and pulled her hands behind her back to handcuff them.

"You're under arrest," he told her again.

"It was self-defense."

"Didn't much look like self-defense to me," he sneered.

Kelli didn't bother arguing.

"Stay there!"

She didn't move. He went on and, with the help of late-arriving cops, got Lizzie and her crew handcuffed as well. It was a different cop who returned to retrieve Kelli. He pulled her to her feet. He was kind of cute for an older guy, with red cheeks and black hair just long enough to form messy curls. His name badge said Halloran. Halloran's eyes went over her, stopping briefly at the red-purple splotch on her face. He checked her pockets, pulling out her keys, change, and deck of cards and dropping them onto the ground next to her. He held on to her student ID card for a moment longer.

"Kelli Munroe."

"Yes."

"Sixteen?"

"Uh-huh."

"What happened here?"

Kelli gave a shrug. "Those three ambushed me. I just defended myself."

His eyes went to the other three teens and he shook his head, doubting her story. Kelli took a glance at each of them herself. She wasn't a big fan of violence, but she couldn't suppress a little surge of pride at what she had done. She had held the three attackers off. If the police hadn't shown up, she would have been out of there, back home safely. *That* was why she took martial arts.

Sensei would be proud. Not of her having a street fight, but of the good job she had done.

The street was bristling with emergency vehicles. Not just the police cars that had answered the initial call, but also ambulances bringing paramedics to evaluate everyone's injuries and to decide whether anyone needed to go to the hospital, and maybe a few more police cars who had brought cops who were just walking around the scene gawking, acting like they were doing something important.

A paramedic approached Kelli and Halloran. "Hey, my name is Dustin. You got this tigress under control?" he asked Halloran with a laugh.

"You can have a look at her," Halloran said without cracking a smile.

Dustin moved in to examine Kelli's face first. "How are you feeling? Any dizziness? Blurred vision?" He shone a penlight in her eyes.

"It's not a bruise," Kelli said. "It's a birthmark."

"What? Oh…" He was taken aback, and prodded Kelli's cheek for swelling or tenderness, as if he didn't believe her. "Oh, it is."

Halloran held Kelli's student ID where Dustin could see it and verify that in the picture she had an irregular red-purple mark painted over the space under her right eye, taking up most of the lower-right quadrant of her face.

"Oh, I see," Dustin said lamely. "Uh… Kelli. Do you have any injuries? Where did you get hit?"

Kelli moved her body experimentally. She had taken a few blows, she knew. She hadn't focused on them during the fight, and she was used to taking hits during practice.

"No, nothing major," she said.

He shone his light in her eyes again, examined her face more carefully for any recent injuries, and took her pulse. He shrugged at Halloran. "All clear."

Dustin moved on to help deal with the others. Michael had a broken nose and was escorted to one of the waiting ambulances. Lizzie and Clark didn't appear to have any serious injuries, though they were both complaining as if Kelli had worked them over for no reason, trying to make her out as the aggressor.

"You're claiming self-defense?" Halloran demanded. "Three against one?"

Kelli nodded. "Yeah. That's what happened. I was just going home after school."

"Where's home?"

Kelli gave him her address and his eyes went across the park, pinpointing its approximate location.

"Why would they attack you? What's the history?"

"I've known Lizzie since kindergarten. She's always been a bully. Usually, we just stay away from each other. I leave her alone and she leaves me alone. But today I got in the way when she was picking on someone else. And she didn't appreciate that."

"Picking on who? When did this happen?"

"A guy I know. Nothing happened. Just exchanged words. But she didn't like being shown up in front of her posse, so she came after me on the way home to remind me of my place."

"Who is this boy?"

Kelli shifted. She knew Les wouldn't want her bringing him into it. He just tried to fly under the radar. Avoid any kind of trouble.

"A guy I know."

"We're going to need to gather all of the relevant details and talk to everyone involved," Halloran pointed out. "I need his name."

"I don't want to get him in any trouble. If cops come knocking on his door, his mom is going to be really pissed. You could get him beaten up or thrown out."

Halloran considered this, but didn't waver from his goal. "I still need his name."

"Les," Kelli sighed. "Les Broke."

"Goes to your school?"

"Yeah. Lives in the projects."

His eyes located the slums to the west of the park, and he nodded.

"What's your relationship with this guy? He your boyfriend?"

"No. Just a friend. Known him for a long time."

"And why was Lizzie picking on him?"

"Because that's what she does. That's what bullies always do. Look for any sign of weakness, and then hone in on it. I didn't like her harassing Les, so I told her to cut it out. She did, but she was pretty steamed that I would stand up for him."

"Have the two of you been in any physical altercations before?"

"No... not since second grade... nothing the police were ever called about."

"Why today? You've known each other since kindergarten, you haven't had an ongoing feud. Why start today?"

"I didn't like her making fun of Les," Kelli insisted.

He stared into her face. Kelli looked steadily at the ground. She hated people looking at her. They would stare at her face as if fascinated by the purple birthmark. As if they'd never seen anything like it before. It wasn't like port wine birthmarks were that rare. People had them. Why act like she was some kind of freak just because she had a mark on her face?

"You're sure Lizzie wasn't making fun of *you?*"

"What's the difference? If she was making fun of me, I'd tell you. Who cares?"

"If she was making fun of you, maybe you were the one who instigated the physical fight. Maybe you got tired of her verbal harassment and decided to take action."

"I got tired of her verbal harassment a long time ago. I learned to ignore it."

"And today, something snapped. She just pushed you a little bit too far."

"No. I didn't snap. They attacked me. Michael attacked me first," Kelli nodded toward Michael. "All I did was defend myself. There were three of them!"

"You're the one who seems to have done the most damage. Maybe you attacked Lizzie and the others came to her aid."

"That's not what happened! Talk to the witnesses. There's a whole park full of them!"

Halloran's eyes went to the gawking bystanders. Plenty of people had been attracted by the lights and sirens and now wanted to know what was going on, to be involved in the excitement. Never mind that everyone had just stood by when Kelli was under attack. That was why she had needed to learn how to fight. She needed to be able to protect herself when the rest of the world was content to just stand by and watch her get beaten down.

"We will interview witnesses. But in my experience, people don't want to get involved in a thing like this. No one will admit to having seen how it all started. Who threw the first punch. All of those eyes, and no one admits to knowing what happened."

"Well, they know what happened. I didn't attack Lizzie. She and her goons attacked me. And I'm sure if you looked at her school record, you'd see that she was a troublemaker. She likes to hurt people, and I'm not the first one. Just check her record."

"We'll see what we can get access to." He gave a little shrug. "Privacy laws, you know. This wasn't on school grounds. The school is going to resist getting involved."

And Lizzie knew that. She had avoided attacking Kelli on school grounds. Too many witnesses. Too many cameras. Too many adults who might spill the beans on Lizzie.

———

There were TV cameras there before the police finally finished their investigation and took Kelli and the others to the police station. Kelli tried to keep her face averted from the cameras. No surprise, but she didn't like having her birthmarked mug broadcast all over TV. But it didn't look like she was going to be able to avoid it. The local channels needed something to spice up their newsfeed. Some fresh mayhem straight out of the projects would do nicely.

They tried to get some quotes, rushing in and blasting questions at Kelli, boom mikes held close overhead and cameras practically pressing themselves against her face. Lizzie made some noise, complaining about how Kelli had attacked her, that she was out of control and had a history, and someone needed to take her in hand. Kelli just tried to keep turned away from the camera, face pressed into her own shoulder for camouflage, and didn't give them a sound bite.

But even so, when she got into the car, she could hear the anchor approaching the police officers and witnesses with questions on the 'ninja girl going wild in the park.' Kelli rolled her eyes. Did TV anchors ever get stories right? It made her question everything she had ever heard on the news. Each story twisted a little more this way or that, some details misinterpreted, rumor reported as fact; she couldn't ever trust that a story reported was actually true in every respect.

Ninja girl? She took it as a compliment, but she studied Jujitsu, not Ninjutsu. Sensei would want to know why she hadn't corrected them, maybe pointed people toward the dojo. He could always use fresh blood, more people signing up, even if it was just for one of his weekend self-defense workshops.

Kelli had thought that once she was in the police car, they would immediately drive off to the police station. But she had forgotten how long it took the police to do everything. Even a routine traffic stop when her mother was pulled over for speeding could make her an hour late for an appointment. Her mother might not care about being late, but Kelli did. She was always embarrassed when her mother got her somewhere late. People should always follow through on their commitments and be where they were supposed to be when they said they would be. It was just common courtesy. Like not staring at people who were different or disfigured.

So instead, Kelli sat there in the car, watching the circus that played on outside the car. The police walked around the grassy area, making their observations, writing in their notepads, talking to each other. Probably discussing Sunday football more than what had actually happened in the park. How long did it take to figure out that Kelli had been ambushed, had fought for a couple of minutes, and then had been shut down by the arrival of the police? There wasn't that much evidence. There weren't that many witnesses. The whole thing had been over in a few minutes.

———

"Where did you learn to fight?" asked Bloggs, the cop who had introduced himself to her after she was taken to the police station and put in a conference room, where again she sat for what seemed like hours. He was an older cop, looking near retirement age, and had a nervous habit of stroking his hair back while he was thinking. Maybe the reason he was getting so thin on top.

"Golden Dragon Dojo," Kelli told him.

She could see the surprise cross his face. He smoothed his hand over his head. "You've had actual training, then? What kind of place is Golden Dragon?"

"Jujitsu."

He scribbled something down in his notebook. "How long have you been going there?"

Kelli thought about it. "Two, three years."

"These other kids, are they a part of your dojo?"

Kelli snorted. "No! They don't know anything about martial arts. They're just… thugs. They think they're tough. It's easy to be tough when you gang up three-on-one."

"Not always so easy…" Bloggs said, the corner of his mouth quirking up into a smile. "Sometimes you end up at a disadvantage."

Kelli smothered a smile of her own. "It's not that easy. I'm good, but three-on-one still isn't… sporting."

"Have you ever had the opportunity to use your Jujitsu training before?"

Kelli wasn't sure how to answer that. It was the first time that she had ever been picked up like that in a fight. It was the first time that she had been jumped in the park. But it wasn't exactly the first time she had used Jujitsu outside of the dojo.

Bloggs was waiting. "Well…?"

"I don't know. I guess."

"What do you mean, you don't know? Is this the first time you've used it, or not?"

"No…"

"Tell me about when you have used it before."

"I don't know. Not anything like this. Just… you know, somebody grabs me, I break their hold, get the hell out of there…"

He studied her, frowning. "Is that the truth?"

"Yes," Kelli insisted. "I've only ever used it to protect myself. Get out of a bad situation. That, or practicing. That's all."

He turned a page in his notepad and started asking her questions that she had already been asked at the scene. How did she know Lizzie and the boys? What had happened to prompt the fight? How had it all gone down? Kelli tried to remember all of the details, but it had happened so fast that a move-by-move description of the fight was impossible. She kept stumbling over the details.

"You admit that you made the first move," Bloggs said.

Kelli shook her head. "No! They ambushed me. Surrounded me and then attacked."

"But you landed the first blow."

"There were three of them attacking me! If I waited for them to land the first blow, I'd be on the ground with two of them holding me down!"

"You are the one with training. I think you could have dealt with that."

"It's not magic," Kelli protested. "I don't have superhuman strength! If they have me pinned, there's not a lot I can do!"

She didn't say that there was nothing she could do. There was almost always something. Not entirely effective, maybe, but something she could try.

Bloggs kept asking questions. Kelli's body was aching and getting stiff. The fight had been short, but it tired her out more than sparring with the others in her dojo. Sensei had always said that it was different in a real fight. Adrenaline, no mats or props, hitting with all of your strength rather than sparing your partner and working through the forms. He had been right. Kelli was exhausted after a two-minute fight like she had never been after twenty minutes on the mats.

———

Bloggs had left and Kelli closed her eyes, trying to rest her brain and recover some equanimity. She had been in fight-or-flight mode for hours, despite her attempt to slow down and move on after the fight was finished. Dealing with the police was stressful. Thinking about being on TV. Wondering how her parents were going to react to the whole thing. If the police would even call them. Kelli did breathing exercises and tried to center herself. The calmer she was the sooner she would go home.

Bloggs returned to the room. He threw a clipboard down on the table. It had a small stack of computer reports attached to it, topped with one that showed Kelli's mugshot.

The birthmark stood out starkly under the harsh lighting. It was so ugly she could barely look at herself.

But Bloggs hadn't brought it to her to critique her photo. He had a point to make. And Kelli knew what it was without being told.

"You've been charged with domestic abuse."

"The judge threw it out."

"You told me you've only used Jujitsu to get out of a bad situation."

"Yeah."

"Domestic abuse isn't a bad situation."

She glared at him. "Then what is it?"

"If you're being abused, sure. But using Jujitsu against your parents…"

"Why do you think I needed to learn to protect myself? The police have a stupid rule that if you hit someone else in a domestic, you get arrested. It doesn't matter if you started it or if you were just protecting yourself. Everyone involved goes to jail."

Bloggs nodded, obviously aware of this policy. "Leave it to the courts to sort it out," he agreed.

"And the court threw out the charges against me."

"Why? Because there was not enough proof or because you were acting in self-defense?"

Kelli crossed her arms over her chest. She rolled her eyes. "Can you prove who threw the first punch out there?" she demanded, jerking her head in the direction of the door.

"With so many conflicting stories, all we can do is give it our best guess," Bloggs admitted. His mouth tightened. "But we still have more witnesses to interview and leads to follow, so that doesn't mean you're going home anytime soon."

"Just don't judge me by that," Kelli pointed to her mugshot and the other papers on the clipboard. "Because that was thrown out. All I did was protect myself. Just like I told you."

He looked back at the clipboard again. "There's a bit more in there than just the domestic."

Kelli cleared her throat. She gave a shrug, like it didn't really matter. What difference did it make to the assault charges against her? "Yeah, so?"

"Sounds like you're quite the little con artist."

"A girl's gotta eat. Better cons than turning tricks."

"You're not living on the street. You don't have to con people out of their money in order to eat. You just go home and eat there."

"Anyone ever tell you you're naive?"

"No," Bloggs said flatly. "Even if your parents are down and out, there are breakfast and lunch programs at school, food banks, food stamps; there's a whole variety of programs available to make sure that kids like you aren't starving."

She didn't bother arguing with him over it. He wasn't living it; he didn't know what it was like. And it was irrelevant to the assault charges. Running a con didn't make her any more likely to start beating up people randomly in the park. He knew what had happened. It was time for him to decide what to do about it.

CHAPTER 2

All things considered, Kelli's stay in the jail had been uneventful. Just like when she was arrested for domestic assault, they put in her a cell by herself, away from the adult population, and the biggest problem she had to deal with was boredom. She wouldn't be sent over to juvie until a judge had had a chance to consider the charges against her and decide where she should be while awaiting trial.

But as with the domestic assault, once the judge had a chance to review the evidence that had been assembled against Kelli, he dismissed the charges.

"No previous violence and no trouble at school," the judge pointed out. "This is not the kind of kid to just go attacking random groups unprovoked. If it's three against one, then you can bet it wasn't started by the one, unless she's insane." He looked at Kelli over square-framed granny glasses. "She doesn't strike me as insane."

The judge shuffled through the papers in front of him. "She already had that bruise when she was arrested?"

The lawyer who had been assigned to Kelli's case rose to his feet. "Err… it's not a bruise, your honor, it's a birthmark."

"Oh." The judge cleared his throat. "Fine, then. I don't see any evidence that Miss Munroe has committed any crime. Self-defense has always been a legal defense to assault charges. Please see that she is released to her parents immediately." His eyes scanned the courtroom. "Are her legal guardians here?"

The lawyer at the other table stood up. "Her parents were notified of the situation, your honor, and the hearing time. But they did not make an appearance…"

"What's the situation?" The judge turned his attention back to Kelli's lawyer. "Has Social Services been brought in?"

"No, your honor, there isn't any indication that Social Services needs to be informed. Her parents are in the picture, they—"

"They just couldn't make it," Kelli jumped in. "People have to work. My mom doesn't want to get fired from her job because they think she isn't dependable because her daughter got in trouble. And my dad is disabled…"

"It would be a good idea to get Social Services in for a follow-up," the judge said. He banged his gavel. "Case dismissed."

———

"Kelli!"

Kelli turned at the sound of her name. Les hurried up the steps of the courthouse toward her. A fringe of messy curls peeked out the bottom of his omnipresent beanie, bouncing as he took the stairs two at a time.

"Les! What are you doing here?"

He reached her, and gave her little a punch on the shoulder by way of greeting. "Heard it was your hearing today. I had to come, didn't I?"

"Well…" Kelli shrugged. "Not really. And you missed it."

"I don't mean so I could be here for the hearing, I meant so I could be here when you were released. And I was right; here you are!" He gave her a wide, self-satisfied smile.

"Oh, okay. Yeah you were right; here I am."

If anything, Les's grin got wider. They walked down the stairs together. Without discussing it, they both headed toward the bus stop. Kelli went to work as soon as they got there.

"Does anyone have a bus ticket I could use? I don't have any money. I had to go to a hearing at the courthouse and I don't have any way to get home."

She looked at each of the people standing around the bus stop, studiously ignoring her.

"Come on, please…? Can anyone help?"

There was a woman standing with her toddler in her arms, jiggling him to keep him quiet.

"I had to go to a hearing," Kelli repeated. "They just took my baby away from me!" She squeezed out a couple of tears. "Come on! This is like the worst day of my life! Can't anybody help me? Some change? A bus ticket?" She scrubbed at both of her eyes with her fists. "You think I'm going to buy drugs or something? With a few cents?" She indicated the purple mark under her eye. "My boyfriend knocks me around like this, and *I* lose custody? What kind of sense does that make? Now I can't even get home." She sniffled, letting a few more tears escape her eyes. "Never mind. I guess I got feet, I can get there by dark."

The woman with the toddler caved. "I've got a ticket," she offered. "Just give me a second to get it out for you."

Kelli stood patiently waiting while the woman juggled her toddler and bags and found a spare bus ticket for Kelli. Kelli gave her a brave smile.

"Thank you so much. It's really nice of you to help a stranger. I don't know what I would have done." She tousled the hair of the toddler. "You take care of this little guy. You don't want to know what it's like to lose one." Kelli wiped one final tear from her face and went back to join Les while they waited for the bus to arrive.

Kelli noticed that the woman was still watching her, seeing whether she was actually going to catch the bus, or if she was going to sell the ticket in order to buy drugs or support some other vice.

"People are so distrustful," she told Les.

Les laughed and gave her a little shove. "Tell me what happened in the park," he urged. "I want to hear all about it. I hear you mopped the floor with Lizzie and her boys."

Kelli gave a modest shrug. "Well, I don't know about mopping the floor with them. After all, we were outside. But… let's just say they were all down when the police got there."

"That's my girl," Les cheered. "Next time she'd better bring more than three!"

Kelli's stomach clenched at the thought. Three had been hard enough to take care of. If Lizzie did bring a bigger posse next time, say six people, the outcome would be very different. She was going to have to be careful.

Hopefully, Lizzie would stay away from Kelli and Les after the fight. If she didn't, Kelli could be in trouble.

"You should just stay away from them," she told Les. "I mean it, okay? If she does bring more next time… I could be dead."

Les's expression sobered. "I didn't mean anything," he said quickly. "And I never asked you to jump in and stand up for me. I was okay. Nothing would have happened."

"I—I know. But she's such a bully, it just drives me nuts sometimes. I couldn't listen to her for a second longer. I just blew."

He nodded. "I'll try to avoid her. But I can't be obvious about avoiding her, or she'll just get worse. You just stay out of it next time."

Kelli agreed.

But she knew she wouldn't.

———

They got on the same bus as the lady who had given Kelli the ticket. Kelli was glad the woman saw her actually use the ticket. Not that it mattered what a random stranger on the street thought about her, but it did make Kelli feel a little bit better about herself. A little bit less like a con. The woman didn't have as far to go as Kelli, traveling only a few stops before getting off again. Kelli sat back, watching the city go by outside.

"Everything okay?" Les asked. "You're quiet."

"Sure. I'm fine."

"Nobody messed with you at the jail, did they?"

Kelli shook her head. "Noooo. I was all by myself. The only people I saw were the guards. They always take care of me just fine."

"Your mom come see you?"

"No. Why would she? She knew I didn't do anything wrong. That they'd release me in a few days. It's not like she has money to waste on bail."

"You're a hero! You were on the news and everything. It's all anyone was talking about. The crazy ninja girl that took on a whole crowd of marauders in the park. Not even so much as a split lip. The reporters didn't come to talk to you in jail?"

"They couldn't. I don't think. Not allowed."

"You saw them at the courthouse when you got there, though."

Kelli shook her head. She had arrived pretty early on the courthouse transfer bus. It was still the gray light of dawn when they had pulled up to the deserted building. There hadn't been any reporters there to visit her.

"What were they saying?"

"How brave you were. How people should stand up for each other, and people at the park should have stepped in to help you. How you were so good and protected yourself. It was great. My phone was ringing all night with people from school saying, 'that's the girl you know, right?'"

"And did you admit it?"

"What? Why wouldn't I? You're my best bud." Les wrapped one arm around her and gave her a squeeze. Kelli laughed. His face was close to hers, and for a moment she stared at it, wondering how he would react if she gave him a peck on the cheek. Then he released her shoulder and Kelli looked out the window again.

"I wish I'd seen it," she said. "That would be cool."

"Maybe you can go online and see it. They must let you watch footage online."

"Yeah. Maybe. I'll look."

They got off the bus at Les's stop and Kelli walked him home. Les slowed as they got closer to his house.

"I should be walking *you* home. What if Crazy Lizzie and her posse are out there, waiting for you to get home? She must have seen everything on TV too. She'll know that your hearing was today."

Kelli laughed it off. "She's not going to do anything. Too much risk that there will be cops or TV reporters hanging around, trying to get more information. Don't worry about me."

"You'll be careful?"

"I always am." At Les's look, she quickly amended. "Yes. I'll be careful."

"Don't cut through the park? Stay on the road where there's lots of traffic?"

She sighed. Cutting through the park was so much easier and faster. "Yes. I'll take the road."

"Okay. Good. Call me when you get home?"

"I don't think so, Les. It's the end of the month, I doubt my mom has any minutes left on her phone."

Les looked for a way around this and then shook his head, unable to think of an argument. "I'll see you tomorrow, then?"

"What's tomorrow?"

"School."

"I mean, what day is it? I lost track."

"Friday."

"Oh." Kelli considered this. "I've kind of missed the rest of the week and Friday is a lax day. So maybe I'll wait until next week. Clean up the house tomorrow."

Les gave her a disbelieving look. But Kelli was thinking about the judge's suggestion that Social Services needed to be brought into the equation with Kelli's mom not showing up for the hearing. If they decided to make a surprise visit, Kelli didn't want them walking into the pig pen that the house was currently in.

"One day isn't going to make that much difference," Kelli pointed out. "Especially not a Friday. No one wants to work on Fridays, even the teachers."

"Okay… guess I'm probably not going to change your mind. Do you want some help? I could come over?"

"No." Kelli hesitated, searching for words. "I don't think my dad really likes people coming over. He's been kind of weird about it. I think… I should just do it myself. Thanks, though."

Les nodded. "After school, then? Where are you going to be?"

"The park?" Kelli suggested. "Over at the chess tables."

"You sure you want to be at the park? After what just happened?"

"That was across the park, not at the tables. There are always people there. Even Crazy Lizzie wouldn't be stupid enough to attack me in front of that many people."

"I don't know…"

"I'll see you tomorrow."

———

It was weird being home so early in the day. Kelli would normally still be in school. And she didn't usually even go home once school was out, not until later in the evening, when night started to fall. Being home mid-afternoon made it feel like a holiday that nobody else was observing. Or maybe like an undeserved sick day, faking flu when she had a test or an assignment due.

Kelli walked in and looked around the living room with critical eyes. Looking at it like a social worker would. It was worse than she had realized.

She had gotten used to the disorder, ignored what she couldn't change. Became blind to it all. There was debris everywhere. Clothing mixed with dirty plates and food wrappers on the floor and every surface. Spills and stains long turned black with dust and dirt. The smell of rot and the sound of flies buzzing.

Kelli swallowed and walked through it. The TV was on, but that didn't mean that anybody was home or awake. It pretty much stayed on twenty-four hours.

Her mom was in the kitchen. There were stacks of dirty dishes everywhere. The dishwasher hadn't worked in years. There was no more food preparation area, which didn't really matter, because no one actually prepared food there. Other than throwing something in the microwave or boiling up a pot of macaroni on the one free element on the stove.

Patricia Munroe was older than the parents of most of the other kids Kelli knew. She had already been in her forties when she had Kelli. Her hair was still blond only because she dyed it. Her pouchy face was wrinkled and her eyes always looked tired. She turned around as Kelli came in.

"Oh, it's you," she observed. "Thought you'd finally come home, did you?"

Kelli didn't bother to point out that it was the first chance she'd had to go home. She made a gesture to include the room.

"They're talking about sending a social worker. This place needs to be cleaned up."

Patricia looked around the kitchen and grunted. "What business is it of anyone else what this place looks like? How am I supposed to keep it tidy when no one else does a lick of work? Why is it all up to me?"

"I'll help. I don't want them poking their noses in here either, but we can't help that."

Patricia sprinkled cheese over what looked like a full bag of Doritos on a plate, and shoved it into the microwave.

"What's all this about you getting into a fight in the park? It was all over the TV."

"Some kids from school." Kelli lifted dishes out of the sink in order to plug the drain, her stomach turning at the smell of mold and signs of movement under the dishes. After pressing the drain down, she ran the water as hot as it would go. "They ambushed me."

"What for?" Patricia looked Kelli over. "Are you okay?"

"Yeah, I'm fine. Just stupid school stuff. You know, bullies."

"Should I talk to the school about it?"

"Oh, yeah, like that would help," Kelli sneered. "Don't talk to the school. They're inept and it will only make the bullies retaliate."

Kelli found some soap to squirt into the water, and it started foaming up. Patricia took her nachos out of the microwave. She offered the dish to Kelli. Kelli took a few hot chips off of the plate. The food at the jail had been dull and bland. Kelli crunched the spicy chips and the cheese burned the roof of her mouth.

"Oh, ow! Be careful, they're hot!"

"Do you think I don't know that?" Patricia demanded. She popped out the upper plate of her dentures with her tongue. "At least with this, I never burn the top of my mouth anymore." She put it back into place.

"Yeah, bonus," Kelli agreed.

When she was younger, Patricia had had normal teeth like everyone else. Kelli remembered Patricia in hospital after the 'accident' that had smashed in all of her front teeth. She had looked horrifying with a mouthful of jagged, bleeding teeth. Like a feeding shark. And then when the stumps were all removed and they had to wait for her gums to heal before she could be fitted for dentures. Eating nothing but soup and oatmeal and other liquids, because that was all that Patricia could eat. Kelli took more chips from the plate before Patricia headed back to the living room to watch TV. The crunch made her feel better after thinking about those weeks of nothing but liquids. She didn't burn herself this time.

"When you're done, pick up all the dishes out there and bring them in here," Kelli instructed. "I'll wash. Just don't leave more dirty dishes out there."

Patricia made a noise of agreement and shuffled out of the room. Kelli turned back to the sink and gingerly fished around in the hot, soapy water for the slimy dishcloth.

———

She washed two sinks full of dishes at a time. Washed them, filling up the drying rack and the other side of the sink with clean dishes, drained the dirty water, filled the sink back up with dirty dishes and fresh water while she dried off the clean dishes and put them into the cupboard. Repeat.

Repeat. Repeat. She tried to follow the talk show that Patricia was watching in the living room. She could only hear snippets of the families yelling and cursing at each other, and tried to piece them together into something that made sense. Only there didn't seem to be any order to the screamed comments about abuse and infidelity, and she couldn't tell when one story ended and another started. The audience clapped and cheered when the women talked and booed when the men were brought in, no matter how justified the men seemed to be in their accusations against the mothers of their (or someone else's) children.

It was tedious, mind-numbing work. Why didn't they all just clean their own dishes as they used them? Or wash everything at the end of the day? Why did they just leave the dirty dishes on the counters or floors and only scrape and wash off a dish when there was nothing else to put their food on? They lived like pigs.

When she was finished all the dishes in the kitchen and her hands were sore and chapped, Kelli made her way back to the living room. Patricia sat in her armchair, head tipped back and snoring. There was a pile of empty cans and bottles beside her chair. How many she had emptied this round and how many were from the last few days, Kelli didn't know. She did know that none of the bottles was over a week old, since Kelli regularly took empties to the bottle depot to claim the refunds. If they could claim money for the rest of the trash and dirty dishes and empty containers in the house, Kelli would be rich and there was no way the house would look like it did. If Kelli could pick up the empties, why couldn't she clean up the dirty dishes too? She berated herself for letting things get to the state they were in. She needed to be more diligent in the future. Social workers could be called at any time, and if they found the house like that, there would be consequences.

CHAPTER 3

Kelli tended to forget about her dad being home. It had been just Kelli and Patricia for so long, it was always a surprise to find her dad there too. There had been other men too, while her father had been gone, but none of them had ever stayed for long. Most lived somewhere else and only visited or stayed over sporadically. The rest of the time, it was just Kelli and Patricia. Two single girls, Patricia used to say. Even though she wasn't single. She was in the sense that she wasn't legally married to Axel Ivanovich, but they were still a couple. Patricia still visited him every week. His clothes still hung in her closet and his old beater was still parked in the yard behind the house.

After washing up all the dishes Kelli could find in the kitchen and living room, and wiping down the unidentifiable gunk on the counters, and the identifiable rodent droppings and bugs along the backs of the counters and in the corners, Kelli had grabbed a couple of garbage bags and started throwing out everything she could put her hands on. Trash, flyers, mail, broken bits of electronics, stained and torn clothing. Everything. She had filled five garbage bags and put them back behind the fence. Then she was too exhausted to do anything else. Her whole body was sore and tired and she felt indescribably gritty and grimy. She wished she'd had gloves. Both for washing up the endless dishes and for picking up the garbage. The filth was awful.

She was reaching for the closed bathroom door when it was opened from the inside. Kelli jumped and strangled back a shriek of surprise. Axel looked back at her, nearly as startled by her as she was by him. It was a good thing that he was coming out of the bathroom. She hadn't even thought about him being home and would have walked right in on him. Kelli's faced flamed in embarrassment.

"Oh. Hi." Kelli swallowed. "How's it going?"

He looked at her without speaking. Axel was a scary guy. Even people who saw him for the first time and didn't know anything about him were scared of him. The fringes of hair around his bald head were buzzed short. He had a gray mustache and goatee. The lines of his face were deep and his expression hard. It was no surprise to anyone who saw him that he was a convicted felon. Or had been, anyway. He'd lived a hard life. Ten years in prison had chiseled away any softness that he'd had before being sent away. She could remember playing with him when she was a little girl. She could even remember him laughing, pulling her close to cuddle. It was unimaginable now. He was distant and remote and almost always angry.

He grunted at her and pushed past. Back to his room. Or maybe downstairs to get a bite to eat or to bother Patricia. Kelli didn't wait to see. She entered the vacated bathroom and shut the door. The bathroom was her sanctuary. With the door locked, Kelli was safe and alone.

She started the shower running in the tub, to get the rust out of the pipes and give the water heater a chance to start working. As she peeled off her clothes, she realized that the bathroom was in just as dismal a state as the rest of the house. Toiletries and garbage littered the counters. There were yellow stains on and around the toilet. She always wiped the seat, but she didn't worry about the rest of the toilet, and it was really gross. The plush bathroom rug smelled rank, and it was dirty and all trampled down. Kelli had started to make a pile of clothes downstairs that needed to be washed. Stuff that was salvageable. The bathroom rug would have to go in the washer too. Kelli grabbed a less-smelly towel from the towel bar and laid it over the rug to give herself a clean surface. All the towels would have to be washed. Who knew when the last time they had been done was. And it would take at least a couple of garbage bags to clear out all the junk and empty soap and shampoo bottles filling the bathroom. Kelli finished stripping and jumped into the shower. She soaped up, scrubbing all the grit and grime away. The tub needed to be cleaned too, and after she was done washing herself, she wiped around the surround and the tub itself to wipe away the worst of the mold and mildew. She needed scrubbing bubbles for the soap scum ring, and bleach for everything. Maybe there was some under the sink. If not, she would have to come up with a plan to beg or borrow some.

After getting out of the shower, she wrapped a towel around herself and peeked out the door to make sure that no one was nearby. Her bedroom was only one door down, and somehow, she always forgot to get fresh clothes to change into before showering. She sneaked down the hallway.

"Hey! What are you doing here?"

Kelli froze at Axel's shout. She glanced over her shoulder at him.

"What? I'm just going to get dressed."

"Who are you? What are you doing in my house?" he demanded.

Kelli turned around to face him fully. How could he not know who she was? "It's Kelli! I live here!"

His eyes bored into her. She watched him take in the towel wrapped around her, and then go up to her straight brown hair and the large purple mark on her cheek.

"I know who you are," he growled. "It was just a joke. Doesn't anyone around here know how to take a joke?"

He turned around, retreating to his bedroom with a plateful of mac and cheese. Kelli stayed there for a minute longer, frozen, staring at his closed door, hearing the muffled noise of the bedroom TV behind it.

What was that about? Axel's behavior since his return home a year ago was often bizarre. At first, she had thought it was just antisocial habits he had picked up while in prison. That he would soften up and start to behave more normally once he had been home for a while. She stayed out of his way, gave him as much room as she could, and waited for her old dad to return.

But he hadn't. If anything, she had started to see more warning signs. More bizarre behavior. 'I was just joking' was a common refrain, when it was patently obvious that he had been serious. He often seemed confused or disoriented, scowling angrily at her as if it were Kelli's fault. She accommodated him sometimes without even realizing she was doing it. Taking longer to explain things to him. Telling him how to perform simple tasks, as if he were two years old. Spring something on him unexpectedly, and he was likely to go off like a roman candle. Anger was a common aftermath to confusion. He seemed furious at least half the time.

Kelli knew he had a series of sessions arranged with a psychologist, trying to unravel the series of events that had led to his incarceration, and ten years later, the reversal of his conviction. She hoped that the psychologist would have some answers for them, something that would help them to manage things at home.

Sighing, Kelli went the rest of the way down the hall to her room. She would get dressed, lie down for a quick nap to get her energy back, and then she would tackle the housework again. With any luck, by the end of the next day, the house would at least be presentable.

————

The following day was spent in a marathon cleaning session. Kelli managed to scrape up a few more cleaning supplies from neighbors. Some gloves to protect her hands. Lots of sprayer cleaner and bleach. 'Don't mix them,' Mrs. Rawlings had warned. 'Only use one at a time and clean it up well before using the other.' She didn't want to end up gassing herself mixing chemicals.

She stopped occasionally to sit down and eat, her entire body pulsing with pain. Maybe it was an exercise that Sensei could add to his 'toughening up' practice. If Kelli worked like that every day, she'd have the body of a gymnast.

She was excited to see the improvement the cleaning and decluttering was having on the house. It hadn't looked so good in years. Kelli had started disposing of the garbage bags full of junk and clutter in the neighbors' garbages, all the way up and down the block. She couldn't put it all behind their fence. There was way too much.

Kelli had the windows open to air the house out, so she heard the voices of the school children as they let out and headed to their homes or their friends' houses, or played in the streets. She had cleaned all day. She'd never worked so hard in her life. It was time for a break from it. Kelli took a couple more bags of trash out of the house with her, walking two blocks down before disposing of them.

Les was already waiting for her near the chess tables. Kelli grinned at him as she claimed an empty table and set up her game. Not chess, but Three-card Monte. Very quick to set up and take down and move to another location where she could find a fresh mark. She started her patter, showing off the queen of hearts and encouraging bystanders to find the lady, turning cards over, switching them back and forth, using sleight of hand to hide and reveal the queen at will.

At first, there were no takers. Maybe people had seen her there too many times before and weren't about to be taken in by her trickery. Maybe they were just too shy, or had heard of other people being taken in by similar street cons. But there was a lot of street traffic past the chess boards and she would draw someone in sooner or later.

Les approached to play his part, throwing down singles to bet on the game. Sometimes he would win several games in a row, making Kelli look like an easy take, and other times he would lose a number of games, making bystanders think that they could easily do better than Les. One psychology worked for some, the other for others. But it wasn't long before a couple of teenagers who looked like they were downtown to shop at the trendier stores stopped and gave it a try. Kelli took them at several games, and when they looked like they were getting ready to make a fuss about the game being rigged, Les told her "Look out, cops!" and she pocketed the money and her cards. They separated to move on to a new location, leaving the aggravated teens behind to stew over their losses.

Les met Kelli by the drug store.

"Nice," Les complimented. The teens had been good marks. Impulsive, with plenty of cash for spending money, and the egos to think they could beat the house.

"Thanks. You too. How about over on fifth, beside the bodega?"

He nodded. "See you there."

They split up again, and Kelli headed over to the spot she often played. But when she got there, Kelli spotted a police car. When she looked up and down the street to see what was going on, she could see that they were patrolling foot traffic, looking for any trouble. Bad news for Kelli; they would never allow her to play right under their noses. She kept moving and went on to the picnic tables outside of the downtown swimming pool. Lots of executives who wanted to keep in shape frequented the place throughout the day. The ones who couldn't afford private clubs and didn't want to spend too much time away from the office. A quick run to the swimming pool, a few lengths, maybe some free weights in the weight room, and then back to the office again for a coffee and more meetings. They were the type of people always in a hurry, with a little extra money in their pockets, and just reluctant enough about going back to the office to linger for a few minutes over a game of find the lady. As long as Kelli mixed up the days and times that she worked the area, she didn't usually run into the same marks repeatedly.

She was there for half an hour before Les showed up. He rolled his eyes at her.

"You need to get a phone so I know where to find you!"

"Too expensive. You found me. Sorry, there were cops by the bodega."

"Yeah, I saw. Asked them if they knew where you had gone, but they didn't know."

Kelli stared at him for a moment before deciding it was a joke, and she laughed. Les was just brave enough—or stupid enough—to do such a thing.

"Any action so far?" Les inquired.

"Pretty soft so far." Kelli whipped the cards back and forth, resuming her patter and inviting Les or nearby pedestrians to follow her hands and find the lady. It wasn't long before Les was engaged in the game, and humans being the social animals they were, other people soon joined in.

"Two bucks a try, or five bucks for three," Kelli invited. "Follow the cards and find the lady…"

Les won twice in a row and then lost three. A mark jumped in, losing ten bucks before walking away in disgust. The traffic was pretty steady until the sun started to get lower in the sky and people got leery about approaching her. Kelli pocketed her cards and she and Les headed back toward home.

"Good take today." Kelli was pleased with the amount of cash she'd been able to pull in. And that was on top of a productive day cleaning the house. She imagined what it would be like when she was out of school. Every day could be like that. Making things nice for herself and making a steady income. She shuffled through their take, sorting out the bills and counting it up. She gave Les his split.

"Thanks." Les nodded at the money Kelli retained. "See, you could buy a phone. One of those cheap prepaids at the corner. Then I could reach you."

Kelli shook her head. "I gotta get some food."

"You're done your stamps already?"

"Dad keeps using them. Which would be fine if he bought regular food, but…"

"What's he buying?" Les asked, his eyes alight with curiosity. He knew they couldn't buy alcohol with their assistance card. But there were still a lot of nonessentials that a person could spend it on.

"Mac and cheese."

"Mac and cheese?" Les repeated blankly. "What's wrong with mac and cheese?"

"The fact that we already have a couple hundred boxes of it. Every time he goes to the store, he comes home with a cartload of mac and cheese. If I want to eat anything else, I gotta buy it. And believe me, mac and cheese for breakfast, lunch, and supper every day for two weeks gets pretty old."

"You can get school breakfast and lunch," Les pointed out. "That's some variety, anyway."

"Yeah? What did they serve for school lunch today?"

"Uh…" Les thought back. Then he grinned. "Mac and cheese."

Kelli laughed.

"But they don't serve it every day," Les protested. "They have a variety."

Kelli shrugged. "I still don't like mac and cheese every day."

"No. I wouldn't either," he admitted. "I really don't even like the stuff. I only eat it when it's the only option. That processed cheese powder… I'm not sure it even comes from cows."

"What? It comes from cows?" Kelli gave a mock shudder. "Why didn't you tell me?"

"I don't think you need to worry. It's mostly just chalk."

Les stopped in front of his house. "You want to come in? I'm sure we've got something other than mac and cheese to eat."

"No, it's okay." Kelli knew that the row of snotty-nosed children that came after Les were always hungry. She wasn't about to take food out of their mouths. "I'm going to pop by the store. Maybe even get some fresh fruit."

Les sucked in his cheeks and wiped his mouth with the back of his hand. "Sounds good," he agreed. He gave a little wave. "See you tomorrow."

Kelli watched him into the house before going on.

Before going to the store, she needed to stop by Golden Dragon. There were no lessons on Friday, but she needed to pay another installment toward her training and get a bit of practice in. Friday evening was a good time to find someone at the dojo and pick up a couple of extra hours of practice.

———

Brittany counted up the bills that Kelli handed her, and input the numbers into the computer. "Okay, you're paid up until the end of next month," she advised. "Thanks for paying ahead."

When Kelli heard the name Brittany, she always pictured a blond white girl. But Brittany was a tough-as-nails, middle-aged, black and Asian woman. Her skin was dark, her black hair tightly curled, with the most amazingly exotic eyes Kelli had ever seen, slanted, with one brown and one blue iris. Les had once asked Kelli if she felt a kinship with Brittany, because of her two differently-colored eyes, and Kelli had had no idea what he was talking about.

"What do you mean?" she demanded. "I don't have eyes like that."

"No, I mean…" He shifted uncomfortably. "I mean, because of… you know… your birthmark. And she looks different too, because of her eyes."

Kelli shook her head in disbelief. She would never have considered Brittany's incredible eyes a disfigurement, like Kelli's birthmark. They made her beautiful. Kelli wanted to stare at her not because she was ugly, like Kelli with her mark, but because she was so intriguingly gorgeous.

"I saw you on TV," Brittany said, breaking Kelli's reverie. "What happened?"

"Oh. Well, you know, I was jumped in the park. Three kids from school."

"And…?"

Kelli shrugged. But her heart sped up and she was excited to share it with someone else who was an expert on fighting.

"It all happened really fast. I didn't have any time to think about what to do. I was really glad for all my practice time, because it was… it was all instinctive; muscle memory."

"That's why we practice," Brittany agreed. "There isn't any time to think. It has to be automatic."

"It wasn't a big fight. They're making a big deal of it, but it was over in two minutes. Not like the fight sequence in some action film. Just bang, bang, bang—everybody down, and all over."

"You did good, if it was three against one and you had them all down in two minutes," Brittany pointed out. "Really good. Sensei will want to hear all about it."

"Yeah." Kelli was nervous to talk to him about it. Would he want details? To deconstruct the fight and tell her all of the things that she had done wrong, like he would for a sparring session during class time? She didn't really want to think of all of the things that she might have done wrong. All the split-second decisions that she had made that might have put her in more danger.

She looked around the dojo to see who was there to practice with.

"Well, I gotta work out. Talk to you later."

"Later," Brittany agreed, turning her eyes back to her computer.

CHAPTER 4

Saturday mornings, Kelli liked to sleep in. There was no school, the streets were too quiet to drum up any money until afternoon, and the dojo was busy with the beginner classes and weekend workshops. So she stayed up late watching TV Friday night, like any normal teenager, and slept Saturday morning away.

But she awoke to the doorbell ringing repeatedly. Not just a persistent salesperson, but a sustained, insistent ring. Kelli finally dragged herself out of bed, checked herself to make sure she was decent, and stumbled down the stairs to the front door. She looked out the peephole before opening the door. She didn't want to be facing Lizzie or a local gang banger before she'd even had her morning coffee. But it wasn't a teenager—it wouldn't be, so early on a Saturday morning—and it wasn't a salesperson or news reporter. It was a man, a tough-looking guy in a suit. Maybe somebody there to see Axel. A parole officer, sponsor, or police detective.

The insistent ringing hadn't stopped. Kelli opened the door and blinked in the bright sunshine.

"What is your problem?" she demanded.

"Are you Kelli Munroe?"

"Yeah."

He tapped the name badge clipped to his lapel. "DCFS. Are your parents home?"

Kelli swore mentally, but kept it in her head. She rubbed her leaky eyes.

"I dunno. You got me out of bed. They could be out running errands." Kelli stepped back from the door so that she could see into the living room. Patricia was conked out in her armchair. "Yeah, Mom's home, at least. I didn't check to see if Dad was."

"Is there somewhere else he would be at this time of day?"

Kelli considered. Axel wasn't working. He spent most of his time in his room watching the smaller TV. But he did go out shopping and he had those psychologist appointments. There were other places he could be.

"Probably sleeping," she said. "We all sleep late on Saturday. That's what civilized people do." She glared at him, hoping he'd get the message.

He stared back at her, his eyes on the birthmark. "Since your mother is home, I'd like to come in. Take a look around."

"Yeah, okay," Kelli agreed. She yawned widely without covering her mouth. "Come on."

She opened the door the rest of the way for him. She gestured at her mother. "I don't know if she's gonna want to wake up. She was up pretty late last night." This to head off the idea that Patricia was just drunk or drugged up. There was a single beer can on the floor next to the armchair. Kelli had picked up the rest before going to bed, stowing them in a garbage bag in the closet to take in for refund at the next opportunity. She'd bought a few things at the store after her Jujitsu practice, but they still needed a few more things. She had to return the neighbors' gloves and cleaners, but she wanted to keep the house up if she could. She liked being able to walk through a room without tripping over something or putting her foot into the middle of a plate of leftovers.

And she still had to figure out how to get rid of all of the vermin. It would help that there was no longer food on every surface.

While DCFS went into the living room to have a chat with her mother, Kelli headed for the kitchen and put on a pot of coffee. They didn't have one of those fancy one-cup machines, but at least she didn't have to suffer through instant. She had cleaned up the ancient machine and bought fresh filters for it so she could make nice fresh coffee whenever she wanted.

There was a big mouse turd in the middle of the clean counters. Kelli glanced over her shoulder in panic to make sure that DCFS hadn't followed her into the kitchen. She grabbed a paper towel from under the sink and quickly picked it up and threw it all into the garbage. She could hear DCFS talking loudly to Patricia, trying to get her up. Patricia's replies were slow and whiny.

As the coffee pot was filling, DCFS walked in. He took a glance around the kitchen.

"You want coffee?" Kelli asked.

"Sure, I could go for that."

She watched him take a brief walk around the room, opening and closing a couple of the cupboards and the fridge. He stood and looked at Kelli as they waited for the coffee to finish dripping.

"Tell me about yourself," he said.

Kelli shrugged. "Nothing much to tell. I just live here, go to school, try to keep my head down and work hard."

"How are your parents?"

"Fine."

"Tell me about them. Your mom seems a little… under the weather."

Kelli shrugged. "It's Saturday morning. You woke her up. Lots of people have a drink or two Friday night. Lots of parents do a lot more than have a beer or two in front of the TV."

"And your dad? Is he home?"

"I haven't checked yet. He doesn't go out a lot, so probably."

"What's he like?"

Kelli poured them each a cup of coffee. She didn't offer him any cream or sugar. Kelli took a sip of the piping hot coffee. She looked sideways at him. "You didn't look him up before you came around?"

"I might have," he admitted. "What do I need to know?"

Kelli stared off into the distance over the brim of her cup. "He was in prison for ten years. Most of my life. He's been out for a few months. They're still trying to sort it all out."

"Sort what out?"

"How he got convicted when he didn't do it."

He nodded slowly and took a careful sip of his coffee. "How *did* he get convicted?"

"They didn't have any evidence. They got him to confess. So, he pled out. Never went to trial."

"And for ten years, everyone thought they had the right guy?"

"I guess. Until they got the girlfriend of the guy who had really done it. She spilled the whole story for a deal. They went back to the evidence and it all fit into place. Dad's story had never quite fit the facts. So they did DNA testing and proved it wasn't him. It was this other guy."

DCFS shook his head. "Why did he confess if he didn't do it? Was it coerced?"

"He still thinks he did it. They're looking at the old interview tapes and trying to figure out if it's something called implanted memories. The investigators might have suggested details that he later thought were his own memories…"

"That's a scary thought."

"They're supposed to be specially trained not to do that kind of thing. They're supposed to be taught the right way to conduct an investigation… but I guess it still happens. Especially with kids and teenagers. Not that Axel was that young, but younger suspects are more impressionable."

"What has it been like since he came home? Things must have changed a lot around here."

"Kind of weird at first. I'm still getting used to him being here. But it's nice that he's out."

"Do you feel safe around him?"

Kelli answered carefully. "Just because he was convicted of a violent crime… that doesn't mean he's actually violent. Since he didn't actually do the crime."

DCFS considered this, taking another sip of coffee. "You didn't exactly answer the question."

"I feel… I don't know. Off balance. But I'm not scared of him. And I'm not neglected. The judge thought because my parents didn't come to the hearing that I was neglected. But you can see that I'm not." Kelli gave a little gesture that included the kitchen, the coffee, and the food.

"Why don't you take me on the tour?"

"What tour?"

"Show me around the house. Your parents' room. Where you sleep."

"Oh. Okay."

Kelli poured a third cup of coffee, which she handed to Patricia as they walked back through the living room. Patricia looked at her with bloodshot eyes. "What's this all about, then?"

"Just a social worker. The judge who heard my case sent him," Kelli explained, giving a shrug. She went around Patricia's chair and to the stairs to take DCFS upstairs. He followed her up the long staircase. Kelli stopped at the door of the master bedroom. "He's probably sleeping." She tapped on the door with her nail and cracked the door open to peek in at Axel.

The room was messier than she had left it. Obviously, he hadn't wasted any time in spreading his crap around the room again. But it just looked disorderly, not unsanitary.

"Dad...? Dad, are you awake?"

DCFS shifted impatiently, but Kelli kept the door blocked with her body and didn't let him past.

"My room is down there. Why don't you take a look at it?"

The man didn't look like he was going to accept the suggestion, but Kelli stood firm, waiting for him to go. He nodded and walked down the hall toward her room. Kelli went into the master bedroom.

Axel was lying in bed, the sheets a twisted mess around him. The areas of his face usually shaved clean were scrubby with dark whiskers. He scowled even in his sleep, his face set in hard lines.

"Dad. Dad, wake up." She gave him a little shake, standing as far away from him as she could, worried that he might be angry and violent if startled. His upper torso was bare, and she could see the dirty gray hairs that curled across his chest. She couldn't tell whether he had anything on under the blanket. "Dad! You need to wake up."

His eyes opened and he looked at her. An angry, hard glare. Ready for a fight.

"It's Kelli," Kelli said, not sure if he would recognize her right off. He had just woken up and might be disoriented. "Listen, there's a social worker here, and he wants to make sure everything is okay. You need to get up and tell him everything is good. All right?"

Axel scratched his chest and looked around the room, taking it all in, figuring out where he was. She wondered if he still expected to wake up in a small gray prison cell every day. Did it surprise him every time he woke up and found himself in the bedroom? Or was he used to it by now?

"Kelli. What's going on?"

"You just need to tell the social worker that everything is okay. That you guys take care of me, feed me, and drive me around and stuff. So he'll write up a report saying everything is fine."

Axel nodded. He pulled the sheets around him, tucking them around his body. "Hand me that." He gestured to a ratty old robe. A robe that must have been old when he had left it in the closet ten years earlier before going to prison. Most days, that was all he wore, shuffling around the house like a refugee, not knowing what to do with himself. Kelli handed it to him and he put his arms through the holes and drew it on before climbing out of the bed and tying it closed. Kelli caught a glimpse of dingy white boxers as he got it on. At least he was up and decent. DCFS could see that everything was fine, just like any other normal family, and then he would leave.

She went down the hall to her bedroom.

"Is he up?" DCFS asked.

She nodded. "Just give him a minute to get mobile. You know, he probably wants to use the john and splash some water on his face."

"So… this is your room."

Kelli nodded. Everything was neat and tidy. Like she kept it that way her whole life, and didn't eat in her room or leave crap around and laundry all over the floor. There was still a ton of laundry in the basement waiting to be washed, folded, and put away. She wasn't sure where she was going to put it all. She would probably have to send some of it to Goodwill, because they didn't really have room for everything if it was all cleaned and put away.

"No pictures, trophies, hobbies…?"

Kelli opened her mouth. She hadn't even thought about any of those things. She thought he would only be making sure that she had a bed, clean clothes, food, and enough supervision. Did he really care about her personal effects? Looking around the room in a panic, she realized that it looked like a prison cell. She had cleared out all of the clutter. Anything she didn't use anymore. All of her toys from when she was a kid. Any craft junk or clay pots she made in kindergarten. And she had never been one to collect posters of cute boy bands or sci-fi movies she liked.

"Uh… I don't really have any hobbies," she said. "I have schoolwork and studying, and that really takes up all my time."

"You don't read? Have a computer?"

"No. Maybe watch TV with Mom sometimes. I'm not really into sports. Except for Jujitsu! I'm really into Jujitsu," Kelli said with relief, glad to find an interest that she could show him. And it was even related to her hearing, tying everything up in a neat bow. "Here, look." She opened her closet door and showed him her gi neatly hung up. "See? That's my uniform. And I keep all my belts," she opened a drawer to show him the neatly rolled-up belts. "I have…" she scanned the room. "I have Jujitsu books and videos. I go to the dojo at least three or four times a week."

"Do you fight in tournaments?"

"No… that takes money, and travel. I just stay in my own dojo. Work with my sensei and the other people who go there."

"You must have been doing it for a few years now."

"Yeah. It's really helped me. Given me confidence."

"And the ability to fight off three attackers at once."

"Well… yeah. If I'm lucky. If they'd been skilled, that would be a different matter…"

DCFS seemed to be satisfied with her hobby and he headed out of the room, back into the hallway.

Axel faced DCFS in the hallway. His eyes darted to the stranger and then to Kelli, his eyes searching. He looked back at DCFS and studied the ID tag.

"You're a social worker."

"Mr. Ivanovich, it's good to meet you."

"No one calls me mister. Just call me Axel."

"Axel. Your daughter has been very kind to give me the tour."

"We take good care of Kelli. You don't need to worry about her."

"I'm glad to hear that. How have things been for you the last little while? It must be quite an adjustment for you."

"What is?"

Axel had been born in the States, but when he was angry or belligerent, his Russian accent showed through. He had grown up speaking Russian with his parents, and while he usually spoke English without an accent, sometimes one came out.

"Living at home, after… uh… being incarcerated for so long."

"Oh, that." He gave a heavy shrug. "I try not to think of that. I am happy to be home. Spending time with my girl." Axel reached out to pat Kelli's arm and it took all her control not to flinch away from his touch. "We go out for ice cream. Watch movies. Play football." He mimed throwing a ball and cocked his head slightly. "She's not so good at football. She throws like a girl." He laughed at his own joke.

Kelli stared at him. Went out for ice cream? Watched movies? Played football? There was no sign of deception in Axel's face or manner. As if it were all true and he were the best of fathers to Kelli, affectionate and attentive, trying to make up for their time away from each other. Was he a psychopath? Who else would be able to lie so convincingly?

DCFS chuckled. He appeared to accept Axel's words. "Well, even if she does throw like a girl, she can whip the butt of anyone who criticizes her for it."

Axel gave a smile, his eyes sliding over to Kelli. "Did you hear about the fight in the park?" he said suddenly, as if it had just occurred to him. "She really knows how to take care of herself. It was all over the TV."

"Yes, I did hear about that," DCFS agreed.

"They put her in jail. For defending herself. But she's out now." Axel looked around before reaching for the handle of the door to his room. He opened it part way. "Her mother is very happy to have her home."

"I imagine so." DCFS took a glance into Axel's room, but didn't insist on entrance. "Well, you have a nice day, Mr. Ivanovich. Axel."

Axel grunted. "You too."

He closed the door and was gone again. Kelli wondered whether he was headed back to bed, not even sure why he had gotten up in the first place. Or maybe he just wanted to watch TV. His days were full of lounging around in bed and watching TV.

DCFS nodded at Kelli and headed toward the stairs. "He seems like a nice guy."

"Yeah."

She followed the social worker down to the living room again. Patricia levered herself out of her chair and waddled over to him. "Did Kelli show you everything you needed? I'm sorry… it just takes me time to get warmed up in the morning. But as you can see, everything is fine. Kelli has everything she needs and we take good care of her."

"Yes. Everything seems to be fine," DCFS agreed. "I'll write up my report and the incident file will be closed. I don't see any need for follow-up. Sorry to have bothered you."

Kelli let out a sigh of relief. DCFS shook hands with her. Kelli nodded and squeezed his hand.

"Great. See you. Or not, I guess. Thanks."

"Take care, Miss Munroe. And you can call if there is anything you need. If you have concerns… you know how to reach us. Whether it's for you, or one of your friends or neighbors." He held her hand still, no longer shaking it. "I left a business card in your bedroom. If there's anything at all."

He met her eyes. Kelli nodded again and forced a smile.

"Great. Thank you. See you later."

He finally left. Kelli let out a long, slow breath. Patricia looked at her.

"Now that he's gone, maybe I can get my oven mitts back," she said nonsensically.

Kelli frowned, her brows drawing down. "What?"

"My bottle. Where did you put the vodka I had here?"

"You finished it all," Kelli said. "I just picked up the empty."

"I finished it?"

"Yeah."

"I don't remember that."

Kelli rolled her eyes. "You had a lot to drink. I'm surprised you remember anything"

———

Patricia shuffled her way into the kitchen. She looked around vaguely, then headed toward the coffee pot for a second cup.

"Did you do all this?" she asked, indicating the room with a gesture.

"Well, it wasn't you and it definitely wasn't Dad."

"Did I ask for a smart mouth? It's lucky you did it before that snoop showed up, is all I'm saying."

"Yeah. *Lucky.*" Kelli leaned back against the cupboard, sipping what was left of her coffee.

"Did you know he was coming?" Patricia looked surprised.

"Yeah. I told you that."

"You didn't tell me."

"I told you when I got home. Thursday."

Patricia shook her head stubbornly.

———

Kelli stopped at the convenience store to grab a bottle of juice before heading out to set up her game. A weekly tradition. A ritual that brought her luck. Something about having to spend money before she would be able to earn more. She couldn't remember when it had started, it was just one of those superstitious little things people did, even if they didn't really believe them.

The store owner, a sweaty, overweight middle-eastern man, had worked there forever and knew everyone in the neighborhood. So he didn't stare at Kelli's birthmark as she carefully counted out her coins on the counter to pay for the drink. A few times when she had been short, he had let it ride, and she always paid him back immediately on her return. He knew she would always pay.

"Hey, pretty girl," said a voice.

Kelli startled. She turned around to see who had spoken. It was an older boy with long black hair wearing gang colors. Kelli's stomach twisted anxiously. What did he want from her?

As soon as she turned around, he saw that he had made a mistake. His eyes went to her disfigured face and his jaw dropped. His expression changed from teasing to disgust.

"Oh. I thought you were someone else," he spat.

It could have been worse. He could have called her ugly straight out. It was written all over his face. She'd heard it all before. Kelli's hand was curled tightly around her bottle, ready for trouble. Ready to fight her way out of it if she had to. But he didn't raise his hand to her. Kelli scattered a few more coins on the counter, not bothering to count them, and quickly walked away. She heard the banger swear and say something to the store owner with a low laugh. But the man knew Kelli and he didn't say anything in response.

Kelli's face was hot and her eyes stung. She didn't know why she still reacted emotionally to encounters like that. She had born the mark her whole life. She was used to things like that happening. She knew she should have a tougher skin. People weren't going to stop being jerks. They were going to continue to stare, to make inappropriate comments, to target her because of the way she looked.

It wasn't going to stop.

She shouldn't react to it. It should just roll off like water off of a duck's back. Because that's what she was, the ugly duckling. Only she was never going to turn into a beautiful swan.

———

Kelli met up with Les, and they spent the afternoon running several cons. Three-card Monte tended to be Kelli's favorite, but the shell game appealed to a younger crowd. Kids out with their parents for Saturday shopping would drag their minders over and beg them for change. Twenty-five cents a round was such a small thing to keep a child quiet, so most would stay until they ran through all of their pocket change, and then move on. Kelli let them find the pea often enough that they would stay excited about the game and stick around. Some were repeat customers who she often saw on weekends.

"Mommy! Mommy, I want to play the pea game!" Kelli heard one of her regulars and scanned the sidewalk for him.

A little boy of about six, tow-headed, wearing a blue windbreaker. He was tugging on his mother's arm, but she wasn't paying any attention, intent on making her way through the crowds to get to the next store.

"Mommy! The lady with the face," the little boy insisted. "I want to play with the lady with the face!"

"What?" She looked down at him in irritation. "What are you talking about?"

"The lady with the face!" The little boy pointed at his own cheek and then at Kelli. "The pea game, please!"

The woman shook her head, scowling. "We already gave money to the guitar man. I don't want to have to stop for every panhandler you see."

"But the pea lady is nice, I want to play the game. I brought cents from my piggy bank!"

The mother relented and let him drag her over to where Kelli sat. Kelli smiled at her young customer. "You all ready?"

He nodded eagerly.

"Watch it, then. Here's the pea." She lifted a shell to show him. "Keep watching." She started sliding them back and forth, whirling them around each other in a complicated pattern. "Where is it? Is it here? Is it here?" She lifted empty shells. "So where is it?"

He pointed at the remaining shell. Kelli lifted it to show him the pea, smiling.

"Okay, you all warmed up? You think you can do it today?"

He nodded again. Kelli waited for a coin from the mother, then ran through a few games with her little friend, letting him win a couple of times, playing until his mother shook her head, indicating that she wasn't paying any more.

"I have my own money," he protested, when he realized his mother wasn't paying.

Kelli glanced at the mother, then back at the boy.

"I'll give you two more games," she said. "No charge. You keep your piggy bank money."

He gave her a brilliant smile, happily lost two more guesses, and then they went on their way. Kelli had noticed there were always more takers after one of the kids played with her. Maybe they thought if a kid could win now and then, they had a chance to beat the house. Or maybe they just appreciated her being nice to the little ones. Whatever the psychology was, she was kept busy for a while after the little boy went on his way.

Les circled close and gave her a sign. Time to pack up and move on. She didn't know whether he had seen something, or just figured they'd been in one place too long, but at his signal, she immediately pocketed the tools of her trade, shrugging at the people who were watching or waiting to play.

"Sorry, got to go."

People drifted away. Kelli and Les walked together.

"Good day for it," Les observed.

"Yeah. Sunshine brings everyone out."

"What happened with the social worker?"

She had told him she'd had a visit, but hadn't discussed any details.

"Went fine. He came, had a look around, Mom and Dad were both home. He decided everything looked okay."

"Yeah?" He raised his eyebrows. "You must have really cleaned."

Kelli nodded. Her face burned, embarrassed by his comment. She knew the state of her house was pretty bad, but she had a 'nice' house, in a better neighborhood than Les's, and for him to take notice of how dirty it was, considering his slum house and twenty or so siblings, made her feel pretty bad.

"You should come see it. It looks really good now."

He nodded, but didn't act like he intended to. They rarely went to each other's houses, spending most of their time together either out making money or doing schoolwork at the library. 'Schoolwork' being a euphemism for messing around on the internet until it was nearly closing time and then panicking about not having any assignments done.

"Hey, look at that!" Kelli stopped outside a pawnshop window, pointing to an old-style oil lamp on display.

"Cool," Les acknowledged, barely slowing.

"I gotta have that!"

He stopped and turned around to look at her. "What? Why?"

Kelli peered in at it. "It's like Aladdin's lamp, or something. Isn't that so cool?"

"Uh, yeah. If it had a genie in it. Come on, Kelli. What would you do with a lamp?"

"I don't know. Sell it."

"You think that's going to have any street value? A watch or a necklace, something anyone can use, that's a good buy. An ancient oil lamp? No one is going to want that. It's probably not even genuine, it's some Disney knock-off. If it is genuine, you could never afford it or make anything off of it."

It was another common con for them. Going to the dollar store or pawnshop to find something sparkly and selling it on the street with a sob story for more than it was worth. Or selling one item and substituting one of lesser value when wrapping it up. They often switched from one con to another during the day to avoid getting bored or being in one place for too long. But Les was right. The lamp would be a terrible investment. And Kelli couldn't afford to get something that would just sit on her dresser at home.

She sighed, and they walked along the sidewalk again.

Les glanced at her. "Sorry. That was harsh."

"No. You're totally right."

"Yeah... but I didn't need to say it like that. You could have gone in to look at it."

"Well, like you said, unless it's got a genie in it, there's not really much point, is there?"

They walked along in silence. Kelli was out of sorts. She didn't feel like setting up again. Maybe she'd just go home early.

"What would you get?"

Kelli looked at Les. "What?"

"If you had a genie. You know. And three wishes. What would you wish for?"

"Money," Kelli said instantly. "Lots and lots of money. More than I could ever spend."

"Yeah," he agreed. "Then you could buy everything else you could want, right? What would you wish for the other two? Something you couldn't buy."

"No birthmark. I'd wish I never even had it. Ever. Even when I was a baby. You?"

"Huh…" Les shook his head slowly. "I can't think of anything that I couldn't just buy."

"Money can't buy happiness," Kelli quipped.

"Okay, then I'd wish for happiness. How about that?"

"You can't wish for happiness, it's against the rules."

"Says who?"

"I don't know. You just can't. You can't wish for happiness, only the things you think will make you happy."

"Fine then. I'd wish for a life that would make me happy."

"You can't… oh, brother. That's just the same as wishing for happiness."

"What's your third wish, then?"

"You haven't made your second yet!"

"I made my second. What's your third?"

Kelli pondered on this. She knew what she really wanted. But she didn't know what to say. "Um… okay, then… I'd wish… for a parent who would love me."

She rolled her eyes, knowing she had exposed herself. People just didn't say things like that. She and Les knew all of each other's secrets, but revealing this even to him was a risk. She waited for him to laugh at her.

But he didn't.

Kelli ventured a look at him. They both stopped walking.

"I'd wish that for you too," Les said.

"You can't use your third wish on me. Use it on your family."

"I can wish whatever I want. For me, for you, for anyone. And I'd wish for you. And your mom. Or dad. Do you care which?"

"No, I don't care which. Because it's never going to happen anyway. Do you know what he said?" she demanded, stopping suddenly, her voice rising. "When the social worker was there. He said he takes me out for ice cream. Or the movies. Or to play football together! Can you believe it? Where would he come up with something like that?"

Les's eyes went wide. "Really? And did he buy it? The social worker?"

"Hook, line, and sinker!"

"Well… I guess we know where you get your skill for deception."

Kelli was shaking her head, thinking back to the way Axel had spoken. Perfectly naturally. As if he believed every word himself.

"It was amazing. The guy must really be a sociopath. Who else can lie like that?"

"You."

"Not me! Even I get nervous. But he wasn't. Just said it like it was the truth."

"Lucky for you."

They walked to the bus stop. Kelli thought maybe they'd go to the library. She didn't feel like playing anymore, but she wasn't ready to go home.

"If he can lie like that, how did he get convicted?" Les asked.

"I dunno… he confessed. He still acts like he thinks he did it. Maybe he did."

"But the DNA says he didn't."

"Right," Kelli agreed.

"Maybe he's like that guy on TV the other day. He had two different DNA profiles. What do they call it?"

Kelli shook her head. "I don't know. How can someone have two different kinds of DNA?"

"It's a medical condition. I don't know."

She thought about the suggestion, then shook her head. She didn't know a lot about Axel's case, but just enough to discount the theory. "The DNA was for someone else they had in the system. Dad couldn't have someone else's DNA, even if he did have two kinds. He couldn't have someone else's."

"Unless he's a shapeshifter." Les closed his eyes and spread his hands, making an imaginary picture. "All he has to do is touch someone, and he can change into them, down to the last molecule. Even DNA—which is bigger, molecule or DNA?"

"Uh… DNA. I think." Kelli started walking again. "But I don't think Axel is a shapeshifter."

"He could be. He looks just like an alien on Men in Black."

"The aliens that look like people?"

"Exactly!"

Kelli sighed.

CHAPTER 5

The time passed too quickly. The next thing Kelli knew, it was Sunday night, and returning to school the next morning loomed up before her. She was sixteen, so why didn't she just drop out so that she didn't have to deal with all the crap that school entailed? The whole thing seemed to have been designed just to torture her. But as much as she wanted to just dump it, she wanted a better life and didn't see how she was going to get one without a high school diploma.

"What are you pacing around like a caged animal for?" Patricia demanded. "You're driving me up the wall."

"Just restless," Kelli said. "Don't know what to do with myself."

"Why don't you go outside? Run off some energy?"

Kelli looked at her. "It's after dark," she pointed out.

"Well, Miss I-beat-up-bad-guys, I didn't think that would stop you."

"I don't go looking for trouble."

"It finds you often enough."

"I'm not looking for it," Kelli repeated. "I'm sorry. I'll try not to bug you."

"Then go up to your room and find something to keep yourself occupied."

Kelli didn't want to be confined to her room. She did feel like a caged animal. That was a good description of how pent-up and anxious she felt.

She would have gone outside in a second if it had still been daylight. She hated to have to go to her room and not even to be able to roam the house.

At another glare from Patricia, Kelli nodded. "Just let me get a snack and I'll get out of the way."

She retreated to the kitchen and looked through the fridge and cupboards. In spite of the groceries she had purchased over the past week, there wasn't anything that struck her as appetizing. She could cook up a box of mac and cheese, but just the thought of it turned her stomach. Axel might be able to eat the stuff every meal, but Kelli couldn't. Kelli spread some peanut butter on toast and put it on her plate to take it up to her room. She wouldn't leave the plate in there. She would bring it back down at the end of the night or the next morning and wash it. No plates piling up in her room. No crumbs to attract vermin or to get moldy. Her room was going to remain in pristine condition.

Kelli mounted the stairs and walked past the master bedroom. She heard the bedsprings squeak as Axel got up, and quickened her pace to get to her own room and shut the door. Axel yanked his door open and glowered at her.

"What are you doing?"

"Just getting a snack and going to my room, Dad."

"Were you fighting with your mother?"

Kelli wasn't sure whether their raised voices had caught his attention, or whether he was just being paranoid or delusional.

"No. Just talking. I was getting a snack and she's watching TV." Kelli smiled at him and kept moving down the hallway.

"Why are you eating *that?*" Axel caught her arm, preventing her from going back to her room.

"It's just what I felt like. Peanut butter on toast." Kelli raised her eyebrows, still smiling like a mad person. "Do you like it? Do you want me to get you one?" She swiveled back toward him. "Do you want this one, and I'll make myself another?"

"Are you making fun of me?" he barked.

"No. No, just asking if you want some. It's okay if you don't. It's okay if you do." She didn't know which way to go with it. Nothing she said or did seemed to be calming him down. "Do you want me to get you something?" she pressed again, hoping that he would decide there was something he wanted. She tried to ease her arm out of his grip, but it was becoming increasingly obvious that he wasn't going to be distracted this time. Kelli was starting to weigh all of the points for and against her. He was bigger than she was, but she could use leverage to turn his own weight against him. They were in a tight space. She could use her smaller frame to an advantage in the hallway. But what she really wanted to do was just to get away from him. She didn't want to have to fight him. Why did he have to get up and confront her?

Axel called her a nasty name and tried to push the plate into her face. Kelli blocked it and stepped back, maneuvering for a better advantage.

"Dad, just leave me alone," she pleaded.

"You hang around here, making trouble for your mother, picking fights with me. You think I'm going to put up with that kind of lip?"

"I'm not doing anything to you. I'm not picking a fight. I'm just going to my room. That's all."

He shoved her into the wall and swore at her, calling her filthy names. Maybe he would leave it at that. Maybe if she weren't confrontational, he would just wind back down again and leave her alone. Kelli inched toward her bedroom.

"You want to fight?" Axel challenged. "You want to prove how tough you are? Your mother told me how you were on the TV. You think you're bad, that you're so tough. Everybody thinking you're a hero because you got into a fight at the park. Show me how tough you are."

Kelli blocked a blow aimed at her chest. She stood there, balanced on her toes, waiting for him to make another move. He wasn't winding down. If anything, he was getting himself more excited. Had he been drinking? Taking drugs? She hadn't seen him with anything worse than headache pills from the bathroom cabinet, but she wouldn't put it past him. He was a convict. He might have gotten a taste for illegal drugs somewhere along the way. It would explain his paranoid behavior.

"I'm sorry, Dad," she tried. "I'm sorry for being such a pain. I'll just go to my room and stay out of your way."

He moved in, battering her like a boxer at the speed bag. First one side, then the other, in rapid succession. Kelli blocked a few blows, but still took one hard fist to the cheekbone. She repositioned her leg behind his body and tried to shift him over it. It wasn't as easy as practicing the move in her drills. He was slippery, pulling away from her and moving in an unexpected direction. Still aiming blows at her face and head instead of grappling her like one of the other fighters from the dojo would. Kelli moved in closer to him. If she could just get a good grip on his arm, she could throw him. She could get close enough to grapple him and take him to the ground, where she could get the advantage.

She grunted, taking another blow to the face. She swore and shoved him back, throwing him into the wall. It wasn't the same as taking him down, but at least it gave her a few seconds to regroup.

Axel growled angrily and bounced back at her.

"Just leave me alone!" Kelli shouted.

He tried to hit her face again and Kelli went for his eyes. Jujitsu wasn't always clean, like watching it on TV or in a tournament. Sometimes it was messy. Defending yourself against attack didn't mean following a set of rules. The unarmed combatant went for tender parts. Eyes, nerves, groin. She couldn't be squeamish about it, or she'd end up too badly hurt to get to school in the morning. Maybe even all week.

Axel backed up a couple of steps, his hands going up to protect his eyes. With his hands too close to his face to see what was going on, Kelli moved in again, and managed to get her foot behind him this time. A quick flip, and he went crashing to the floor. Kelli jumped past him and retreated to her room.

Breathing hard, her heart pumping like a piston, Kelli ran into her room and slammed the door behind her. She locked the door and listened for a moment, her ear pressed against it. She could hear Axel moving and groaning, swearing at her, and slowly getting himself to his feet. Without wasting any more time, Kelli got to the other side of her dresser and pushed it in front of the door, so that even if he picked the lock or kicked the latch through the frame, he couldn't get into the room. She got to the other side of her bed, and pushed it into place behind the dresser, like two steps in a Chinese puzzle box. She sat down on the bed to add her weight to the barricade, and was still.

She could hear Axel going up and down the hallway, grunting and groaning. He tried the handle once, but didn't try to force or break it. Just rattled the knob and went on again. Kelli heard him go into the bathroom. Into his bedroom, and back out again. He went back in and complained loudly about the mess the room was in.

"I'll get demerits and no yard time," he said angrily. "Who tossed it? I'll kill whoever left it like this!"

Kelli closed her eyes. He was back in prison. That was why he had come after her. He thought he was back in prison again, and she was... who? Another inmate challenging him? Some kind of enemy or gang member? She had no idea what it had been like for him in prison. She had visited with him, but the sanitized visitor room was no reflection of what the rest of the prison was like. How he lived every day. She could only glean a word here or there when he would mention it offhand. Or she would see or hear one of the other inmates being fractious and get just an inkling of what it would be like to have to live with people like that. She had never felt close to Axel, even as a child, but she still felt sorry for him living in those conditions.

Axel paced up and down the hallway, breathing heavily. She heard him start down the stairs. Hopefully, he wouldn't start beating on Patricia. If he did, should Kelli go down and try to stop him? Put herself back in harm's way to protect her mother from further abuse? Patricia had never been very good at keeping herself safe. She picked violent mates and opened herself up to them. It wasn't fair of her to put Kelli in the middle. She should never have allowed Axel to come back again.

There were raised voices, but she didn't hear any noise of crashing furniture. No screaming. Kelli was too far away, and the door was closed so that she couldn't hear whether there were any blows or not. She stayed on her bed, cowering there, listening for further hints of danger.

In a while, she heard Axel making his way back up the stairs and Patricia's voice with him. She couldn't tell whether she was going with him willingly, or whether he was forcing her. But they both went into the master bedroom and the door was shut. Kelli picked up a book and put in her earphones, playing a repeating loop of music on her cheapie mp3 player.

———

Before she knew it, it was morning. Kelli had slept only fitfully. She never turned the light off, afraid of what would happen if she did. She didn't want to be in the dark. If something else was to happen, she wanted to be in the light, where she could see exactly what was going on. She awoke, lay there listening to the silence of the house or to sirens in the distance outside, read for a while, until she fell back asleep, face in her book. She slept and awoke in a restless cycle, never feeling safe enough to sleep soundly.

When morning came and her alarm went off, Kelli dragged herself out of bed. She pushed her bed back into place, and pushed the dresser away from the door. She made a trip to the bathroom, ears pricked for any sound of Axel or Patricia. She looked at herself in the mirror.

Axel had bruised her face. The opposite side from her birthmark. Though, touching the birthmark with careful fingers, Kelli realized that it was probably bruised under the birthmark too, only the discoloration wasn't visible. She did her best to make up her face so that the new bruising wasn't visible. But from experience, no one really paid any attention to any new bruises. They were so used to avoiding looking at her face and birthmark, they didn't notice any new marks.

Kelli slipped down the stairs to the kitchen. Patricia's TV was still playing to the empty living room, but apparently, she hadn't made it back down after joining Axel. Hopefully, that meant that she had fallen asleep with him, both of them calm and satisfied, rather than that she was knocked out or throttled to death.

Kelli put ice on her face while she waited for a fresh pot of coffee to perk. She could hear the neighborhood beginning to stir. Traffic picked up as parents took the younger kids to school. Children shrieked and called back and forth to each other. She liked the sounds of their playing. That was how kids should be, happy and carefree on their way to school.

She didn't go back upstairs to get her schoolbooks, worried that any noise outside Axel's bedroom door might wake him up and set him off again. She'd have to hand in her assignments late. But that was better than not getting to school at all.

Les was already hanging around Kelli's locker. He had a smear of blueberry in the corner of his mouth, which told Kelli that they had blueberry muffins for the school's free breakfast program. She didn't like blueberries. And she didn't like being seen at the free breakfast program. Kids knew that she lived in a better neighborhood, not in the projects, so they took exception to seeing her making use of the free breakfast program that they thought should be the exclusive right of the poorer neighborhoods.

"How's it going?" she asked Les, opening up her locker and surveying the contents.

"Good. You all set? Where are your books?"

"Left them at home."

"Your report too?"

Kelli nodded. Les didn't ask her why. He gave her a grimace. "You okay?"

"Yeah."

"You sure?"

Kelli waved a hand at him. "Let it go, Broke."

Les put up both hands in a 'surrender' gesture. "When crazy ninja girls says let it go, I let it go."

Kelli picked up a couple of books that had remained in her locker since before the fight, and she scrounged through the rest of the junk there until she found a pen. Hopefully one that would work. "People aren't still saying that, are they?"

"Crazy ninja girl?"

Kelli nodded.

"Of course. You think they're going to let something like that go this century? You're stuck with it now."

"Well, I guess it's better than poopface."

"A change is always nice."

The early bell went, and Kelli closed her locker and did up the lock. "What would be really nice is—"

Her words were cut off when one of the bigger boys, a halfback on the football team, went crashing into Kelli, bouncing her into the metal lockers with a huge crash. Completely unprepared because she hadn't even finished turning around, Kelli wasn't able to brace herself. Head spinning, she tried to get reoriented. Les put his arm around her, holding her up.

"You okay?"

Kelli swore weakly. "Did somebody get the license plate of that truck?"

"I think it said, 'jerk face.' Seriously, did he hurt you?"

Kelli looked at the lockers, a brand-new dent where her body had landed. "I guess that makes him a big man, that he can body check crazy ninja girl when she's not looking. Lucky I didn't hit it face first and get my teeth knocked out."

Saying it brought back an image of Patricia when she got her teeth knocked out. The bleeding, broken stumps in her mouth. It had been terrifying. For Kelli, anyway. Patricia had probably been too drunk to care at the time. Not until later, when she sobered up.

"I gotta get to class," Les said apologetically. "You be okay?"

"Yeah, go, I'm fine."

He still looked guilty about separating from her to get to his own class. They didn't share much of their schedules. Kelli tried to take the advanced classes when she could, and Les was happy to drift along in the remedial streams.

"Go," Kelli told him again.

He went, winding his way through the mass of bodies to find his class. Kelli took a deep breath. She hadn't even dropped her books, so it was just a matter of straightening up and walking it off. She was fine. No permanent harm done.

"Oh, look." One of the prima donnas pointed Kelli out. "Munroe is back. You get tired of being on TV, Munroe? Decided to come back and associate with the serfs again? Are you sure you're not too good for us?"

Kelli ignored her. She didn't know why the cheerleaders had to attack her. It wasn't like they could feel threatened that she was going to take their spots on the squad. She'd never tried out for cheerleading and she never would. Even if she'd had the looks, it wasn't something that had ever interested her, and she had no desire to even be seen with the Barbies. She liked Jujitsu, not dancing around with a pom-pom, baring her legs up to her crotch and wearing a skin-tight body suit to show off all her assets. The very thought put her teeth on edge.

"Why don't you go home, Munroe?" the fake blond went on. "Nobody wants you here."

"I'm not here because I want to be with you," Kelli said. "Why don't *you* go home?"

"Because I belong here. You… don't. Nobody wants you here. Why don't you do us all a favor and just kill yourself? Next time someone tries to beat you up, why don't you just die?"

"Seriously?" Kelli demanded. "Is that really the best you can come up with? They don't teach you much verbal repartee in cheer, do they?"

The girl looked at Kelli blankly.

"Which word didn't you understand?" Kelli asked sweetly. "Verbal or repartee?"

Her nose wrinkled. "Why don't you just die?" she repeated. Brilliant repartee.

Kelli shook her head sadly at the lack of education in her generation and walked to class.

———

It wasn't until evening that Kelli got home. She and Les spent some after-school time at the library, then picking up business until it started to get dark. Kelli headed for home with a knot in her stomach. Things would probably be quiet. Chances were good that they would not have two wild nights in a row.

The house was dark. Just a couple of flickering TVs going inside. Kelli opened the front door and looked in for Patricia. She was not in her usual chair, though the driveling TV and a pile of empties said that she had spent time there during the day. Kelli walked through to the kitchen, expecting to find Patricia there refueling, but there was no sign of her. Kelli started the water running in the sink, determined to tackle the day's dishes before they had a chance to pile up any higher.

As she shut off the water, there was a noise behind her. Kelli whirled around to face the attack, but there was no one there. The noise had come from the bathroom. The pipes knocking because she had been running the hot water? Or a mouse or Patricia? Kelli held still, listening. After a minute, a groan from her mother. Kelli shook her head. She walked over to the small bathroom.

"Are you okay, Mom?"

No response.

"Are you sick?"

Kelli waited again for an answer. When there was none, she knocked sharply on the door. "Mom, are you okay? Do you need anything?"

Another groan, but nothing coherent. Kelli bit her lip. She had work to do. Dishes to wash. Homework that she hadn't finished at the library. And she had been looking forward to holing up in her room and just reading and listening to music without any interruptions or worries about anyone else.

She went back to the sink and started washing the dishes. But her mind was on Patricia and what sort of disaster Kelli was going to find if she opened the bathroom door. Did she really want to get involved? Did she want to face a new drama that would probably take most of her evening to deal with?

Kelli went to the kitchen to gather up the empty cans and bottles. She made a second trip to get the dirty dishes and put them into the hot, soapy water. She grabbed the bits of dirty clothes on the floor and threw them down the stairs to land somewhere near the mountain of laundry she still had left to do. It wasn't washing itself. She needed to get to it soon, before rats started nesting there.

Finally, Kelli drained the sink and looked back at the closed bathroom door. She could ignore the fact that Patricia was in there, maybe sick, maybe hurt, and just go upstairs to veg out and selfishly enjoy the rest of her evening. Chances were, Patricia would be all right. She would take care of herself. It wasn't like Kelli was the mother and Patricia the child.

Except it *was* sort of like that. Over the years, their roles had become reversed, and Kelli did feel responsible for her mother's welfare. Could she really go to bed knowing that Patricia might be in trouble?

Dragging her feet, Kelli went back over to the bathroom and pounded loudly on the door.

"Mom! Are you okay?"

The door opened inward. After picking the lock, Kelli had to push the door open, trying to avoid crushing Patricia behind it, yet still get it open far enough to do something for her. Patricia lay on the floor, moaning as Kelli pushed and tugged at her through a crack in the door, trying to get her repositioned to get the door open. She needed leverage, but had none. Finally, she got Patricia wedged into the space in front of the toilet and got the door open the rest of the way.

Patricia was a mess. Kelli cataloged the issues. Patricia had bruises on her face that were obviously from the day before. She and Axel apparently had come to blows sometime during the night. Patricia's breath and body stank of alcohol, and her shirt was crusted with vomit. The biggest problem, though, was the big purple goose egg on her forehead. If she had to guess, Kelli figured Patricia had either fallen off of the toilet head-first into the wall, or had passed out throwing up over the sink or toilet. The bruise was nasty, but Patricia was still at least semi-conscious, trying to answer Kelli.

Kelli felt Patricia's pulse. It was nice and strong. No worries there. She could probably get by just getting Patricia relocated for the night. She'd wake up with a killer headache, but she'd be fine.

"Let's get you back to your chair," Kelli prompted, trying to pull Patricia to her feet. "Come on. You're missing your programs."

It was not easy getting her arm around Patricia to try to lift her up. She wrapped Patricia's arm around her neck to provide a second lifting point. Patricia's movements were clumsy and she was too drunk to support her weight properly even when Kelli did get her to her feet. It was no wonder she had fallen down. What was surprising was that she had even made it to the bathroom first.

"Come on, Mom. Just to your chair, and then you can sit down and rest."

They shuffled along. Kelli tried to go slowly so that Patricia could do some of the work herself. Eventually, they got to the chair and Kelli turned Patricia around and dumped her into it.

At that point, Patricia's eyes flickered open, drawn to her TV screen. Kelli bent over, looking at the bump on Patricia's forehead. It was nasty. She got an ice pack from the freezer and settled it over the bump, making Patricia moan in protest.

"You gotta keep that there. Try to take down the swelling. Okay?"

Patricia felt beside the chair for a bottle. It was a wonder she could still feel anything with how much she reeked of drink. Kelli considered trying to clean her up, but decided to just leave hygiene alone for the time being. If she cleaned Patricia up, chances were, she'd just be wallowing in her own filth again by morning. Better to just leave it alone, and maybe the next day Patricia would be able to manage changing and showering without assistance.

Kelli left Patricia where she was happiest and headed up the stairs. She tried to creep as quietly as possible, not wanting Axel to open the door when she got to the top of the stairs. She didn't need another confrontation with him.

She held her breath slipping past his door, and didn't start breathing again until she reached her room.

CHAPTER 6

Kelli slept restlessly. Things were quiet, but even that was unsettling, as she never knew how long it was going to last. Having slept so little the night before, she was able to get a better night's sleep, but still kept waking up listening, thinking she had heard Axel or that her mother was in trouble. But she wasn't going to keep getting up and checking on Patricia. Walking up and down the hallway that many times would be too risky.

Morning came around and all was quiet. Kelli always felt relief when the sky started to get lighter and she was still alive and unhurt. The early morning hours were good to her. Parents that had drunk themselves unconscious or dropped from exhaustion after fighting all night. Peace and quiet. A fresh new day to look forward to.

She got up and showered, keeping one ear open for trouble, but feeling pretty relaxed. If Axel were going to pick a fight, it would have been during the night. He was rarely active in the early morning hours, even though he must have had to get up early in prison. From what Kelli remembered, they had to be up at four o'clock for showers and breakfast. Kelli liked early morning, but four was a bit much even for her.

After pampering herself with hot water, soap, and fresh clothes, Kelli went down the stairs. She picked up the warm ice bag from the floor and leaned over Patricia for a look at the lump. It still looked pretty bad. Darker than it had been, but no less swollen. Patricia's eyes fluttered open and she gave a little yelp at seeing Kelli right over her face like that. Kelli put her hand on Patricia's shoulder to try to calm her.

"It's okay. It's just me. Just checking on the bump on your head. How is it feeling? Pretty sore this morning?"

Patricia groaned. She brought her hand up to her face to prod at the other bruises, but didn't touch the bump.

"My head is killing me. Get me something."

Kelli nodded. "Sure." She went into the kitchen and started the coffee going, and pulled a bottle of painkillers out of the cupboard. She had hidden them away before the social worker's arrival, knowing that it was a forged prescription and that the social worker might be suspicious seeing them on the shelf. But now that the inspection was done, she had moved them back to where she could keep track of them. A couple pills with a mug of fresh coffee should get Patricia started on her day.

"Did you fall down last night?" Kelli asked, delivering them to Patricia in her chair. "Do you remember how you got the bump?"

"I just got dizzy," Patricia slurred. "Must have a bit of the flu or something."

"Or something," Kelli agreed. "Are you still dizzy this morning?"

"No." Patricia poked at the vomit dried to her clothes. "I must have been sick. What a state I am in!"

"You can get cleaned up, if you're not still too dizzy," Kelli said. "I'm already done my shower, it's all yours."

"Everything is wavy," Patricia complained. "Where are my glasses?"

"You don't have glasses. Is it a concussion? You've got a pretty bad bump."

"Yes, definitely a concussion," Patricia agreed. "That's why I threw up. From the concussion."

Kelli glanced at Patricia's clothes, but didn't really want to look too closely. Kelli thought that Patricia had probably thrown up again after being settled into her chair the night before. So maybe some of it was from the concussion. Good thing she hadn't choked to death during the night, especially reclined in her chair like that, unable to move in any direction without effort.

"Concussions are bad for you," Patricia wandered on in the discussion. "They say that if you have too many concussions, it can do permanent damage. Forever. All those times I've fallen down…"

Or been knocked down. They both knew very well that most of Patricia's concussions had not been accidental. Why she always seemed to pick abusive men, Kelli had no idea. Maybe there was something wrong with her from a long time ago. Maybe her own father had been abusive and that was what she thought she wanted in a man.

"I'm not a child!" Patricia insisted suddenly, her voice angry.

Kelli drew back from her. "No one said you were," she countered. "I didn't say anything!"

"You think you have to take care of me and baby me, and you don't. I'm the adult here, not you."

"Yeah," Kelli agreed dryly. "I'm going to have some breakfast. You want anything?"

Kelli wasn't sure what she was going to have. Another peanut butter on toast, maybe. She didn't really get hungry in the morning, but she hated not eating until noon.

"Cereal. Do we have any kind of cereal? Good stuff?" Patricia asked.

"Lucky Charms."

Patricia nodded eagerly. "That's what I want."

"With milk or without?" Kelli wasn't quite sure how Patricia could manage the sugary cereal when she was hung over, but she wasn't going to argue about it. It was good if Patricia was having something other than alcohol all day long. At least the cereal was fortified with vitamins.

"No milk. Just put it in a cup."

"Put the cereal in a cup, or the milk in a cup?"

Patricia looked at her as if she was being dense. "The cereal!"

Kelli shrugged. "Okay. Get it to you in a minute."

She retreated to the kitchen. Kelli put stale bread in the toaster for herself and scooped a cup full of Lucky Charms cereal out of the box for Patricia. She had put the cereal into a plastic container to keep the mice out. Apparently, mice liked the rainbow marshmallows as much as Patricia. She took the cup of cereal in to her mother, and watched for a minute while Patricia picked all of the marshmallow bits out, leaving the cereal behind. Patricia glared at her. "What's your problem?"

"Nothing. How are they?"

"They taste like they always do."

Kelli went back to put peanut butter on her toast and to wait for the coffee to finish brewing. Then she sat down at the kitchen table to eat her breakfast in peace.

———

Done her breakfast, Kelli headed back up the stairs to gather her books together and get ready for school.

"Where are you going?" Patricia demanded.

"Getting ready to go."

"Go where? The appointment isn't until ten o'clock."

Kelli stopped and looked down at her mother from the stairs. "What appointment?"

"At the doctor's. That's today, isn't it?"

Kelli went back down the stairs again. She looked at her mother and then walked over to the calendar on the wall where they scribbled appointments and important dates. Did Patricia have a doctor's appointment? Had she set something up for Kelli? It had been years since Kelli had seen anything other than emergency room doctors.

Patricia's messy writing was on the calendar. The name of Axel's psychologist, and what might have passed as the number ten.

"An appointment for Dad," she said. "You don't need me there for that."

It was impressive that Patricia had even remembered about the appointment. Kelli was surprised that she knew what day it was.

"He wanted everybody in the family there," Patricia said. "You too."

"What does he need me there for?"

"I don't know. He said that they need the whole family to do a proper evaluation."

Kelli shifted uncomfortably. She didn't want to miss school, she didn't want to spend the time with Axel, and she didn't want to be stuck in a doctor's office for no particular reason.

"I was just a baby when Dad went to prison," Kelli protested. She'd been bigger than a baby, of course, but she'd only been a child. What impact could a little child have on Axel's decision to confess to the crime? What input could she have on the psychologist's evaluation of Axel?

"That doesn't have anything to do with it," Patricia said, scowling. "He wants everyone in the family there to finish his evaluation. You have to come."

"You didn't tell me ahead of time! I have school today."

"You can miss one day of school. You get good marks."

"I missed most of last week, I'm already trying to get caught up."

She knew there was no point in arguing. Patricia expected her to go, and she would go. But she wanted to voice her protests anyway. She wanted Patricia to know how inconvenient it all was and that she couldn't just spring things on Kelli that way.

"You are going," Patricia said in a determined voice.

Kelli sighed. There was no point in going upstairs to get her books. Since she had the time and had to be cooped up at home, she should probably get to work on the laundry. She could get a few loads washed before it was time to go to the doctor's.

"Are you going to go get Dad up, then? He needs to get ready."

"Not yet. It's early."

Kelli shrugged and went downstairs to start sorting laundry.

———

To begin with, Kelli just sat in the doctor's waiting room while Axel and Patricia had sessions with him. The evaluation had been going on for several months, but it was the first time that Kelli had been asked to attend. She wondered if Patricia had even gotten it right, as no one seemed to pay her even the slightest attention.

But eventually, a young nurse or receptionist with a friendly smile approached Kelli with a clipboard.

"You're Kelli Munroe?"

"Yeah."

"Would you come with me, please?"

Kelli swallowed and stood. It was good to get to her feet, but she wasn't looking forward to meeting with the doctor. She'd talked to psychologists before. Mostly through the school. They were always friendly and prodded with all kinds of personal questions, trying to dig out any issues. The woman led her through a series of corridors that got Kelli turned around, eventually taking her into a blue-carpeted room with some comfy chairs, and the doctor sitting behind a large table in a heavy office chair.

He stood up as Kelli walked in and reached out to shake her hand. "You must be Kelli Munroe. Kelli, I'm Doctor Siddal. It's nice to finally meet you."

His eyes went immediately to her birthmark. Just like everyone's. Thinking about the goose egg on Patricia's head, Kelli didn't want him getting the wrong impression.

"It's a birthmark."

"I know," he agreed. "Axel has told me all about his daughter."

What exactly had Axel told the psychologist? Real things or made up things? That his daughter was the crazy ninja girl from the park? Or that he took her out for ice cream and played football with her on Sunday mornings? Or something completely different? Kelli made a noncommittal noise and looked at the furniture.

"Have a seat," Siddal invited. "Whatever looks comfortable."

She wondered if it was the first test. Psychologists could read motives into anything. Everything they said was a test. She just chose the nearest chair and plonked down. Let him read what he liked into that.

"I don't really know why I'm here," Kelli said. "I didn't have anything to do with Dad's confession."

"There's more involved here than just a confession. The confession is just one symptom of what's going on in your father's brain."

"I'm not a doctor."

"No. I want you to relax, Kelli. This isn't anything bad. I just want to talk to you. Ask you some questions about your parents. Get a complete picture of how Axel functions at home."

Kelli looked around the room. It was hard to think of anything she wanted to do less.

"We've done lots of testing on your father over the past months, as you probably know." Siddal seemed to be waiting for a response, but when he didn't get any, he went on. "As well as the psychological and functional testing that I have been doing, he has had brain imaging done, a full medical, and a review of his medical history."

Again, a pause. Kelli nodded impatiently. "Yeah?"

"Tell me, Kelli… does it surprise you that your father would confess to something he didn't do?"

"Well… yeah. If he didn't do it, then why didn't he fight it? Get his DNA tested in the first place?"

"It's odd behavior for an innocent man, isn't it?" Siddal agreed. "Did you know that one in four people who were later found to be wrongly convicted had actually confessed to the crime?"

"One in four? Really?" She shook her head, amazed. "Then… why are you so interested in Dad? If it's so normal?"

"Most of those confessions fall under two headings. The convicted person was either persuaded that they did it or had some culpability, or they were afraid of what would happen if they didn't confess."

"Okay…"

"Knowing your father, which side would you put him under?"

Kelli already knew the answer to that question. "He thinks he did it."

Siddal nodded. "That would appear to be the case. So why does he think he did it? After a man is exonerated like your father, this Foundation attempts to identify the points where the justice system broke down, so that they can be addressed in the future. We've effected changes to the way that detainees can be questioned to try to prevent false confessions or other miscarriages of justice."

Kelli had seen plenty of crime TV. She knew all about people who were questioned for hours on end, how they eventually would break down and confess to anything. And she had learned about implanted memories. Questioning a subject in a way that fed them the details and made them think they remembered something that hadn't happened. Researchers said they could make just about anyone remember doing something that they hadn't done, with a few techniques.

"We have at our disposal all of the recordings of Axel's interrogations when he was first detained and later arrested. We have studied hours of interactions to try to determine where things broke down, what might have happened to convince your father that he had done something he hadn't."

"What's this got to do with me?" Kelli demanded. As interesting as it was to sit there and listen to Siddal pontificate about something that had happened ten years ago, Kelli was ready to move on. She didn't want to be there in the first place.

"Your dad's case is quite unique. Prison officials noted some odd behaviors during his incarceration. And looking back over the tapes of his interrogations… it's difficult to identify any coercive methods used by the arresting officers or the detectives that questioned him. In fact, during most of the discussions, the conversation between Axel and his interrogators was very calm and civil."

Kelli knew the charming, civil Axel. As long as he wasn't drinking, he could seem like a very nice man, in spite of looking like he'd walked directly out of a mug shot book or vintage mob movie.

"Have you ever heard the word confabulation?"

Kelli blinked at the sudden change in direction. "Uh…. Yeah… telling tall tales, right? Making up fantastic stories."

Siddal nodded, beaming at her.

"It actually has a medical meaning. Have you ever met someone who seems like they're lying all the time? They come up with bizarre, unbelievable stories, and even when confronted, won't back down?"

Kelli was glad that he had said 'someone' instead of Axel, though she knew he would circle back eventually.

"Yeah."

"Someone who will continue to make things up even when you've caught them in a lie and can prove that they are lying?"

Kelli nodded again.

"There are cases where the person in question doesn't even know that they are lying. They don't know that they are making things up. Their brain is, in fact, supplying them with information that logically fills gaps in their knowledge, and they don't realize that they've just made something up."

Kelli chewed on her lip, thinking about Axel. She never knew that about him when she was a little girl. And it had not become obvious to her while he was in prison. She knew that he told stories. Some of them she believed and some she didn't, but she thought mostly that he was bored and was just entertaining her with made-up stories. It wasn't until he came home that she started to see how he really was. That he actually believed the stories he told.

Like the one about taking her out for ice cream. Kelli couldn't remember him ever, in his lifetime, taking her out for ice cream. Not even when she was little, before he went to prison. Yet when he said it, there was no hint that he didn't believe it. No wink or nod or snicker with her after the fact over how gullible the social worker was.

Siddal leaned back in his chair, making it creak loudly. "I was reviewing a case recently about a woman who was found to have no episodic memory. She couldn't remember anything that happened to her, her experiences, like you or I would. She could remember facts. She knew the way things worked. But she couldn't actually remember any sensory information or details about the specific events that had happened to her."

"So she lied?" Kelli asked.

"She told colorful stories. She said she thought that was what everyone did. She didn't realize that she actually had a deficit. Instead she was like a blind person discussing brilliant colors. She had the knowledge, she mouthed the words, she made it up as she went along."

"And some people… don't even know they're making it up."

Siddal nodded. "Exactly."

"You think that's what's going on with my dad?"

"I do."

Kelli sat and stared at him. Axel not recognizing her in the hallway. Making up stories to the social worker. Not knowing where he was. Confessing to a crime that he hadn't committed.

"How does that happen? Is someone just… born that way?"

"Some people are born with differences in their brains. Some are injured, maybe in a fight or an industrial accident. We learn some fascinating things from people with penetrating brain injuries. Those ones who walk into the emergency room with a knife or a pole sticking out of their heads."

Kelli liked doctor shows and those were some of her favorite cases. She grinned. "But Dad never had anything like that, did he? Was he born that way? Or did something happen?"

"Going back over his medical records… he had an infection."

"Like the flu or a hangnail?"

Siddal smiled. "He had dental surgery to remove an impacted molar, and he ended up with an infection down in his jaw. It spread through the bone and into his brain."

Kelli felt her eyes get wide as she pictured it. It must have been horrific, grotesque, like some zombie movie. She'd never considered that something so dire could result from having a tooth pulled. An infection in his brain that had wiped out his ability to form memories?

"Gross," she murmured.

"They had to remove pieces of his jaw and skull. He was on some very strong antibiotics to try to get it under control, but it seems that it left him with some significant damage."

Axel had scars on his jaw, neck, and head. Kelli had always assumed that they came from fighting. He'd never said a word about the infection or the fact that it nearly took his life and left him handicapped. But maybe he didn't know. Maybe he had no clue what effect it had on him. Maybe all he remembered was that he'd had an infection, and the hospital had fixed him up. He wouldn't have been conscious of what was going on at the time, would he, if it had been that bad?

Kelli twisted her fingers together. "So… you figured it all out. You know how he got convicted now. Why he confessed when he didn't do it."

Siddal sat his chair upright again, nodding. "Yes. We've solved that piece of the puzzle. What's in the future for him… I don't know. I have some concerns about Axel moving forward."

Kelli stared at a divot in the carpet. Someone had moved the furniture around recently, and the indentation in the carpet was still there.

"How have things been since he moved back home?" Siddal asked.

"I dunno. Fine. Weird having him back. But he mostly keeps to himself. Watches TV in his room. It's hard for convicts to get jobs. Probably harder if they're brain-damaged."

"I would guess so. How do he and your mom get along?"

"Pretty good. She visited him every week when he was in prison. Lots of women wouldn't do that. They'd just go find someone else, and he wouldn't have anywhere to go when he got out. But she never got rid of his stuff."

"Very admirable." Siddal was silent for a few moments.

Kelli twisted uncomfortably. But she knew he was trying to use silence against her. Trying to make it so that she would jump in and fill it up. She knew how shrinks worked.

"Your mother has a pretty bad bump on her head today."

"Yeah." Kelli raised her eyes to him. "But Dad didn't do that to her. She was sick. She fainted in the bathroom and hit it on the sink."

"Really. Does that happen very often?"

"She's kind of clumsy. She drinks more than she should. And lately… she drops things a lot, even when she hasn't had much to drink. She's been…" Kelli trailed off. She didn't know what to say. Things hadn't been good for Patricia lately. But Kelli wasn't about to blab about all of their troubles and end up being put into foster care. She didn't want Siddal to think that Axel was beating on Patricia all the time, but she didn't want him to think that Patricia wasn't capable of taking care of Kelli, either.

"Your mother was present for a lot of the psychological testing that we have done," Siddal said. "And I've had the chance to talk to her at length. While your dad's memory issues are concerning, he is stable and I think we can help him with some strategies. Maybe we can help him to find work that would suit him. But your mother... I'm quite concerned about her."

A lump swelled up in Kelli's throat. Her eyes burned. She wasn't prepared for this. All she had come for was to hear what the doctor had to say about Axel. She had been dragged out and had no interest in getting involved in Axel's life. But her *mother*...

"You've been worried about her?" Siddal asked. He pulled a couple of tissues from the box on his desk and handed them to her.

"Well... some..."

"She's losing words?"

"Yeah. Not a lot. But... she never did before."

"She's more emotionally labile? That means that she can change moods very quickly. Happy to crying or screaming for no apparent reason?"

Kelli nodded. "I thought that was just... well... drink."

"Drinking won't help. I sense from talking with her that she drinks a lot. There are certain eye movements and other behaviors that someone experienced with alcoholics recognizes."

Kelli didn't dare confirm or deny. He obviously knew what he was talking about. But she didn't want to go home to social workers ready to take her away.

"You said she fainted. Does she fall more than she used to?"

"Yeah. But I just figured..."

"She is experiencing early dementia, Kelli. We can help her. Try to slow it down. But there is no cure. Sooner or later, she will not be able to take care of you. Or herself."

"I'm sixteen. I'm old enough to take care of myself. And I can help her. Whatever. She doesn't need... she doesn't need to go to a home."

"Not yet," Siddal agreed. "But at some point, months or years down the road, she will. You need to be prepared for that. Start working on a plan now. She's going to need supports."

Kelli's stomach twisted. She felt like she needed to find a bathroom. Or maybe throw up. Who did Siddal think he was, evaluating Patricia when he was supposed to be looking at Axel? It wasn't his job to say what was wrong with Patricia or that she needed to go to a home. No one had said anything to complain about her. Siddal was the only one who thought there was something wrong.

"Can I... is there a bathroom I could use?"

"Why don't we take a short break? I'll show you where it is."

He walked her to it, and also showed her to a little kitchenette where she could help herself to coffee, tea, or juice boxes. There were even cookies on the counter. In spite of herself, Kelli was feeling hungry after having only toast for breakfast, and helped herself to a couple cookies, along with some tea that she hoped would calm her down and settle her stomach. She didn't really want to go back in to talk to Dr. Siddal again. She was done with that.

———

Dr. Siddal brought them all into the same room to discuss his findings. Kelli sat awkwardly, trying to inch her chair outside of the circle. She didn't want to be a part of it. She was just a kid. The daughter. She didn't need to be involved in decisions about what to do with Axel or Patricia. She wasn't the parent.

Dr. Siddal went over the tests in detail, discussing what he had learned from each one. Neither Axel nor Patricia seemed to take a lot of this in. They sat side-by-side, Patricia with her hand clutched in Axel's. When Dr. Siddal told Axel that he had memory problems, Axel shook his head.

"I remember everything. I remember everything just fine. I don't have a problem with memory."

"The things that you are remembering are not true. They are artifacts of your imagination. Your brain provides a likely scenario, and that's what you remember happening."

Axel scowled and continued to shake his head. "What are you talking about? Nobody complains about my memory. I don't make things up. This is all just because of mixed-up DNA tests. No one knows how to interpret DNA tests anymore."

"Maybe you can confirm that you have noticed this behavior," Siddal said to Patricia.

She looked at him in alarm and shook her head. "No. I don't know what you're talking about."

"Kelli?"

Kelli just put her head down and refused to answer. What was he bringing her into it for? He was the expert. He was the one with the training and the tests. Kelli was just a kid, and she didn't want to be the target of Axel's anger. In a few minutes, he was going to blow his top, and then Siddal would see what he was really like. If Axel wasn't careful, he was going to be going right straight back to prison for assault.

"Mr. Ivanovich, maybe you can just think about that for a few minutes. See if it makes some sense to you. I know it's a bit of a shock, and it's going to be hard to accept that your brain has been lying to you all this time."

Siddal turned his gaze to Patricia. Kelli swore under her breath, too quietly for anyone to hear her. It was not going to be pretty.

"Mrs. Munroe… it has been very helpful having you here during Axel's testing. You have been instrumental in helping us to sort things out."

Patricia nodded, smiling. That smile was going to be wiped right out in a few seconds.

"During those interviews, though, I couldn't help noticing that you are experiencing some cognitive issues."

Patricia just looked at him, still clutching Axel's hand, her smile looking pasted-on. Siddal took a deep breath and continued.

"You are experiencing some early dementia. I am hopeful that it is early enough that we can treat it, slow down the progress to give you some more time… There are medications, therapies…"

None of them said anything. Axel looked at the doctor and then at Patricia. "We're here about Patricia?"

"That wasn't the goal in the beginning, of course, but I couldn't ignore the signs…"

"I don't have Alzheimer's," Patricia argued. "What are you talking about? I'm too young for that."

"I don't think it is Alzheimer's. I suspect that the combination of your drinking, and perhaps past head injuries…"

"I'm not an alcoholic!"

"That's good, because I'm going to ask you to cut out the drinking completely. I think it will make a big difference to the speed of progression of your dementia. Alcohol is very bad for the brain."

"I'm not giving up drinking," Patricia said with a laugh. "That's ridiculous. I don't drink very much. A few drinks before bed. The doctors say it's healthy, a moderate amount of alcohol. I'll cut back… but I'm not stopping…"

"You forget things all the time," Axel said, looking at Patricia. He put his other hand over hers, sandwiching her smaller hand between his larger ones. "I didn't know what was going on… now, I know…"

"I don't forget things," Patricia snarled. "You're the one who doesn't know what's going on. Tell them, Kelli. I don't forget things. I'm as sharp as I ever was!"

Kelli hunched down in her seat, wishing she could just be absorbed into the blue carpet. Siddal gave her a sympathetic look.

"This is going to take some work," he said to them all. "It will take a little while to sort things out and figure out how to best help you. We'll assign a case worker to each of you, and we'll have a multi-disciplinary team to work out a schedule…"

Patricia started swearing. She got up and stormed out of the office. Siddal looked at Axel and Kelli and sighed.

"It's never easy, telling someone things are starting to slip. How are you doing, Mr. Ivanovich? Are you going to be okay?"

"Why wouldn't I be okay?" Axel gave a shrug. "Patricia is the one who is sick." He stood up and looked for a minute at Kelli. She could almost see the gears turning as he tried to process what the two of them were doing there. "Are you going to drive us home?"

CHAPTER 7

Kelli looked up from the library computer and glanced around, looking for Les again. Maybe he was sick or had been coerced into babysitting at home. He hadn't been at school and it didn't look like he was going to make it to the library either. It was irritating, because she seriously wanted to talk to somebody about the trip to the doctor's office the day before. Her head was still muddled from all that had happened. She felt like everything had been turned upside down.

She turned her attention back to her computer and opened a search screen. Everybody kept talking about how she had been on TV because of the attack at the park, and she had never actually watched any of the footage. If she was going to be famous, she should at least see what they had to say. She typed her own name and 'news' into the search field, and clicked.

The profile of the reporter she had seen at the scene when she was arrested popped up in the first few searches, and she clicked and watched the breathless report of one girl getting attacked by three other teens in the park and kicking their butts. They actually got it right, indicating that she had been jumped, and expressing outrage over the fact that she had been arrested for defending herself.

Kelli watched the little bit of footage they had of her being escorted to the police car and pushed in. And she grinned as she watched Lizzie and her goons being taken from the scene as well. They'd been remarkably quiet since the attack. She'd expected retaliation at school, but they were keeping their heads down. Maybe Lizzie was worried about incurring further charges or getting a worse sentence if she were caught making trouble for Kelli or Les again.

A couple of people had caught snippets of the fight on their cellphones. It was weird to watch herself fighting from another perspective. It didn't look like any Jackie Chan movie. There were no acrobatics. No finesse. It was dirty and brutal, desperate. Over in a few minutes. It didn't seem like the blurry person on the screen could really be her.

She went back to the search results and started checking through the other reports. She had repeatedly been told that it was 'all over' TV, and she saw that all of the local networks had, in fact, picked it up. There were even a couple of national channels that had rebroadcast the local reports.

Kelli saw a popular talk show in the results, but it was way down the list. She saw by the URL that it was an old, archived show. But it was her name. It had to be someone else with the same name. But it was funny that it was even the same spelling. She clicked the video out of curiosity, interested in seeing her namesake.

As the host introduced the day's show to the live studio audience, there was a long shot of a blond woman. The camera zoomed in, and Kelli found herself looking at Patricia. A much younger Patricia. Thinner, not as deeply wrinkled, not so tired and worn looking. Kelli watched in disbelief as the host announced that Patricia's boyfriend was challenging her over the paternity of her daughter. Over Kelli? A photograph of Kelli's wide-mouthed gummy baby smile replaced her mother's image on the screen. Definitely Kelli. Her heart went out to that baby, too innocent to know yet how ugly she was. The birthmark was brilliant red.

She felt sick looking at it. Why did they have to plaster her disfigurement all over the screen? There was a drawn out 'awwww' from the audience. They felt sorry for her. Did they know what kind of life she was doomed to live with that birthmark? Or were they just responding to a prompt?

Kelli's picture shrank and another picture appeared beside it. Patricia's boyfriend. Only it wasn't Axel. Kelli stared at the picture, trying to see Axel's face. He had changed over time. Especially with his time in prison. He had aged badly. But she knew it wasn't him. There was nothing familiar about the face. It wasn't Axel, and he didn't look anything like Kelli either.

His name was John. John didn't believe that the baby was his, the host announced. A recording of John played.

"She just doesn't look like me. I mean, look at her. Even look at my baby pictures." Instantly, John's baby picture replaced the one on the screen. Kelli couldn't see any resemblance. But then, she could rarely see any resemblance between babies and their parents like other people claimed to. She thought it was mostly mass hysteria when they did. "And that birthmark! Nobody in my family has ever had one. Nobody in Patricia's family. Where did that come from? I know she's been fooling around on me. That baby is not mine!"

The pictures disappeared, replaced again with the image of Patricia sitting on the stage. She dabbed at her eyes. The host questioned her gently about her relationship with John and the birth of Kelli.

"I've never been with anyone else," she sobbed. "Only John. I love him and I haven't cheated on him!"

"Was he there when she was born?"

"Yes. We had plans. We were going to get married. Be a family."

"When did that change?"

"When her birthmark started coming in… it was just light pink at first, they said it was a bruise from the delivery… but it started to darken, and they said it was a birthmark, a port wine stain, and he decided he didn't want anything to do with her."

"Well, let's hear what John has to say." The host raised his voice. "John, come on out!"

John came out. He was throwing his fists and shouting, to the boos of the live studio audience.

"That is not my baby!" he insisted, pointing an accusing finger at Patricia. "You know that is not my baby! She doesn't look anything like me! And nobody in my family has birthmarks like that!"

"It's not inherited," Patricia argued. "The doctors said it's just one of those things. It didn't come from me or you, it's just something she was born with."

"You insist that you haven't been with anyone else," the host said calmly to Patricia, when everyone was seated and quiet again.

"No, I haven't." She sniffled.

"Man, that is not my baby," John shouted. "All you have to do is look at her to know she's not mine!"

"And you took a lie detector test," the host said to Patricia, as if John hadn't said anything.

"Yes."

The host pulled papers out of an envelope with a flourish, looking at them as if he'd never seen them before.

"You were asked, 'have you had an affair with anyone other than John?' You said, 'no.' The lie detector determined… that you are telling the truth!"

The audience howled, booing at John, who again was on his feet, shaking his finger in Patricia's face. "A lie detector isn't enough! The reason they can't be used in court is because they are unreliable! I don't care if she passed a lie detector."

"You wanted a DNA test," the host said.

"That's right, man. I know that baby's not mine. A DNA test will prove it."

"What are you going to do if it shows that you *are* the father?"

"If that's my baby, I'll do right by her. But she isn't. I know that. I know it in my heart."

"She is," Patricia insisted. "She is your baby, I was never with anyone else."

The host turned to the audience. "We did get a DNA test. The results, after these commercials."

Kelli was happy she didn't have to sit through the inane daytime television commercials about diet aids and feminine leak protection. The video jumped immediately to the next scene, where the host summed up everything that had been said so far, and threw a few more softball questions at Patricia. Then he tapped the new envelope in his hands.

"I have here the results of Kelli's DNA test. Are you ready for the results?"

"You'll see she's yours," Patricia told John.

The host tore the envelope and slid out the test results. "The results are in. John, you… *are not* the father."

The studio was filled with screams. The audience, John standing up again and gesturing at Patricia, yelling at the top of his lungs. "I knew it! I knew that baby wasn't mine!" Half of his words to her were bleeped out but Kelli could read his lips.

Patricia sat there, the blood drained out of her face, looking completely stunned. She started to cry, her hands over her face, wailing loudly. "That's not true! I know she's John's. I wasn't with anyone else. How could the test be wrong?" She actually grabbed it out of the host's hands. Kelli had never seen a guest on the show do that before. She and Les had watched such shows before, always laughing at the men and women who appeared on it. How could anyone be stupid enough to appear on the show? They had to know what would happen. The women knew they would get caught. The fathers knew who they were. It was ridiculous.

Patricia stared at the DNA results. The camera zoomed in close to her, so her eyes could be seen going back and forth as she read the results, looked at the top of the page, turned it over and back again. She held it out in front of her at arm's reach, as if she couldn't believe it was real.

"It's not true, John! I don't know what happened. They mixed up the results. It's wrong! I swear to you, I was never with another man!"

"I caught you," John screamed. "Admit what you did! I knew it and I caught you!" He continued to rail at her, using language deemed inappropriate for network TV.

Kelli watched her mother, fascinated. It was horrible to see her mother crushed like that, in front of a studio full of people. In front of the national and international audience. She was ruined. Her life with John was over. She had been humiliated in front of millions of people. She had thought that she could play the odds, that she could get away with cheating on her boyfriend and he would never find out. But he had. He challenged her in a public venue, and the whole world knew what she had done. Kelli couldn't look away.

Patricia seemed so genuinely shocked. White as a ghost, she sat there, shaking her head and staring at the offending test. It couldn't be an act. Kelli had seen her mother lie before, and she wasn't that good of an actor. Kelli started going through the possibilities. Her mother had messed around, but hadn't thought that she could get pregnant. They'd used protection or she'd had some other reason to believe that pregnancy couldn't result. Or maybe she'd been drugged and raped and didn't even know it. Maybe she'd miscounted the months and didn't think she'd been with anyone but John during that time. But she had been. She'd been with Axel or someone else.

That thought gave Kelli pause. Where was Axel in all this? He wasn't up on stage, offered as an alternate daddy. Was he her biological father? Had a second DNA test proven his paternity, and so he and Patricia had settled down together? Or was it someone completely different? Someone that Kelli had never even met? She tried to remember if either of them had ever told Kelli that Axel was her father. Had she just assumed it? They called him Dad, and she just assumed?

The talk show segued to the next story and the segment ended. Kelli just sat there, staring at the empty frame.

Everything had changed.

And nothing had changed.

For years, Axel had been distant and remote. She saw him a few times a year for special occasions. She fought with the kids at school who tried to tease her about him. She wasn't the only one in school with a family member in prison. There were others with incarcerated parents or siblings. She didn't let them get her down about it.

The latest developments, with him being released and moving back home had not made them a nuclear family. Axel's reclusive, bizarre, and sometimes violent behavior had not endeared him to her. He was no different from the dozen or so boyfriends who had passed through the doors before him.

Except that she had thought that he was her father.

———

Kelli walked home in a daze. She wasn't usually home so early in the evening, so when she walked in the door, Patricia started up and turned to look at her, brows drawing down.

"What are you doing home already? Did you skip school?"

"School ended hours ago, Mom," Kelli pointed out. What time did Patricia think she was in school until? Maybe she thought Kelli stayed after school to watch football or go to yearbook club. Or some other program that hadn't been cut.

"Well, what are you doing home?"

Kelli sat down on the little-used couch, shifting to find a comfortable position in the worn, lumpy seat. Patricia's eyes widened in alarm and she looked around the room, obviously wondering what was going on.

"What happened to John?" Kelli asked.

"John? Who is John? What are you talking about?"

"The man you told he was my father. Whatever happened to him?"

Patricia's mouth dropped open. Kelli waited for a fly to buzz right in.

"How the hell did you hear about that?" Patricia demanded in a screech.

"I just watched a recording of when you were on TV. Flunking a DNA test in front of millions of people."

Patricia swore, covering her face, just like she had when she first heard the words 'you *are not* the father.'

"So," Kelli persisted, "what happened to him?"

"He left." Patricia shook her head helplessly. "We never spoke to each other again. He went home, and he took his things, and he left. I never heard from him again. I don't know what happened to him."

"And you couldn't exactly pursue him for child support payments."

Patricia shook her head. Obviously not.

Kelli sat there, looking at Patricia and waiting. Patricia blinked at her. "What?"

"Who *is* my father?"

Patricia weighed her answer. "Axel is your father," she said. "You know that."

"Axel." Kelli let the idea roll around in her head for a while. "Where was he when John was around?"

"He was… he was around too."

"And he moved in when John moved out?"

"Yes."

"You lied to John in front of millions of people, when you said that you hadn't cheated on him. You said you hadn't been with anyone else."

"Yes," Patricia admitted. "It was a lie."

Kelli put her feet up on the couch in front of her, knees to chest, and studied Patricia through narrowed eyes. Patricia wasn't a good liar. She looked guilty as sin. But on TV, she had not looked like she was lying. She must have been mistaken, then. That was the only other explanation. She thought she was telling the truth. She hadn't thought that she'd been with anyone else when Kelli was conceived. She miscounted, or she was drugged, or there was some other reason she hadn't thought that anyone else could be the father. Did she have the beginning of dementia even back then? Kelli didn't know, but she thought that dementia progressed faster than that. Someone couldn't live with it for fifteen years and not be institutionalized.

"I don't get it," she said. "Why don't you just tell me the truth? Tell me what it really was that happened."

"It was Axel," Patricia repeated. "I just told John that you were his. Because… he seemed like he would be a better father. I wanted him to be your father, so I said he was."

Kelli didn't say anything. She still didn't believe it.

"He had a car," Patricia said. "A place of his own. I wanted that. I was still living at home with my parents and I wanted out."

That rang true. Kelli wondered briefly why Patricia would still be living at home at forty. Why hadn't she found her own place before that? There was no reason a single woman had to stay home. She could have gotten a job and earned enough money to rent her own apartment. But then, Patricia had never managed to stay gainfully employed in Kelli's memory. She had brief periods of employment here and there. She'd work at something for a few months, rarely making it past the three-month probationary period, and then she'd be back at home, grumbling about her employers and looking for something else again. Maybe she had never been able to hold down a job.

"If I asked Axel," Kelli said, "he'd say that he was my father? My biological father?"

Patricia nodded. "Of course. Because he is." She turned her attention back to the TV, and despite the attempts that Kelli made to question her further, Patricia refused to talk any more about it.

———

Kelli went up to her room to try to study and finish her homework. She hated doing it by herself. It was a lot more fun when Les was with her. It took three times as long, but it was a lot more fun. If she had a phone, she would call to make sure he was doing okay. She worried about him missing the day. Hopefully he wasn't sick or hurt. Maybe he just felt like skipping, or his mother had asked him to stay home to look after a sick kid so that she could go to work.

She managed to keep her focus on the work. Mostly. Then she really had to go back down to the kitchen to get something to eat. She hadn't yet had supper, and had mostly skipped eating the rest of the day, so she needed to get herself something. She tiptoed past Axel's door and went downstairs and started going through cupboards, trying to decide what to eat.

While she was starting a new pot of coffee, still undecided as to what to eat with it, she heard the front door bang, and Axel's voice. She hadn't even realized that he wasn't home. She was so used to him being in his room. Had the TV been playing behind the closed door? She couldn't even remember whether it had been quiet or whether the usual background noise had been there.

With a pot in her hand, Kelli went to the doorway of the kitchen, and smiled at Axel.

"Hey," she greeted. "I didn't know you were out."

Axel looked at Kelli and nodded a greeting, saying nothing. His eyes went to the pot in her hand.

"Uh… you want me to make you something?" Kelli suggested. She would probably get a lot more out of him if she softened him up first. Attract more flies with honey, as the saying went.

"You making supper?" Axel asked.

"I could. If you want something, I can put it on. Maybe… mac and cheese…?"

"Are you really going to make it?" Axel questioned suspiciously.

Kelli nodded. "Sure, why not? Who doesn't like mac and cheese?" She gagged at the thought. But she wanted him in a happy mood.

"Mac and cheese would be great," Axel acknowledged, scratching his scarred jaw, fingernails rasping across his stubble. He looked at Patricia and the TV, and apparently decided it would make more sense to wait for his dinner downstairs, so he sat down on the couch. Patricia gave him a look, and then scowled at Kelli, as if Kelli had broken a house rule by offering to make Axel supper, leading him to stay where he wasn't wanted. Kelli gave a little shrug and retreated into the kitchen.

It didn't take long to boil the pasta. Kelli let it boil on high instead of turning the element down, wanting it to cook as quickly as possible. She didn't want Axel to change his mind and go upstairs. Then she would either have to take his dinner up to his room, or to forget to take it to him and hope that he forgot as well. It was better if she could talk to him outside of his room, with other people—or one other person—around.

She mixed in the powdered cheese and gave it several swirls to dissolve it. Then she heaped half of it into a big bowl for Axel and added a spoon.

He was still sitting on the couch when she took it in to him. Patricia gave Kelli a baleful look, but Axel actually smiled a genuine smile and took it from her, slurping the first spoonful from the bowl with relish.

"Mmm, perfect," he told her. He gave a little sigh, settling into the couch and shoveling several bites into his mouth before chewing a couple of times and swallowing the big wad of noodles.

Kelli held back a grimace of disgust.

"Used to have mac and cheese every day for lunch when I was a little boy," Axel told her. "Every day I would run home from school to have my KD and then get back to school to play until the bell rang."

Was it the truth? Kelli hadn't thought to ask Siddal whether Axel still had memories from before his brain infection. Did he really remember eating macaroni and cheese at lunch, or was it just a hole that his brain had filled in for him?

Kelli sat on the arm of the couch, considering her approach.

"Dad… how old were you when I was born?"

Axel raised his eyebrows, surprised by the question. He rubbed his goatee. Then his eyes went to Patricia for help. "I guess I must have been… forty… forty-five?"

"Forty-four," Patricia snapped.

"Forty-four," Axel repeated, nodding. "I remember; I had just turned forty-four that year."

"Yeah? What else do you remember about the year I was born?"

He blinked at her and took another bite of macaroni.

"Did you have a good birthday that year? What did you do?"

"We had some friends over. It's not a big birthday, so we didn't do anything really special… your mom made me a cake. Of course. She was pregnant, so we couldn't do a lot…"

Patricia nodded her agreement. "Yes. I made a cake."

"But you weren't living with Mom then, were you? I thought she was living with John then. Until I was almost one."

His eyes darted to Patricia. He stirred the macaroni to incorporate some of the cheese powder that hadn't dissolved.

"Well, just because she was still with John, that didn't mean we couldn't do something together. Just the two of us. A little… risky…" He gave a little smirk. "But that just made it more fun."

"So, you didn't have some friends over. The two of you went out on the sly."

"We met up with some friends. At a club. Patricia couldn't drink, because she was pregnant, but that didn't mean we couldn't have a little fun."

Kelli's skin crawled. She was sure not a word of it was true. He was just inventing it out of thin air. Whatever sounded good to him. Then making little adjustments here and there, like a dressmaker adding a little tuck or stitch.

"And Mom made a cake…"

"She brought it with her to the club," Axel finished for her.

Kelli shook her head in disbelief. "Do you remember the day I was born?"

"Of course." Axel smiled at Kelli, baring sharp teeth. "How could I forget the day my daughter was born?"

"But she was with John then," Kelli reminded Axel. "She told John it was his baby, and he was with her at the hospital that day. They were planning to get married." Kelli looked at Patricia. "That's what you said on the show. You and John were going to get married. *He* was the one who was with you at the hospital."

"Axel came later," Patricia advised. "He waited until John was gone home. He even brought you a teddy bear. Do you remember that bear?" She directed the last at Axel.

"Yes. Had to bring something for my little girl."

"You weren't seeing Axel then," Kelli argued. "You said on the show that you weren't with anyone else. You said you weren't cheating on him. So, what's this crap about sneaking around together on his birthday and both of them seeing you at the hospital? Did you tell both of them that they were my daddy?"

"It's not like that. Don't be smart. Axel and I were just friends then. We weren't together, but we stayed friends. Right?"

Axel slurped some more macaroni. There was sauce in his goatee. "We broke up, but we still saw each other. As friends. I didn't know you were my daughter yet. But I remember how pretty you were, the day you were born."

"No, you don't."

"Of course I do."

"I wasn't pretty. I was ugly then, just like I'm ugly now. Ugly baby with a big old birthmark across half her face. I'll bet I was hideous."

Axel looked at Patricia.

"It was just pink to start with," Patricia said. "Not very visible at all.

They said it was just bruised, from the birth. I thought maybe they used forceps. It got darker and darker…" Patricia shook her head, her lip curling in distaste. "Until it was… like that."

"See?" Axel's head went up as if he'd just won the gold star. "You were pretty the day you were born. I knew it. I remember."

"You didn't care about my birthmark?" Kelli asked him. "When John left, I mean, and you and mom moved in together? You didn't care about having an ugly daughter?"

Axel gazed at her, unflinching. To give him his dues, Kelli never had felt like he cared about her mark. He never grimaced at it like Patricia did, or acted embarrassed, or told her she should hide it better with makeup. He acted like he didn't even see it.

"It's just a birthmark," he said. "Why would I care about that?"

"John thought it meant that I wasn't his daughter. But you don't have a birthmark. Does anyone in your family have one?"

Axel stared off into the distance. "I have an uncle with a big brown birthmark on his arm," he said deliberately. "And a second cousin… he's got one on his face, like you, only it covers most of his head, and it's blue."

Patricia smiled triumphantly.

"How come I've never met them?" Kelli demanded. "Why wouldn't you introduce me to your family with birthmarks, so I wouldn't feel so different? So ugly? If you really had relatives with birthmarks, wouldn't you do that?"

"They don't live around here," Axel said logically. "Or maybe I would have. I haven't seen them for years and years. Hardly even remember them. But when you asked about birthmarks… yes, I remember there are birthmarks in my family."

"You can stop fussing now," Patricia said. She picked up a beer from the floor beside her chair. "You can see that Axel is your father. It doesn't matter that we weren't living together when you were born. It's not who's around when you're born that matters," she gave a sloppy grin. "It's who was around when you were conceived."

"And you said that was John. You swore up and down that he was the only one you were with when I was conceived."

"I was wrong."

"How can you be wrong about something like that?"

"I was wrong. Now I told you to quit fussing, Kelli Anne Munroe, so you cut it out before I decide to knock some sense into you."

"You can't lay a finger on me," Kelli warned. "You know I won't let you hit me anymore."

"Get on up to your room and quit bugging your parents. Go do your homework. I don't want any calls from the school saying that you're falling behind in your work."

"I'm keeping up," Kelli grumbled. She slid down from her perch on the arm of the sofa. She still hadn't had anything to eat. The smell of the cheese made her nauseated, and she had been in too much of a hurry to get it done before Axel went upstairs and her opportunity passed. "I just have to grab a bite," she said. "That's what I came down here for."

"There any more of this macaroni?" Axel asked.

"Yeah. Come help yourself. I just have to figure out what to make for myself."

He didn't object to the suggestion that he could serve up his own macaroni, and followed her into the kitchen. Kelli looked through the fridge and the cupboards again, finally settling on a can of beans and pork. She could have that, and a piece of toast, and a fruit cup. That would make a nice, round, nutritious meal, to make up for the fact that she'd pretty much just had coffee the rest of the day.

CHAPTER 8

Kelli told Les about the video she had found. And she realized that he wasn't up to speed on what she had learned at the doctor's office and filled him in on that. Les listened with wide eyes. He shook his head in disbelief.

"It's like you suddenly stepped into a daytime soap," he said. "What's going on? One day you're just Kelli, crazy ninja girl, and the next… both your parents are losing their minds… if they really are your parents… it's all pretty crazy. How long did it take you to think all this stuff up? You must have been pretty bored without me around yesterday," he joked.

"It's all so weird," Kelli agreed. "Here I am walking down the street with you, just like any other day, and everything looks just like it always does. But inside… everything is all mixed up. I can't believe that no one else knows all this stuff."

"Well, they probably didn't move here until after everything happened," Les pointed out. "How long have you guys lived in that house?"

"I don't know. Since I was two or three. I'm not sure. After she got back together with Axel. I don't know if he was the one who bought the house. He must have, I mean, 'cause my mom couldn't have, she was just living with her folks."

Les's brows drew down as he stared at Kelli.

"What?" Kelli asked.

"They own the house? Nobody around here owns."

"Some people do."

"No. Who told you your folks own?"

"They don't pay rent. There's no landlord."

"They pay mortgage?"

"I dunno… they pay bills."

"That doesn't make sense," Les said.

Less sense than Kelly not even knowing who her father was? She never stopped to think about the family's finances. She knew they were better off than Les's family, or anyone over in the projects. But she didn't think there was anything that set her off from anyone else on her street.

"Anyone who owns houses around here is either a slumlord or their family has owned the house for three generations," Les insisted. "No one can afford to buy anymore. If they could, they wouldn't buy here. And you've got a pretty nice house."

Kelli had been so focused on getting it cleaned out for the social worker, she hadn't really thought about the bones of the place. But it was a nice place, when you got down to it. It must have looked pretty good when the carpet and paint were fresh. She tried to remember what it had looked like when she was a child, but gave up. Her memory must be as bad as Axel's. She just couldn't remember back that far.

"So, what's Mom trying to hide?" she asked Les, returning to her previous thoughts about her beginnings. "I think… Axel obviously didn't come into the picture until after the DNA test. You've seen those shows. If there was any other guy hanging around her, John would have named names. They're always making accusations. He never suggested anyone when he was accusing her of being a lying… liar. He never said who he thought my father was. If she was making cakes and sneaking out with Axel, wouldn't he have said?"

"She obviously *was* sneaking around with someone."

"Well… I guess…"

"It wasn't virgin birth. The stork didn't drop you down the chimney."

"I just mean… it's not Axel. She's not telling the real story. I saw her face when they announced that John was not the father—my father. She was so shocked. She's not a good liar. I know she's lying to me now. But she wasn't lying on that show when she said she hadn't been with anyone else. Or didn't think she had been."

"Succubus?" Les suggested. "You know, like from Shakespeare? Or was it incubus?"

"I think incubus," Kelli said. "But no… I don't think some demon came to her in her sleep. Though she could have been drunk. Or drugged."

"Did you ask her that? Maybe she's just afraid to say, but if you acted like you understood…"

"I'm not going to suggest it. Then she'll suddenly remember, 'oh yeah, that was what happened.' Between her lying and Axel's… confabulating, I'm never going to get the truth out of them."

They walked in silence for a while. As they approached the school, Les spoke again. "Does your mom keep important papers somewhere?"

"Not really." Kelli looked at him, wondering where he was leading.

"I'm just thinking… maybe she has papers showing how she bought the house. Or Axel, if he did. I mean, he was convicted of armed robbery, maybe they bought the house on the take from some big heist. But you might be able to unravel part of the history… maybe it will lead somewhere."

"Murder," Kelli corrected.

"What?"

"He was convicted of felony murder. Not armed robbery."

"Because he shot someone during a robbery."

"Yeah. Except… it wasn't him. He wasn't the guy."

Les rolled his eyes. "Well… that doesn't mean he wasn't involved in another heist…"

"But…" Kelli looked for a way to argue the leap of logic further, and shook her head. "Whatever."

"Maybe she's got papers somewhere. What about your birth certificate? Does it have John's name on it? What about contacting him and finding out if he ever figured out who she was with?"

"If he suspected anyone, he would have said on the show," Kelli insisted.

"Maybe… or maybe he found out afterward. You know, a million people see the show, maybe one of them emails him afterward to say that they know who your mom was fooling around with."

Kelli stopped at the bottom of the steps leading up to the school doors. "Yeah. Maybe." At least this suggestion made sense. But she didn't have any desire to make contact with the screaming, swearing man who had been on the talk show. Why Patricia had ever gotten together with him in the first place, she would never understand.

Or maybe Patricia had gotten letters after the show. She didn't have a computer or email address, so there was nothing for Kelli to hack, and surely Patricia wouldn't still have fifteen-year-old emails anyway. But she might have old letters tucked away somewhere. Actual physical letters.

Kelli just had to find them.

———

The day dragged on. Even her after-school time with Les, the few hours of freedom that she always cherished, seemed to take an eternity. She didn't tell Les that she wanted to go home and see if she could find any evidence about who her real father was. They hadn't had any time together for a few days. It would have been rude to abandon him for her own selfish pursuits. And she needed the extra money. The fresh food in the fridge had dwindled and disappeared. Kelli wasn't sure where it all went so fast, when Axel ate only macaroni and Patricia only her booze, but one or the other of them must be raiding the fridge during the day, consuming Kelli's few purchased items.

Her time with Les always zipped by, but it crawled instead. Kelli was relieved when it finally started to get dark.

"Better head home," she told Les.

"How much did we bring in?" Les asked tentatively as they walked home.

That was when Kelli realized that she hadn't split it as usual. She had just pocketed everything, and Les had to be wondering if something had changed and he wasn't going to get his cut for some reason. He needed it just as much as Kelli did. She swore.

"Oh, yeah. My brain is somewhere else tonight! I'm walking around with my head in the clouds!"

She immediately went through her pockets to count up and split the money. She gave Les a bigger cut than was actually his share, feeling guilty about forgetting him in her distraction. He eyed her, but didn't protest. He shoved his share into his tight jeans pocket.

"You okay?"

"Yeah," Kelli assured him. "Just fine. Why?"

"Just… you seem off tonight. All this stuff with your folks?"

"Yeah. I'm sorry. I haven't been much company tonight."

"No, it's okay. I just want to make sure that you're all right. You know… I'm here for you, right? Always. If you just want to talk. Whatever you need."

Kelli punched him lightly in the shoulder. "Course I know that."

Les smiled. "Good."

She watched him up the walk to his house, then walked quickly on to her own. It had taken longer than she had expected to get back, and with clouds moving in, it was much darker than she liked it to be when out on the streets.

———

On arriving home, Kelli went through the motions of putting on a pot of coffee and finishing the last of the beans with a piece of toast. Patricia had not had anything to say to her when she came in, and she assumed that Axel was upstairs shut away in his own room as usual.

Where would Patricia put important papers if she had saved something? There was no filing cabinet full of neatly-labeled and alphabetized folders. No shoebox full of old photos. None of the old stand-bys that she had seen on TV. Patricia didn't keep copies of the bills that she paid. Most mail went directly into the garbage. It was all junk anyway. Any letters that Patricia had gotten after the talk show would have been disposed of long ago. Wouldn't they?

Kelli took her supper up to her bedroom. She had eaten about half of her toast when she thought about the third bedroom. Across the hall from hers, the third bedroom housed broken furniture, Patricia's overflow of clothes, and various odds and ends that no one had any use for but which Patricia would not allow to be thrown away. Dubbed the 'guest room,' the third bedroom had never, in Kelli's recollection, housed a guest. It was just the place to stash old papers.

Leaving her supper unfinished on her dresser, Kelli opened her door quietly and sneaked across the hall to the empty bedroom. She half-expected the door to be locked, but it turned easily in her hand. Kelli groped for the light switch and turned it on. She hadn't touched anything in there in her recent house cleaning. It was disorderly, but not dirty. Kelli slipped in and pulled the door shut behind her, not wanting to attract attention.

She scanned the room. Where would Patricia put important papers? There was an old writing desk hidden in the corner under piles of clothing, boxes of junk, and a crystal vase. That seemed like a good place to start. Kelli shifted the furniture in front of the desk so that she could access the drawers. The bottom two were filled with baby clothes and books, and a few old toys that Kelli vaguely remembered from her childhood. She straightened to open the top drawer and banged her head on the drop-leaf of the open desk. The crystal vase rattled and wobbled, and Kelli reached out quickly to steady it.

"Ow! Damn." Kelli rubbed her head. It wasn't a bad bump. Probably wouldn't even swell up. But it did smart.

In order to get into the top drawer, the drop leaf had to be closed up. And to close it, Kelli had to clear away the boxes, clothes, and vase. She stacked what she could on the bed and the rest on the floor. She closed the drop-leaf and opened the drawer. She expected more baby things, but instead found a morass of medical supplies. Old pill bottles, pressure bandages and swabs, and other bits and bobs that Kelli couldn't identify. There was a brown envelope with a sheaf of papers in it at the bottom of the mess. Kelli pulled it out eagerly.

Kelli flipped through the disorderly, dog-eared documents. Hospital bills, medical after-care instructions, physical and occupational therapies, letters to and from lawyers, a few x-rays and other tests. All about Axel's brain infection. It was fascinating stuff, a window into the past, but not what she was looking for. Kelli checked the drawer for any further paperwork, and not finding any, slid the medical records back where she had found them and closed the drawer.

The closet seemed the next most likely place to find papers. She was half hoping that there would be a file case or a box neatly labeled on the floor or up on the shelf, but she already knew there wouldn't be. She never went into that closet for anything, but she had seen it sitting open before when Patricia was looking for some lost outfit. It was jammed full of clothes. Not just hanging on the rod, but also piled on the floor that rose two feet into the air. Anything could be buried in there. And it didn't smell nice. Kelli was afraid if she started poking through the clothes, she might find a rat's nest.

She looked up on top of the shelf instead. A jumble of boxes and plastic shopping bags full of all manner of junk. Kelli started taking them down one at a time, trying not to start a landslide. There were Christmas ornaments she didn't even know they had. Clothes, including a lot of scarves. Patricia never even wore scarves. Old schoolwork of Kelli's. Wood shavings for an animal cage. Immunization records.

Kelli slowed when she saw the immunization records. She pulled the wad of papers out of the shopping bag and paged through them slowly. There were medical records for Kelli. A couple of emergency room admissions. A letter from DCFS instructing Patricia to take Kelli to the dentist. Kelli was sure she was getting close.

There didn't seem to be any order to the papers, they were all shuffled together in random order. Eventually, Kelli teased out a DNA test. The cover letter confirmed that the candidate DNA was excluded as a parent to the subject. Which was convoluted language for 'you *are not* the father!'

She looked at the details on the test, and paused. Kelli would have been two at the time of the test, older than she had been at the time of the show. Patricia had done a second test to confirm the first.

Or had she tested someone else the second time?

Axel, or some other candidate?

Kelli studied the DNA results form, looking for the name of the man they had tested. She couldn't find anything that gave his name. Did they keep it confidential? Just connected with a file number? If a woman had several potential fathers, wouldn't she need to see the name on the test results to know whose tests had been negative and whose had been positive?

The only names on the form were Kelli's and Patricia's. Kelli's was in the 'subject' field, and Patricia's in the 'applicant' and 'candidate' fields.

Patricia was the candidate?

Kelli stared at the name in the field. That couldn't be right. She was reading it wrong, or it had been filled in wrong.

If Patricia was the candidate, then it wasn't a paternity test. It was a maternity test.

And if it was negative, then Patricia was not Kelli's biological mother.

———

After a long time, Kelli put the test to the side and continued to look through the rest of the papers in the bag. She wasn't sure what was going on, but there had to be adoption paperwork or something else that would explain it.

She could understand John not being her father, even if Patricia couldn't. She could imagine scenarios that fit the facts as she knew them. A new one came to mind. What about a fertility clinic? Patricia had been old when Kelli was born. Maybe she'd had problems conceiving, and had artificial insemination. They could have used the wrong sperm.

But surely if that had been what happened, John would have been accusing the fertility clinic instead of Patricia. He would know that it could have been the clinic's fault rather than Patricia fooling around on him.

Kelli's head whirled. None of it made sense. She needed to be methodical and look through each page in that bag, through every paper in the closet or in the room, if it came to that. Something would explain what had happened.

There was a thick package of papers clipped together with a black foldback clip. Something from a law firm. Kelli leafed through it. Settlement. The cover letter mentioned a check with more zeros than Kelli had ever seen on a check before. The Claim and Affidavits attached gave the name of the hospital where Kelli was born. There was a smaller clipped section with the name of the TV network on it, which had apparently enclosed another large check.

Kelli put them down.

Patricia had sued the hospital. And the network. They had paid her off.

Kelli wasn't John's daughter. And she wasn't Patricia's daughter either.

The hospital had switched babies.

———

Kelli sat on the floor looking at the papers for a long time. She went over it and over it, and couldn't see any other explanation. The claims and settlements were full of legalese, but Kelli could tease out the main points. Patricia sued the hospital for giving her the wrong baby. Pain and suffering. And she had sued the television network for humiliating her in front of millions of people. Slander and defamation of character. And she had won.

Kelli hadn't thought that there was anything to Les's puzzlement over

Patricia owning the house. People bought and sold houses all the time. It had been Axel's money. Or one of them had come into money. Or had pulled some kind of con that had landed them a big windfall. The kind of con that Kelli and Les were always talking about.

"We need to do something big," Kelli would say. "You hear about teenagers pretending to be doctors or airplane pilots and getting away with it. I don't want to do that. I don't want to put anyone's life in danger. But I want to pull something big. Something memorable."

"Something expensive," Les would add. And they'd laugh. That was the dream. To pull off the biggest imaginable con, and have enough money for whatever they wanted. Not just a few groceries in the fridge. Not just some fresh fruit or a pay-as-you-go phone. But landing a real fish. A big mark.

"Someday we will," Kelli promised. One day she would think up the biggest, most brilliant scam, and she and Les would pull it off.

Her mother had done it without even trying. She had threatened her marks with exposure, and they had paid up big time. Enough to pay for a house. A house that, as far as Kelli could tell, had been nice at one time, and was still better than the townhouses in the projects like Les lived in. They didn't have to come up with rent each month for some slumlord, and hadn't had to pay a mortgage either. Les would be pleased. He had called it.

Eventually, Kelli gathered the papers up and went downstairs. She did something that she would normally never have considered doing, marching over and shutting Patricia's TV off.

Patricia sat upright, making a squawk of objection. "What do you think you're doing?" she demanded. She grabbed the remote and turned the TV back on. Kelli turned it off and stood in front of the TV so the remote wouldn't work. Patricia stood up, advancing threateningly. Kelli stood her ground.

"You can't hit me."

"Get out of the way and let me watch my TV!"

Kelli held up the papers. "I want to talk to you about these."

"What are those?" Patricia stared at the sheaf of pages. She grabbed at them and Kelli let her pull the DNA test out of Kelli's grasp. Patricia looked at it, studying it closely. Then her jaw dropped and she looked at Kelli. "Where did you get these?"

"From the closet."

"What are you doing going through my personal, private papers? Those aren't yours. They're mine."

"They're about me. I think I have a right to look."

"No, you don't. You are a child and it's none of your business. It's only mine. You quit poking your nose into things that don't concern you."

"How does this not concern me?" Kelli demanded, motioning to the papers. "How can you say that's not any of my business? Who my parents are is none of my business? The fact that you kept me, when you knew I wasn't even yours? That's not my business?"

"No," Patricia said flatly. "I raised you. I'm your mother. And I say it's none of your business."

"Did you ever even find out who my biological parents really are? What happened to your biological child?"

"None… of your… business!"

Kelli flapped the thick settlement documents at her. "Are you telling me that you took their money, you let them pay you off, without ever trying to make things right? Without even knowing whose life you screwed up?"

"You haven't had it so bad," Patricia scoffed. "You don't go hungry. You run around at will, wherever you feel like. You have two parents. That's better than most of the world, you know!"

"Yeah, things have been just dandy for me growing up," Kelli snapped. "Looking like a freak. Treated like an outcast. Ignored by you. It's no wonder you didn't want anything to do with me. I always thought it was because I was so ugly, but it's because you knew I wasn't even your child."

"You never lacked for anything. That money meant you had everything you needed. You've got nothing to complain about."

"Yeah, you took me to the dentist whenever someone complained to social services. Let me live in this rat's nest. Provided me with a steady parade of daddies. What do I have to complain about?"

Patricia gave a nod. "You grew up with more than I ever had. You're lucky. You look at any of the kids living around here and you'll see. You're one of the lucky ones." She motioned for Kelli to move out of the way of the TV. "We're done talking. Move your butt."

Kelli pointed at the DNA results. "You found out you weren't my biological parent fourteen years ago. So, what did you do then? Who did you talk to? Did you go right to a lawyer?"

"What I did is none of your business. I raised you. I was a mother to you. It doesn't matter what a stupid test says." She threw the DNA test back at Kelli. "Just forget about it. Don't make waves."

Patricia managed to get the TV turned back on, but Kelli was still standing in the way of the picture.

"You don't care that you're not my real mom?"

"You never had any other mother."

"But I should have had. You kept me away from her."

"You've got nothing to complain about. I've been a good mom to you."

Patricia sat back down in her chair and leaned over to pick up a bottle. Kelli looked down at the papers in her hand and almost didn't notice that Patricia had picked up an empty bottle, not a full one. Kelli brought her hands up to protect her face just in time. The bottle hit her hand and spun to smack against her teeth. Kelli yelped and covered her mouth. Patricia cackled with laughter.

"Take that, ninja girl! Now get out of my way before I try a bigger one!"

Kelli stared at Patricia for a few seconds, angry and humiliated all at the same time. She could take Patricia on. Kelli could smack her around just like Patricia had smacked Kelli when she was smaller, before she started training at the Dragon.

Patricia was an old, sick woman. She couldn't defend herself against Kelli, even with a bottle. Even with a broken bottle.

Kelli took a few long, deep breaths. That wasn't the way that she had been trained to fight. She knew that her Jujitsu was for self-defense. It was dishonorable to attack someone weaker, no matter how hurt and embarrassed Kelli was.

Patricia's decision to keep Kelli and keep quiet had happened a long time ago. It was a fresh betrayal in Kelli's mind, but it had happened years go. Patricia was a different person then.

Kelli swallowed her anger and moved out of the way of the TV.

"That's right," Patricia muttered. "I'm still your mother."

Kelli started up the stairs.

"You're not my mother. You never were."

CHAPTER 9

Are you kidding me?" Les's voice rose in disbelief.

They were in the school library and several voices shushed Les at the same time. He didn't even look around to see who had objected. He just stared at Kelli, waiting for her to laugh that she was just conning him. That he had fallen for the best joke ever. But Kelli just sat back, folding her arms and waiting for him to take it all in.

"So, not only are John and Axel not your dad, but your mom isn't even your mom? I don't understand how that could happen!"

Kelli had already explained it to him and didn't think it was that difficult to understand. But Les still looked baffled and disbelieving.

"The hospital switched me with another baby. Sent me home with the wrong parents."

"But there must be systems in place to prevent that. There are computers. Every baby has a bracelet and a leg band. How do you mix two up?"

"I don't know. They both get bathed at the same time. I don't know how it happens, but it does. All the time."

"Not all the time," Les said with a laugh.

"All the time," Kelli insisted. "I looked it up," she gestured to one of the library computers. "One in eight babies goes home with the wrong parents."

"One in eight?" Les shook his head. "No way."

"Most of them, someone figures it out right away, and they get it sorted out. A few days at most. But some of them…" Kelli spread her hands apart in a shrug. "Some of them don't figure it out until years later. Or never."

"Not one in eight!"

"In busier hospitals, as many as one in four."

"No way," he repeated.

Kelli didn't say anything. She couldn't do much about him not believing it. The numbers sounded crazy to her, too. She'd never heard of it happening to anyone else. And with numbers like that, she should know lots of people who had been switched, for a few hours or days, anyway. How was that not in the news?

"But even if they do accidentally switch babies," Les said, "your mom figured it out, so why wouldn't she… why wouldn't she return you to your real parents, and get her own baby back?"

"She didn't figure it out right away. Not until I was two."

"Still… that's young enough that you could bond with another family…"

"The hospital paid her off. She took the money and kept quiet, instead of making a fuss about it. She didn't want her other baby back badly enough… the money was more important."

"That's harsh."

"But true."

He gave a little nod, conceding the point.

"I don't know if the other family even knows," Kelli said. "The hospital paid Mom money to keep quiet. She never met with these other parents, this other little girl. What if they didn't tell the other family either? And they still don't know that they have the wrong child?"

"How is that legal? When you find out that someone has the wrong baby, don't you have to go to court? I mean, I know it's not kidnapping. Not intentionally. But don't you have to sort out custody? You'd have to go to family court and decide who was supposed to have which baby, wouldn't you? I've seen cases like that on TV."

"Maybe that's only when they make a fuss. If the hospital can keep it quiet, then why would anyone go to court?"

"Because you can't just keep the wrong baby. It's not… it's not fair!"

Kelli chuckled. "Since when is life fair?"

Les was scowling and Kelli tried to figure out what was wrong with him.

It was upsetting, sure. More to her than it should be to him. What was he so angry about?

He noticed her inquiring expression and, still scowling, drummed on the table top, drawing another chorus of shushes from the other students in the library. Kelli caught Mrs. Finch, the librarian's eyes on them, and put her hand over Les's to stop him.

"What?" she whispered.

"I was just thinking about Sudi," Les said.

Kelli tried to follow the segue. What was he frowning about his little sister for? What did it have to do with their conversation?

"Uh… what about Sudi? Is she… sick?"

"No. One in eight babies goes home with the wrong family. That's what you said."

"Well, higher in bigger, busier hospitals, so that means lower in ones like ours, where it's quieter."

"But still…"

"What?"

"We've got ten."

"Ten what?"

"Ten babies," Les said, looking at Kelli like she was the one being stupid for not following him. "We have ten kids in the family, so odds are, we would bring home the wrong one at some point. Right?"

"No… not really…"

"And Sudi… you know how she's not like the rest of the family. We're always making jokes, you know. About the milkman. About how she doesn't look or act like the rest of us."

Kelli blinked at him. "And now you're thinking… maybe she's not really your sister? That she was switched from another family?"

"She could be," Les insisted.

"Yeah, I guess… She is kind of the odd one out in your family…"

"Right?"

"Yeah. But just because someone is a bit different, that doesn't necessarily mean she's not yours. She could just be more like a grandparent, someone a couple of generations back. Genetics are funny."

Les scratched at a mark on the table, thinking about it.

"If you're worried, you could mention it to your mom," Kelli suggested.

"Are you kidding? She would freak. I wouldn't be able to sit for a week."

There weren't a lot of boys who would admit that their moms could still whip them. But everyone knew how tough Les's mom was. Ten kids, several of them bigger than she was, and she could still whip the hell out of them. And did, whenever occasions warranted. Kelli probably wouldn't have dared talk to her about Sudi either. Kelli was a good fighter, good at defending herself, but she was still a little scared of Mrs. Broke.

"Don't be dissing my mom," Les said quietly.

"I'm not. I get it. But I'm sure Sudi's just a throwback. She's a Broke. She's just a little different than the rest of you."

He nodded, but didn't look convinced. Kelli looked at the books they had spread out on the table, like she was planning to do some work. But the fact was, they were skipping classes because she had wanted to talk to Les. The books were there only for show, so that Mrs. Finch wouldn't harass them.

"What are you going to do?"

"Do? What can I do? It's a little late for anything to change now."

"Aren't you going to try to find your biological parents?"

"No… how would I? Mom isn't going to tell me who they are. It's all been hushed up."

"What hospital were you born at?"

"The General," Kelli said automatically. But something tickled at the back of her brain. General? "No… the court papers were for Central, not General." Kelli heard the outrage in her own voice. "She even lied to me about what hospital I was born in!"

"Well, you know the truth now. Can't you find out what other babies were born that day or in the time before you were released? There's public records, right?"

"I don't know. I guess."

"It has to be a girl that was there while you were there. Unless you think Patricia wouldn't notice that her baby boy turned into a baby girl."

Kelli's face burned. "No, I don't think she was that bad."

Les frowned. "What about… your birthmark? Didn't she notice that?"

"She said it was only faint when I was born. Just pink. They told her it was a bruise. It didn't look like this right away."

She hated talking about her birthmark to anyone. It shouldn't bother her to talk about it with Les. He was her best friend and she knew he didn't care about it. But they had always talked around it, pretending it didn't exist. Unless Kelli brought it up. Which she didn't.

"Are there pictures? You know, lots of people do pictures of the baby right after it's born, in its mom's arms. Does she have any pictures of the… real baby? That we know was before you were switched?"

"I don't know. She doesn't have many pictures of me. You know, because of this." She gestured to her face.

"But they must have taken pictures when you were first born. And if it was just faint to start out with, they wouldn't care, right?"

"I don't know. I'll have to see if I can find any pictures. I guess there were probably some in the closet, but I was looking for papers about my biological father then, not baby pictures."

"Guess the joke's on John, leaving because you weren't his baby, when his baby is still out there somewhere. He did have a baby with Patricia, it just wasn't you."

It boggled the mind. Kelli rubbed her eyes. They were dry and sandy. Gritty from lack of sleep.

"I'll find some pictures… you really think that will help? And you think I can track down my biological family?" Kelli stared at the open school-books. "What would they say to me? What would I say to them?"

"I dunno. But don't you want to meet them?"

Kelli tried to rein in the immediate flight of fancy. A loving mother and father. Siblings. A comfortable middle-class school. Clean home and fresh food. Friends. Chances were, her biological family wouldn't be that much different from the one she was in right now. And they wouldn't want her to become part of their family. They might be mildly interested to know that they had had another daughter, a daughter that had grown up somewhere different from where they had, but they wouldn't be welcoming her into their family like a cat that wandered off ten years before in a move. People were different. They would be attached to the daughter they had raised, and Kelli would be a stranger, alien to their family circle.

"I dunno. It all sounds good, but I'm not so sure it would be. They might not want anything to do with me. I don't know how I would feel about them."

"Well, you have to try. Otherwise, you'll never know."

"What if I don't like them? What if they're… I don't know… awful people."

"Then you don't have to have anything to do with them. You go home and kiss your mom and thank her for keeping you."

Kelli laughed. Somehow, that didn't seem like a likely scenario. "Yeah, okay."

"Then you'll do it? You'll search for them?"

Kelli nodded.

"Sure. Why not?"

————

Searching public birth records was not as difficult as Kelli had worried it would be. The lady at the registry helped her to fill out the forms properly, and went over the results with her. But all that Kelli was left with was a list of names. There were no associated addresses and she didn't have their parents' names. As Les had said, she could eliminate the boys, but she couldn't be sure of anyone else. What was she supposed to do, hire a detective?

The lady at the registry apologized for not being able to provide her with the more detailed records. But it seemed those were only for the people named on the record. And while technically Kelli was the child named on the record, she didn't know which one it was and had no way to prove it.

"There's no way I can even find out the parents' names?" Kelli demanded.

The child's name was not going to get her far. She could look them up on social media, but they wouldn't have addresses or phone numbers registered in their names. And what would she do if she did find someone on social media? How would she know by looking at them whether they were the one she was switched with? She couldn't just message them to ask them if it was possible they were switched at the hospital.

"Not through the registry," the woman said, her voice still apologetic. "You could try checking birth announcements in the paper. Not a lot of people do it anymore, but you might be able to find something."

She sounded doubtful. Kelli didn't expect to find anything. It was a long shot. So much for thinking she could just waltz in and find out all about her biological family. But she had the names of the girls that had been born the same week as she had been. It wouldn't hurt to search online birth announcements, just in case.

Kelli found birth announcements for three names. With the parents' names in hand, she was able to track down addresses for two of them. The third had probably moved out of the city and lived somewhere with a divorced or remarried mother, going by a new name. If Kelli were left trying to track her down, it was going to be difficult.

Unsurprisingly, the two girls that she could track down were not from Kelli's part of town. Her class of people didn't announce births in the newspaper or online registries. Families like the Broke family added another child to their families with a mixture of joy and regret. One more child to help support the family and have a chance of 'making it' one day. One more mouth to feed until then. More dirty diapers to change, midnight awakenings, and snotty noses. A new child was a hope and a curse.

Kelli chose the girl who was the closest to a main bus route to visit first. She decided it probably wasn't right to contact the girl before her parents, so she determined to talk to the mother first. That was the safest route. She would explain about the hospital switch, and see if the woman thought there was any chance that her daughter might be the other girl involved in the mix-up. She wouldn't ask for any future contact, or for anything. Just to figure out whether this was her biological family or not. So she would know. Then she would go home again.

The house was in a nice, middle-class neighborhood. People mowed their lawns and kept them free of debris and car parts. The houses were clean, with nice drapes or blinds behind the windows. None of them had broken or taped-over windows, plywood in place of the glass, or cardboard or newspaper taped up on the inside. A nice little street in the suburbs.

Kelli halted in front of the house, back on the city sidewalk, not going up the cobbled pathway to the front door. She had been trying to hold back the anxiety over meeting these people for the first time. But looking at the house, she couldn't suppress it any longer. Her stomach knotted and cramped. Instead of going into the house, she just wanted to turn around and go home. Lie down in her bed and pull the covers up over her head. Hide from the world like she used to hide from monsters when she was a little girl. As if a thin blanket could protect her from anything. Like it was a magical barrier. She felt stripped and defenseless standing in front of the house.

What would they think of her, coming boldly to the house with no warning, no investigator or lawyer or cops? Just a teenage girl, trying to find a new family. It was stupid. She had been stupid to listen to Les about finding her biological family. Maybe when she was older. Maybe when she was forty and had kids of her own.

She turned around to go home. But that felt even stupider. All the time and effort to track down a girl born on the same day at the same hospital, to find out where she lived and make the trek to her house. And then Kelli was just going to turn around and abandon the quest before its completion?

She turned and looked at the house again. It was a nice house. They would be nice people. People that lived in neighborhoods like this didn't drink themselves into a stupor or beat their wives. They didn't whip their children with cords or coat hangers or whatever else was handy. They lived normal, middle-class, suburban lives just like on TV.

She didn't believe her own line. She knew it was a con. But she had to tell herself something to convince herself to go to the door. These were nice people. They would be happy to meet her. They wouldn't care that she came to the door without some kind of warning.

Kelli walked up the sidewalk, swallowing hard and keeping her breathing slow and even. She worked on a breathing and meditation exercise she'd learned at the Golden Dragon. Learning Jujitsu wasn't just about fighting. It was about life. About learning how to cope. How to make a good life for yourself.

When she rang the doorbell, she could hear the deep, rich gong inside the house on the other side of the solid door. It was a stately ring, not the screechy clang of Kelli's front doorbell that always set her teeth on edge.

She waited. Maybe they weren't home. Both parents might work. They might both be out. She couldn't tell whether there were any cars in the garage. She might be wasting her time coming so early in the afternoon.

There were footsteps inside. Kelli breathed.

The door opened, and Kelli was faced with a pleasant-looking woman in her forties. A tall, slender woman with skin like ebony. Kelly hadn't even thought about race when looking at the names on the birth register. There hadn't been a baby picture beside the birth announcement for Chelsea Rose King.

"Uh..." Kelli fumbled for words. She didn't even know if the woman was Chelsea's mother. Maybe she was a maid or a visitor. A house sitter. "I'm looking for a Mrs. King...?"

"Yes, I am Mrs. King," the tall black woman confirmed.

"Oh... I... I think I have the wrong house..."

Kelli started to withdraw. The woman looked at her, forehead wrinkled. What kind of sense did that make? To ask for the home owner by name and then say she was in the wrong place? Kelli berated herself for her stupid tongue, but she didn't take back what she had said.

"Are you sure I can't help you?" Mrs. King asked.

"No. Sorry. No, I shouldn't have come here."

Kelli withdrew from the house and ran away, across the lawn, and down the street. She didn't stop running until she had left the house far behind.

CHAPTER 10

Kelli just wanted to get out on the street, playing Three-card Monte, like it was a normal day and nothing had happened. She was still the same person. Living in the same circumstances. Drumming up enough money to eat and survive for a few more days.

Her patter and the feeling of the cards moving from hand to hand were familiar and calming. It was all routine. Maybe she couldn't go back to the ignorance she had lived in prior to finding she had been sent home from the hospital with the wrong parents, but she could move on and put it behind her.

"Kelli! Where were you? I haven't seen you!"

Kelli glanced up at Les. It was just like any other day. He was there to shill for her. They would play the game and split the winnings, just like any other day.

"Hey. How's it going?"

"Did you find anything out? Did you track down—"

"Not now." Kelli stopped him. "Just play."

"Does that mean that you found anything out? Or not?"

"Find the lady," Kelli called, as if he hadn't spoken. "Is she here…? Is she there…? Find the lady, win a buck."

He stood there staring at her. Finally, he pointed to one of the cards. Kelli showed the Jack. "Oooh, bad call. Try again."

Les finally got the idea and they fell into their usual routine. When they decided to move on, though, Les tried again.

"What happened?" he demanded. "Did you find anything out? Did you talk to anyone?"

Kelli sighed and told him about visiting the house. Les started to snicker.

"And you're sure you're not black?"

Kelli scowled at him. "I just ran away. I was so embarrassed. What am I thinking? I can't just go up to someone and tell them I think I'm their daughter! It's crazy!"

"Well, yeah, it kind of is. But what else are you going to do?"

"I'm not going to do it anymore. That's it. I'm forgetting about it. I'm living with my mom and dad, just like always. Nothing changes. None of this stuff matters. What did I think? That I was in the middle of some magical fairy tale?"

"I don't think you should drop it! This really is happening. No, it's not a fairy tale. No one is going to turn you into a pumpkin. But you should know the people you came from."

"I don't know what I'm doing! I just about walked up to a family that has nothing to do with me and told them I was their daughter."

"So you do a little more research on the next one. Find out about them. Find pictures on the net and see if you look like them. You shouldn't run away, just because one family was the wrong race. You're not related to all of them, just one."

"I dunno. I'm kind of freaked out."

Les nodded, his eyes on the sidewalk in front of them as they walked. "I can imagine what it must be like... but I know that I don't really know anything about it. I just keep thinking... what if it was my family? What if we really were missing one of my siblings, because of some hospital's mistake? Wouldn't I want her to come and meet us? Just to know who she was?"

"Did you talk to your mom about Sudi?"

"Yeah..." He scuffed his shoe on the pavement. "Sort of. I didn't tell her about the whole switched at the hospital thing. I just asked her... if Sudi was like anyone else in the family. She said that she's just like one of Mom's sisters. They could be twins. I guess... it *is* just genetics."

Kelli breathed out. "That's good. I don't know if I could handle knowing that someone else was going through the same thing."

"Wouldn't it make you feel better? If you knew that you weren't the only one?"

"No. Too stressful. Thinking about someone else going through this… especially Sudi… no, it's just too hard. I don't want anyone else doing this."

Les walked along beside her, frowning. Kelli pointed to a new location to set up. Les had to know that meant no more personal conversation, but that didn't seem to deter him.

"I never thought about how hard it must be," he said. "I thought… it's kind of cool. It would be fun. To see what kind of family you had, and if you were like them. Maybe… clicking with someone like you don't with your mom and dad…"

Kelli sat down and pulled out her cards. "No. I feel like I'm drowning and there's nobody to pull me out. I just keep going under…"

He opened his mouth to say something else, and she motioned to him to cut the talking. Les looked like he was going to continue, but then he shrugged and walked away from her. He'd come back once she got started, so it wouldn't look like they were in cahoots. Kelli settled back into her game, immersing herself back into her old, familiar role.

———

Kelli knew that she would eventually go back to looking for her biological family. It was inevitable. Knowing that she had another family, she couldn't just ignore the fact and go back to ignorance. Les had said to research the next family she was contacting, and she decided to do that. It was best to know what she was getting into, and not to disrupt a family that couldn't possibly be hers, like the Kings.

The Foresters were even further from Kelli economically than the Kings had been. The Kings had at least been middle class. Well-to-do, without being exactly rich. She could be comfortable in that neighborhood. Not feel like an outsider stepping into their living room, if invited. But the Foresters were a different matter.

Justice Emerson Forester was the father's name. Everywhere Kelli found his name, it was all three together. Justice Emerson Forester. He was a judge, but she wasn't sure whether Justice was also his name, and he'd been encouraged by it to go into law, or whether it was just a title, but had been applied to him for so long that no one ever used Emerson Forester without first prefixing it with Justice. Even the birth announcement had been written that way. 'Justice Emerson Forester and Preston Brooks are pleased to announce the birth of their daughter, Elisa Eleanor Brooks Forester.' It was a mouthful. Kelli repeated it to herself several times, getting the taste of the name in her mouth. Elisa Eleanor Brooks Forester. Should that have been her name? Had she spent the first day or two of her life as Elisa Eleanor Brooks Forester? It had a very different feel from Kelli Munroe. Kelli with an 'i.' Munroe with an 'e.' She read through biographical information on Justice Emerson Forester. There were plenty of sources listing his job history, the charities he supported, important cases he had ruled on, and the society he kept. There was far less on his wife, and only the birth announcement for his daughter. His wife, Preston Brooks, had served on several charitable boards. She was listed as a donor on various campaigns.

But there weren't many pictures of the two of them together. By far, most of the pictures were of Justice Emerson Forester. On the bench. At the courthouse. At events for charities, universities, and political actions. Any pictures taken alongside his wife were ten years old. None of the biographies said that he was separated or divorced, but Kelli had her suspicions.

Since he was a public figure, it was fairly easy to figure out where Justice Emerson Forester lived. He had inherited his family home. It was on an 'estate' far past any bus routes. It took some planning for Kelli to figure out how to get there.

Once she was standing on the long driveway in front of Forester Cottage—which Kelli would call a mansion or a castle rather than a cottage —she started having second thoughts again. Just as she had when she had reached the King house, she suddenly felt like turning tail and fleeing home. What was she thinking? That a millionaire judge would be happy to see her? That he wouldn't throw her out on her ear? He'd see her as a threat, maybe even a blackmailer, snooping around his life and trying to hold herself out as his child.

Kelli stood by the iron gates and took out the pictures. She had a newborn picture. As Les had suggested, they had taken pictures of the baby moments after she was born and cleaned up to be presentable. All swaddled up, capped, and cuddled in a glowing Patricia's arms. Then there was a later picture, a few days to a week, as far as Kelli could tell. Baby in a frilly pink dress. The faint blush of a birthmark on one side of her face. Kelli stared at the familiar shape. It was lighter, but even at a few days of age, it was clear. What would her life have been like if it had stayed light like that? Or faded away, like the doctors had said it would?

The picture from the Forester birth announcement showed no birthmark. A long-faced baby with a lacy headband.

Kelli wasn't sure enough to match the newborn picture with either of the days-old pictures. Red-faced and head misshapen, there was little to guide her in selecting either one. There were similarities between the two babies. Both had scant, blond hair. Both had blue eyes. Baby blues, not yet the color they would become. Kelli's had turned brown. What about the other baby's?

Kelli put the pictures back away and looked again at the mansion, her insides knotted. Was she really going to do it? Could she go through with it? She started walking down the long driveway. Her shoes crunched in the shale, and sharp bits got into her sneakers. It seemed like the house was a mile away, and Kelli knew she was slowing more and more the closer she got. Finally, she was at the door.

Arguments flew through her head. He wasn't going to be home. Did she think that a judge just sat around in his dressing gown watching TV all day? When he wasn't in court or at the office, he would be at an event. Not just sitting around waiting for the long-lost daughter he didn't know he had.

She pressed the doorbell. She couldn't hear it ring through the thick door, but she imagined it anyway, bells playing Beethoven or Bach throughout the house, letting everyone know there was a visitor. Or maybe it only played on the main floor or in the servants' quarters, so that the master of the house would not be disturbed. She was tempted to press the bell again. Not being able to hear it ring made her feel like it wasn't ringing, and she needed to press it harder, or use the antique door knocker, to let someone know she was there. She clenched her fists at her sides to avoid doing so. She had been right to start with. The judge wasn't home. Nobody was home. Who would want to stay cooped up inside all day? He was out at the country club. Or taking his daughter somewhere cool.

The door opened suddenly, making Kelli jump. A short, middle-aged woman looked at her. Hispanic. Not Preston Brooks. Not Elisa Eleanor Brooks Forester.

"Uh… hi. I'm looking for Justice Emerson Forester." Kelli swallowed and waited. The maid would tell her to go away. Of course Justice Emerson Forester was indisposed. Didn't take callers without an appointment. Didn't see anyone at all. He was out or on vacation or even out of the country.

"May I tell him who is calling, miss?"

"Kelli Munroe. But… he doesn't know me."

"He's not expecting you, miss?"

"No."

"Will he know what this is about?"

"No."

The maid waited to be told what it was all about. But Kelli could only shake her head. "It's… personal. I'm sorry. He's probably not at home…"

"Wait here, miss."

The maid walked away. She didn't close the door, but she didn't invite Kelli in, either. Kelli looked around the grand front hall. It was big enough to hold a dance in. Maybe they did have dances there. Surely it didn't sit empty all the time. Kelli felt awkward standing there, neither in nor out. She didn't know what to do with her hands. Should she hold them at her sides? Fold them? Put them together in front of her? She knew she shouldn't fidget, but that was exactly what she was doing, standing there trying to figure out what to do with herself.

There were footsteps from off to the side, not the direction the maid had gone in. Kelli looked in that direction, preparing herself to have to explain the situation again to a butler or someone else. Personal business? They would want more details. She wouldn't be able to get in to see Justice Emerson Forester on such skimpy details.

The man walked into the hall from a side room, and smiled politely at Kelli. Kelli turned to face him, stammering for an explanation. It wasn't another employee. It was the judge himself. He was even handsomer in person than in the pictures. In a beautifully-cut blue suit, silvering hair looking like he had just come back from the barber, a short, distinguished mustache and goatee that put Axel's to shame. He smiled pleasantly at Kelli, raising his eyebrows.

"Uh, sir, uh, my name—"

The coffee mug in his hands went crashing to the floor. Kelli looked at it in dismay, her mouth open. Had she caused that? It was broken, the spilled coffee seeping into what was probably a priceless hand-woven silk rug. The judge was staring at her. Kelli clapped a hand over her birthmark, swearing.

She'd startled him with the birthmark. He was so disgusted and distressed by it that he'd fumbled his coffee. Kelli was mortified. She hadn't imagined anything like that happening. She should have tried to disguise the mark. Makeup, an artfully arranged hat or scarf. He wasn't used to freaks walking in through his door.

"What is your name?"

Justice Emerson Forester held out both arms and grasped her by the shoulders, still staring intently at her face. He wasn't upset or disgusted. He was smiling. His eyes sparkled.

The maid came from another direction and made a noise of dismay at the broken mug and spilled coffee. The judge stepped around it, shaking his head. "Just take care of it, Felicia. It's only coffee."

Kelli stared at the man, not understanding what was happening. He touched her hand, encouraging her to move it away from the birthmark again. He swore. Or prayed. Maybe both.

"Come in. Come in and sit down and tell me what you came here to tell me."

He held her by one arm, tugging her into the hall and then leading her into a smaller room with plush carpet and a fireplace. He escorted her to a chair and made sure she sat down. He sat down across from her. There was a small coffee table between them, something ornamental and probably hand-carved, but he might as well have been two inches from her face, his eyes were so intense.

Kelli swallowed. "My name is Kelli Munroe," she said hoarsely. "And I think... maybe... that I could be..."

"My daughter."

———

Kelli stared at Justice Emerson Forester. She shook her head slightly.

"How could you know that?"

He reached toward her. Toward the birthmark on her face. Then dropped his hand, flushing. "I held you when you were born. I remember the shape of your birthmark. I remember looking at it. Memorizing it. I thought it was a birthmark. But the next day, it was gone, and when I asked about it... they said it had just been flushed or bruised a little from the delivery. And it had faded."

Kelli stared at him. She hadn't known how she was going to tell her story to him. Or how she would ever prove any of it without a DNA test, which he would naturally refuse. And instead of having to talk him into anything, he had dumped it right into her lap. He knew who she was and he didn't need anything to be proven to him.

The judge shook his head. "I didn't... I didn't really think anything of it at the time. So much happened. It didn't worry me. I never thought of it again."

"Until now."

"Until now," he agreed. "Kelli Munroe. How did you figure it out? How did you find me? You're only... you're only sixteen. That's some detective work."

Kelli turned her face away from him, hot from him staring at her mark so intently. "It is and it isn't," she said. "I guess my mom figured out the hospital switched the babies fourteen years ago. I didn't know... until recently."

"She knew fourteen years ago?" he repeated in disbelief. "Why didn't she tell anyone?"

"Well, she did. Just not you. She went to the hospital, and there were lawyers, and a big settlement. They paid her off to keep her quiet."

"And they never contacted us? That's outrageous! They knew a mistake had been made, and they didn't even tell us? Give us a chance to get to know our own biological child?"

Kelli nodded. She felt numb. She didn't know what she should feel. She couldn't have imagined the reunion progressing any better. But she didn't know what to do or what to say.

"And she never told you?" Justice Emerson Forester asked. "You never knew that you weren't her biological child?"

"No. Not until recently... when I found the paperwork. And then I didn't know who my biological family was, I had to figure out who else was born at the same time, in the same hospital..."

"Which eventually led you here. You were very smart to figure it out."

"Are you really...?" Kelli stammered. "I mean... are you sure?"

"I'm sure," he insisted. "I held you for hours, staring at that birthmark. Its shape is impressed on my memory." He looked around the room. "We have pictures. Of the day you were born..."

"I have these," Kelli pulled out the pictures from the shoebox. And the one she had printed out from the birth announcement. The judge took them from her and studied them.

"I can see how they got confused," he said. "You and Lisa do have similar features. And your birthmark wasn't as prominent then as it is now."

Kelli held her hand over it again, her face hot. Her father looked at her.

"Don't do that. You don't need to be embarrassed by it. I don't mean to make you self-conscious. It's just… how I know you are who you are."

"It's always caused me trouble." Kelli tried unsuccessfully to pull her hand away from her face. "You know… kids at school make fun and bully… my mom—the mom who raised me—hates it, says how ugly it is. People on the street… stare or look away… spit at me for no reason…"

"That's despicable. People behave like animals sometimes."

He handed her photos back to her.

"I'd like to get copies of those sometime, if you wouldn't mind. And other pictures of you, your growing-up years…?"

"Uh… yeah, sure. Of course."

"Did your mother ever try to have anything done with your birthmark?" He leaned back in his seat, crossing one ankle over his knee and straightening his pant crease fussily. "Laser surgery or anything?"

"I had a few treatments. Nothing ever helped and… well, we couldn't really afford it."

The maid came into the room with a tray. Coffee service for two. To replace the cup that her father had dropped. The judge motioned for her to put it on the table between them, and poured himself a cup.

"Please help yourself. If you drink the stuff. You shouldn't, of course, but…"

Kelli couldn't help grinning. "I can't live without it," she admitted. She poured herself a cup and added just a touch of sugar and cream from the containers on the tray. More for the ceremony than for the taste. She usually drank her coffee black. Black, burnt, cold, day-old. Any way she could get it. It was like an addiction for her.

She sipped the rich blend and gave a little whistle. "Wow! I've never had coffee like that. It's wonderful." She took a longer sip, even though it was piping hot.

Her father chuckled. "Must be genetic. Lisa will never be a coffee drinker. Tea, sometimes, but coffee, never."

"Lisa…" Kelli looked around. "Does she live here?"

"No. Her mother and I separated a long time ago. Well, that is, Preston and I separated a long time ago. I guess technically, Preston is *not* her biological mother…"

Kelli gave her head a shake. "It's so weird."

"Tell me about your family. The family who raised you. They were good to you, I hope?"

Kelli again became self-conscious. Not of her birthmark this time, but of the holes in her shoes and in the knee of her jeans. The stains on the t-shirt she wore. Her flat, drab brown hair. All the little things that emphasized that she hadn't been raised in the kind of home that his daughter had been.

"Well… I guess. It wasn't like I had the perfect family…"

"No family is perfect," he assured her. "I just hope they didn't hurt you. That you were provided for."

Kelli didn't know what to say. She avoided his eyes. Justice Emerson Forester's voice dropped to a lower register.

"Oh… I see… I'm so sorry, Kelli. I'm sorry… I never knew."

"What could you do even if you had? You wouldn't have wanted to send Lisa back there. No one could have made everything right."

He sighed. "You're probably right. But I still feel bad about it. Did you have two parents? A single mother? You said there was a big settlement from the hospital, so hopefully that provided you with some of what you needed…"

"Mostly it's been me and my mom. My biological dad… Lisa's biological dad… left when he had a paternity test that showed I wasn't his daughter. My mom hooked up with Axel sometime after that… I'm not really sure when… and he was around for a bit when I was little. But then he went to prison for felony murder. He was there for ten years…" The judge's expression was horrified. Kelli hastened to add, "But he didn't actually do it… the conviction was overturned and he was released, because of DNA evidence. So, he's back now. But he and my mom are both sort of… they have some problems… my mom was just diagnosed with early dementia. And Axel has some kind of brain damage, from back before the armed robbery…"

"Then what are you doing? Are you in a foster home now?"

"No, I'm still with them. I wouldn't want to go into foster care. It's… well, things happen in foster care. I'll just stay where I am. Take care of myself. And my mom, for as long as I can."

"You can't do that. Not with them both… disabled. We'll have to work something else out. I don't know if there is anything that can be done for either of them, but if there is…"

"I don't think so." Kelli sighed. "Mom's a pretty heavy drinker. And she's had a lot of concussions. Once you kill brain cells, they don't come back."

"No. What can I do for you, then? You could come here. I can't let you just go back to a home where you are neglected or abused…"

"I don't want any trouble. And there would be. I'm okay where I am, really. I just… wanted to meet you. See where I really came from."

Justice Emerson Forester sipped his coffee. His brows were settled low over his eyes as he stared off into middle space. "You'll want to meet your mother as well, of course. I'll… try to arrange that for you. Break the ice. I don't know how Preston will react. She and Lisa are very close, so you'll have to be prepared that she's going to see you as an imposter. She'll think you're trying to take something away from Lisa."

"I'm not, though. I'm not asking for anything from you. Either of you. It was just… I don't know… I had to know who you were. That's all. I couldn't go my whole life without at least trying."

"I hope you will keep in touch. You won't just disappear, will you?"

Kelli's face warmed. She felt so comfortable sitting there with him. Not because the couch was soft and the room was the perfect temperature, even though they were. But she just felt a connection with her father. A spark that she had feared would not be there. He had just met her, and yet he cared about her. Not that she was going to put the touch on him. Or threaten to take the story to the press. But he really cared about her welfare and that she keep in touch with him. Far from ejecting her from the house and telling her never to contact him again, he was afraid that she was going to leave and never come back.

"If you want. I didn't know… what you would think."

"I don't know what I think! I never expected this. Never thought for a minute that Lisa wasn't mine. She doesn't take after me, but how many teenage girls can you say do take after their fathers? But I *know* you. And maybe this is a second chance for me."

Kelli nodded. It could be a second chance for both of them. Kelli loved her mother, but wasn't really bonded with her. And Axel… she was afraid of him more than anything. He was someone to avoid. Which wasn't easy, when he lived just down the hall from her.

"You aren't that close to Lisa?" she asked tentatively. "I guess when you and her mom broke up…?"

"It's been a long time since she lived with me. And even when they were living here… I was too involved with my work. I didn't spend enough time with Lisa or Preston. Didn't give them enough attention. I always thought that I had to spend time building my career, and I would give them more of my time once I was more established. Now… I have career success, but they are gone."

"Do you still have visitation? You get to see her?"

"Yes, of course. And I pay spousal and child support. But it's hard to have a close relationship when you are only seeing someone occasionally, and only because of the threat of withdrawing financial support. I don't know if she'll have anything to do with me once she's an adult. Unless it's to ensure that she is in my will."

"That sucks."

"It does."

"So, I guess… you're a judge…?"

"Yes. I am. It's not as much fun as you might think… most of the time it's pretty tedious. Have you ever been in a courtroom…?"

Kelli swallowed. She took a sip of her aromatic coffee and tried to think of what to say. She made a noncommittal noise, encouraging him to go on.

"Well, anyway. Most days it's just routine cases. Hearing the same arguments over and over again. Seeing people ruin their lives and relationships with poor choices. It's not very often I get one of those golden cases. The ones that can set precedent and change the direction of a person's life or the way that cases will be handled in the future. Mostly, it's just grinding away, waiting for those bright spots. But they are few and far between."

Kelli thought about the judges that she had appeared before. Most were brusque. They barely seemed to skim the papers they were given, and stared off into space as the lawyers made their arguments. It had never occurred to her that it must be boring and depressing, listening to tedious tales of bad decisions over and over again.

"Huh. I never thought of that. So, why do you still do it? Why don't you do something else?"

"I do other things as well. Being a judge isn't my whole life, thank goodness. I have other business interests, investments, hobbies, personal interests. I don't spend all my time in a stuffy courtroom."

"That's good. It doesn't sound like it would be a good idea."

"Judges have been known to crack up!"

Kelli had heard of such cases. She opened her mouth to tell him about Judge Cardel, a juvie court judge who had started to bring his pet potbelly pig to his private chambers, then she thought better of it. Justice Emerson Forester might have more questions than she wanted to answer on the matter.

CHAPTER 11

Les didn't usually get up until late on a Sunday, but Kelli had to talk to him, so she threw pebbles at his window until his face appeared and he waved at her. Kelli paced up and down the sidewalk, waiting for him to get dressed and washed up and to grab something for breakfast. It was stretching on toward a full hour when he finally exited the house and walked down the sidewalk toward her.

He yawned without covering his mouth and scrubbed at his eyes with his fists. "Sorry, I had trouble getting out of there. Some of the littles were up and I had to look after things." He ran his fingers through his hair, mussing it rather than straightening it. "What's up? Why so early?"

Les pulled an apple out of his pocket to eat and Kelli waved it away. "I'm treating you to a real breakfast this morning."

His eyes widened. "You're treating me to breakfast? Like, not a Pop Tart?"

Kelli nodded. She pulled out a folded-over wad of bills, and after he had glimpsed it, shoved it back away again, looking around to make sure no one was watching them. Who would be watching? All the gang bangers were sleeping after a night of revels. Teens were sleeping in. Drug dealers and other punks were all hung over. Sunday morning was a safe time.

"Where did you get that?" Les demanded. "What con are you already running at nine in the morning? What brings in moola like that?"

"Not today. Yesterday."

"Yesterday? I thought yesterday you went to see…" Understanding flooded over his features. "You put the touch on the biologicals? Tell me all about it!"

They started to walk. Kelli led the way to the nearest pancake house. Les could have however big a stack he wanted. And bacon and sausages and eggs, if he wanted. They could both eat their fill without worry about there not being anything to eat the next day.

"He's flush," Kelli said with a shrug. "Big mansion. Fancy cars. Servants. He's a judge."

"No, way! Talk about the perfect mark! What story did you give him?"

"Nothing. Mostly he asked the questions and told me about himself. I didn't have to ask for anything. In fact," Kelli laughed, "he insisted!"

"Suh-weet. How did you convince him you were his daughter? I mean, you couldn't do a paternity test yet. You must have told him something pretty convincing."

Kelli told him about how her father had recognized her birthmark as soon as he had seen her at the door. She dug a photo out of her pocket.

"Look. This is me right after I was born."

The infant in the picture was wet-haired and squalling, face squished, body elongated. And most importantly, she had a pink splotch over her face that would later darken into the port wine stain they were both so familiar with.

Les swore in wonder, and nodded his head. "That's you. You can tell, can't you? Even though it's not dark, it's still clear."

Kelli nodded, staring at it once more herself. That was her. In her biological mother's arms, not Patricia's. The child that Justice Emerson Forester should have taken home from the hospital. But if he had, where would she be now? She wouldn't just be meeting him and getting to know him. She'd be the spoiled brat that didn't want to see him unless she was paid to do so. Her father hadn't said much about Lisa, but from what Kelli gathered, she was a socialite who wasn't interested in much except parties and looking good. She had her own car and whatever she wanted, and still only saw her father when he insisted.

They walked into the restaurant and, after staring at Kelli's birthmark, the hostess showed them to a table and gave them their menus. The smells of pastries and maple syrup made Kelli ravenous.

"Coffee," Kelli said to the woman before she could retreat. "Please."

Les opened his menu and pored over the possibilities. "What did you talk about? Are you going to move into the mansion?"

"No!" Kelli made a face. "He'd like me to, I think. But I couldn't just leave Mom…"

"Sure, you could. I know her. She'd be happy to get you out of the house. Wouldn't she?"

"Well… yeah, probably. But she needs someone looking out for her… making sure she's okay."

"Let the axe-murderer do that."

"I don't know if he can… and… I dunno about going to live with someone else. It would be weird. I don't know anything about this guy."

"You know he's rich and likes to give you money."

Kelli snorted. "Yeah. But I don't really know what kind of guy he is. I mean, it might all be show. He might be a totally different guy once he takes off the mask. Or he could change his mind. Decide that he doesn't want some 'long lost daughter' hanging around the place. He might talk to his lawyer, who will say not to have anything to do with me."

A harried waitress arrived at their table, banged two coffee mugs down, and sloshed burnt-smelling coffee into them. She left again without a word or a smile.

"He could be totally different," Kelli reiterated, going back to her original line of thought. "He could be abusive. A drinker. Handsy. I don't know."

Les had to concede the point. "Yeah, I guess. But once you get to know him better. You'll consider it, won't you? This is your big chance! It's what you've been waiting for."

Kelli flipped slowly through the menu, hungry but not sure what it was she really wanted. "It doesn't feel real. I don't think I believe it's really happening. I'm just going to wake up, and I'm going to be plain old Kelli Munroe again."

"Well, please don't wake up until I've had a chance to eat my pancakes."

Kelli laughed. "Okay."

A waitress wandered over. Not the harried-looking one, but a lazy one who looked barely awake. She took their orders, but Kelli wondered whether she would get them right or come back with something completely different.

"When are you going to see him again?" Les asked.

"He wants me to go over for dinner tonight. I guess I will, but it's not exactly easy to get out there."

"You're having pancakes with me and then dinner with him? Probably lobster or something. You'd better not have any lunch, or you won't be able to stuff it all in."

"Lots of time between now and then. I'll be hungry again."

"What do you think it will be like? A big, long table with a white cloth? China? Servants? Do you think it will be lobster or caviar?"

"I hope not," Kelli wrinkled her nose. "I don't like seafood. I didn't think to ask. You know, someone offers me food, I just take it…"

"Will you eat it if it's something really gross? Like, I don't know… calf's liver or snails?"

"I don't know." Kelli shifted uncomfortably. "He won't pick something like that, will he? He knows I'm just a teenager, I don't eat stuff like that."

"Maybe his other daughter does and he doesn't know the difference. Or maybe he wants to introduce you to all these new delicacies, since you haven't had them before."

"Ugh." Kelli rubbed her stomach. "Stop it, or I'm not going to be able to eat my pancakes."

———

Kelli wondered before leaving if she should tell her mother what was going on and where she was going. She should, at some point, tell Patricia that she had made contact with her biological family. Would it be better to do it sooner or later?

She paused in the living room, where Patricia was deeply engrossed in a rerun of Dallas. After a minute, Patricia swiveled her head. "What do you want?"

"I'm going out… I'll be late getting in."

"Late? Is this a date?" Patricia dropped a candy bar wrapper on the floor. "Who would take *you* out?"

Kelli's anger flared. What kind of mother spoke to her child that way? Kelli had made a lot of excuses for Patricia over the years. She'd had a hard life. She was too old when she had Kelli and didn't have the energy a younger mother did. Her addiction was a disease, not a choice. But how did any of that excuse her dislike of Kelli and her hateful remarks about Kelli's birthmark?

Kelli had asked the question many times, but it was the first time that she had an answer.

Because Kelli wasn't really Patricia's daughter, and she knew it. Because the birthmark was more than a skin condition, it was a constant reminder that Kelli was not the daughter she had borne. She was a changeling. A concession that Patricia had made for money.

But no matter what Patricia said, it didn't get her her biological daughter back.

Kelli teetered on the edge. Walk out and slam the door, or stay and fight?

"I'm having dinner with someone," she said. "My biological father."

Patricia stared at her, obviously not understanding what Kelli was telling her. Her eyes went to the side, up to the ceiling, back to Kelli again.

"What are you talking about?" she demanded. "Your biological father? John?"

"John isn't my biological father. The DNA test proved that. You know what I'm talking about. My real biological father."

"You can't run around meeting men that you don't even know," Patricia said, scowling. "That's dangerous! Anything could happen."

"What? Nothing is going to happen. I'm just having supper. At his place."

"You're going to his house?"

"Yes. I was there before. It's fine."

"Where?" Patricia looked behind her, toward the living room window, any view of the street always blocked by dirty, bent, horizontal blinds. "Where does he live?"

"Nowhere around here. I wouldn't go to someone's house in this neighborhood," Kelli conceded. "But he's not… he's got a nice place. It's safe."

"When will you be back?"

"I don't know. Late. I can't help that, we're eating late and it's a long ways out. You'll be asleep before I get back."

"Why don't you stay there if it's going to be that late? You shouldn't be out on the street after dark. Not around here."

First Patricia said that Kelli shouldn't go meet her father for supper.

Now she was suggesting Kelli sleep over. Did it even occur to Patricia how inconsistent she was?

"I'm not staying there," Kelli said. "I'll be home. I'm just not sure when." She held up her new cell phone. "I have a phone if there's any trouble."

"Where did you get that?"

"I had some money."

"Are you dealing drugs? You never had money for a phone before!"

Kelli laughed and rolled her eyes. "I'm not dealing drugs! How stupid do you think I am? I just… came into a little money. That's all."

Patricia's eyes narrowed and glittered. "Came into a little money, eh?"

"It's got nothing to do with you," Kelli warned. "He's my father and you keep your distance. You got your money from the hospital when you agreed to drop the lawsuit."

Patricia's eyes turned back toward the TV. She sat there staring at it with a sullen frown. Like a child who had just been told she couldn't have the new bike or puppy she wanted. Kelli looked at her for a moment before walking out. It was a good thing that Kelli hadn't spilled Justice Emerson Forester's name or any details about how rich he was. If Patricia figured those details out, she might try to put the touch on the judge herself, and Kelli didn't want that complication.

"See you later."

Patricia stared at the TV and didn't answer.

———

Kelli arrived at the mansion a little early. She hadn't wanted to show up late and have her father worrying about her or their dinner getting cold. But arriving early was a problem too. There wasn't exactly anywhere for her to go and kill time before ringing the doorbell. No nearby parks or stores or coffee houses to hang out in. No friends to drop in on and visit for a few minutes. Just long driveways leading to other mansions. People who didn't know her from Adam and didn't want to be disturbed by wandering strangers. Kelli could walk up and down the road a bit, but she thought people might be leery and call the police. Then she'd have a lot of explaining to do, and she wasn't sure the judge was ready to reveal his new relation to the public.

She finally walked up the lane to the house and rang the doorbell. The maid let her in, smiling in recognition and greeting her cordially.

"Come in and have a seat. Mr. Forester isn't down yet."

She led Kelli into the room that she had previously met with her father in. Kelli sat down, but once the maid was gone, she stood back up and wandered around the room, looking at the paintings, vases, lamps, and other decorative touches. Everything was so beautiful and had such depth. They weren't just department store buys and reproduction posters. Everything looked as if it had a history, a named artist, and papers to prove its provenance. Kelli tried to read the signatures on the paintings. Were they famous names that she should know? Most of them she could only read a letter or two of. If they were well-known, she had no idea who they were.

"Kelli."

Kelli jumped and whirled around, feeling as guilty as if she'd been caught with her hand in the cookie jar.

"Oh… hi…" She didn't even know what to call him. Father? Justice? Mr. Forester? "I'm sorry… I got here earlier than I meant to. I hope I didn't interrupt anything…"

He sat down in the same place he had the first time they had met. He was dressed more casually this time. Sweater and slacks instead of a suit. He still looked as neat and crisp as if he'd just stepped out of a salon.

"No, not at all. It's just fine." His lips pressed together, and Kelli wasn't sure she believed him. Something appeared to be bothering him. "I… didn't see your car."

"I don't have a car."

He looked stunned. "How did you get here, then?"

Kelli wandered back over to her seat and sat, turning the answer over in her mind. She had a feeling that he wasn't going to like it. He didn't understand the kind of life she led.

"I took the bus, hitched, and walked."

"I had no idea! I wouldn't have asked you back here if I knew how difficult it was for you. I didn't realize when you were here before that you didn't have a car."

"Sorry…"

"There's nothing for you to be sorry for. I should have thought about it. I'm so embarrassed. It must have taken you half the day."

"A few hours."

"And you still got here early!"

"Yeah, I misjudged. Wanted to make sure I wouldn't be late."

"A very admirable quality. So many people I know are intentionally late."

"Really? I get it if something happens and you can't help it, but why would someone be late on purpose?"

"To thumb their nose at the host. To express dominance. To make an entrance." The judge shrugged. "Not good reasons, but reasons."

Kelli nodded.

"From now on, you take a taxi to get out here. I'll get you an expense card. Until we can work out something more permanent. Do you know how to drive?"

"I have my license. But I don't get much opportunity to drive. Just my mom's car, now and then, if she needs me to run an errand."

"Would you like a car of your own?"

Kelli looked at his face. Would it be nice to have her own car? Or did she want him to get her a car? Which question was he asking?

"Someday," she hedged. "Can't afford anything right now. I have to save up."

He pursed his lips. He didn't pursue it any further at that point, and Kelli was relieved he'd let it go. They didn't really know each other well enough to discuss her finances.

She asked him questions about himself, and they discussed the weather or other unimportant topics until the maid came in to announce that dinner was ready. The judge stood up. He didn't offer Kelli his arm, just smiled at her.

"This way."

They exited through a different door from the one Kelli had entered through. She tried to look at all of the opulent furnishings discreetly as they walked by, not gawping at everything. They entered a dining room which did, as Les had predicted, have a long table with a white cloth. But there was no fancy china, and the two chairs that they were obviously intended to take were both at one end of the table, on perpendicular sides, rather than opposite ends of the long table.

And Kelli could immediately relax her anxieties about being served steak and kidney pie or blood pudding. A couple of pizza boxes were on the table, a popular chain. She grinned, relieved.

"Les—my friend—he said you were probably going to serve me lobster and caviar or something really gross. He figured since you didn't have a teenager at home, or maybe if they were Lisa's favorite foods…"

Justice Emerson Forester chuckled. He motioned Kelli to a seat, and pushed her chair in for her. Then he sat down himself.

"You're in luck. Lisa happens to be a staunch vegetarian. The kind who doesn't eat seafood, so I wouldn't dare feed you lobster or caviar without asking first. I even got a vegetarian pizza, just in case." He motioned to one of the boxes. "You didn't say you had any dietary restrictions when I asked you to dinner, so I hoped that you didn't have any… no allergies or anything."

"No. I'll eat most normal stuff. Except mac and cheese. Pizza is great," she assured him. "Any kind."

The judge opened both boxes. Kelli helped herself to a slice of 'everything' pizza and a slice of vegetarian.

———

"I have a question," Justice Emerson Forester said slowly, "and this is very forward of me, and maybe awkward for you. Do you mind…?"

Kelli dabbed at her greasy lips with a cloth napkin. "Well… long as you understand I might not answer it."

He looked relieved. "Yes, of course. Don't feel compelled to answer."

"Okay."

"You said that you have had laser treatment on your birthmark before, but it didn't really help."

"It doesn't always work," Kelli agreed.

"I had one of my assistants look into alternatives."

Kelli raised her eyebrows. "Alternatives to laser treatment? Not much. You don't want to damage the skin, and end up with a worse problem. I could cover it up with makeup, but it doesn't cover really well and tends to wear off by the end of the day. People still look, they still know something is wrong. So… I just go natural. People are gonna stare. So, they're gonna stare."

"There are some clinics that are having good results with microtattooing."

"Tattooing? I know some people that put tattoos over top."

"This microtattooing is coloring your birthmark so that it is the same color as the skin on the rest of your face. Not making a picture, just... coloring over the birthmark with the color it should have been in the first place."

Kelli frowned. "I've never heard of that."

"It's pretty new. Not a lot of places are doing it. Would you... be interested...?"

She waved her hand in dismissal. "It's probably really expensive."

"It would be my gift to you. Something that I would have done for you if I had raised you."

Kelli took several bites of pizza. She was full, but she didn't want to answer him right away, and a full mouth was a good excuse. Her face burned, knowing that he was looking at her. Knowing that he was looking at the big purple birthmark and wondering what she would look like without it. How many times had Kelli looked at it and wondered the same thing? It wasn't wrong for him to ask the question. But it wasn't comfortable.

"I told you it might be awkward," he reminded her. "And you're allowed to say no, or say you don't want to talk about it."

"Not... right now..." Kelli said, relieved. "I don't know... I have to think about it, and I don't want you doing a bunch of stuff for me. I don't really... know you yet."

He nodded. "I understand. I just wanted to put it out there. You can bring it up again whenever you like. I don't know if you even want to have it removed—or covered—you might want to just leave things as they are. It wasn't necessarily your own decision to have laser surgery as a child."

Kelli sighed. "I hate it," she admitted. "It makes me feel like a monster. Ugly. Less than human. Everyone stares. People make fun." Kelli thought about Patricia's comments before she had left. "Even my mom, she tells me how ugly I am." She swallowed the bitterness, trying to keep down the lump in her throat and not let tears come out. She was a big girl. She hadn't cried in years. Not real tears, just cons. She accepted her birthmark. It was part of who she was.

Justice Emerson Forester's expression was so sympathetic, Kelli nearly did lose control. She shook her head at him.

"Don't look at me like that," she ordered. "Seriously. Don't feel sorry for me. I know who I am, and I'm strong. Don't make me weak."

"Sorry. New topic."

Kelli nodded.

"When you leave, it's going to be dark. I don't think it's safe for you to go home in the dark. Certainly not walking and hitchhiking."

"Well… it will be okay. I don't think anything will happen. And I know Jujitsu. I can protect myself."

"You can protect yourself in some circumstances, maybe, but why put yourself into a dangerous situation when you don't have to? If you want, I can drive you home. Or you could stay here and head home in the morning."

"Oh, no. I wouldn't want to put you out!"

"Neither one would be putting me out. And I would be much happier knowing that you were okay. I couldn't sleep tonight if I had to wonder if you got home safely. Which is it going to be?"

Crap.

Kelli could tell by the steel in his voice that he wasn't going to back down on the issue. She wasn't hitching home and that was that.

She didn't want him driving her home. She couldn't bear for him to see where she was living. He could probably track her down and find out where she lived more easily than she had found him, and maybe he already had. But she couldn't let him drop her off there. And dropping her off somewhere close but still outside the neighborhood probably wasn't on offer. Patricia had told her to stay overnight, so it wasn't like she didn't have permission. Patricia probably wouldn't remember in the morning, but Kelli knew.

"Uh… let me think about it," she hedged, not wanting to seem too eager to stay with him.

The judge nodded. "As you can see, the place is plenty big enough to house one extra visitor for the night. I have several guest rooms. I would like to turn one of them into your room, your own place for when you stay over. Just like Lisa has her own place here."

"I don't know…"

"You will have a room here. Whether or not you make it your own is up to you."

Kelli coughed. "Uh… okay."

Her father laughed. "I'm not going to be a big rule enforcer. Obviously, I had nothing to do with raising you and I'm not going to be able to step into that role now. But you should know that I am stubborn and there are some things I just won't back down on."

"Must be a family trait," Kelli laughed.

———

After a leisurely meal, Justice Emerson Forester took Kelli on a short tour of the castle—the cottage, as he referred to it. He took her upstairs to where the bedrooms were. Kelli was having a hard time keeping her eyes calm and steady, instead of whipping her head back and forth to try to look at everything at once. There would be time for exploring. She would get to know the place a little at a time. If she let herself get overwhelmed, she would just end up lost and confused. So she watched for landmarks and tried to block out the overstimulation of the artwork on the walls, delicate-looking ornaments on tables, and the carved wood around the doors and ceilings. The carpet was thick and soft and looked like it had just been vacuumed. Like a museum.

"That is Lisa's room," the judge said, indicating a bedroom farther down the hall. "And this one is yours." He opened the one on the right. Kelli followed him anxiously into it. Her room. In spite of the fact that they barely knew each other, that they had just barely even met, he had assigned a room to her. Whether she made use of it or not. He was going to pretend that she was his family, before they even had a chance to decide if they liked each other or not. He didn't know anything about her. He hardly knew anything about her background or what kind of person she was. She shook her head.

"You don't like it?"

"Oh—" Kelli looked around. She hadn't even taken the room's furnishings in. It wasn't decorated for a child or a teenager, but the walls were a deep rose, with lots of the ornamental wood moldings, and there was a rich-looking bed with a cover she thought was silk, and a matching dresser and wardrobe. "No, it's lovely. It's really nice."

"Then what were you shaking your head at?"

Kelli bit her lip. She didn't know how honest to be with him. He wasn't like anyone she knew, and she wasn't quite sure of their roles and how to behave with each other. "Well… it's just that… you're too trusting. You shouldn't let me stay over like this. You don't even know who I am. I could be planning on stealing all your valuables. Letting someone else in to clean you out. I could be planning on blackmailing you. Seducing you." She shook her head. "You're not protecting yourself. You're being… naive."

He laughed explosively and gave her a hug around the shoulders. Not too intimate, just a friendly, good-humored squeeze. "Is that what's bothering you? Kelli, whatever you want is yours. I wish I could give you more. For sixteen years, you've been… away… and I've given you nothing at all. I'm estranged from my wife and daughter. I have no other children or family. Nobody special to leave my fortune to. So take it. Whatever you want. It's yours."

Kelli shook her head firmly. "I couldn't do that. I'm not taking advantage of you. Taking anything away from your family. It wouldn't be right. You don't even know me."

"I know who you are, Kelli. What more do I need? I knew the instant I saw your face that you are my daughter. You can't fake that. I don't need any further proof. I know how much you've lacked… and I know I can't make up for it."

Kelli hadn't told him much about herself or her home life. She didn't know how much he could have gleaned from what she said and didn't say, but he seemed to know more. He didn't sound like he was guessing that she had had a bad life. Kelli's full stomach gave a lurch. He'd investigated her. Of course he had. Why wouldn't he? She had investigated him, what little she could on the internet. He had plenty of resources at his disposal. Much more to lose. Of course he had run background on her.

Just how much did he know?

"Would you like to see the rest of the house?" Justice Emerson Forester asked her. "Or do you want to stay in here?"

"I just think…" Kelli gestured at her surroundings. "I'll get ready for bed. Need to get up early in the morning so I can get back in time for school."

"Okay." Her father kissed her on the forehead. "Have a good night. There are a few sundries in the drawers. Toothbrush and toothpaste. Let me know if you need anything, or ask Felicia, if you prefer. Anything you need."

"Okay, thanks."

He released her and departed without asking any further questions.

Kelli stood there for a long time, just listening to the sounds of the house, before finally moving. She checked the drawers and wardrobe, finding not just toothbrush and toothpaste, but deodorant, t-shirts and sweat pants that she could use as pajamas, an extra pillow and blankets, and a few other surprises. She realized that the door to her right was not a closet, but an ensuite bathroom. Not huge, but serviceable, and it meant she didn't have to go traipsing around looking for one, especially in the middle of the night. She pulled back the blankets on the bed and felt the cool, clean sheets. Were they ironed? They looked like they must be right out of the package, but were uncreased.

Kelli got ready for bed. Before turning off the light and closing her eyes, she tried calling Patricia to tell her that she would, after all, be sleeping over at her father's house.

There was no answer.

CHAPTER 12

The bed was so comfortable, Kelli couldn't sleep. She tossed and turned, but couldn't seem to settle her mind or her body. Her mind warred over whether the judge was the perfect mark, or whether he was canny, one step ahead of her and keeping her off-balance. Was it wrong to take advantage of him? Or wrong to refuse his gifts and his attempts to coddle her? Her body was sore after walking, her stomach too full, and the bed was too soft and smooth and foreign against her skin. Every time she moved, she felt perfectly enveloped in its coziness, yet she couldn't sleep.

Eventually, she must have dropped off. Because she awoke in the morning to a light tap on her door. Before she could get up to answer it or even get her head on straight to call out to the visitor, Felicia the maid was bringing in a coffee service tray, which she set down on the top of the dresser.

"Morning, Miss Kelli," she whispered. "Mr. Justice wasn't sure what time you needed to get up, he asked me to make sure you had your coffee."

Kelli stretched and rubbed her eyes. "What time is it?"

"Just six o'clock."

Kelli forced herself to sit up. "I'd better get moving, then. Thanks, this is just what I need."

"Mr. Justice said he would drive you into the city when you're ready. He has a meeting at the courthouse, so he's heading that way anyway."

"Uh… okay. Is that the truth, or did he just make up an excuse to drive me in?"

Felicia gave Kelli a little smile. "I don't know. But he has to be in the city early most mornings."

"Okay." Kelli pushed her blankets away. She knew that if she remained in bed, she would just go back to sleep, and then she'd be late to school. She couldn't keep up her marks if she were late, and she needed a high school diploma to get somewhere in life. So she'd get up. Shower off the cobwebs, have a couple mugs of coffee, and get into the city with Justice Emerson Forester.

"What would you like for breakfast? I will have it ready when you finish getting ready."

Kelli hesitated. She didn't usually have breakfast, and she didn't like to put anyone out cooking for her. But it would be nice to head off the hunger and have something other than just coffee before school.

"Umm… gee, I don't like to put anyone to any trouble…"

"That's what we get paid for. It's no trouble."

Kelli noted the 'we.' How many servants did the judge have working behind the scenes?

"Well… I dunno. Maybe just some toast and eggs? I won't have a lot of time to eat…"

Felicia nodded. "That's just fine. I'll see to it."

———

Kelli managed to find her way to the dining room, where she had breakfast with her father, and then they headed out to the garage. Kelli hadn't even considered what it was going to look like being dropped off at school by a man no one had ever seen before, and was relieved when they climbed into a dark blue fuel-efficient compact rather than a long sleek luxury car or little red convertible. At least it wouldn't stand out.

It started with a purr and they made their way along the long driveway.

"We should stop by your house first to pick up your schoolbooks," the judge suggested.

Kelli had already thought of that. She shook her head. "No, it's okay. I've got everything I need in my locker."

He glanced sideways at her. "You must have some work at home that you need to take in with you."

"No."

Under no circumstances did Kelli want Justice Emerson Forester to see where she lived or have the opportunity to meet Patricia or Axel. Those cards were not on the table. He might have had her background checked out. He might have even been given pictures of her house and parents by a private investigator. But that wasn't the same as seeing it and being there himself. He had to know that there were boundaries.

"Are you sure?"

"I said no," Kelli insisted.

He looked back at the road and didn't pursue it any further. "Where is your school?"

Kelli chewed on the inside of her cheek. Was he playing her? Did he really not know, or was he just trying to put her at ease? Did he know the address, but not the part of the city it was in? Or maybe he knew what neighborhood it was in, but hadn't taken note of the address?

She knew she was being paranoid. It didn't make any difference whether he knew or not, he was going to see it. But she liked to know if she was being conned.

She told him the general area. "I'll give you directions when we get close."

He nodded his agreement, and they traveled for a while without speaking. The radio was playing quietly. The temperature inside the car was perfect. There were no sounds from the road outside. Kelli watched the scenery fly past as they made their way toward the city.

"We will need to get you a car."

Kelli looked at him. "What?"

"It will make things much easier for you coming out to see me. I don't want you hitchhiking. It's too dangerous. And it must take you hours to get out there on the bus. How many transfers do you have to make?"

"A couple. And I'm careful hitchhiking. I don't get in with just anyone. Really, it's okay."

"Remember how I told you I could be stubborn sometimes?"

Kelli swallowed and looked out her side window. They were just entering the city. With rush hour traffic to contend with, it would still be another half hour at least to get to the school.

"Yes."

"You can pick out a car that suits you, or I can pick something out."

Kelli didn't say anything. She imagined having her own car. No more buses or walking for miles. She could drive to the good grocery store instead of the convenience store, and be able to carry home enough groceries for a week. She and Les could drive to any likely location to play their cons, ranging farther afield to places the cops wouldn't recognize her. Her birthmark always made it way too easy for the locals to recognize her and stamp down any new enterprises. With her own car, there were so many more opportunities.

"Do we have an understanding?" the judge questioned.

"Yeah. I get it."

"Do you have something in mind, or do you want me to look around?"

He wouldn't have a clue what kind of car would be appropriate for her neighborhood. She could just see him getting her something new and flashy that would get stolen or stripped the first day.

"Let me."

"Okay. But it needs to be before you come out to the cottage again, and I don't want that to be too long." He shifted his grip on the steering wheel. "I want to see you again soon."

Kelli felt awkward. She'd never had a boyfriend to demand her time. Her parents didn't expect her to be around. There was Les, but he had never been pushy. They just hung out together whenever they were both free. They had their routines, but she rarely felt like she had to be anywhere because of him.

"Yeah. Sure."

She could see Justice Emerson Forester turn his head to look at her, but Kelli kept her gaze focused out her side window.

As they pulled into the neighborhood, Kelli gave the judge directions, until they pulled up into the no-stopping zone in front of the school, where dozens of cars were stopped for drop-offs.

"Just pull in there," Kelli advised.

The judge looked wryly at the no-stopping signs and looked as if he were going to say something, but then he closed his mouth and just pulled in like everyone else. She saw his eyes go over the school, taking in the old brick building, the high fences, the morass of students smoking outside or flowing into the building. She felt herself flush, seeing it through his eyes.

"You enjoy school?" he asked.

Kelli shrugged. "No. But I do okay."

"An education is important."

"I know. I'm going to graduate. I work hard."

He nodded. Kelli didn't know whether to shake hands or kiss him good-bye. She didn't know him that well, despite his determination to spend thousands of dollars on her. He patted her on the shoulder and gave it a little squeeze.

"Have a good day, Kelli."

"Yeah, you too… Judge…"

He smiled. Kelli got out of the car and headed up to the doors of the school. Les was standing there watching, his mouth open.

"Is that him? Your bio dad?" he demanded.

"Yeah."

"He's picking you up now? Did you have breakfast together?"

"We had breakfast… I actually stayed over his place last night."

"At the mansion?"

"Cottage, they call it. Yeah."

"Things are moving pretty fast. I thought you said you didn't want to move in with him?"

"I'm not. Yet. He wanted me over for supper, and that made it too late to get back home, unless he drove me, and I didn't want him… to know where I lived."

"He already knows where you live," Les said with certainty. "That would be the first thing he'd check into."

"Well, I didn't want him there. Knowing about it is different than… seeing it."

"Yeah," Les agreed. "For sure."

They went into the school. Les looked Kelli over. "No books again?"

"No. I'll have to sort things out better next time. I didn't get home."

"You want to skip?" he offered, raising his eyebrows hopefully.

"No. I've missed too much lately."

"Teachers are just going to give you hassle for not having your books."

"I can handle them."

———

And handle them she did. Kelli's first-period teacher, Mr. Hurst, jumped on her as soon as she walked in. She waited until after the bell, hoping that he wouldn't want to interrupt his own lecture to hassle her, but it didn't work.

"Kelli. You're late. And where are your books?"

Kelli slid into her seat, keeping her head down. "Sorry, Mr. Hurst. I'll have them tomorrow."

"Maybe you'd like to talk to the principal this morning."

"No, sir. I really don't want to have to miss. Can I… talk to you privately? Later?"

He scowled at her. Hurst was always rumpled-looking, even first thing in the morning. He peered at her through thick lenses that warped his eyes. She wondered sometimes, with the mistakes he made on the board, whether he could actually see what was right in front of his face. But he seemed to be able to see the middle of the classroom just fine. Maybe he was farsighted.

"Come into the hallway." He motioned for her to leave the classroom ahead of her. Kelli slid reluctantly back out of her seat and left the room. He followed her, closing the classroom door behind them with a bang. Kelli could hear the chatter that started immediately on their exit.

"Let's have it, then," Hurst prodded. "What's your excuse?"

"I had to leave… suddenly yesterday…" Kelli sniffled and worked a sob into her words. "There wasn't time to take anything… just the clothes on my back. Even then, I was cold." Kelli rubbed her arms. It had been chilly the evening before. Humid and colder than she had expected it to be. It was a good thing she *hadn't* slept on the street overnight. "I haven't been back there yet. I'll try… this afternoon. Take someone with me. Okay?"

She sniffled again and wiped her nose with the back of her hand. Hurst stared at her. Or past her. He stepped back a pace, looking down at her through a different part of his glasses.

"Is this something I should be reporting?"

They all knew that teachers were required to report if they suspected abuse, and Kelli hoped she hadn't pushed it too far. In a school half-filled with at-risk kids, teachers could spend all their waking hours making unnecessary and sometimes damaging reports.

"No, sir. I'm okay. And I have a safe place to go, now. Really. It'll just cause me more trouble if you say anything."

They heard a crash in the classroom and Hurst's eyes flickered back to the door.

"We'd better get back in there. You'd better have your books tomorrow, or make some other arrangements."

"Yes, sir. I will."

He opened the door and ushered her back into the classroom, his hand resting briefly on her back. Face hot, Kelli went back to her desk and took her seat, everyone staring at her and attempting to look innocent for Mr. Hurst. He went back to the board and started into his lecture.

CHAPTER 13

It was everything that Kelli could wish for. Everything that she *had* wished for. Her own room at the cottage and a new car were just the beginning. It wasn't long before Kelli was spending more nights at the cottage than she was at home with Patricia and Axel. It was weird, the atmosphere at Forester Cottage. Although she knew she was safe there, and that her father hadn't turned out to be abusive or any of the other things she had feared, she couldn't help feeling anxious at the silence of the house.

Kelli was headed to the library to see if the judge were reading a book in his favorite room when a figure darted out in front of her. Kelli reacted instantly, her many hours of training kicking in before she could even think.

Almost before she could blink, she had Manuel, the head gardener, down on the floor, Kelli's hand pressing over his throat. Manuel stared up at her, eyes wide and round, unable to cry out or protest because of the pressure on his throat. Kelli swore, pulling her hand back and offering to help him to his feet.

"I'm so sorry, Manuel! You startled me. I'm sorry, I didn't mean to. Are you hurt?"

He got back up.

"Kelli?"

Kelli turned at the sound of her father's voice behind her. She whirled around, hands up in defensive posture. Panic sped her heart at being pincered between the two men, even though she knew logically that neither one was going to hurt her.

"Are you all right, Manuel?" Justice Emerson Forester asked, his voice low and even. As soothing as he could make it.

Manuel nodded vigorously. "Yes, sir. I'm fine. I'm sorry, Miss Kelli, I didn't mean to startle you."

Kelli swore again. She breathed heavily, trying to slow her breathing and settle down her heart. "Does everyone have to walk around here like cats all the time? I need bells or traffic signals or something."

"You can go, Manuel," the judge said.

Manuel apologized again for scaring Kelli and retreated. Kelli watched him go, then turned her back to the wall. No one was going to hurt her. She wasn't being ambushed. She wasn't the target of anyone's rage. She had just been startled. It was a little thing.

"Are you okay?" her father asked, not getting any closer.

Kelli realized she was still holding up her hands, ready to attack or defend. She forced herself to lower them.

"Seriously," she said. "Does everything have to be so quiet around here? It gives me the heebie-jeebies!"

"The heebie-jeebies?" he repeated, without cracking a smile.

"I'm climbing the walls. It's so quiet. Can't anyone whistle or talk to themselves? Or leave a TV playing?"

"Is it that quiet?" He cocked his head to the side and listened for a moment. "I don't even notice it. I guess I've been living on my own for too long. You're welcome to leave a TV or radio on if you like. It won't bother me."

Kelli sighed. She leaned against the wall behind her, relaxing her tense muscles and listening to her own breathing.

"Yeah, okay. I might just do that," she agreed.

"Were you looking for me?" He motioned to the library door beside him.

"Yeah." Kelli followed him into the room.

They both sat down in comfy chairs and the judge picked up a book from the table next to him. He fidgeted with it in his lap.

"Did you ever think some more about that microtattooing?" he asked. "To get rid of your birthmark?"

"Yes," Kelli admitted, feeling as if it were a fault. Vanity was one of the deadly sins, wasn't it? She hadn't stopped thinking about it. It was like a fairy tale, and she was afraid that if she accepted that gift, everything would change. She would be giving in to the wicked witch. Selling her soul. Maybe she wouldn't be herself anymore.

"And do you think it is something you want to do? Or look into further? You certainly don't have to make a decision right away. But maybe you'd like to talk to someone who does it. Get an evaluation. Or am I pushing you? You don't have to get it done."

"Maybe… talk to someone about it," Kelli said slowly. "I don't think I'm ready yet. But… I'd like to know more about it. Success rates. Risk. If I'm going to regret it after…"

"I don't want to push you into anything. I just wonder if it is something you want done."

Kelli nodded. "If you know someone who does it, I'd talk to them."

Justice Emerson Forester nodded. He opened his book and fanned the pages. Not reading it, or even really looking for something. Just fiddling.

"I do want to ask you about school, though."

"What about it?"

"How are things going?"

"Okay. I get good marks. I'm handing in all my assignments."

"I'm impressed with your efforts. I don't think your mom and dad are really the supervisory type, but you've really stuck with it, against all odds."

"I want to get a diploma. I never figured I'd be able to go to college, but I thought if I could at least get good marks and a diploma… maybe I could get somewhere."

"It's very admirable. Would you like to go to college? Do you have ideas of what you want to do with your life?"

"Yeah, I'd like to, someday." Kelli didn't want him jumping in and saying that he'd pay for everything. Maybe she could get a job and at least earn part of her tuition. She didn't want to be indebted to him for everything. "I don't know what I want to do. Maybe work for a couple of years, then go back to school when I have a better idea of what I want to be."

He nodded and didn't argue that she had to go straight into college immediately, and that he'd see to it. But Kelli had the feeling he hadn't quite gotten to where he was going yet. There was something else on his mind. She turned her eyes to the side and studied the spines of the books on the shelf next to her.

"I'd like to get you out of that school you're in," he said slowly. "And get you into something that will prepare you better for college."

"Oh…" Kelli looked at him. "I never thought about that. I mean… that's where my friends all are."

"You never talk about your friends."

"That doesn't mean that I don't have any," Kelli shot back.

"Of course not. You could have friends over, you know. If they don't have cars, you could pick them up and bring them out. You could have a sleepover, if you didn't want to do that much driving all in one day."

Kelli pictured herself having a sleepover at the cottage. It was laughable. Besides the fact that she was way too old for sleepovers, he was right; she didn't have any friends. Not like that. The other girls shunned her; she was the ugly, unpopular girl. Her martial arts training made her a bit better than just a bookworm, but she was still a geek. Still too much of a tomboy and too contemptuous of the popular crowd and things like football and cheer-leading.

"You could have a party. Maybe for the end of the school year?" the judge suggested.

Kelli shook her head. "No… I really don't go in for that kind of thing. And the kids at school… they don't know about *this*, and *you*…"

He raised his eyebrows at that. "Really? I would think that was the kind of thing that you'd want to tell everyone. No one knows?"

"Just Les. I wouldn't want anyone else to know… At a place like PS2, it isn't an advantage to come from a rich family. People would think that I was… looking down on them all… putting on airs."

"Well, all the more reason to get you out of there. I don't think it's a good atmosphere and it doesn't offer the advantages that I want to give you."

"I don't want to go to some private froo-froo school."

"Hmmph." That irritated him. He had probably expected her to jump at this opportunity, just like he expected her to jump at all the rest of the gifts that he offered her. But there was more to it this time. It was more than just Kelli being reluctant to take a gift. She was putting down his society. A private school that offered all the advantages was part of his world. The world that he wanted her to be a part of. And Kelli was disparaging it. Disparaging him.

"It's like the car," Kelli explained. "It has to be something that fits me."

He'd been pretty good about the car, understanding that she couldn't be driving a late model vehicle all over her neighborhood, to the school, leaving it parked on the streets. It had to be something old. Understated. Practically a junker. Every time she pulled it into his garage, she imagined him wincing in pain. But that was the way it had to be.

"Your education can't be a 'beater,'" Judge Emerson Forester said sternly. "You can't go to a nothing school and expect to get anywhere. You have to have a quality education. No matter what your friends might say about it."

Kelli opened her mouth to protest that she didn't care what anyone else thought, then stopped. Then why didn't she want to go to the best school he could give her? If she wanted to get ahead in the world, make as much of herself as she could, then why wouldn't she let him put her into the best schools?

"I don't know," she said. She pressed her lips together hard, thinking about it. "I'm not going to fit in at a place like that." She covered the birthmark with her hand, feeling like she could already feel the humiliation of their stares. "Even if I get this removed, I'm still not going to be the same as those other girls. They belong there. I don't."

"There will be an adjustment period. But you're a bright girl. I don't think it will last long."

"I really don't want to."

He flipped through pages in his book, barely looking at them.

"Wherever we settle on," he said, "you're going to need some upgrading. What do you think of some tutoring over the summer?"

"Ugh. Really? I don't need tutoring. I keep up with everything."

"Getting an A at PS2 is not the same as getting an A at one of the more prestigious schools. That may be a classist thing to say, but it is the truth. They're scraping the bottom of the barrel for teachers. They don't have the money to run any extracurricular programs. They don't have the technology other schools have. They'll give just about anyone a pass, even if they don't show up for classes. Is that the kind of education you want? Because it doesn't impress anyone on a college application."

"I don't know. I never really thought about it. I thought it was all standardized."

"Not like you would hope, no. You all write the same final exams, but guess where your school sits in the standings?"

Kelli grunted. She didn't really have to guess when he put it that way. "I don't want to spend my summer doing schoolwork."

"It won't take up all your time. A couple of hours a day, maybe. One-on-one tutoring isn't the same as sitting in a classroom of thirty or forty students. You'll pick things up quickly, and we'll be able to identify where the problem areas are. Okay?"

"Two hours a day *including* homework time?" Kelli demanded.

He nodded. "Including any homework time. No more than that."

"Fine then." Kelli sighed. "I thought I was going to have such a good summer this year… but I've never had to do summer school before."

"Think of it as enrichment," the judge said with a smile. "It's not a punishment. Learning can be fun."

"My new motto."

———

———

"So, you never guessed that Lisa was switched at the hospital?" Kelli asked Justice Emerson Forester over breakfast one day.

He looked up from his paper and held her gaze for a few uncomfortable moments. "Do you honestly think that I would be able to ignore the fact that I had a biological daughter out there, and not move heaven and earth to find her? That would be unconscionable!"

Kelli stabbed at her eggs and runny yolk pooled on her plate. She swiped the toast through it. "My mom did. She knew when I was two."

The judge shook his head. "I never knew. It never crossed my mind even once."

"Even with the birthmark?"

"Even with the birthmark. They said it was just trauma from the birth. It was just a bruise that faded on its own. There was no reason for me to be suspicious about anything."

Kelli nodded slowly and took another bite of her toast.

"I *did* know that Lisa was not my child."

"What?" Kelli dropped her toast right in the middle of her plate. "You knew? How?"

"I had my suspicions about Preston's… fidelity. I had her investigated. Had a DNA test done quietly. It confirmed that I wasn't Lisa's father."

"Just like with me! Is that when you broke up with… my bio mom?" Kelli hadn't yet met Preston, and didn't feel comfortable referring to her by her first name. "Because Mom's boyfriend, the one she said was my dad—Lisa's dad—John—he left when the test confirmed he wasn't my father."

"No. I let Preston call the shots on that one. We are legally separated, not divorced. And I still support Preston and Lisa." He looked at the toast that Kelli had dropped in the middle of her plate, and took a small bite of his own toast spread with marmalade. "I never told Lisa that she wasn't my biological daughter. I can't imagine that Preston would have."

"You never told her?" Kelli couldn't believe it.

"No. What good would that do? It would only hurt her. I didn't have any bitterness against her. It wasn't her fault she wasn't my daughter."

Kelli fished her toast out of the puddle of eggs and took a couple of big bites of the messiest bits. "Wow."

"Your mom still raised you when she knew that you weren't her daughter. And she never told you."

"But that's not the same. She kept me because she wanted the money from the hospital. And she didn't tell me or anyone else because she signed documents saying that she wouldn't tell anyone."

"But she still raised you. She could have put you up for adoption or foster care. She could have tracked us down, like you did, instead of taking the money. She loves you."

Kelli laughed and shook her head. "Oh, no. I don't have any illusions about that. I don't know if she ever loved me, even before she knew I wasn't hers. Maybe she did way back then. But not anymore."

Her father frowned as he continued to eat. "It can be hard for children to tell how their parents feel about them. The depth of their feelings."

"You think I'm just being a brat about it? I'm not. She always beat on me. Told me I was worthless. Her nickname for me when I was a little kid was Poopface. Because of this." She gestured to the birthmark. "How do you think it felt when the other kids picked it up from my own mother? Or who I thought was my own mother. No, she didn't love me. She never loved me."

He shook his head back and forth slowly. "I'm so sorry that you had to deal with that growing up, Kelli. I really am. I hope you know that. If I had known about the mistake… I would have found you. I would have found a way to take you back, or to protect you. I'm a judge, I know the legal system. I would have found a way to help you."

"Well, it's all good now," Kelli said lightly.

They both ate in silence. Kelli finished her plate and pushed it away from her. Her waistbands were all starting to get tight. She was going to need a new wardrobe if he kept feeding her all the time. Of course, as far as he was concerned, she needed a new wardrobe anyway.

"I'm glad that you brought Preston and Lisa up," Justice Emerson Forester said, before she could leave the table to go fetch her school things. "Because I wanted you to know… they're going to be coming for a visit."

CHAPTER 14

Kelli was not thrilled to learn that her biological mother and her almost-twin were going to be coming to the cottage and she would be forced to meet them. She knew that she should be excited about meeting the other parent in her life. The other half of the missing puzzle pieces. But she really wasn't.

The judge had, of course, called his ex-wife to advise her of Kelli's reappearance and what had happened at the hospital. It was the proper thing to do, and he was all about doing everything the right way. But Preston hadn't made immediate plans to meet her long-lost biological daughter. She had stayed out of the picture, and had not been to the house since Kelli had been reunited with her father.

Kelli didn't really see the point in meeting her. She already had Patricia. She didn't need more than one angry, cold mother in her life. Kelli had one parent now who cared and doted on her, and that was all she needed.

She paced back and forth across her room. She was afraid to go out into the hallways or down to the dining room too early. Preston and Lisa could be anywhere, and Kelli didn't want to run into them. She hadn't actually seen or heard their car arrive yet, but she didn't feel alone in the house. She could feel their presences there already.

Eventually, some time after the prescribed dinner hour, Kelli heard a car pull into the yard. She looked out the window for an instant, hoping neither of them would be looking up at her window at the same time. It was a white convertible. Maybe a Camaro? Kelli wasn't really a car person so she wasn't sure. Both of them got out of the car. Lisa was almost the same height as Preston. Both blonde. Both dressed in tight shirts and short skirts, with tiny purses on strings on their shoulders. They had on high heels, but didn't wobble.

Kelli looked down at her own outfit again. Pants and a knit shirt. She figured since it had a collar, she was dressed up. But Preston and Lisa obviously had different ideas.

The door was opened for the two ladies without waiting for them to ring. Kelli cracked her door open and listened to their muffled voices. All light tones and giggles. No confrontation. No anger. Kelli breathed out slowly. There wasn't going to be a fight. They were just going to have dinner together. Kelli was going to get to meet her biological mother. All good.

Felicia came down the hall to get Kelli and found her standing listening at the crack. "They're ready for you, miss."

"Okay." Kelli cleared her throat. "Felicia, does this look okay? I mean, I saw them when they got out of the car, and…" Kelli made a motion indicating her own clothes.

Felicia gave a blink of understanding. "It will be fine, miss. They're always overdressing. Mr. Forester is not even in a suit."

"Are you sure? I don't know what I should do. I don't even have makeup or jewelry or anything, and they're going to be staring at my face…"

"Do you want me to get you something from Lisa's room? Some accessories…?"

Kelli shook her head, aghast. "No! She'd know. I don't want anything of hers. No, no, no."

"They're ready for you, then."

Kelli took several slow breaths, and went downstairs to meet her mother.

———

They were in the annex rather than the dining room. It was the room that she and Justice Emerson Forester had first met in when Kelli had shown up the first day. A comfortable meeting room for pre-dinner drinks, informal discussions, and unexpected guests.

The two ladies had their backs to the door, a sure sign of disrespect to the last guest to arrive. Only her father was facing the door and saw her come in.

"Ah, here she is. Kelli, this is Lisa and Preston," the judge introduced, stepping up beside Kelli, and gesturing to each of the others as if she didn't know which was which.

Kelli did her best to swallow her anxiety. She nodded to them and forced a smile. "Hi. Nice to meet you."

Preston had turned, but wasn't even looking at Kelli. She stared over Kelli's shoulder as if looking at something off in the distance. Lisa did look at Kelli's face, and despite having been warned ahead of Kelli's birthmark, Lisa's jaw dropped open and she stared at the purple birthmark.

"I'm sure," Preston murmured.

"Lisa?" the judge prompted.

"What? Oh, yeah, very nice to meet you, I'm sure," Lisa parroted.

They were both beautiful. Preston looked quite a bit younger than Patricia. A woman in the prime of her life rather than one who had spent her strength on drink and spite. She looked younger than Justice Emerson Forester by at least ten years. Her ash blonde hair fell around her face to just below her shoulders, a very attractive color that Kelli suspected came out of a bottle. Her face was smooth, with no visible lines. Her makeup was subtle and expertly applied, coming off as natural even though she had probably spent an hour on it. Lisa's complexion was like fine porcelain, looking as though she had never in her life had a pimple or a bruise. Her hair was a strawberry blonde, falling into ringlets around her shoulders. She was slim without looking waifish and she didn't go overboard on the makeup like the cheerleaders Kelli knew. She looked like a model.

Kelli felt very much the ugly duckling in the presence of the two women. Her hair was neatly combed and fell straight to her shoulders without even a wave. She didn't have a speck of makeup on, a fact she was sure they could tell as soon as they looked at her. If Preston had been looking at her. She wasn't wearing one of her grubby hoodies, but she might just as well have been, as underdressed as she was in comparison.

"They both have the same eyes," the judge observed.

Kelli and Lisa looked at each other curiously to verify the fact. Preston still didn't look at Kelli. Their eyes were not only the same color, a medium brown rather than the baby blue the birth pictures had shown, but they were the same shape and size, uncomfortably similar. Lisa's mouth turned down in a pouting frown, apparently not pleased with this development.

Preston had a wine glass in her hand. No one made any offer to shake hands or kiss cheeks. Kelli couldn't help but remember how her father had fallen on her the first time he saw her, before she'd even had a chance to tell him who she was. Had she expected the same kind of reaction from Preston? If so, she was disappointed. The woman had no intention of greeting her like a daughter.

"Well, there is an excellent meal awaiting us in the dining room," Justice Emerson Forester observed. "Let's adjourn there and have our dinner, shall we?"

Preston gave a sigh and put down her wine glass. They all headed over to the dining room. Justice Emerson Forester put his hand on Kelli's back as he walked with her, escorting her and giving her a little encouragement. She jumped at his touch, and then tried to relax and give him a smile of appreciation. She did appreciate the gesture, but she wondered if he could have any idea how she was feeling. She was certain that he'd never been put in such an awkward position.

The dining arrangements were more formal than when Kelli and the judge ate together. But he still didn't have people seated at opposite ends of the long table. Instead, the place settings were all at one end of the table. Kelli made her way toward the seat she usually took, and Lisa and Preston headed for the two seats on the opposite side of the table, with the judge presiding at the end. At least there was no fighting over seats. Kelli stared down at her empty plate and turned her head ever so slightly so that the birthmark would not be so visible to Lisa and Preston.

The dinner was, Kelli was relieved to see, not seafood. Then she remembered that Lisa was vegetarian, so it couldn't be. They started with some kind of vegetable stew with spices that reminded Kelli of a pizza. She spooned the soup carefully, in small bites, not slurping from the spoon. She might be from a less affluent home, but that didn't mean she didn't have table manners.

"Kelli is an expert at martial arts," Justice Emerson Forester offered. "She studies... which one is it, Kelli?"

"Jujitsu," Kelli said, not raising her eyes. "And I'm not an expert... just a beginner."

"Well, I don't know if that's how I would classify you," he said with a smile. He didn't bring up the ambush in the park, but Kelli had a feeling he had watched all of the available coverage. "But it seems like a fascinating discipline. Lisa is on the cheerleading squad at her school."

No big surprise there. Lisa gave a look that was either a simper or a pout, Kelli wasn't sure which.

"What school do you go to?" Lisa asked.

"Uh… well, I'm just finishing the year, and then I'm not sure where I'm going to be in the fall. We're… looking at options."

"As long as you don't come to Michael's," Lisa sneered.

"Elisa…" Preston murmured.

"Well, I have to say it, don't I? Otherwise that's exactly where he's going to send her!" Lisa directed a glare at the judge.

"It's not appropriate in this company."

Lisa rolled her eyes and continued to eat her soup.

"I was just pointing out that you are both athletic," Justice Emerson Forester said. "Although in two very disparate sports."

Kelli eyed him. Was he going to spend the whole evening pointing out similarities between the two of them? Like maybe if he did, they would come to see how alike they were and bond as sisters? Or Preston would accept Kelli as her daughter? If that was what he thought, he had better think again.

Her father caught her gaze and looked away sheepishly. He knew his not-so-subtle plan had been discovered. Kelli shook her head mentally. He needed a lot more practice before he could pull a con over on her.

"Daddy," Lisa said suddenly, "remember how we used to play croquet in the yard on Saturday afternoons? And we'd have a tea party in the garden?"

He flushed and glanced at Kelli. "Of course I remember that," he said. "We had a lot of fun together, didn't we?"

Daddy. Kelli didn't remember ever calling Axel or any of the other men Daddy. She wasn't sure what she would end up calling the judge, but she was pretty sure it wouldn't be something so juvenile. She knew that Lisa was just trying to assert her relationship as Justice Emerson Forester's dominant daughter. Kelli would never be able to reclaim the past. Lisa would always have that over Kelli.

"Croquet?" Kelli repeated. "Isn't that like… what they played with flamingos in Alice in Wonderland? I didn't think anyone played that for real."

"Not in your circles, obviously," Lisa returned sweetly.

The claws were out and neither one of them was bothering to be subtle about it.

The judge gave his ex-wife—or estranged wife—a look. She smiled a determined smile.

"How about your social life, Kelli?" She deigned to speak to Kelli directly for the first time. "Do you have a boyfriend? Take part in any clubs? Volunteer activities?" There was a pause. "Church, maybe?"

Kelli looked at the judge, alarmed. Was she expected to be religious now? He gave her a smile that attempted to be reassuring, but he didn't jump in to her rescue.

"Mostly I just focus on schoolwork," Kelli said. "I don't do any clubs or anything."

"Doesn't sound like you have a boyfriend either," Lisa observed smugly. The voice and her expression said what her words didn't. Who would want an ugly dog like Kelli? "I have a steady boyfriend. Truman Sharp. I just love that name, don't you? I think it sounds so… perfect. Just like he is."

Kelli saw Preston dart a glance at Justice Emerson Forester. This was apparently news to him and she was watching him for his reaction. The judge raised his eyebrows and wiped his mouth with his napkin, laying his spoon in his bowl of unfinished soup.

"Is that Anthony Sharp's son?"

Lisa nodded, smiling. She looked at Kelli. "He's a *very* powerful man."

"He's a very dangerous man," the judge said flatly. "How long has this been going on?"

"We've been going out for… how long, Mom? Two months? We just decided to be exclusive." She looked like the cat that had swallowed the canary.

Her father was obviously not happy about this, but was making a valiant effort to keep his mouth shut and keep his thoughts to himself. Nothing like forbidding your daughter to see someone to drive her straight into his arms.

What kind of a person would the judge call dangerous? How was he dangerous? Was Lisa in physical danger? Was her beau's father violent? In organized crime? Or was it meant in another sense? Some kind of social or political danger for the judge? Preston looked completely unconcerned that her husband thought Lisa's boyfriend's family might be dangerous. Did she think he was overreacting or were they both trying to wind him up?

"If he's dangerous, you should be careful," Kelli told Lisa. Cheerleading wasn't a very practical skill if Lisa was in physical danger. But who was she to give Lisa advice? A girl she'd never even met before. But she couldn't ignore the knot in her gut over the thought of Lisa being hurt or taken advantage of.

Lisa laughed. "Oh, Daddy's just being silly. He never likes anyone I'm dating. It's how dads are supposed to be."

Kelli gave a nod and finished the last spoonful of her soup. It was Lisa's life, after all. Kelli didn't have any kind of influence over her.

Felicia unobtrusively gathered up the soup bowls, and another part-time servant whose name Kelli didn't know, came in with a salad course. Kelli watched the others to see which fork to use and tried to eat slowly. It wouldn't do for her to look like a ravenous wolf. The initial courses were so light that she was worried there wouldn't be enough to eat; but she'd been eating so much lately, it wouldn't hurt her to be left a little hungry for once.

"So… what's he like, this Truman?" Kelli asked. If the spotlight was on Lisa, then it wasn't on Kelli. She could relax and not answer questions that might be embarrassing to her or to the judge. "What do you do together?"

Happy to be the center of attention, Lisa immediately launched into a long description of all the events that she and Truman had attended recently. She had quite the social calendar. As she half-listened, Kelli realized that it was all safe, public stuff. Nothing was going to happen to Lisa at fundraisers and tennis tournaments. Kelli felt her father relax. Lisa wasn't running around the country with this boy, spending time in dark streets and crack houses. Not that Kelli could tell, anyway. She was sure that Lisa and Truman were sneaking their share of stolen kisses and intimate moments, but it sounded like she was safer making the social circuit with him than she would be hanging around with the star quarterback on the school football team.

Lisa went on and on. Kelli caught Preston's eyes on her birthmark. Preston looked quickly away, pretending that she hadn't been caught.

"Why don't you tell us about yourself, Kelli?" she suggested. "After all, that's what we're here for. You must have so many interesting stories, growing up the way you did."

Lisa folded her arms, pouting at being interrupted. But under Preston's glare, she feigned interest.

"Yes. Tell us. Did you have tea parties with *your* dad?" She looked possessively at her father.

"What exactly do you do at a tea party?" Kelli asked. "It always sounded pretty boring to me."

The judge gave a little chuckle. "You can only pretend to sip tea with stuffed animals for so long without your brain imploding. Then… duty calls and you have to go to the office."

"Daddy!" Lisa protested. "You liked having tea parties with me!"

"Of course I did, sweetheart," he agreed. "I enjoyed spending time with you. But they *were* boring."

Lisa sniffed.

"The animals were always fighting," Justice Emerson Forester said to Kelli. "Somebody was always best friends with someone else, and somebody wasn't invited to a party, or sat in the wrong seat. I think there was a secret romance between the turtle and the caterpillar…"

"There was not!" Lisa said in a horrified tone. "It was a frog, not a turtle, and she hated the caterpillar! The frog didn't get invited to—"

All of them but Lisa laughed. Which just made her pout more. Kelli suspected that Lisa spent most of her time sulking over one thing or another. As demonstrated by the slights to her stuffed toys.

She had a funny feeling watching Lisa and her father interact. It was a few minutes of grasping before she could figure out what she was feeling. It was obvious from the way they talked to each other that they were remembering the same thing. Justice Emerson Forester didn't suddenly go off on a tangent, describing some other story of what had happened. He didn't look blankly at Lisa like he didn't know what she was talking about. Instead, they were *sharing* memories. Their memories fit together, like a jigsaw puzzle, his and hers.

Kelli pushed away from the table abruptly. "Excuse me. I need…" She didn't know what excuse to make. "Bathroom. I need the bathroom. I'm… sorry!"

She stumbled away from the dining room, trying to keep the layout of the house straight in her head so that she didn't blunder into a closet or the kitchen instead of the downstairs bath.

"Miss Kelli?"

Kelli waved Felicia off and grabbed the handle of the nearest room. The lights came on automatically, making the marble, glass, and brass fixtures sparkle. She shut the heavy door behind her and turned the lock. She needed space and privacy of her own to get settled down.

She wanted to hit something. She wanted to hit Lisa in the face, but failing that, to hit anything. Preferably something that would crash and break. Something that would hurt. Something that meant something to someone. She tore the thick towels off of the towel racks and threw them on the floor. There wasn't much satisfaction in that. She stomped on them. Threw herself down on the floor and pounded them with her fists. She wanted to scream, and despite all her efforts to remain quiet, little squeaks of protest came out when she tried to hold them back.

It wasn't fair! It wasn't fair that Lisa had grown up with a father who would play tea parties with her no matter how mind-numbingly boring it was. That he could remember all the details and they could talk about it like it happened only moments before. All while Kelli had been growing up with a cold mother who would have nothing to do with her and a father who went away to prison, who was damaged beyond all repair and would never be able to have that kind of relationship with her, even if it were what he had wanted.

Tears were streaming down Kelli's face. She was glad that she wasn't wearing any makeup that would smear all over her face. When she was finished her pointless tantrum, she could wipe away the tears and return calmly to the table as if nothing had happened.

She lay there, spent, face buried in the towels in the middle of the floor. There was a polite knock on the door.

"Kelli? Are you okay?"

It was her father's voice. Concerned. Understanding. Apologetic.

Kelli wiped her nose on one of the towels. "I'm fine. I'll be back in a minute."

"Take however much time you need. I understand."

He could try, but he could never understand. Never in a million years.

"Just a few more minutes. Don't hold up the next course for me. Just eat."

"Let me know if you need anything."

She could tell that he continued to hover there for a minute or two, waiting for her to make a reappearance. Eventually, he left.

Kelli hung up all the towels except for the one that she had blown her nose on. She left that one on the floor, over beside the big jetted tub. Standing in the center of the room, she tried to still the frantic whirling of her mind, to achieve a meditative state. She started practicing her forms. Exercises and stretches and practices she had learned at Golden Dragon. Familiar movements that her body knew, that she didn't have to think about. She matched her breathing to her movements.

Eventually, she felt more peaceful. She splashed water on her face and returned to the dining room.

"Kelli." Her father stood up immediately. He held her chair for her as she sat back down again. "Are you okay?" he murmured.

"I'm fine. Sorry," she told the other guests. "I just… took a turn. I'm okay."

Lisa and Preston stared at her. Or, Preston stared in her direction. Somewhere over Kelli's shoulder.

"You have nothing to apologize for," Preston said graciously. "I'm glad you're feeling better."

"Don't know what she's being such a baby for," Lisa whined. "What's she crying about? I'm old enough not to go around crying at everything and we're the same age."

"Things are *different* for Kelli," Preston said. "She has not been brought up the same way as you were."

"There's nothing wrong with me." Kelli looked down at the stir fry and rice on her plate. Had they made it to the main course? Her stir fry had chicken in it, but when she looked over at Lisa's, hers did not. "It might be hard for you too, if you were going through all this."

"I *am* going through it," Lisa pointed out. "Everything you're going through, I am too. Finding out that I was switched at the hospital. That my mom and dad aren't my biological parents. It's exactly the same for me."

Put her in the same room as Axel and Patricia and see where her airs went then. Kelli took a couple of deep breaths and went back to eating her dinner.

———

When the last course was cleared away and dinner was finally done, Justice Emerson Forester invited everyone to join him in the games room for some fun games, talk, and treats. Kelli looked sideways at him, trying to figure out if she were required to stay there, and if so, what she had to do. Was she expected to entertain? To put on a happy face? To play games and be a good sport when she lost?

"Justice, it's been a long day," Preston said. "I was up early this morning to work on the summer foundation fundraiser and I've just been going all day. I can't possibly stay up any longer. We'll have to do more visiting another time."

"Me too," Lisa chimed in, patting a polite yawn. "I have to be up early tomorrow for breakfast with my darling Truman. If I don't get to bed now, I won't be able to put two thoughts together for him. Good night."

The judge looked at the two of them, and then at Kelli. "This was supposed to be more than just dinner."

"I don't think any of us realized how emotionally draining it would be, "Preston said, patting her husband's arm. "You must be beat too. You had cases to hear this morning, didn't you?"

"Yes, but I'm fine to play for a couple more hours—"

"You and Kelli, then. I'm sure she's starving for some daddy-daughter time." She dropped her voice, as if she didn't want Kelli to hear, but she clearly did. "The poor little thing."

Mother and daughter both begged off and went to their rooms. They were staying the night, not driving all the way home, so it wasn't like it was too late to do anything.

The judge sighed. "Well, there you are. I hope you weren't… too disappointed."

Kelli tried to take it all in. She knew that Preston had just been faking when she said how emotionally drained she was, but Kelli *was* exhausted by it all. Preston had kept herself aloof, putting little effort into getting to know Kelli or keeping the conversation going. But Kelli had been anxious and fully engaged all night and she was crashing.

"Could we go to the library instead of playing?" she suggested.

Justice Emerson Forester smiled. He patted her on the back. Kelli tried not to shy away, but she still flinched at his touch.

"Let's," he agreed. "I never turn down the opportunity to curl up with a good book."

They walked to the library together in silence. They picked up their current books and sat in their favorite chairs.

"I did try to warn you," the judge said. "I told you what they were like."

Kelli nodded and didn't comment. It had been traumatic enough, without having to debrief and go over it all again.

"I'm sorry she doesn't have any interest in you."

"Yeah. Thanks. It's okay."

"It's not okay. But it is what it is."

Kelli shrugged, not sure what that even meant, and sank into her book.

———

Kelli hadn't expected to see or hear any more from Preston or Lisa that evening. And maybe if she played possum, she wouldn't have to see them in the morning either. Lisa had said that she had to be up early. Kelli hoped if she slept late, she would be able to avoid them for the remainder of their visit.

But after she was in bed, she could hear noises in the house around her. She was getting used to the normal noises of Justice Emerson Forester and the staff moving around, and their usual activities, but she didn't normally hear any noise from Preston's or Lisa's rooms. Kelli shook herself awake and put her head out the door.

Lisa's door was shut and there was no strip of light under it. It would appear that she had gone to bed. Preston's room stood empty. The door was open and the light was on, but there wasn't anyone inside. It must have been Preston that Kelli had heard.

Kelli walked back to the other end of the hall and listened. Where had Preston gone? What was she doing up, wandering around?

There were low voices. Kelli followed them. They were on the move, eventually ending up in the annex room, where Kelli imagined Preston was having another glass of wine.

"You have to get rid of that girl," she said, tones strident. Gone was the fake, cultured voice that she had used over dinner. Her real voice was harsh and clipped. Impatient. "Pay her whatever you have to, but get rid of her. I won't abide having her around the house."

"You don't have any say as to what happens in this house," the judge pointed out.

"That's what you think. Just because I'm not on title, that doesn't mean I don't have any say."

There was a period of silence while the judge considered this.

"Kelli is staying," he said finally.

"Why would you want that wretched little ragamuffin around here? She's an embarrassment. She has no upbringing. She'll rob you blind or murder you in your sleep."

"A little melodramatic, don't you think?" Justice Emerson Forester's voice was dry.

"That's the way she was raised. Why would you expect her to behave any other way?"

"You don't know how she was raised."

"Do you?" she challenged.

"I think I have a better understanding than you do. She's a child, Preston. She needs love and support and encouragement."

"You're being naive."

"She's your child. Don't you feel any affection for her? No attraction?"

"No. Why would I? I'm not a cat; it's not like she still has my scent on her. She's been gone for sixteen years. Raised by trash. I don't want someone like that in this house."

Kelli could hear the judge moving around. Getting himself another drink. How much had he consumed already? Would he get violent when he had enough in him?

"Pressy. I told you. It's not your place. You can't control whether I let Kelli stay here or not."

"There are ways."

"She's your daughter and you should be happy that she's being taken care of properly."

"Being taken care of. Is that what you call it?"

"What else would I call it? I want to give my daughter what she has been missing all these years. I want a chance to get to know her. And unlike Lisa, she actually wants to know me too."

"I'll tell you all you need to know about her. She will take advantage of you. She will bleed you dry. If you're lucky, she might not ruin your reputation too. She's a leech. A parasite. That's all."

"She's not taking advantage of me. I have to talk her into taking anything."

"She knows her psychology. The more she resists, the more you want to shower her with gifts. You've already given her thousands. A car, cash, the tutors you have lined up. Where are you sending her in the fall? How much more is it going to take to pay off her other parents so that they'll stay out of the way? And not only all of that, but you take her into your home. You let her live under the same roof and put yourself at risk."

"What is she going to do?"

"She has a record of violence, Justice. You might think that you and your judge friends can wipe the slate clean, get rid of any mark against her, but people will still know. She has been charged with domestic violence. With assault. You yourself said she is trained in karate. She could kill you if she took it into her mind. You refuse to give her what she wants, and see how she reacts then."

There was a clink as one of them put a glass down.

"You don't know what she's like," Justice Emerson Forester said in a calm, measured tone.

"Oh, no? You're shutting your eyes. Refusing to see what's going on under your own roof. She's stealing from you."

"Kelli is not stealing from me."

"Yeah? Have you looked through the drawers in her room? Under her mattress? Do you know how many little trinkets she has stashed away?"

Kelli's face got hot. They couldn't see her, but she flushed anyway. She held her hand over her mouth to avoid making a noise that might attract their attention. Preston had searched her room? She made that big show of being so tired she had to go to bed, and then she had gone and searched Kelli's bedroom while Kelli read with the judge in the library. And she had the nerve to suggest that Kelli was the dishonest one!

"I told Kelli that anything she wants is hers," the judge said. "She's not stealing from me. I told her she could have those things."

"Family heirlooms? Priceless pieces of jade? You can't let her take those things!"

"She's my heir. She can take what she wants."

Kelli supported herself against the wall. *She* was his heir? There was silence and Kelli imagined that like she, Preston was gaping at this news, unable to believe what he had said.

"*She* is your heir? Lisa is your heir! She is the child we raised. She is the one who is your daughter."

"I've given Lisa everything she needs for sixteen years. I'm not going to stop supporting her. But she is not my child. And she hasn't wanted anything to do with me for years. You think I don't know the only way to get her over here is to bribe or threaten her?"

"She's a teenager," Preston said. "All teenagers are like that. They want to do their own thing and think they don't need their parents anymore. I'm sure you went through the same thing before you left home. I know I did. Visit Grandma at the rest home? No thanks. Have Sunday dinner with the parents? Other things to do. You did it. They all do it."

There was the squeak of leather as Justice Emerson Forester sank into his favorite chair. "It's more than that. You've alienated her affections. Yes, she comes when I call, but only because you tell her that I'll disinherit her if she doesn't. So, let's take my estate off the table. See if she wants any relationship when she no longer stands to inherit."

"You can't cut her out of your will!"

"She'll get a bequest. But that's all."

"That's insane! It's cruel! I'll contest it every step of the way!"

"I'm sure you will."

"How could you want that horrible, disfigured changeling for a daughter?" Preston demanded. Her voice had changed again. It was guttural and desperate.

"Disfigured?" the judge repeated blankly. Then understanding crept into his voice. "You mean her birthmark?"

"She will never be able to be a part of society like Lisa. She will never fit in. People will stare at her and talk about her. She'll never be able to hold any position of authority. She can't be in publicity photos. She'll never be able to go anywhere without people pointing and staring."

"Do you really believe all that? Are you so desperate to raise Lisa up above everyone else that you'd crush your own child to do it?"

"She's not my child!" Preston ranted. "She can go back where she came from! She can make good in her own society, the brave child risen from the gutters. But she'll never be anything but a freak show in our circles."

There was a long period of silence. Kelli closed her eyes, waiting for his reply. She knew he would defend her. He already had, and he was stubborn. He wasn't going to change his line. But she wondered what was going through his mind as he sat there. What Preston said was true. As long as Kelli had the birthmark, no one would look at her as a real person. She'd just be the fodder for gossip. She had resisted going to any events with him, even though he had invited her. He seemed comfortable with the prospect of presenting her as his daughter, but he hadn't lived her life. He had no idea what it would be like for her. He thought everyone would be as accepting and open-minded as he was.

"I think we're done here," Justice Emerson Forester said coldly. "You should get off to bed. I know you were saying earlier what a tiring day you'd had. Maybe you'll see things differently in the morning, when you are well-rested."

Kelli forced herself to move from her position. There was an old saying that eavesdroppers never heard good things said about themselves, and it turned out it was true. She should never have followed them downstairs and listened to their conversation. She should have stayed in bed, blissfully ignorant of what was being said about her. She stumbled ahead of them, back up the stairs and into her bedroom. She stepped into the dark room and shut her door, not all the way, leaving it open the barest crack. Despite all that she had overheard, she wanted to know if there were any parting salvos before Preston and the judge went to bed. So she stood there and listened for one more minute.

They paused outside her door, as if they knew she was standing there. Kelli tensed. If they made one movement toward her, she would have to run and jump into bed. But then when they came in, she would be sweaty and out of breath. It would be obvious that she hadn't been asleep. Better to feign they had just awakened her, and she had come to the door to see what was going on.

"You have no idea how damaged she is," Preston whispered.

"I know what she's been through… you and I are responsible for that… that's on us. I want to do everything I can to help her now."

"Did you know she has food in there? Hidden in the drawers and wardrobe?"

Kelli swallowed. She pressed her knuckles to her teeth. What right did that woman have to search her room? And to tell her findings to Kelli's father?

The judge's voice was low. He cleared his throat, choking up. "Children who have been starved often hoard food. I talked to a psychologist about it. He said to just let her have it, as long as it's not something that's going to go bad or attract vermin."

Preston stood there for a moment longer.

"Damaged," she repeated. "That girl is never going to fit in. She is more likely to murder you in your sleep."

CHAPTER 15

Kelli was still in bed when Felicia came and knocked at her door. Kelli buried her head under the covers.

"Miss Kelli? Are you coming down for breakfast…?"

Kelli groaned. "No. I'm not feeling good. Tell them I can't. Tell—my father—I'm sorry."

"Of course. Can I get you anything? Maybe some tea would help?"

Kelli's stomach was already rumbling, expecting the regular breakfast it had become accustomed to. She lowered the blankets.

"Yeah. I mean, yes, please. And some toast…?"

"Of course. I'll bring it up in a few minutes."

"Thanks."

Felicia withdrew. Kelli closed her eyes and pulled her blanket up again. But she was too wide awake to convince her body that she wanted to go back to sleep again. She moved around restlessly until her tea arrived. Then she gave up and got up to the bathroom, returning to the comfort of her covers to sit and sip her tea and eat the toast. It wasn't enough to fill her, since she wasn't really sick, so she dug into her hidden supplies and had a sleeve of cookies as well. She contemplated the cookie box as she ate, thinking about Preston's words.

She could never fit in. She was too damaged. She was too disfigured. She could never be part of the judge's society.

Anger rose within her, supplanting her depression. She had overcome every obstacle placed in her way, and Preston thought that she couldn't break into society? Kelli was the consummate con. They thought she couldn't convince a few muckity-mucks that she belonged? She had the lineage and that was the hardest part. Everything else was just a matter of attitude and presentation.

————

When the judge got home from his meetings in the city, Kelli was ready for him. She headed him off at the door.

"Can we talk before dinner?"

Justice Emerson Forester juggled his briefcase to give her a brief sideways hug. "Of course, Kelli. I think I'm going to change out of this suit. I'll meet you in the library?"

"Okay," Kelli agreed.

She was sitting in her favorite chair with a book when he came down, but she wasn't taking in anything on the page. Her father had changed into a sweater and slacks. He slid into his chair with a sigh. Apparently, it had been a long day for him.

"Are you feeling better?" he asked.

Kelli marked her place on the page with her finger, but really she hadn't even been reading it, it was just for show.

"I decided… I want to go ahead with the tattooing," she said as casually as she could. "For my birthmark," she added, as if he might not understand.

"Certainly. I'll make arrangements." She knew from his expression that he was trying to decide whether to ask her why she had made the decision. "We can get it done after school lets out."

Kelli realized she was going to have to make a decision about school for the next year too. She sighed. "What are my options for school?"

"Well… I'm assuming that you don't want to go to the same school as Lisa."

"I think that would be a safe assumption!"

The judge pressed his fingertips together, his expression darkening. "I'm sorry about last evening… I had hoped that it would go better."

"Yeah. It kind of sucks when your own mother doesn't want anything to do with you." Kelli paused. "Neither one."

"Your mom…" Justice Emerson Forester trailed off, not sure how to complete the question tactfully. "How has she been? With you staying here more often."

He said it as if she hadn't moved in completely. As if she were only visiting on weekends and spent the rest of her days at home. But Kelli hadn't even spoken to Patricia in a couple of weeks.

"She's probably glad to be rid of me. She hasn't tried to get me to go back."

"It hurts me to think of all that you had to go through with them."

His eyes were distant. If it hadn't been Kelli, it would have been Lisa. He couldn't very well say that he wished that the babies had never been switched, and that Lisa had been subjected to poverty and abuse instead.

"It's just a bad situation all around. All we can hope is… that in the end, everyone can come to some sort of peace… I'm afraid that Preston will probably never get to a place where she's willing to be a mother to you. But hopefully… she can accept you as a member of our extended family."

Kelli tried to keep her voice from showing her emotion. He didn't know, after all, that she had heard everything that had been said the night before.

"I don't care whether she ever accepts me. You do, and that's enough."

He looked at her. "Is it?"

Kelli nodded.

"Okay."

———

Kelli had been given a number of warnings by the tattooist. The birthmark might still be visible on close examination, but it would be camouflaged better. There might be some redness after the tattooing. She might have burning, itching, and scabbing afterward. She had to keep the initial bandage on for eight hours, and then keep it very clean and protected until it was fully healed.

She was both eager and terrified to take the bandage off and see how well the tattooing had succeeded or failed.

She could feel her father hovering outside the bathroom as she looked in the mirror at the bandage, too paralyzed to remove it.

"Quit it!" she said.

"Kelli?"

"Quit standing out there waiting for me."

"Are you okay?"

"I'm freaking out a little bit!"

"How does it look? They said we could go back for more work, if it needs more done…"

"I don't know yet."

"You don't know?" he repeated.

"I haven't taken the bandage off yet."

"Can I come in?"

Kelli conceded and opened the door for him. He sat against the counter, studying her.

"You know I love you no matter how you look."

"Uh-huh."

"You didn't have to get this done to please me."

"No. I didn't. I did it for myself. But I'm scared. I don't want to see it now."

"When she was working on it, it looked really good. Are you afraid that it will still look the same? Or worse?"

"No… I know you said it was looking good and she said it went really well. But… it's stupid. I'm more afraid… I won't be *me* anymore."

He nodded, looking at her and waiting for more, then staring off into the distance to consider it.

"No matter what you look like on the outside, you will always be your-self on the inside. For better or worse. It's the same for everyone, in one way or another. We age and we lose our looks. We have accidents… scars…" He stroked back his gray hair. "Believe me, I didn't look this *distinguished* when I was twenty."

Kelli laughed. It wasn't really funny; she was just really, really anxious. She appreciated her father for trying to understand how she felt, but he couldn't know. He'd never had a disfigurement like hers, much less had it removed.

Kelli reached up and fingered the edges of the surgical tape. "It's time to take it off."

"Do you want me to do it?"

Kelli considered, then nodded. She turned away from the mirror, so that her back was to it, and Justice Emerson Forest walked around to the front. Kelli closed her eyes.

He tugged at the edge of the tape and peeled it slowly away. Kelli winced and flinched, and brought her own hand up to assist with the process. Together, they pulled the bandage off. Kelli's eyes were still closed.

"Well… what do you think?" she asked.

"It's beautiful, Kelli. It's amazing."

She cracked her eyes open to look at her father. He was beaming, looking at her face where the birthmark had always been. She was used to people looking at her, but not with that expression.

"I'm still scared to look."

"Close your eyes again."

Kelli obeyed. He turned her around, so she was facing the mirror. "Okay. Whenever you're ready, have a peek."

Kelli just stood there with her eyes closed. She tried to talk herself into it. He said that it looked good, and she had to assume by his expression that he wasn't lying. She needed to see for herself what it looked like. She couldn't walk around with her eyes closed and avoid reflective surfaces for the rest of her life.

"This was a mistake. I shouldn't have had it done."

"But you did. So look and see."

"No. I just can't."

He walked out of the room. Kelli's eyes flew open, looking after him. Had she offended him? Was he angry? She had been rude to him, curt when there was no reason to be. He'd done everything he could to help her.

"Wait!"

He turned and looked at her. Kelli realized she had opened her eyes. She turned her head slightly, glancing at the mirror, more a reflex than anything else. At first, nothing was different. She saw her profile as she always saw it. One half of pretty. Then she realized she was looking at her bad side. The birthmark side. She stepped closer to the mirror and turned her head, looking at her face straight on. Both sides smooth and unmarked. Tears filled her eyes and she wiped them impatiently away. She put her face right up to the mirror. She could see the faintest outline of her birthmark if she was looking for it. Maybe it was just the redness that the tattooist had warned her about, and it would go away in a few days. Or maybe she would always have that little reminder of the big, purple birthmark that she had carried for sixteen years.

Justice Emerson Forester walked back to her side. He put his arm around her and gave her shoulders a squeeze. "What do you think? Was I right?"

Kelli shook her head. "I can't believe it. Is that really me? Is this real, or is it just another dream?"

He squeezed her again. "Do you dream that you don't have a birthmark?"

"All the time."

"Well, I guess dreams really can come true."

"It's real?" Kelli repeated.

"You know it's real. If it was a dream, would you be wondering if it was a dream?"

"Sometimes I do. Or sometimes I think, 'every time this has happened before, it has been a dream, but this time it isn't.' And then I wake up." Tears were streaming down Kelli's face and she was afraid to wipe them away. Afraid that the tears or the action of wiping them away would ruin the tattoo, and the birthmark would be back. She had succeeded in hiding the birthmark with gobs of makeup before, but it always came off again as soon as she touched it. Apparently, there was a special kind of makeup that could be used to camouflage birthmarks, but it was too expensive. Or it had been. Now she didn't even need that. Kelli pulled out a tissue and dabbed at her face carefully. The tattooist had said that she needed to be careful of infection. Not to be touching her cheek or putting anything against it. Keep it clean and away from everything and just give it a couple of weeks to heal.

"It's not going to wipe off," her father teased, watching her dab carefully.

"I know… I think. It's… it's amazing, I didn't think it would work."

"Didn't you?"

"The laser surgery never worked. They would say that it would lighten up, that they could help me, but it never worked. Sometimes it burned, but it never made it any better. But this…" Kelli's fingers hovered over the affected area, just about touching the surface, but afraid to get too close. "I don't believe it."

"I'm so pleased it worked."

Kelli felt an immediate jolt of anger and rebellion at his words. She knew that he meant he was glad for her, but that didn't stop the emotions from bubbling up in her. He didn't want a disfigured daughter. He wanted a daughter that he could show on his arm. That he could take to parties. That could appear in publicity photos. He didn't want her to have a birthmark because it would reflect badly on him.

She knew it wasn't true, but that didn't stop the feelings.

Maybe some of it was true. It wouldn't hurt to have a pretty daughter instead of an ugly one. Lisa hadn't worked out so well, but now he had a functional replacement.

———

Over supper, Kelli stared down at her plate and tried to ignore his looks. Justice Emerson Forester couldn't stop smiling. He kept looking at Kelli, a wide grin on his face. He was more excited about the erasure of her birthmark than Kelli was. He wasn't trying to stare, he was just enthralled with the results. His money had paid for it, so he had the right to look at the results and be proud of it. But it was driving her buggy.

"I would say that a celebration is in order," he said, realizing that she had caught him looking at her yet again.

"Like what?" Kelli asked.

He considered for a moment.

"I have just the thing!"

Kelli picked at her dinner while he left the dining room and went to get or arrange whatever it was that he had thought of. She wasn't really in the mood for celebrating. She wasn't sure how she felt about her unmarked face. Whenever she looked in the mirror, she stared, wondering who that was looking back at her. How long would it take before she got used to her own reflection? How many days would it be before she believed in her heart that it really was true and she no longer carried the disfigurement that had marred her for so many years?

The girl in the mirror was pretty. Kelli had never felt pretty. Any time any boy noticed her, it had only been for however long it took him to see the other side of her face. Then everything had changed. Like she was some kind of mutant monster.

Justice Emerson Forester returned to the dining room, carrying a bottle. He showed it off to Kelli.

"How about some champagne?" he suggested. "I've been saving this bottle for a special occasion, and I think we've earned it today!"

Kelli just stared at him in disbelief as he uncorked it. She clamped her mouth closed.

She knew that he drank. Usually just one or two glasses in an evening. She'd never seen him drunk. But she'd never seen him drink a full bottle, either.

The judge got two wine glasses off of the sideboard and placed them on the table in front of himself. He poured the sparkling liquid with a flourish, and reached across to place one in front of Kelli.

He froze. "What is it?" he asked. "What's wrong?"

"I don't drink," Kelli said icily.

"It's just champagne," he protested.

"No."

"Just one glass. To toast."

"No."

He stood there with the glass in his hand, staring at her.

"Kelli…" He slowly sat himself down in his chair, putting the glass down in front of her plate. "It's common for children to have a sip of wine on a holiday or special celebration. I know there are those who don't approve, but I think that if alcohol is completely withheld, the child doesn't learn how to drink responsibly. They don't see it used in a socially acceptable way, and when they finally are allowed to have any, they react by drinking irresponsibly."

Kelli took a couple more bites of her dinner. If she hadn't still been hungry, she would have just left him there at the table by himself and gone to her room.

"Just a sip," Justice Emerson Forester said. "Just toast with me. To you, and your new tattoo."

"No. Not even one sip. Not even one toast," Kelli said. There could be no question in his mind that she was serious. She was not drinking even a drop of his champagne.

"I don't understand," he said. "Why don't you explain to me what the problem is? Are you afraid that you'll get addicted? With just one sip? Did something happen to a friend? Did you make a promise?"

"My mom drinks."

"Yes…?"

"I've seen what it does to her. I am never touching a single drop of alcohol."

"One drink doesn't make you an alcoholic. One drink doesn't change you. I'm sure you know from experience that it takes more than just one drink to make your mother… tipsy."

"I don't care. I'm never going to drink. Ever."

"All right…" The judge picked up his own glass. He nodded to the glass of milk by Kelli's plate. "Here's to you, and your new look."

Kelli picked up her milk and tipped it toward him in acknowledgment of the toast.

They didn't clink glasses.

The milk tasted sour to Kelli.

CHAPTER 16

Kelli read in her bed instead of in the library. Before she put down her book to go to bed, there was a tap on her door, and the judge poked his nose in.

"Can I come in? Do you mind?"

Kelli shrugged. She felt a little like a child who had thrown a tantrum, even though she was sure her choice had been the right one. She hadn't had a fit or said anything to him in anger, but there was still a pall hanging between them. He had tried to do something nice for her, sharing an expensive champagne to celebrate her new face, which he had also arranged for her, and she had slammed the door in his face. She had not been willing to compromise even an inch.

He came in and sat on the edge of the bed. Kelli found herself cringing away from him, her stomach twisting into a tight, hot knot of anxiety. She tried to mask her reaction and pretend that she was used to bedtime visits. She was sure it was as natural to him as sitting on Lisa's bed to read her Curious George when she was a little girl. But Kelli couldn't help her automatic defensive response.

"There are some events that I would like you to attend with me this summer," he said.

"Because I look good enough to come along now?"

Frown lines appeared between his brows. "Because you're out of school now and have more free time. And because… I felt like you were starting to get more comfortable with me. I didn't want to ask you too soon and… make things weird."

"Oh." Kelli nodded, admitting that those were both perfectly natural reasons for him to wait until then to ask her. "Yeah, I guess… So… what are these functions?"

He gave her a long, assessing look before setting out to outline the fundraisers and dinners that he hoped she would attend with him. Pretty posh events, but if Kelly were determined to prove Preston wrong and fit in with her father's society, then she had to start doing things with him. Not eating dinner at home and reading in the library, but going to events and being seen in public.

"What if people get the wrong idea?" she asked. "They don't have a clue who I am, and suddenly you start showing up at things with me? Aren't people going to think…"

He laughed. "That I'm dating someone young enough to be my daughter? Well, yes, I supposed that's a real possibility. But I'll have to introduce you, and word will get around pretty quickly that you're my daughter, not my much-younger girlfriend."

"But we don't have the same last name. People won't believe it, will they?"

"It's always possible that someone will set out to prove it wrong, but the deeper they dig, the more convinced they will be that it is the truth. Because it is the truth. And in the end, truth will prevail."

Kelli snorted. Truth was not a magic pill. It had never gotten her anywhere in the past.

"If I'm going to go to these things…"

"Yes?"

"You're going to have to help me. Explain what's expected. What you're going for. I'm going to need new clothes. A makeover."

He smiled, his shoulders dipping down as he relaxed. "That all sounds doable."

"I've seen enough 'country mouse' movies to know that things are a lot different in your world. I might not have had all the advantages, but I still had a TV. I don't want to look like an idiot."

"I can't see that happening."

"Not if you help me."

"You want me to take you out shopping tomorrow?" he offered.

"Uh… no."

"No?"

"I need someone else. A woman. Someone who knows what they are talking about."

The judge grinned. "You don't think I know what I'm talking about?"

"In women's fashion? I doubt it. How long are skirts this year? What colors are in? What styles? What's being worn for formal and for semi-formal?" It was a world that Kelli had never been concerned about before. She'd never had the money to afford stylish things, even if she had been interested. If she could find something that was clean and comfortable and didn't have many holes in it, that was what she wore.

Not that she had ever gone to any parties. She supposed that there had been parties. Football after parties. Proms at school. Dances. Kids with keg parties when their parents were away from home. Kelli had never gone to any of them. Nor had she ever been invited. There had been one or two invitations passed on through intermediaries, but Kelli had correctly seen them as nerd bait. Get one of the geekiest, most awkward kids at school, and convince her that she has been invited to a popular party. Then humiliate her in the most spectacular way possible. Kelli wasn't falling for it. She stayed away from anything like that.

Justice Emerson Forester rubbed his chin thoughtfully. He was obviously going through his mental contact list to find the right woman to help Kelli out with her preparations.

"I have a friend, Melinda Kravitz. She is also a judge." Kelli was about to object, but he went on. "She has a daughter that clerks for her part time. She always looks well-turned-out at the courthouse, and very pretty whenever I see her at family functions with her mother. She might be a good fit."

"How old is she?"

"I'm not sure. Eighteen. Nineteen. Young enough to know what the cool kids are wearing."

"Well… she might work. Do you think… she wouldn't be too busy?"

"She should be off school for the summer. I think she's clerking full time over the summer. Not traveling to Guatemala or anything like that."

"Can you ask her without it being awkward?"

"Leave it to me." He patted Kelli's leg, making her jump at the unexpected contact. "I'll work it out."

He stood up and bent over to give her a kiss on the forehead. Kelli wanted to pull away, worried about the possibility of germs near her tattoo, but she steeled herself and stayed still. The spot that he kissed was nowhere near the tattoo. She was just obsessing over it.

"Goodnight," Kelli whispered.

"Goodnight, sweetheart. Thank you for agreeing. We'll make sure that you'll fit in. Don't worry about it."

He left, pulling the door shut behind him. Kelli rubbed her leg where he had touched her before leaving. She breathed deeply and tried to control the effects of the spike of adrenaline that coursed through her.

———

Things had progressed quickly, and Kelli was introduced to Melinda's daughter, Cassia Kravitz. Cassia had graciously agreed to help Kelli out. Justice Emerson Forester said that she had been eager to meet Kelli and see that she was all ready for the summer.

"Mom told me a little about you," Cassia said. "But I guess I didn't get the full story."

Oh, boy.

"I'm not trying to pry," Cassia said, lowing her voice a little. "I just wondered… you know, the basics… Mom said that you are Judge Forester's daughter, but you've been estranged, and you just recently came to live with him…?"

"Yeah."

Cassia led Kelli to her car. It was a pretty, sleek, sporty white car, far different from the car that Kelli had chosen to get to and from the city and not stand out in her old neighborhood. It seemed sort of silly that she'd been so worried about it. Since she ended up moving out of the neighborhood completely in just a few weeks. And since school had ended, she had no reason to go back for anything. She should probably upgrade her vehicle, if she were going to fit in with the judge's crowd. She expected that she and her father would not show up for all events together. There would be times when they would each come from somewhere different and meet up at a function. She'd need the right vehicle to get her there.

Kelli slid into the warm leather seat and put on her seatbelt.

"I didn't grow up around here," she said. "What happened was… well… you know his other daughter, Lisa?"

Cassia nodded, her mouth pressing into a thin line. Apparently, Lisa rubbed her the wrong way too. Kelli warmed a little toward Cassia.

"She and I… were switched at the hospital."

"What do you mean?" Cassia asked, turning on the engine. They pulled out, driving slowly down the long driveway, and then speeding up once they hit the main road.

"I mean, he and Preston took Lisa home, and my mom took me home."

"Yes…"

Kelli scowled, not sure why Cassia wasn't immediately getting the picture.

"But they each took the wrong baby. I… was Judge Forester's baby."

Cassia's jaw dropped. She glanced over at Kelli, eyes wide. "But that means… Lisa *isn't* his daughter."

"Not biologically, no."

Cassia gave a low whistle. "Holy crap! Are you serious? You're not kidding me, are you?" She gave Kelli another look. "You're not kidding! Freaking princess Forester is not even his baby? I mean, I always suspected there was something 'off' there, but a hospital mix-up is not what I thought."

Kelli looked at Cassia curiously. "You suspected what?"

"Oh, I don't know. That there was an affair. That she was an alien. Virgin birth. Just something. Judge Forester has always been such a great guy, and he's really good to her, but she is… oh, man… such a little snot. She's a mini Preston. Nothing like the judge."

"But she's not Preston's, either."

This part of the equation hadn't seemed to have sunk in yet. Kelli didn't think that Cassia's eyes could get any wider, but they did. She swore under her breath.

"When this gets around, Preston is going to be madder than a wet hen. She dotes on Miss Lisa Forester. She would move heaven and earth for that little girl. Honey, I'd watch my back if I were you!"

"I know," Kelli agreed, thinking back to Preston's vitriol the night of their dinner together. She had done everything she could to persuade Justice Emerson Forester to give Kelli the boot. And chances were, she wasn't done yet. She wouldn't stop at that.

"Wow. That's incredible. Well, good for the judge, for not being afraid of all of the fall-out, and taking you in. That's pretty amazing of him."

"What fall-out?"

"Well, there's bound to be people who say he should have known, that he was in on it, that you're really a child of one of his affairs, whatever. You know how catty people can be, especially when they envy the person involved…"

"Do you think so?" Kelli hadn't considered that there might be any negative consequences for her father. But what Cassia said made sense. People were always willing to take up a rumor and to twist it into something worse. People who didn't like him would be happy to take up the torch. And as much as she hated to admit it, there would be people who didn't like the judge or were jealous of his position. "I guess you're right."

"Oh, don't you worry about it. He'll handle it. He's one of the good guys."

"Yeah."

"Well… this makes things really interesting. You probably really don't know anything about our little community. The who's who of the court circuit and elite of the elite."

"No. I told… uh… the judge… that if he wanted me to go to some of these events with him, I'd need someone to show me the ropes. And I guess you were elected."

"No problem! It's going to be a ton of fun. Not just because I love a good makeover. I am really going to enjoy knowing that we're putting little Lisa in her place."

"I'm not actually…" Kelli stumbled, searching for words. "I'm not doing it to spite Lisa… I don't think it's her fault, the way she is, and that she got stuck in the middle like this. And she still is… the judge's daughter, the one he raised. I don't want to hurt her."

Show off to her, maybe. Show her up. Show her that a person didn't have to be raised a Forester to put on a good showing, maybe. But she didn't actually want to be mean to the girl. It wasn't Lisa's fault that she'd been swapped at the hospital any more than it was Kelli's.

"You're a bigger person about it than I would be," Cassia said. "But then… you don't really know her, either."

Kelli watched the scenery whip by along the now-familiar road. "Do you?" she countered.

They were a few years apart in age. How much did a nineteen-year-old really know about a lowly sixteen-year-old, even if they were in the same social circles? Kids tended to only associate with those in their own grade.

"Well," Cassia considered. "I mean, she's not my best friend or anything like that. But I see her around at stuff and I know her reputation."

Kelli nodded. She refrained from asking what kind of a reputation Lisa had. Obviously, it wasn't good. And with Lisa dating someone named Truman Sharp, now exclusively, there was probably plenty of fodder for the gossip mill.

"I'm just going to focus on me," Kelli said. "Lisa can do what she likes. I just want to do whatever I can to fit in. Help my… father… look good."

"Okay," Cassia agreed. "You got it."

———

It was a long day, and it became apparent to Kelli that she wasn't going to be ready in just a day. It was going to take several sessions before she understood all of the intricacies of the social structure around the judge.

Cassia took her to a hairdresser named Pria, a beautiful Asian woman with colorful eyeshadow who examined Kelli's hair with a scowl and shaking head, clicking her tongue over the limp, drab tresses. She acted like Kelli was a street urchin who might have lice or fleas.

"Let's give her the works, Pria," Cassia urged. "What do you think? Some highlights and a wave, a good trim…"

Pria ran her fingers through Kelli's hair. "Maybe some layers for volume. Do you want it short?"

Kelli shook her head. "Not too short," she said anxiously. She'd always had long hair. Shoulder length or longer. She used it to screen her face from view, to hide the birthmark that was no longer visible. She would feel naked without long hair. She already felt conscious enough of the changes to her face.

Pria nodded at Cassia. "The works," she agreed. She gave Kelli a forced smile. "You are going to be thrilled with it, honey."

"Yeah… Cassia said you're the best." Kelli forced a smile of her own. If she was going to pull it off, she needed people like Pria on her side. Pria serviced many of the elite in Justice Emerson Forester's circles, and what she had to say about a client would be spread far and wide.

Pria's smile softened slightly. "Well, who am I to argue with Cassia?"

Kelli tried to just relax while Pria worked on her. It was like a spa day. Not that Kelli had ever done such a thing, but she tried to think of it as pampering rather than tampering. She closed her eyes and pretended to be asleep while Pria primped and snipped away. Pria talked in a hushed tone to Cassia, getting the scoop on who Kelli actually was. A few times she stopped what she was doing to look at Cassia in shocked disbelief, but kept her exclamations quiet.

"Lisa isn't even Preston's? I can't believe it!"

It was of interest that neither of them expressed surprise that Lisa wasn't actually Justice Emerson Forester's daughter. Kelli supposed that they had been estranged for long enough that it didn't come as a shock that there had been an affair. Maybe the judge had made it known to a few close acquaintances that he knew Lisa wasn't his biological daughter and word had spread. That sort of thing was far from being unusual and must happen regularly, even among the upper crust.

When Pria announced she was done and pulled the cape off of Kelli, she opened her eyes. She had a good stretch to give veracity to the idea that she'd been sleeping through the whole thing, and looked anxiously at the mirror. It wasn't like when she had had to look at her face after the tattooing of her birthmark, but she was still nervous about it.

Instead of flat, drab hair, Kelli's hair surrounded her face with soft, shining waves. The highlights were similar to what she got when she spent the summer outdoors, sun-bleaching her hair. But that had still never given her hair the body and bounce and feminine curliness that it had now.

"Wow," Kelli murmured. "That's really… that's pretty!"

"You're no ugly duckling," Pria said. "It's been there all the time. You've just never done anything with yourself."

Kelli covered the right side of her face, under her eye, imagining how it would have looked if she had that hair while she still had her birthmark. Would she have been pretty then? She shook her head. No. Even with pretty hair, she couldn't be good looking with the birthmark. It would have been pointless. She had been right to get it taken care of, like the judge had advised.

"What is it?" Pria asked, studying Kelli with her brows drawn down in a scowl. "Did you get something in your eye?"

"No, no, it's fine," Kelli said, wiping her eyes quickly and moving her hands away from her face. That was what she looked like now. That was her, looking back out at her from the mirror. A pretty young blond. People wouldn't look at her and then turn away when they saw her full face. She was just like anyone else.

"You're looking good, but this is only the start!" Cassia reminded Kelli. "Pria will show you what to use to keep it looking nice, and then we'll move on. We've still got to do makeup, and clothes. I don't think we'll be able to get it all done today. And I have to tell you about everyone, who they are and what to expect. You brought the list of events the judge wants to take you to in the next few weeks, right?"

Kelli had been given detailed instructions. Cassia needed to know all of the information if Kelli were to be properly turned out. She pulled the folded-up piece of paper from her tight jeans pocket. Cassia unfolded it and skimmed the list.

"Yeah, okay. We've got our work cut out for us. You ever been to a fancy-dress party before?"

"No."

"You'll have a blast." Cassia folded the paper back up. "You have a phone, right?"

"Yes…?"

"Start using it. All those dates belong on your calendar, not on a piece of paper in your pocket. And you need to start inputting names and phone numbers. All the hostesses of these events. People that you run into that you say you'll keep in touch with. People you might ask a favor from or do a favor for. You won't be able to keep them all in your head. It's all about connections. Don't just write down their name and number. Everything important. What you find out about their families, the foundations they support, their professions. Age, birthday, anything that you might want to bring up again the next time you talk to them. People are impressed when you remember things about them. Their kids' names and what they're doing. Mommas always love to have people ask about their children."

"Okay." Kelli tucked the list of dates back away. She was going to have to learn how to use her phone properly. So far all she had done was to dial numbers on the keypad. If she were going to play her role properly, she needed to up her game.

Cassia withdrew, tapping away on her own phone, while Pria told Kelli how to take care of her hair, giving her bottle after bottle of product, and plying her with various combs, brushes, curling irons, hair dryers, and everything else in her salon.

While Pria rang everything up, Kelli wandered back over to the mirror to look at herself again, to refresh her memory and try to convince herself that she was just as pretty as she remembered. It wasn't an illusion, that image was her now.

But inside, she still felt just the same as she always had. Ugly. Useless. Worthless.

Pria was chatting with Cassia, who was off her phone again. She glanced in Kelli's direction and lowered her voice, but Kelli still heard her words. Probably Pria fully intended for her to overhear.

"She's even prettier than Lisa."

———

Kelli went home exhausted. She was glad Cassia was driving her, because she wasn't sure she would have been able to manage even that. Her entire body was tired and sore from being turned this way and that, tramping through stores, trying on countless shoes and outfits, until they all blurred together and she couldn't remember where one store ended and the next began.

"*This* one for Fourth of July. *This* one for Miss Dimity's barbecue. *This* for the hospital fundraiser." Kelli was worried about being buried in an avalanche of clothes.

They had stopped at some specialty store, a stylist of some kind, who had done all kinds of measurements, commenting on each of Kelli's features and how she could enhance them or hide them, depending on whether they were good or bad. She put Kelli under burning hot lights and held color swatches next to her, analyzing the colors that were best for her to wear. And she sat Kelli on a high stool, dabbing and sponging at her face while working through endless palettes of makeup to decide which one was just right for Kelli. She curled, tweezed, and brushed every feature into submission.

"You have a slight shading difference here," she had pointed out Kelli's tattooed birthmark before starting. "Have you ever noticed that?"

Kelli felt her face heat up. She wondered, with the birthmark and the tattoo, whether she turned an even shade of red all over her face, or whether the tattooed side remained exactly the same tone.

"I know. I had a port wine birthmark. I just had microtattooing done to cover it up."

"Really?" Sophia leaned in close, studying Kelli's skin from only a hair's breadth away. "I've heard about it, but I've never seen the results. How obvious was the birthmark? How big was it?"

Kelli pulled back from her. She glanced over at Cassia, who also seemed interested in hearing the answer. If Kelli wanted to be able to put her best face forward—literally—she needed to have a good relationship with the stylist. After a minute of hesitation, Kelli dug into her wallet, and handed Sophia her driver's license.

"Wow!" Sophia stared at the picture, and then looked back at Kelli's face in disbelief. "That's amazing! Look at that!" She handed the driver's license to Cassia. "Can you believe it?"

Kelli covered her face, wishing she could just sink right into the floor.

"No, no," Sophia protested. "I'm just amazed at how good you look! They really did a good job of it. Lots of people have different coloring from one part of their face to another. No one is going to notice it. And a dab of makeup will even out the imperfections. Nobody has perfect features, dear. Anyone who tells you differently is lying. We all have things to cover up."

"Can we just get on with it?" Kelli begged, reaching out her hand for her license to hide it back away. Cassia handed it back slowly.

"You need to get a new one."

"What?"

"A new license."

Kelli tucked it back away. "I don't care that it shows my birthmark. That's who I really am. I still am, you know."

"Yes, but your license has to be an accurate reflection of what you look like now. If you show that to a cop that pulls you over, he's going to arrest you for identity theft!"

"Really?" Kelli frowned, thinking about it. She had hated getting the driver's license picture taken. She always tried to keep her birthmark from showing in pictures, but the DMV woman wouldn't let her turn away, and kept swearing when Kelli instinctively pulled away at the flash and shutter click. It had been such an ordeal. And she needed to do it all over again? It didn't seem fair.

"Yes. If you have a major change to your appearance, you have to update your license."

Kelli wasn't happy about it. Just one more thing to add to the list of tasks to complete.

As she sat there only half-listening to all that Sophia was telling her about her skin type and face shape and color palette, Kelli's mind wandered to Les. It seemed like years since she had seen him last. What was he doing now? Was he running cons on his own now, since she was no longer there to split the work with him? Were he and his siblings getting enough to eat without the supplemental income Kelli brought in? Had he been advanced a grade at school, or had they really flunked him, like they had been threatening to do before they wrote final exams? She hadn't even seen him since writing those last few tests.

When Sophia had finished and Kelli had stopped to stare at the stranger in the mirror once more, and had gushed to Sophia over how wonderful she now looked, Kelli pulled out her phone and tapped Les's phone number into the texting app. She composed a quick greeting, and pressed send. Sophia and Cassia were sorting through the makeup and brushes Kelli needed to buy to maintain her face, and Kelli's phone buzzed. She dropped her gaze to it, expecting to see a text back from Les, but instead there was an error message. *Delivery failed.*

She checked the number again, but it was right. Had Les changed his number? Been unable to pay for the month? She felt guilty for having gone so long without contacting him. They had always seen each other every day when she was living with Patricia. They had been at school together every day, and on the weekends, they had spent all their free time together. What kind of a person was she, to have gotten so wrapped up in herself that she lost track of her best friend?

"Kelli?"

"Hmm?" Kelli looked up and saw Cassia and Sophia looking at her expectantly. "Uh… sorry, off in my own little world there for a minute. Thank you so much Sophia, I can't believe what a great job you did. This really means a lot to me."

Sophia's expression relaxed into a smile. "I had a lot of fun torturing—I mean working with—you," she joked. "You feel free to come by any time you need anything. If you have an event you need something extra-special for, or a question or want a new look, or more product. I'm here for you."

"Thanks!"

Kelli and Cassia departed. Kelli took the shopping bag from Cassia and they headed for the car.

"Everything okay?" Cassia asked.

"Yeah, fine. I was just trying to get ahold of someone. But I guess he changed his number…"

"He? You didn't mention you had a boyfriend!"

"He's not my boyfriend," Kelli protested. "It's not like that. He's just… my best friend. And I haven't talked to him, with everything that has been happening. I don't want to lose him, just because I moved in with the judge."

"Can't you call him Dad?" Cassia demanded. "It's really weird that you don't. I mean, a lot of kids call their parents by their first names, when they're not in front of them, but you don't even do that. Won't he let you call him Dad or Justice?"

"Uh… I guess. We haven't really talked about it, and I'm not sure what I feel comfortable with. I already had a dad, you know, so… it would be weird to call him that too. Wouldn't it?"

"Lots of people have more than one dad. It doesn't seem to stop anyone."

"I'll… talk with him about it sometime."

"Soon," Cassia pressed. "People are going to notice right away if you're acting all distant. They'll think something is wrong. You can't be showing up at parties calling him Judge Forester."

"Yeah, you're probably right."

"You know I am. But you distracted me from the important topic. Your boyfriend. What's his name?"

"He's not my boyfriend."

"But he has a name."

"Les."

Cassia nodded. "Les what?"

"What does it matter? It's not like you know him."

"Just information gathering. Always good to know about people's loved ones."

"We're not—"

"Les what?"

"Les Broke."

"Les Broke?" Cassia giggled. "I'll bet he gets teased for that one."

"Enough," Kelli agreed. She heard his common rejoinder in her head. "I wish I was less broke!"

"And the two of you have never gotten together? Never… kissed?"

"No," Kelli said firmly. "He's just my friend. We work together. Help each other with homework. That kind of thing. We are not in love. We are not dating. We are not having… kissing."

"Okay." Cassia shrugged. "None of my business anyway." She sounded like she was going to drop it, but she wasn't. "He's not returning your calls?"

"His phone might be off, or he might not have been able to pay his bill this month. It doesn't mean he's avoiding me."

"Of course not," Cassia gave a knowing look. "These boys, right? They drive us crazy."

Kelli just shook her head and got into the car.

———

It was late when she got in. Kelli wasn't sure if the judge would still be up, or if he would have gone off to bed. She might be off for the summer, but he was still working and needed to be up in the morning. He couldn't stay up waiting for her all night.

"Kelli?" She heard him call from the direction of the kitchen as soon as she stepped in the door. Kelli followed his voice and found him raiding the fridge for a snack to go with his nightcap.

"I know," he said sheepishly. "I'm too old to be eating like this. I need to look after my body. But I didn't have dessert with supper."

They each took a narrow slice of cake. Smaller than Kelli would have liked. She filled a glass with milk to go with hers, and they stood over the counter instead of getting plates or leaving crumbs on the dining room table.

Kelli looked up from her cake to find him staring at her, eyes wide.

"Kelli…" He shook his head. "I love you whether you're all dressed up or straight out of bed in yoga pants. But… you are stunning! You look like you stepped right off a runway."

Kelli laughed. In her mind, her beauty had faded as the fatigue from the day grew. She no longer saw herself when she stood in front of a fitting room mirror. She only saw the body. The clothes. Sometimes not even that, she just stood there while Cassia did the work, too exhausted to make another decision.

"Have you seen yourself?" Justice Emerson Forester persisted. "Honey… you do. You look gorgeous."

"It's just a bit of hair and makeup," Kelli said. "That's not me. That's just… paint. And I'm too exhausted to look in the mirror again."

She popped the last bite of cake into her mouth and washed it down with the rest of the milk.

"I'm glad you like it," she conceded. "I'm flattered. But… you know you're exaggerating."

"I'm not. And I've seen fashion shows, so don't tell me I don't know what I'm talking about. You could give any of them a run for their money. Such a… transformation from the first day you came to my door."

"I'm still the same person," Kelli told him. "Nothing has changed."

"No. Not you. Just the window dressing. But… it's a very nice view. You're a very lovely girl."

"Better than Lisa?" Kelli asked.

His jaw dropped and he dithered about for something to say. Kelli had pity on him.

"That's the kind of question that you just plain don't want to answer," she said. "There's no right answer."

"Sweetheart… there's no question you look better than Lisa. And you actually mean it when you smile. Lisa is always wearing a mask, putting on an act, except when she's pouting about something. I love it when you smile. It's genuine."

Kelli sighed. That just went to show how wrong he was.

And what a good con she was.

CHAPTER 17

The Fourth of July Picnic was the first event that Justice Emerson Forester took her to. It was hosted by Mrs. Wickham, who Cassia had informed Kelli was the mother of a girl around her age. She was the wife of a senator. They had two children. And the mansion they lived in backed onto the golf green at the country club. All of this had been duly noted in the contacts database in Kelli's phone.

The word 'picnic' was a misnomer. It couldn't be further from what Kelli pictured. No sandwiches on a red-checked blanket or tablecloth. No potluck. No lemonade. It was a full formal banquet in dresses and suits. Even the children had on stiff, uncomfortable-looking clothes and were not allowed to run around and play. Kelli felt sorry for them.

She walked in on the judge's arm, feeling awkward and out of place. But she knew she had a part to play, and that was what she was there to do. She would show Preston and Lisa and the judge that she could fit in there just as if she had been raised by him. She would show everyone that she belonged there, no matter how she was raised and how she had looked when she first came to him.

Justice Emerson Forester strutted like a peacock. He was obviously proud to have a pretty girl on his arm, even if she was his daughter rather than his girlfriend or wife. And maybe he had a right to be proud. He had paid for the transformation, after all.

Kelli saw the whispers and glances darted in her direction. No one stared at her in the same way that they had when she had the birthmark, but there were still stares, and she still felt uncomfortable with all the attention.

"And who is this lovely young lady?" asked a woman who bustled over. Sleek like a greyhound, her movements quick and jerky. She thrust her hands out to take Kelli's "I'm sure I haven't seen you here before."

"This is my daughter, Kelli," her father introduced her.

"Your daughter." The woman looked Kelli over again, looking puzzled for a moment. "You know, I did hear a rumor… someone said that you had another daughter who had come to live with you…?"

"That's right," Justice Emerson Forester agreed placidly. "Kelli, this is Mrs. Wickham, our hostess."

"Oh!" Kelli squeezed Mrs. Wickham's hand. "I just can't believe how beautiful it all is, Mrs. Wickham. You must have been planning for it all year. When the invitation said 'picnic'… well, I wasn't thinking of all this!"

Mrs. Wickham laughed, smiling widely. "I'll let you in on a secret, my dear. Even with all my staff and volunteers, it still takes me a full year to get everything planned and executed. I've already started planning next year's!"

"Wow!" Kelli was momentarily speechless. "That's amazing. You put so much into it!" She pulled her hand out of Mrs. Wickham's, hoping that she had not withdrawn it prematurely. But she did not like to be touched. "And how are your children? I think you have a boy, and a girl my age."

"That's right," Mrs. Wickham agreed. "Oh, she's a gem, Judge Forester. She's done her research! Yes, my little Daffodil is just your age."

It was all Kelli could do not to snort, trying to stifle a laugh. Daffodil? Somehow Cassia had neglected to tell her that part. Kelli should have asked. Next time she'd know better and not be surprised by a name.

"I hope I'll get to meet her today. Is she here?" Kelli asked.

"Yes. I'm sure you'll run into each other at some point. I'll tell her to keep an eye open for you. She's probably helping in the kitchen, the dear."

Kelli nodded, and followed the tug on her arm as Justice Emerson Forester started to move away. "It was very nice to meet you, Mrs. Wickham."

Mrs. Wickham was already turning to greet her next guest.

"She'll have a very busy day," the judge observed.

"No kidding. I could never do something like this." Kelli looked around. "A whole year to plan it? And then it's over in a day?"

"She has her finger in other pies too. She's always volunteering on some committee, making phone calls, getting people involved in whatever the hot cause of the year is. But this is the big event for her. Everything else has to revolve around it."

"Wow."

The judge glanced over his shoulder at Mrs. Wickham. "Now that she's been introduced to you, you can bet that the rest of the guests will hear all about you when they arrive. Word will circulate like wildfire."

Kelli looked at him. "Is that what you wanted? Is that why this is the first event that we came to?"

He shrugged and smiled at her. "You picked that up pretty quickly. Mrs. Wickham has… an efficient social network. It puts computer networks to shame. If we want to avoid having to explain over and over again who you are, what better way than to have her pass it on for us?"

"But you didn't explain the whole thing to her. About… the hospital switch, I mean."

"Didn't you hear her say that she had heard a rumor?"

"Yes."

"Well, you can bet that if she didn't hear all the details then, she will have them pinned down in minutes."

———

Kelli lay crosswise on her bed and picked up her phone. She was too tired to change out of her dress, even though she knew she was crushing the fabric by lying down that way. She tapped Les's number into the phone and listened for it to ring.

It went directly to a recorded message saying that the number was out of service. That would be why her texts to him had been undeliverable.

She looked at her watch before dialing his home number. It was still early enough that the little kids and his parents would be up. She wouldn't wake anyone up. But it would also mean that they would all be listening in, wanting to know who he was on the phone with and what it was all about.

She dialed anyway. The phone rang half a dozen times before it was picked up.

"Yeah?" A gruff voice. His mother, probably, but Kelli wasn't sure.

"Les there?"

"Who is this?"

"It's Kelli."

There was no response. The phone banged down, but the connection hadn't been broken. Kelli waited. It was a while before the phone was picked up again.

"Kelli?"

"Les!" Kelli was excited to hear his voice and suddenly didn't know what to say. "Hey… how are you? I tried your cell, but it didn't work."

"Yeah, couldn't pay for it." His tone was breezy, unconcerned. "How's it going with the millionaire mark? You getting everything you ever dreamed of?"

Kelli thought about her life. She had her own car. A clean, safe place to sleep. And no more birthmark.

"Yeah, I guess so," she admitted. But somehow, she didn't feel any different. She still felt like the same Kelli. Lonely, unsure of the future, insecure. "Things are… good. How about with you? What's up?"

"Same old, same old. I'm glad you called. Seems like forever since I saw you."

"Yeah. It's weird. You have to come here sometime. We can hang out."

"Or you could come slumming. I don't really have any way to get out there."

"I could pick you up. You gotta see the place. It'll blow you away."

"I guess. We could do that sometime." He was noncommittal. Didn't offer a time that would work for him.

"I'll see what the judge's schedule is and we'll set something up," Kelli offered.

"Sure."

"He's got me going to a bunch of fundraisers and stuff with him," she explained. "That and tutors over the summer. Ugh."

"Summer school? Lucky you!"

"It's only a couple hours a day, but it's still a pain. Summer is supposed to be the time when you get to just bum around and not do anything."

"I guess things are different for the *riche*," Les said unsympathetically. "The price you pay for unlimited wealth."

"I'd rather be hanging out with you, playing the streets."

"Well, do it then. What's he going to do? Come after you and drag you home? He can't stop you from going out and doing what you want."

Kelli stroked the silky cover of her bed. "I don't want to cause trouble for him. He's been real nice to me. It's not like he's being unreasonable…"

"Well, anytime you want to come back and spend a day in the hood, you know where to find me."

"Yeah. No summer school for you?" Les's mother had threatened in the past to put him into remedial programming over the summer if he didn't shape up. But so far, he'd managed to avoid sweltering in the dreaded classroom when he should be running free.

Les chuckled. "It was a close call," he admitted. "But Ma somehow lost the paperwork, so I didn't get registered."

"Lost it, did she?" Kelli had a pretty good idea how the papers had been misplaced. His mother should have seen that one coming.

"Footloose and fancy free," he confirmed.

"And are you… you're doing okay? Making enough to get by?" He'd never been as skilled as Kelli was. And Kelli thought more people probably thought they could win playing against a girl. Or didn't mind her taking their money so much.

Les took a while to answer. "Don't make as much as the partnership… but I get along."

"Always make more with a shill," Kelli said. "Maybe you should—"

"I got it covered. I've recruited Desi. Brought her into the family business. She's happy with a few coins for candy, so the rest goes to supporting the family. We're fine."

But he no longer had enough to pay for his cell phone. Kelli knew he hated not being connected. He wouldn't have just let his phone go unless it were the only option.

"I'll come get you one day, after I check on my schedule," Kelli promised. "We'll get pizza or something and pig out."

"That sounds good," Les said cheerfully. "I gotta go, Mom needs the phone."

Kelli said goodbye and Les was gone. Kelli lay there, watching the screen dim and then go black.

———

Kelli was looking forward to her father getting home. She had done her schoolwork, and they didn't have any events to go to, so it would just be the two of them for the evening. She was bored from kicking around the house alone since the tutor had left. She'd even read ahead to the next chapter in one of her textbooks. She puttered around in the library, looking for something more interesting than her current reads.

She heard his car roar down the drive, faster than usual.

When he came into the house, he slammed the door shut behind him. Kelli's heart raced. She jumped to her feet, instantly on high alert. He didn't come directly to the library, instead going into his office. Kelli hovered outside the door, not wanting to get in his way, but concerned about his change in behavior. The judge threw his briefcase on his desk with a crash. He turned and saw her as he jerked off his suit jacket and threw it over his chair.

"Something wrong?" he demanded.

Kelli swallowed. She forced herself to step in through the doorway and to smile as if nothing was out of the ordinary.

"No, I'm just glad to see you. Is everything okay?"

"No, everything is not okay." His face was tight, his dark eyes drilling into her. "Preston!" he blurted out, hands clenching into fists.

Kelli's breaths came faster. What had Preston done now? She'd never seen the judge in anything but a calm, collected mood before. Even when he'd dealt with Preston's temper tantrum the day of their dinner, he'd shown little emotion over her vitriol. For the first time, Kelli wondered about their separation. Was it because of Preston's affairs and Lisa's disinterest in having anything to do with her father, or was there something more to it? Had he been abusive, like every other man Kelli had ever lived with?

"What happened?" she asked, trying to keep her voice low and soothing. She took a glance around the room, inventorying space requirements, possible weapons, exit paths. If she couldn't calm him down, she needed to get out of there.

"She's gone to her lawyer," Justice Emerson Forester grated out. "He sent a demand. For a DNA test."

Kelli frowned, trying to put it all together.

"A DNA test? She… doesn't believe that I'm her baby? That doesn't make sense, she has the birth pictures. She can see the birthmark."

"Not a test proving that you are her daughter. Though I'll insist on that loose end being tied up as well so she can't squirm out of her responsibilities. She wants a DNA test for *paternity*."

Kelli shook her head. "I don't get it."

"She's challenging paternity. She says… you're not my daughter."

"But you know you are."

The judge slammed his hand down on the desk. "I know we were married when you were born, and my name is on Lisa's birth certificate." His voice was tight, barely under control. "But Preston says she was seeing someone else at the time you were conceived. That she… doesn't think I… fathered you."

The room spun. Kelli looked at him in disbelief. "Could that be true?"

"How would I know?" he growled. "We were trying to have a baby. For two years. We were going to start fertility treatments when Preston finally got pregnant."

"And she thinks… it's because she started up with someone else."

He nodded curtly. He clenched his fists again. "This changes nothing! Even if the DNA test is negative, that doesn't stop me from leaving my money to whoever I damn well please!"

Kelli nodded. But would he want to have anything more to do with her if Preston proved that Kelli belonged to another man?

It seemed like no matter where Kelli went, no one wanted her. Every parent or potential parent pushed her away sooner or later. How many DNA tests was it going to take before she actually found a biological parent who cared? She should stop while she was ahead. Once Justice Emerson Forester realized Kelli wasn't his daughter, she was going to be out on her own. Kelli didn't think she could go back to Patricia and Axel. She couldn't face that life again after living with the judge. There was nowhere left for her.

Justice Emerson Forester picked up the heavy fountain pen on his desk, his favorite pen, and fired it across the room.

It wasn't thrown in Kelli's direction, but she immediately panicked. She'd been on the receiving end of impotent rage too many times not to recognize the danger she was in. She backed toward the door, her hands held up defensively.

"Kelli, I'm sorry…" The judge stared at Kelli as if he hadn't seen her there before. "I'm not mad at *you*."

He strode across the room toward her, his arms held out. Kelli deflected them to the side and grounded herself, keeping low, watching for her chance to throw him. The opportunity for flight was gone. They were nose-to-nose.

He was angry and twice her weight. What he lacked in training, he made up for in mass and rage.

"Kelli." He reached for her again.

Kelli grabbed his closest arm, locked his shoulder joint, and threw him to the floor with a crash. The judge groaned and didn't jump right back up. Kelli didn't think he'd hit his head. He was just surprised, the wind knocked out of him. Not disabled. He still had plenty of fight left in him.

Kelli dashed for her room. Felicia was in the hallway, on her way to see what was going on. Kelli shouldered past her without stopping to explain. Up the stairs. Down the hallway. To her bedroom. Kelli slammed the door and looked around. The dresser was solid oak. She wouldn't be able to budge it through the thick pile of the carpet. The wardrobe too. Every piece of furniture in the room was heavy.

She grabbed a chair and dragged it over to the door, wedging it under the door handle. She didn't want to scratch or dent the fine wood, but she didn't know what else to do. She looked around the room again.

He was a judge.

One phone call, and she'd be out of the house and on her way to jail for assault.

It wouldn't be like before, when she could claim self-defense. The police department's dictate that anyone involved in a domestic was to be arrested and they would let the courts sort out the details wasn't going to hold up in this case. They had a judge right in front of them. A statement from him, and Kelli would be on her way to juvie. She was sixteen; they might even put her through the adult system.

Kelli grabbed a shoulder bag. One of the fancy designer ones that Cassia had directed her to buy. Perfect for a beach party, like the one coming up in a week. She didn't have anything more suitable, it would have to do. She threw her wallet in. A change of clothes. Summer clothes were light enough that they didn't take up all the space. Kelli scanned the top of the dresser. She wouldn't be able to use her credit card, and she didn't have much cash in her wallet. She needed items she could liquidate quickly. Moving as quickly as she could, she grabbed a few pieces of jewelry and shoved them into her pockets.

She was hurrying in the hope of being able to get out of the house before he regained his equilibrium and either came after her again or called the police. She grabbed her keys. She shoved in a bag of raisins that had been secreted in the back of her drawer. She needed some kind of emergency rations.

Kelli jumped at the knock on the door.

"Kelli? I'm sorry, I didn't mean to—" He turned the doorknob, but the chair against the door held it shut. He rattled the knob as if he thought it might be stuck. "Kelli?"

"Leave me alone," Kelli warned.

"I didn't mean to scare you. Can't we talk…?"

"I don't want to talk to you. Go cool off." She clutched the shoulder bag to her like a security blanket. If he would leave her alone, she could sneak out of the house after he fell asleep or once she was sure he was in another part of the house.

"I've already calmed down. I'm fine. I'm sorry I got so angry."

"Leave me alone," Kelli repeated.

He rattled the door again. Fear squeezed Kelli's heart. Would he force it? Would he call the police and have them break in or talk her out?

"Would you move whatever is blocking this door? I only want to make sure you're okay."

"No."

"Kelli!" His voice was exasperated.

She fingered her phone. Should she call someone for help? She didn't know who might be able to talk the judge into leaving her alone. He had a lot of friends, but she hadn't gotten to know more than a couple of them and didn't know how they would react to such a call.

What if she called the cops before he could? The police would be more likely to be on her side if she called and said she'd barricaded herself in for fear that he would hurt her.

"I was angry at Preston, not at you. I would never do anything to hurt you, Kelli."

"Then go away and leave me alone."

He muttered under his breath. She couldn't tell what threats he was making. "You know you're just as stubborn as your old man?" he demanded.

Kelli couldn't help but smile at that, in spite of her anxious state. "Yeah, I am."

"If I leave you alone, will you be okay?"

"Yes."

"Will you stay here?"

She swallowed, looking at the chair under the doorknob. "I don't know."

"Please don't judge me by one mistake. You know I was… provoked."

Kelli said nothing.

"Kelli, I still want you here. You're important to me."

"I know."

"Please give me another chance."

"Just go. Leave me alone." Kelli was frustrated by his persistence. She didn't want to talk. She wanted to run. Having him on the other side of the door, so close, was just amping her up further. He couldn't talk her down. He needed to leave her alone.

"Okay." He sighed. "I promise you I've cooled down. You're perfectly safe here. I wouldn't let anything happen to you. I'll leave you alone." His last words were strangled. "Please stay with me."

Kelli waited. Listening carefully, she thought she could hear him moving away. She slowly approached the door and pressed her ear against it. It was a thick door, and didn't let much sound through. The carpeting was thick, so she couldn't clearly hear his footsteps. All seemed silent as a tomb.

Kelli continued to clutch the bag to her. She sat on the bed, propped up against the wall like she was reading. She didn't change for bed. She didn't put the bag down. She just sat, straining to hear every sound in the house, waiting for him to come back to try to negotiate with her again, or for the doorbell to ring, admitting the police.

Even if he told the truth, they would arrest her. She had pushed him away before he had had a chance to touch her. She had thrown him to the floor without waiting for him to throw the first punch or grab her around the throat. All the police would need to know was that she had lain hands on him. Then she'd be on her way to jail.

———

She fell asleep on the bed, still sitting up, too exhausted to listen any longer. When she awoke in the early hours of the morning, it was with a crick in her neck and the emergency bag still in her arms.

Kelli got slowly to her feet and went to the door. She moved the chair out of the way and opened the door a crack to peek out. Everything was quiet. Taking a deep breath, she crept out of the bedroom into the hallway, and as silently as she could, tiptoed down the stairs and to the kitchen. The kitchen door was the closest to the garage, where her car waited for her.

It wasn't until she was most of the way to the door that she saw her father sitting at the table. She froze.

The judge's head was in his arms, on the table, where he had fallen asleep. He didn't stir. Kelli stood there, watching him, waiting for some sign of life. Her eyes adjusted to the dim kitchen light. There was no bottle or glass on the table beside him. No gun or phone laid at the ready. There was something in his hand. Kelli strained to see it. She took another step toward him, changing her line of sight.

It was a photograph.

She knew without seeing it that it was a photo of her as a newborn.

He chose the kitchen door because he was afraid that she was going to run away. He wanted one more opportunity to stop her from leaving the house. But he didn't sit there drinking himself into a rage or holding a weapon to stop her. He sat there looking at her picture, waiting to talk to her.

Kelli stood looking at him for a while, thinking. She put down her bug-out bag and put a fresh filter and grounds into the coffee maker. When the pot began to fill, Justice Emerson Forester stirred, eventually sitting up and looking around, rubbing his eyes.

He looked at Kelli. At the coffee machine. At her bag on the floor, several steps away from her.

"Morning, honey."

"Coffee will be ready soon," Kelli advised.

"Sounds good. You… okay?"

"Yeah."

He looked at the shoulder bag. "Going out somewhere?"

"No. Changed my mind."

He looked at his watch, squinting at the dial. He swore, his voice gravelly. "A little early for coffee, isn't it? Why don't you go back to bed?"

"I'm awake now. You said you wanted to talk."

He didn't say anything while she filled two mugs with coffee. She sat down, passing one of them to him.

"I won't hurt you, Kelli. I'm not a violent person."

"Anyone can be violent if they're… provoked… enough."

"No. Not anyone. I won't hurt you. Ever. You are safe here."

She didn't argue with him about how threatened she had felt when he threw the pen and then turned on her. Words were lies. Only his actions told the truth and his actions said he could lose control. Kelli sipped the hot coffee after blowing for a moment on the surface.

"I don't care what the DNA test shows," the judge said. "I still want you to stay here. I won't ever have any other children. You need a father and I want to help you, whether you carry my genes or not."

"You'll change your mind. You don't think you will, but you will. You won't see me the same way anymore. You'll see me just like you see Lisa."

"I still love Lisa too. She may not show any interest in me, in actually having a relationship instead of just a title, but I still love her. And I'm not going to feel differently about you."

Kelli took another swallow of coffee. "You set up the test and I'll do it. Then you'll know the truth."

"I promise you—"

"Don't make any promises. Just wait until the results are in."

"You'll stay here until then?"

Kelli stretched her legs out and rubbed a spot on her pants. "I do have some parties to go to," she advised him. "But other than that…"

The judge's face relaxed into a smile. "You'll need an escort to those parties."

Despite her words to him, Kelli couldn't help but feel a stab of pain at his use of 'escort' instead of 'father' or 'parent'. She gave him a smile, hiding the inconvenient emotions. "I think you're right," she agreed.

She would continue the charade until the test results were in. Then she would have to find somewhere else to live.

CHAPTER 18

Kelli searched the bustling streets for some sign of Les and his sister. She slowed down as she went by their favorite places, looking for gathering crowds or the familiar figures on the sidewalk. At least it was easier to search by car than it would have been on foot.

"Come on, Les… where are you?" she murmured aloud.

She decided to go by the library. Sometimes he hung out there. It wasn't a great place for running a game, but on a hot day, it was easy to go inside for a few minutes to get out of the sun, have a drink or refill water bottles at the fountain, and maybe check online for any events that would attract leisurely crowds happy to unload some coin for a little entertainment. And if he had Desi with him, she would probably need breaks more often than Les, not used to working the longer hours out in the sun.

Kelli slowed as she saw a girl skipping down the street. She had the trademark skinny figure, ragged clothes, and curly dark hair of the Broke family. Kelli leaned over to roll down the window on the driver's side and call out.

"Sara Jane!"

The girl turned toward her and smiled.

"Kelli!"

She skipped over to the car and looked in the window. Her smile disappeared.

"Oh. You're not Kelli."

"Yes, I am!" Kelli laughed. "Hop in, Sara Jane, I'm looking for Les. And Desi, if they're together."

"You're not Kelli," Sara Jane countered in a doubtful voice. She took a step back from the car. "I'm not getting in a car with a stranger."

"I'm not a stranger. I'm Kelli!"

"Uh-uh."

Kelli touched her face. "I had the birthmark removed," she explained. "Is that what's confusing you?"

"You couldn't have it removed," Sara Jane argued tartly. She might only be eight, but she knew what she was talking about. Kelli had been around the Broke household long enough that everybody knew she had a birthmark and that she couldn't do anything about it.

"Sara Jane!" A boy's voice snapped from nearby. "You get away from that car! What do you think you're doing?"

Sara Jane took another step back. "I didn't get in!" she protested guiltily. "I was just talking!"

"You get away from there. And you'd better get the hell away from here, you perv—" Les bent down to look in the window and broke off.

Kelli laughed. "She wouldn't even believe it was me," she told Les. "Don't give her a hard time. I told her to get in so we could go look for you, but she wouldn't."

Les looked at her, creases appearing between his brows. He blinked a few times. "Kelli? Is that really you?"

Kelli nodded. "I haven't changed *that* much," she protested. She covered up the lower right quadrant of her face with her hand. "Is that better? Will everyone believe me now?"

Les's face lit up. He pulled open the door.

"Don't get in!" Sara Jane squealed. "Les is getting in the car with a stranger! Get out, Les! It's not really Kelli!"

"Sara Jane, you go home with Desi." Les gestured in the direction he had come from, and searching the crowd, Kelli spotted Desi dawdling, dragging her feet like Les had just made her walk ten miles in tight shoes.

"Do you want me to drop them off?" Kelli offered. "We can drive them over."

"I don't think you're going to get Sara Jane in the car! They can walk."

"You sure?"

Les nodded and pulled his door shut. "Go on, you guys. Get on home."

"I'm going to tell Mom you got in the car with a stranger!"

"Go ahead. While you're at it, make sure you tell her the stranger was Kelli."

"It's not Kelli!"

Kelli laughed and pulled the car back away from the curb. "That's priceless! I can't believe she was so freaked out that I had my birthmark done."

"It *is* pretty freaky," Les said. "I'm still having a hard time believing it myself. Why didn't you tell me you had it removed? You could give a guy a heart attack!"

Kelli bit her lip and pretended to be concentrating on the traffic.

"I dunno. I guess I thought... you might think I was putting on airs or something. Pretending that I was better than I was. I haven't changed. It's just my face. Just the skin."

"It's more than that," Les said, looking her over with pursed lips. "What did you do with your hair? *And* you're wearing makeup. And new clothes."

"That's just outside stuff. So I'm dressing up a bit more. I have to, to go to parties with the judge."

"And I'm pretty sure this isn't the car you were driving when we finished the school term."

"Uh... no," Kelli admitted. She stroked the leather stitched around the steering wheel. "It might be just a wee bit nicer than what I was driving to PS2."

"Just a bit," Les snorted. "That guy is awfully generous. This pizza party you suggested... the loot bag doesn't include keys to a new car, does it? Or season's tickets to the ball game? Maybe just a cool ten thousand in cash...?"

Kelli laughed. "I couldn't say. He's a pretty generous guy. Says he'll give me anything I want. Although..." she tried to keep her expression from changing as she thought about it. "That may be changing."

"What? Why, is he running out?"

Kelli explained about the DNA testing.

———

"His wife says now that you're not his daughter?" Les demanded. "Even though his name was on your birth certificate?"

Kelli nodded. "Says they were infertile, until she hooked up with this other guy. So, I couldn't be the judge's daughter. 'Cause... he couldn't be."

"That's harsh, man," Les said shaking his head. "Why are you going along with it? Can't you just say you refuse to have the test? You're not suing him for paternity, so…?"

Kelli stopped at a light, tapping the wheel with her fingertips.

"I want to know the truth. I want him to know the truth. I don't want to just keep taking from him, if he's not really any more related to me than Axel is. I'm tired of fake dads."

"Axel I can understand, but this one's worth something. You've got it made. Just refuse the test. They can't force you."

"I don't know if they can or not," Kelli said. "There's a demand from Preston's lawyer. I don't know if I'm allowed to just say no."

"You can try."

"No." Kelli shook her head and started moving again. "I told the judge that I'd get it and I'm going to. I want him to know the truth."

Les shook his head in frustration. "What happened to my little con artist? How can you just let a mark like that go?"

"Because he's a nice guy."

"Never stopped you before."

They drove in silence for a while.

"He says that he still wants me to live with him even if I'm not his daughter."

"Yeah, right. That will go right out the window once he knows the truth." Les voiced Kelli's own assessment of the situation. "Unless… he wants you there for other reasons. Is he…" Les trailed off delicately.

Kelli's face flushed. "No!"

"You making yourself all beautiful for him… he could take it the wrong way. You go to all these fancy dinner parties with him, maybe he starts thinking of you as his date…"

"No. He doesn't see me like that. Just as a daughter. Not everybody is that twisted."

Les shrugged. "There's enough of them around. As you know."

Kelli wiped sweat away from her forehead and turned the air conditioning up. "Roll up your window, it's too hot in here."

Les glanced over at her, and complied. "You should have asked for a convertible. Then we could put the top down."

"I'm not taking advantage of him."

"What was wrong with the old car, then?"

"I… I couldn't take it to these social events. It would stick out like a sore thumb. I didn't want to embarrass him."

"Yeah." Les nodded. "Okay."

"What?" Kelli demanded. "You don't believe me?"

"I believe he's the million dollar mark we were always looking for. You found him. I'm not judging you for taking whatever he wants to give you. You've had a crap life up until now. You deserve whatever he'll give you."

"I'm not taking advantage," Kelli repeated. "He wants me to go to these parties and he wants me to look good and fit in. So, that's what I'm doing."

"Until he sees the DNA results."

"Yeah. Until then. Then I'll cut my losses."

"Do you think he'll let you keep whatever he's given you up until now? You can get some good coin for the car, your jewelry, whatever. Enough to go to college."

Kelli saw the sign for the laboratory that was to do the DNA testing and pulled into the parking lot. College. She had been looking forward to the possibility of going to college since she had first met Justice Emerson Forester. She didn't know what she wanted to take or what career path she wanted to follow. But with the loss of her new role looming before her… Les was right. She needed to hang onto the gifts that he had given her so far and make the best of them.

"Yeah. You're right."

They got out, and Les trailed Kelli into the lab. She went up to the reception desk and presented the requisition form. The nurse at the desk looked over it and nodded briskly. "That all looks to be in order. It will only take a few minutes. Can I see some identification, please?"

Kelli took her wallet from her purse and pulled out her driver's license. She passed it to the nurse.

"What do you want to do after this?" she asked Les. "You want to come see the cottage and have that pizza party? It might be your last chance."

He shrugged. "If you want."

Kelli reached to take her license back, but the nurse was holding it and looking at Kelli's face.

"What's your name?"

"Kelli Munroe."

"Birth date?"

Kelli gave it.

"When does your license expire?"

"Uh… I don't know. Two years or something like that."

The nurse tapped the plastic card on the desk, considering. "Would you have a seat, please? I'll call your name when I'm ready for you."

Kelli held her hand out for the driver's license. The nurse didn't hand it over.

"I have some more forms I need to fill out. I'll give it back to you in a few minutes."

Kelli shrugged and went over to the patient chairs to sit down. Les lowered himself into the tubular metal chair beside her.

"Did you get a new picture on your license?" he asked. "Or does it still look… like the old you?"

Kelli suddenly realized why the nurse had been so reluctant to hand the card back. She laughed. "Crap. No wonder! Cassia told me to get it replaced!"

She went back up to the desk to talk to the nurse. "I just realized the problem," she said. "I had my birthmark removed. Tattooed, actually. If you look really closely," she gestured to the border of the birthmark, "you can still see the edge of it, you see there's a bit of a color change there…"

The nurse shook her head. "I don't see anything," she said. "Please go sit back down. I'll bring it back to you when I am finished."

Kelli remained at the counter. "I don't like to let my ID out of my sight," she said. "You know about all the problems with identity theft these days."

The nurse gave her a sour look. She picked up the phone and dialed a number. When the other party answered, she introduced herself briefly. "You recently requested a DNA test," she said. "Can you describe the party who is being tested?" She tapped the end of her pen on the desk as she listened. "Is there any reason she wouldn't look like the picture on her driver's license?"

She finally hung up the phone and handed Kelli's driver's license back to her.

"Sorry for the delay, but we can't be testing the wrong person," she pointed out. "People do try to end-run paternity tests by providing samples from the wrong subject."

"Right. Okay."

"Follow me, and we'll get a swab."

———

Kelli was quiet on the way back to the cottage. She knew that she should talk with Les, ask him about how things were going with him. Keep the conversation going. But she was worried and pensive and wondered how long it would take the results to come in and put an end to her new life. Les didn't push her, watching out the window and making an occasional comment on the scenery. They left the city, and his head swiveled back and forth as he looked at the wide-open areas and clusters of trees.

"It's pretty," he commented. "You remember that camp we went to in sixth grade?"

Kelli nodded. It hadn't been the nicest camp. The grass worn away from all the foot traffic. Broken-down cabins that they hadn't even been allowed to sleep in. Setting up tents on gravel pads that it was impossible to drive stakes into or to sleep on. But it had been the only taste of wilderness the city kids had ever had, and they had drunk it up and talked about it for years after. A waypoint in their lives.

"Yeah, wait until you see his property. It's bigger than the whole camp."

She saw the familiar roads through Les's eyes, seeing it all afresh again. She was going to miss living there. The clean, fresh air, especially after a rain. The quiet roads and lack of traffic noise when she was in the house. It had all been too quiet to her to begin with, but she was getting used to it now.

She shouldn't have let herself get comfortable there. She should have known that it would all end too quickly.

Kelli turned into the long driveway. Les rolled his window down and hung his head out the window, looking around and sniffing at the fresh, green-smelling air. The cottage came into sight through the trees. Les gaped.

"Is that it? That's the cottage? Oh, man…"

Kelli nodded. "Think of the number of families we could fit in that place."

Les was used to sleeping with half a dozen children to a room. They knew houses in the neighborhood that housed entire families in each bedroom. The idea of only two people living in such a huge mansion was mind-boggling, even though Kelli had gotten used to the lifestyle.

"How many bedrooms in that place?"

"Uh… I don't actually know. Maybe… six…? The servants' quarters are separate. And that doesn't include all the extra rooms like the library, study, annex..."

"Sheesh."

They got closer, and his eyes just got bigger. Kelli remembered how she had felt walking up to the door that first day. How she had almost walked away again, too scared to find out if the judge was really her biological father. What had her plan been that day? What was it she thought she would say to him, to convince him that he might actually be her father? What if he hadn't recognized her birthmark and she had had to explain it all to him? She was glad that she hadn't had to. There were enough things that she still couldn't explain to him.

Kelli parked behind the garage rather than pulling into it. She'd be driving Les home again later, so she didn't feel the need to put the car away until then. She got out of the car. Les followed her.

"We'll go in the side."

She didn't want to take him through the huge front hall. Give him a chance to get used to it before showing him the grander areas.

Felicia was in the kitchen and looked over when Kelli came in. Her eyebrows went up at the sight of Les.

"Hey. This is my friend," Kelli introduced nervously. "Les. We thought... I think we'll order pizza tonight. I don't know what the judge had in mind..."

Felicia nodded. "That will be fine, Miss Kelli. I'll let everyone know."

Kelli pulled Les through the kitchen and the back way up to her room. He kept dawdling, stopping to look at things, and Kelli kept dragging him along. "Come on. I'll show you around later. We'll just go to my room for now..."

"This is amazing," Les said reverently. "Did you see that lamp, that was a Tiffany. And I don't think it was a reproduction. And the jade on that sideboard—"

"Okay, don't put prices on everything. Just come. You're not here to appraise the decor."

Les let her pull him along and into her room. He took a slow look around. "So this is how the filthy rich live."

Kelli shut her door. "It still looks like a guest room," she observed, looking around it. "I haven't really changed anything. It's my room, but I don't feel like… I exactly belong here. After the DNA test comes in… I guess it probably won't be anymore."

Les wandered around the generous floor space, looking at the furniture. Kelli had a few things on top of the dresser. Pieces of jewelry and odds and ends. But no personal touches. Les started pulling open the drawers of the dresser. Kelli jumped forward.

"Hey! You don't go through a girl's drawers," she protested, slapping his hand away.

Les gave her a look and kept pulling them open, shifting the clothes around to look behind and under them. Kelli's face got hot as he revealed some of the little items she had tucked away for herself, storing up for a rainy day.

"Les!"

He stopped rifling her drawers and sat on the bed, grinning at her. "I knew you weren't quite as virtuous as you've been putting on. Whatever happened to 'you're not taking advantage of him'?"

"I'm not."

"And those things just wandered into your drawers?"

Les leaned over to reopen one of the drawers and pulled out a package of cookies he had seen there. He ripped it open and helped himself, holding it out to offer one to Kelli. Kelli reluctantly took one.

"He said that whatever I want is mine," she said. "I just… put a few things away… for safekeeping. I'm not stealing, he gave it to me."

Les crunched through a couple of cookies. "Well, that's sweet of him."

Kelli stretched out on the bed. "He's not just a mark," she said. "He's my father. Or maybe he's not. But he's acted like one."

"What does your mom think of all this?"

"I dunno. I called her and left a message the other day. I haven't talked to her, and I felt kind of guilty."

"If he kicks you out…"

"I'm not going back."

"Where, then?"

"I don't know. There's gotta be a shelter or something like that."

"Foster care. Group home."

Kelli shrugged. "Yeah."

"I'd offer you a place, but you know… we're a little crowded as it is. And my mom, I don't think she's ready to take another kid in."

"No. You guys have got enough mouths to feed."

He nodded. "Maybe someone else from school? You cash in a few of your gifts… pay room and board…"

Kelli nodded. "I could pay… but I don't know anyone who would…" she trailed off. "I'm not really friends with any of the girls."

He made a casual movement toward her. "You're all girlie now. They'd accept you as one of them."

"I'm still the same person inside. I don't really want to be friends with the cheerleaders and cliques."

"There *are* other girls around," he pointed out.

"I suppose." Kelli had always focused on the popular girls, because they were the ones who tormented her. Of course, the school was full of other geeks and losers just like she was. She could make friends with one of them, find someone who was willing to give her a room or a half a room for some cash.

"You might as well be thinking about it now. Be ready for when he decides it's time for you to leave."

"I know." Kelli sighed. "I was just getting used to being here."

"Maybe one of your new socialite friends would help you out."

Kelli thought about Cassia and the other girls that she had met at the summer events so far. She couldn't see any of them helping her. She just saw Lisa's sneer and pout, and figured that was how any of them would view her imposing on them. Cassia had been decent to her. But would she help out with something as big as giving her a place to live? Once they found out she didn't actually belong, none of them were going to want her within their spheres. She had been putting on a good act so far, but everyone was working under the assumption that she at least had the right genealogy. When they found out that she didn't have the right blood after all, she would no longer be welcomed. They might express their dismay at her fall from grace, but no one would pick her up again. They would know that she came from the slums and that was where she belonged.

"Wait a minute…"

Kelli recognized the gleam in Les's eye. The gleam that meant he had just figured out a brilliant new con. Something that was going to be lucrative.

"You're missing the whole angle here. You've completely missed it."

Kelli frowned. "What are you talking about?"

"Your biological parents."

Kelli stared at him. "That's why I'm here. That's what we're talking about. If it turns out that the judge isn't my biological father... it's all over."

Les snickered. "You still *have* a biological father."

Kelli closed her eyes. If the judge wasn't her biological father, then he was still out there somewhere. Preston had been with someone. Kelli hadn't just appeared out of nowhere. But who was the mysterious man? Kelli really didn't want to waste her time tracking down yet another parent. What would the next one be like?

"Okay, yeah. But only Preston knows who that might be."

"*She* has money, doesn't she?"

"Yeah... but she doesn't want anything to do with me."

"What difference does that make? She is still your biological parent. She didn't give you up for adoption. She didn't lose custody. There's, like, sixteen years of child support due."

"No..."

"Yes," Les insisted. "One or both of your parents owe you child support. They haven't done anything for you for sixteen years. That will be a nice little lump-sum payment that you can put away for college, and then they need to provide ongoing support for the next two years."

"Preston doesn't work. I don't think."

"She still has money, doesn't she?" Les crunched another cookie and continued to speak with his mouth full. "If she doesn't want to pay, she'll have to name the father."

"It could be anyone. Right from the pool boy to another judge or senator."

"That's right," Les agreed, grinning. "Either she pays to keep it quiet, or she names him and he does. If they refuse, then you leave it to the courts to sort it out."

Kelli flipped over onto her back and stared at the ceiling. "You are devious, Les."

"No more so than you," he said modestly. "You're just out of practice. You haven't been exercising your grade A con skills for a couple of months. You've gotten rusty."

"Seriously rusty."

Kelli's brain had shifted into high gear. It didn't matter that Preston hated her. It was the law. A parent had to support their child. Preston had as much as admitted that Kelli was her biological daughter. And Justice Emerson Forester had insisted that Preston's DNA be included in the testing, to avoid any further issues. When the tests came back, they would have proof that Preston was her mother. If Preston didn't want the judge to support Kelli for fear that it would reduce Lisa's eventual inheritance, then she would have to take over the child support herself. Or name the father. If it would be too much of a social embarrassment to name Kelli's biological father, then they were back to Preston paying support herself. It was only a drop in the bucket, compared to the loss of all of the judge's estate.

Kelli smiled to herself. She was sure that Preston hadn't foreseen this wrinkle when she had set out to prove that Justice Emerson Forester was not Kelli's biological father.

Of course, Kelli didn't want to live with Preston, and she was sure Preston wouldn't want Kelli to live with her, but all the little details could be worked out. Preston could pay for a good boarding school or get Kelli an apartment somewhere.

Kelli wouldn't have to be out on the street after all.

———

Kelli was back in good spirits by dinner time. She was grateful she had invited Les over, so that Les could help her to sort things out. It was a big relief to know that she wouldn't be back with Axel and Patricia or out on the cold hard street by herself. The best con ever was one that the courts would enforce.

She figured they would just eat in the kitchen or out in the garden where they would be out of the way, but the judge insisted that they all eat together in the dining room.

"I want to meet your friend, Kelli. And I like a good slice now and then myself."

"We don't want to be in the way," Kelli protested. "This is just casual. And I told you, he's not my boyfriend."

Justice Emerson Forester smiled. "That's how it always starts," he intoned. "It doesn't have to be a formal affair. I'll dress down and we'll just throw the boxes on the table. Throw a bag of chips and a bottle of pop in for good measure. I promise not to grill your young man."

"He isn't my young man!"

"Bring him down to the dining room," the judge insisted. "I'm not backing down on this. I want to meet him and spend a little time together."

"To convince yourself of his intentions?"

"You explain it however you like. I want to meet the boy. And after a long day at the office, I want to enjoy my daughter's company, not have her hiding in some corner like she's up to no good."

Kelli sighed and gave in. She went back upstairs to explain the situation to Les, and when they saw the pizza delivery car drive up, they headed downstairs to the dining room.

"So, this is Les," the judge said. "Kelli has mentioned you a number of times. I'm glad to get the chance to meet you."

"Uh, good to meet you… sir."

Justice Emerson Forester looked at Kelli, and then back at Les. "Mr. Forester would be fine," he said. "It seems like the least formal option. I know kids often refer to their friends' parents by their first names, but it always grates on me. And I don't know that Justice is any better than Judge Forester or Your Honor."

Les grinned and nodded. "Mr. Forester, then."

"I think Kelli's still trying to figure out what's comfortable for her," the judge said, as if Kelli weren't right there to hear him. "She already has a 'dad,' and like I say, Justice is a bit pretentious. 'Hey, you' seems to cover it for now."

Kelli's face burned. She was quite sure that she had never called him 'hey, you,' but he was right; she still didn't know how to address him. She was embarrassed that he had noticed her awkwardness over the issue.

"Father?" Les suggested. "Pops?"

Kelli opened up the pizza boxes, not looking at either of them. "Let's wait and see the results of the test first, why don't we?" she said.

Justice Emerson Forester looked like he had had a glass of cold water thrown in his face. He grimly took a slice of pepperoni pizza out of one of the boxes and laid it on his plate.

"It's okay," Kelli insisted. "It will all work out. It will. I'm just saying… let's not get ahead of ourselves on the name thing."

The judge opened his mouth to respond, then looked at Les and kept his argument to himself. "Of course," he agreed. "I don't mean to be pushy." He met Kelli's eyes. "It *will* work out."

"I know," she agreed.

CHAPTER 19

Kelli looked around the deck area of Judge Conroy's house. She had already been introduced to or said hello to all the people that Justice Emerson Forester wanted her to speak to, and he had been cornered by Judge Conroy's mother-in-law, who wanted his opinion on some convoluted estate issue. So Kelli was free to wander and talk to whoever she wanted to.

Across the pool from her, Kelli spotted Lisa. Preston and the judge hadn't coordinated events to keep them from showing up at the same thing together. Or maybe Preston had intentionally shown up at the same event to try to crowd Kelli out or to prove that Kelli didn't fit in like Lisa did.

Kelli walked around the pool until she stood in front of Lisa, who was chatting with a couple of friends. Lisa had a nice figure and was dressed in a peach bikini that complemented her shape and skin tone. Kelli was feeling awkward in a one-piece with a sheer toga-style cover-up over top, but Lisa rocked the bikini, looking completely confident and unselfconscious.

Lisa's mouth twisted into a sneer when she realized who Kelli was. She stared at Kelli's now-flawless face and shook her head. "What do *you* want?"

"Is your mom around? I didn't know you guys would be here, but I want to talk to her."

"We've known Judge Conroy since I was a baby. We have more of a right to be here than you do."

"I'm glad you're here," Kelli said with a serene smile. "Is Preston here too?"

Lisa didn't like her reaction. She glanced around. "She's here somewhere. But she won't want to talk to you."

"Doesn't really matter what she wants. Sooner or later she's going to have to deal with this." Kelli gave her another smile. "She *is* my biological mother, after all."

"Why don't you just get lost?" Lisa hissed. "No one wants you around here! You're just messing everything up. Go back to the slums, orphan."

"I think you're getting your terms mixed up. An orphan's parents are dead. Mine are still very much alive. There's a different word for illegitimate children. And for women who fool around while they're still married to someone else." Kelli raised her eyebrows and waited to see if Lisa would be confident enough to amend her insult in front of her friends.

But Lisa just got white and turned away from Kelli. "I said why don't you just go back to the slums," she said poisonously.

Kelli watched Lisa retreat with her sidekicks. She looked around for Preston. She wandered around the pool and through the pool house and the patio where the hors d'oeuvres were set out. Preston was there, speaking to a couple of women her age who Kelli couldn't identify. There were so many people for her to meet, so much for her to learn about. It was exhausting to remember all the names and details of everyone's lives.

Preston saw Kelli waiting patiently nearby and scowled. She continued to talk to the other ladies for some time. Eventually, she broke away from them and tried to make a break for it. Kelli darted across the pavement to catch up to her.

"Wait, Preston! I want to talk to you."

"I have nothing to say to you," Preston snapped.

"Please stop and talk to me. You don't want me to make a scene, do you?"

Preston hesitated, then stopped. She whirled around to face Kelli. "I told you I have nothing to say to you. I don't even know what you're doing here. It's not like Justice is that good of a friend with Judge Conroy."

Kelli shrugged. "I wouldn't know anything about that. I just came because he said he wanted me to be here."

"The girls are out by the pool. You should be hanging out with them."

"With Lisa?" Kelli was surprised to hear Preston make the suggestion.

"No, not with Lisa. There are other girls. Girls who aren't *friendly* with Lisa."

"I want to talk to you," Kelli repeated.

"What is it?" Preston glared at her, finally looking at her now-birthmark-free face for the first time and meeting her eyes boldly.

Kelli took a deep breath. Now that she had the chance, she wasn't sure how to start. "I submitted my sample for the DNA test," she said. "They said it would just be a few days to get back to us."

"Good. I look forward to the results," Preston said with a nasty smile.

"Me too," Kelli said. "I guess if the judge isn't my parent, and you are, you'll be taking over on child support."

Preston's brows arched up. "What?"

"If he's not my father, like you said. Then I guess that just leaves you."

"Leaves me to what? I'm not your parent."

"Biologically. You gave your DNA swab for a maternity test, didn't you? So that will prove that I'm your biological daughter. I'm glad the test won't take too long, because I have to know where I'm going to be living in the fall. With the judge, or with you. I need to register for school and everything."

"Not with either of us. You can go back to that dreadful house in the slums. With your mother. Just go back to where you came from."

"But *they* don't have any responsibility to take care of me. *You* are my biological parent. So, I can come to your place."

Preston's eyes were wide with fury. "You will not be coming anywhere near me or my house. You stay away from me and my daughter."

"You could send Lisa to my old house," Kelli offered. "Since that's where *her* biological mother is. They can take care of her."

Preston struggled for composure. She obviously didn't want a big scene in front of her socialite friends, so she did her best to keep her voice low and not to broadcast to everyone else at the party what they were arguing about.

"You will stay away from me and my daughter," Preston whispered. "We are not going to have anything to do with you."

"There are laws about child support. We could ask the judge, if you're not sure what they are."

"You are a despicable child," Preston hissed. "What do you think your precious judge will have to say when I tell him you are trying to blackmail me?"

"Who said blackmail?" Kelli asked innocently. "I have rights under the law. You can't just abandon your child and refuse to care for her."

"I have cared for my daughter. And I gave—and it was your mother's responsibility to look after you. Not mine. I have no use for you."

Kelli gave a little shrug. "I guess we'll see what the DNA test says. Do you remember the name of this man you slept with? Maybe we'll have to advertise for him, if you want him to chip in on child support."

Preston's fists clenched and Kelli knew that she was barely keeping herself under control. Another prod or two was all it would take for the pressure to build beyond what she could control, and Preston would erupt. Never get between a mother bear and her cub.

Kelli didn't actually want Preston to hit her or shove her into the pool, so she took a step back. She gave Preston a sweet smile.

"I'll be seeing you around. I'm sure the judge will call you when the DNA results are in. Maybe we can have dinner again."

She took another quick step backward before Preston could haul off and punch her in the teeth. As she walked away, she saw Justice Emerson Forester turn away from the conversation with Judge Conroy's mother in law. He scanned the crowd, his eyes meeting Kelli's. Kelli hesitated, then decided there was no point in putting it off and went back over to him.

The judge's eyes were on his estranged wife. He turned to Kelli. "What did you say to Preston?"

Kelli scratched the back of her neck. The beach cover-up was rough and itchy against her skin. "What makes you think I said something to her?"

"I saw you talking to her. And I don't know if I've ever seen her look like that! I thought Cassia was giving you pointers on socially acceptable behavior…" His lips twitched.

Kelli gave him her innocent doe eyes. "I was just reminding my mother that she'd be responsible for child support if you aren't my biological father."

His eyes widened and he choked. Kelli looked around for a waiter and grabbed him a drink. Justice Emerson Forester took a couple of gulps. His eyes were tearing up in the corners. He snorted once.

"You were, were you?" He shook his head and wiped at his eyes. "Well, I can see how that went over." He looked around at the guests at the party. "Do you know… I think I've seen everybody I absolutely had to speak with. It might be a good idea for us to leave early."

"You don't want to stay for dinner? I hear Judge Conroy cooks a mean barbecue."

"I just remembered there's a restaurant near here that I wanted to check out. Doesn't that sound good?"

"I really don't think she's going to bother you," Kelli said, looking back over at Preston, who was shooting laser-beam glares in their direction. "She didn't seem like she was particularly talkative today."

"Come on, Kelli."

He put his hand under her arm and gently tugged her back toward the main entrance. A couple of people stopped them on their way out, expressing surprise over their early departure, but the judge merely reported that an emergency had come up. They got back into his car and headed for home.

———

Things were quiet for a couple of days. Kelli was anxious about the test results, wishing that they would just come in. Having her future up in the air was unnerving, even if she figured that she could still survive without going back to Patricia and Axel or sleeping on the street. She just wanted not to have it hanging over her head.

The judge seemed irritable and on edge as well. He tried not to show it, but Kelli saw the signs, and that made her even more anxious. They didn't have an exact ETA on the test results, just the expected window.

They were having dinner when Justice Emerson Forester's phone rang, and though he was usually quite strict about not answering the phone or dealing with business at the table, he slid it out to glance at the screen. He avoided Kelli's eyes and put it up to his ear.

"Yes, Forester here."

He nodded as the caller identified himself. Kelli waited for the announcement, watching the judge's face for clues.

"Yes… yes…"

Suddenly, relief flooded the judge's features and he broke into a wide grin. The knot in Kelli's stomach relaxed. He reached over to her and squeezed her hand. He thanked the caller repeatedly and hung up.

"She was wrong." He told Kelli what she had already guessed. "I am confirmed as your biological father. And Preston is confirmed as your biological mother."

Kelli blew out her breath in relief and sat back in her chair. "Are you going to call her? I'll bet she's relieved now that you *are* my father."

He laughed. "I can't believe that you told her you were going after her for child support."

Kelli shrugged. "It seemed like a good idea."

Her father reached over and took her hand again, giving it another squeeze. "Now will you believe that you are going to stay here, and I'm not going to turn you out into the street?"

Kelli rubbed the back of her head and neck, trying to massage away the tight muscles. "It would have been different if the results were different," she asserted. "You would have felt differently then."

"Well, I guess we'll never know."

"I guess."

"So, can we talk about school and future plans?"

"Yeah… I guess. But I still don't want to go to the same school as Lisa."

"No, I don't think that would be a good idea," he agreed, grinning again. "You seem to have slightly different personalities…"

Kelli laughed.

"She's very much like Preston. You're more like me," the judge said.

Kelli felt warm. Not her face, like when she was embarrassed, but inside. It felt good. "You think I'm like you?"

"Well, you're an individual, obviously. But we get each other's sense of humor. I can see myself in you. And in your face… my mother, my sister…"

"Really?"

"I kept telling myself that I was just seeing what I wanted to see. But now that the results are in… I can say it aloud. You are my daughter. You're more like me than Lisa ever will be, even though I helped to raise her. I guess some things really are… nature, not nurture."

Kelli scratched her ear, trying not to smile too broadly. Patricia and Axel had never said anything about Kelli taking after anyone or showing any family traits. She had never felt a sense of belonging to them. Her home was her home, and her family was her family, but she didn't feel a connection with them. What passed between her and the judge was electric. She thrilled at his words.

"I also think that you're very smart," he said. "You pick things up quickly. You watch and listen and make quick decisions. For me, those things come naturally. They don't seem like a big deal, because they're just part of who I am. But when you spend some time around other people who don't have those talents… they become more obvious."

Kelli had always thought that the kids she went to school with just didn't apply themselves. Students like Les didn't put the effort into it. They didn't want to do the work required. Didn't pay enough attention. But maybe it did just come more easily to her.

"Yeah, I guess."

"Which brings us back again to the question of school."

CHAPTER 20

Kelli looked in the mirror and smoothed her skirt. She hated mirrors. Somehow, when she got the birthmark removed, she had thought that mirrors wouldn't bother her anymore. She'd finally be able to look in the mirror like a normal person and not be disgusted by what she saw.

But it wasn't as easy as that.

She still saw the birthmark when she looked in the mirror. It was fainter, but she still knew where it was, hiding just below the ink. She kept having nightmares about waking up, and looking in the mirror to discover it was back again, just as brilliant as ever. Or that she went swimming, and the tattoo ink washed off. Or that she went walking in the sun, and it melted off. Every time she looked in the mirror, she expected to see the mark back again.

She felt like a fraud. Walking around with somebody else's face. Funny, despite her life as a con, it was the first time she felt like a fraud. She wasn't true to herself.

Kelli tried to push all thoughts of her birthmark and her now-clear, unmarked face to the side to consider the rest of the image she saw in the full-length mirror. She wasn't used to wearing a school uniform. Uniforms would have made more sense at her old school, where there were such gaps between the haves and the have-nots. Maybe it would have eliminated some of the rivalry between those who could barely keep body and soul together and those who were comfortably off. They would all look the same, at least. At Central, the new school, everyone was well-off. The uniforms didn't need to eliminate class distinctions.

She felt like an imposter in the uniform. Or like she was wearing a Halloween costume. Who was that girl in the mirror? She didn't think that wearing a uniform would be such a big deal when the judge had told her about the dress code at Central. It just meant that she already knew what she was going to be wearing in the morning. Every school day morning. She hadn't foreseen the fight she would have with herself each morning as she got ready for school, telling herself that she didn't belong. She did belong. She was one of them. She just had to fake it until she got used to it. At least that was something she was good at.

Kelli slid a finger behind the waist of her skirt, trying to stretch it out and loosen it. Everything seemed to be getting too tight. She was going to have to get her eating under control. She had never had to worry about her weight before. When food was scarce, overeating was not a problem. Now that she had all the food she wanted at every meal, she was going to have to learn some self-control. Or she was going to be in XXXL clothes by the end of the year.

"You look nice in your uniform."

Startled, Kelli looked up and saw Felicia standing in the doorway. Kelli breathed out and unclenched her fists.

"Thanks," she said curtly.

"Breakfast is ready, miss."

Kelli glanced at her watch. She was overdue for breakfast, which was why the judge had sent Felicia to find out what was holding Kelli up. "Sorry. Tell him I'll be right down."

———

Kelli only planned to have a bit of fruit and toast for breakfast, but everything looked so good she couldn't hold herself back. It was a long time until lunch.

"How are things going?" Justice Emerson Forester asked. "You haven't had much to say about the new school."

Kelli had no idea what to tell him about it. She shrugged. "Okay, I guess. It's school."

"How are you finding the work?"

"Hard to say yet. They're just starting the post-summer work. Getting everyone warmed up for the real thing." Kelli spread a thick layer of jam over her toast. "I'm glad I did the tutoring. I'd be really nervous about how hard all the teachers are saying it's going to be, if I hadn't already studied it…"

"Good. I know you didn't exactly want to do anything over the summer, but hopefully it has given you a head start. If you have problems with anything during the year, let me know right away, and we'll get a tutor to address it. It's best if you don't wait until you're behind."

"Yeah. Okay."

"And you're making some friends?"

"I know a few people from the events over the summer."

If her father noticed that she hadn't directly answered the question, he gave no sign. "Good. I know you must miss the kids from your old school. You can invite them over if you like…"

"Not really. There's Les." She thought about Lizzie and the other bullies and troublemakers. "I didn't… socialize… much."

"Well, you're welcome to have Les over if you like. I know it's a pain being so far from your old neighborhood here…" He stared off into the distance. "But there are a lot of benefits to living here."

"I like Forester Cottage," Kelli hurried to assure him. "I wouldn't want to go back to living in the city… not where I was, anyway. I miss seeing Les… but he needs to be close to his family too. He has a lot of brothers and sisters, and has to kind of keep an eye on things."

"It's good of him to be so responsible. But I'm sure there are times he could arrange to be away, like when he visited us before."

"Yeah." Kelli remembered Les going through her drawers, and wasn't sure how soon she would be inviting him back again. She didn't like people touching her things. And she hadn't done a proper inventory, but she thought that a couple of smaller items might have walked off when he was there. She didn't blame him for it, and was sure no one would miss a couple of knick-knacks. The judge had said that whatever she wanted was hers, which would mean she could give them to whoever she wanted. But she didn't appreciate being stolen from. Even though she might have done the same, had their positions been switched.

The judge looked at his watch. "It's late and I have coffee with Sigmund before court this morning. I'd better get on my way. You'll get yourself to school?"

Kelli got herself to school every other day. She shrugged and nodded. "Yeah. See you tonight."

"I'll be late. I have that museum fundraiser."

"Oh, yeah," Kelli was disappointed she wouldn't be seeing him. It meant supper by herself. Even though she'd always been happy to eat alone at home, without Patricia and Axel within striking distance, she had come to enjoy having meals with her father.

"I did invite you to come," the judge reminded her. "You were worried about not having enough time to get your homework done."

"Yeah. You go ahead, I'll be busy."

He hesitated. "I could tell them I'll be bringing a guest. One person won't make that much difference to the numbers."

"No. Thanks. I'll see you when you get back. Hopefully, I'll be all done my schoolwork, and we can read or turn on the TV."

"Okay." He bent over and kissed her forehead. "See you tonight, then."

As he left, Kelli slurped down the last of her eggs and looked at her own watch. It was getting pretty late. If she didn't want a tardy, she knew she had to get on her way as well.

———

Traffic was good, and Kelli still got to school in good time. She parked her car and walked to her locker, hurrying just a little.

"Thought you were sick today," Daffodil commented, as Kelli spun the combination lock. "You're usually here by now."

"I *am* here now," Kelli pointed out.

"Yeah, but I mean... earlier."

Kelli grunted an acknowledgment. She glanced over at Daffodil.

Daffodil was not the delicate flower her name might have suggested. They had met at the Fourth of July party, and while Kelli couldn't say that they had hit it off, exactly, they did seem to get on together. Daffodil was not the cheerleader type, in the popular cliques. She was overweight, into counterculture films, and didn't fit in very well. Kelli was an outsider because of how recently she had arrived on the scene, and didn't fit into their norms. The two of them, while not exactly rejects, were definitely second-class citizens. It meant that they could talk, but they didn't hang out together outside of classes. Just nodding acquaintances.

"What, did I spill something?" Daffodil looked down at her blouse.

"No. Sorry. I was just off in my own little world," Kelli apologized. "Not looking at you or anything."

Daffodil brushed at invisible crumbs. Kelli ran her thumb along the inside of her waistband to try to relieve the pressure. She really shouldn't have had so much for breakfast when her clothes were already feeling tight.

"You two pigs have breakfast together?" A popular girl named Laura, blond, tall and willowy, sniped at them as she walked by.

Daffodil and Kelli looked at each other and both stopped what they were doing. Daffodil's face flushed.

"At least I'm not sticking my finger down my throat," she retorted.

Laura stopped and looked Daffodil up and down. "Obviously not," she agreed.

Daffodil looked like she was going to take Laura's head off. Kelli laid a hand on her arm. She wasn't going to get in between them, but she didn't want Daffodil to end up in trouble.

"Is it worth getting suspended?" she asked Daffodil.

The bigger girl looked back at her, face still red, struggling for control. She really wanted to pound Laura. But finally, she relaxed and nodded. She turned her back on Laura and dug into her locker, blocking out any further communication.

"You might try cutting back on the carbs," Laura needled. "The two of you might not want to both get on the elevator at the same time."

Kelli and Daffodil just waited. Eventually, Laura laughed and moved on. The first warning bell rang. "Ignore her," Kelli advised.

"I know I should. She's not worth getting upset over. But it drives me crazy. Doesn't she think I'd lose weight if I could?"

"No. I don't think she cares."

"You're right there."

Kelli stacked her books up with a sigh, ready to head to her first class.

"And you're not fat," Daffodil told her. "I don't know what she's talking about. You may not be skinny like her, but you're just... curvy. It's nice. I don't think girls who are stick thin look very good."

Daffodil turned and walked off toward her first-period class. Kelli watched her go, her brain clumsily trying to process what had just happened.

She knew she was gaining weight. That was to be expected when after so many years she suddenly had enough food to eat. Pretty much whenever she wanted to eat it. But Laura calling her a fat pig stung, even if she didn't think it was true. She wasn't going to waste her time worrying about what someone like Laura had to say.

But Daffodil was a different story. Kelli was *curvy?* She had never been called such a thing in her life. Curvy? Kelli looked at her face in her locker mirror. Of course, it was tiny, so she couldn't see anything else. Couldn't see what her body looked like. But her face had rounded out. It wasn't just the lack of the birthmark and her new hair and makeup that made her look different. So different that Les's sisters hadn't even believed it was her. Part of it was her weight too. She hadn't exactly been watching what she ate.

That was going to have to change. She wasn't going to get a new school uniform. She wasn't going to have people telling her she was just chunky or hefty or big-boned. All of that would follow curvy.

———

Since the judge was gone, Kelli took her dinner in her bedroom. Felicia brought it by, and hung around for a few minutes to see if Kelli wanted some company. But Kelli waved her off.

"Sorry, I have a bunch of homework I need to get started on," she explained. "I know it's rude, but I'd rather get it done now so I can spend some time with… my father… later on."

"You don't have to give me any explanation," Felicia said quickly. "I just wanted you to know I was around if you wanted some company."

"Yeah, thanks. But not today."

Felicia nodded and left Kelli alone with her dinner tray. Kelli carved a small portion out of what was on her plate and tried to eat just that. She didn't have to go on any special diet or count calories. She would just eat a little less than what she had been. It wouldn't be a quick weight loss, but she didn't want people to notice and think that she was dieting. Just something slow and gradual so that nobody would notice and it wouldn't be too uncomfortable for her.

But she couldn't stop when she got to the self-imposed cut-off point.

She was still hungry, and the food was really good. Kelli pushed it away to work on her homework. They said that your stomach didn't know when you were full until twenty minutes had passed. She would wait twenty minutes and then see if she were really hungry or not. It made sense on the surface, but the food kept calling to her. Kelli couldn't stop picking at it. Just a little bit… until it was all gone but two bites. At that point, she made herself stand up, and she took the plate to the bathroom and flushed the last two bites.

It wasn't very much, but it was a start. Baby steps.

She sat down and tried again to focus on her homework. But she knew that she had cookies and some other nonperishable foods in her drawers, in case of emergency, and she couldn't stop thinking about them.

"Shut up and focus on your work," Kelli snapped aloud. "No more whining."

She had managed okay when she was at home and there was so little food in the house. She had accepted hunger as a part of life and just went ahead and did her work, empty stomach or not. But it was different knowing that food was there, just waiting for her.

Before she had finished her algebra, the cookies were gone.

———

She kept telling herself that she was hungry and being distracted by food, but once the food was out of the way, Kelli realized that she was not just having trouble with the algebra because she was hungry or distracted. She really had no idea what she was supposed to do. It might as well have all been Greek.

She sat staring at the exercise questions. Then she looked at the answer key in the back of the book. She had the answers, but she still didn't know how to get there. She went back to the beginning of the chapter in the textbook and read through it again, trying to work through the sample questions and the explanation of each step. It sounded easy when she read the text, it sounded like it was obvious and there was only one answer and one way to get to that answer. But when she looked at the exercise again, she still couldn't get it. Another half hour passed, and she was still no closer to getting the answers than she had been to start with.

She pushed the math to the side and instead started in on her history work.

Kelli had always liked history. Liked hearing the stories and about the people who had played parts in it. She sometimes imagined kids learning details about her own life. How she had grown up in the slums, but because she had worked hard and was determined, she had overcome all the odds and had… done something of lasting importance. Someday they would be learning about her.

But Central used a names-and-dates approach, expecting the students to memorize all of the flashcard facts, rather than being able to discuss the larger picture. They were expected to know the larger picture as well, but to be able to back it up with facts. Lots of facts and figures. Kelli figured if she worked on memorizing for twenty minutes every night, she would be able to acquire all the facts that she needed by the time final exams rolled around.

She already knew a lot of things; it shouldn't be hard to memorize a few facts every night. And to retain them. And be able to remember the right ones when she needed to make a reasoned argument.

Kelli sighed and started to write out facts on index cards. She had started out with the plan to memorize twenty facts every night, but that had turned out to be way too lofty a goal. She needed time to herself too. Time to relax and spend with her family. School wasn't supposed to take up all her time.

She still had an English essay to write too. She didn't know what level of work the teachers were expecting or how much of her grade it would count for. It was the first major English language arts assignment since the summer, so they couldn't be expecting too much. They still had to get back into the swing of things.

At least at PS2, she knew how things would be graded. Sometimes there were new teachers who had different ideas, but most of her teachers had been there for years, and everyone knew exactly what was expected.

She could call Daffodil or one of the other girls to find out how Mrs. Henry graded. She didn't want to put too much time and effort into it if it turned out that Mrs. Henry was an easy grader. Or if Mrs. Henry expected to see a lot of improvement over the term, Kelli would be shooting herself in the foot if she came up with something too well-written right out of the gates.

Kelli grabbed her new little laptop and opened it up. She was so excited to have her own computer that she could use at home, making a trip to the library to use their internet unnecessary. She didn't have Daffodil's number, but it probably wouldn't be hard to find. The judge had shared his contacts list with her, which included most of the social contacts in the area, and Mrs. Wickham was bound to be on the list. But she might not like Kelli calling her daughter when she should be working on her schoolwork, so it would be better if Kelli could find her cell number or send her an instant message through one of the social media sites. She opened a browser window and started searching through them.

The next thing she knew, Kelli heard Justice Emerson Forester's car coming down the drive. She looked up from the computer to the clock and realized that an hour and a half had passed as she messed around and chased down rabbit holes. An hour and a half with nothing to show for it. No memorized history facts. No contact with Daffodil. No essay. And no idea what to do about the algebra.

Kelli closed her computer firmly and looked at the stack of schoolbooks. She would tell the judge that she would join him in the library in half an hour. That would give her enough time to put together an outline and a few sources for the essay. She'd read and visit with her father for a while, but beg off saying that she was tired and needed to get to bed so that she'd be bright-eyed and bushy-tailed for school the next morning. Then she would write the first draft of the essay. If it were good, maybe it would only take one draft. If not, she'd have to get up early enough to rewrite it before class.

CHAPTER 21

It was late when Kelli's phone rang, yanking her rudely out of a sound sleep. All of her studying and homework were tiring, and it felt good to get to bed at the end of the day. Getting up in the morning was hard, but sometimes when she hadn't been able to get everything done in the evening, it meant setting her alarm and getting up long before she was ready to.

But it wasn't an alarm or calendar alert that had awakened her. It was a phone call. Kelli fumbled for her phone and pulled it out. It was supposed to be on 'do not disturb' at night. Any calls would go directly to voicemail, unless they were on her exceptions list. And there was next to no one on her exceptions list. Exactly who would she want calling her in the middle of the night?

Kelli blinked blearily, trying to focus on the information on the screen. It wasn't Les, the first person she had thought of when her phone rang. Of course it wouldn't be the judge, because he was already home and in bed. Kelli pressed the green 'talk' button.

"Mom?"

"Kelli...?" Patricia's voice was thready, close to tears. Obviously, she was in her cups, but not enough to black out yet.

"Mom, what's wrong? Is everything okay?"

"How could everything be okay?" Patricia wept. "My own daughter hates me and doesn't want anything to do with me. You never call, you never come home…"

Kelli didn't bother to point out that this was the first time that Patricia had tried to contact her in the months since she'd moved into Forester Cottage. The first time she had bothered to pick up the phone to talk to her daughter. And the only reason she had done it was that she was drunk, and maybe she had watched an episode of 48 Hours with a missing girl.

"I'm here now, Mom. What do you want?"

"I want my life back! I want back everything I had before. You probably think I can't remember being your age, but I can. I remember what it was like. I had a home. I had a part-time job. Everybody knew who I was and said hello to me."

"Yeah? Are you looking for another job? I can help you, if you want."

"I had a family!" Patricia hollered. Kelli pulled the phone away from her ear, wincing.

"Of course you had a family," she agreed. "And you still have a family. I'm not dead, Mom. I'm just not living there anymore. You didn't want me there."

"I never told you to move out. I never said I didn't want you here."

"Yes, you did."

Patricia couldn't prove it either way. Maybe she had told Kelli to go and had just forgotten about it, or maybe Kelli was telling stories, Patricia couldn't know the difference. Kelli had always been able to lie her way out of things.

"I want you home," Patricia insisted. "I need you. I need you here." She moaned, sounding like a cow giving birth.

"What do you need help with? I can come by and help you later."

"I don't want help later, I want you to come home now," Patricia protested in a wail.

"I'll come and visit you after school tomorrow. How would that be?"

"You come here now!"

"Mom, it's—" Kelli pulled the phone away from her ear to look at the time, then returned it. "It's three o'clock in the morning, Mom. I can't come over right now. Do you think you can tell me what's the matter?"

"The matter is that you're living with some man I don't even know. I raised you better than that! You know better than to go shacking up with some boy!"

Kelli laughed. "I'm not shacking up with anyone. I'm living with my biological father. No boyfriends. No sex. Just living with him like I lived with you. So you get a break now. Aren't you enjoying your break?" she wheedled.

"It's not a break. There's no one here to… to help me with anything. All of the cooking, the cleaning. Do you know how much work I have to put into this house and taking care of Axel? Your father is not well, you know. He's not well in the head and he's not an easy guy to take care of."

"I know that," Kelli agreed. "Did he hit you? You call the police and get them to throw him in jail for the night. Don't just let him beat you up."

"You don't know what it's like…"

"I know exactly what it's like," Kelli growled. "Why do you think I'm not living there? Why do you think I spent so much time practicing Jujitsu? Because I got tired of people whaling on me. I decided I wasn't going to stand there and take it anymore."

"I'm not strong like you are. I can't learn all that karate stuff. I have a brain injury, you know. From all those concussions over the years. Always getting beaten up. The social worker and Axel say that I'm forgetting things. I'm not, but if I was, it would be because of the concussions. There was a movie on the TV about hockey players…"

"That's right," Kelli agreed. She yawned, pulling the phone away from her face as she stretched, and then putting it back up to her ear, listening to Patricia ramble on about her sad life and how everything was going down the crapper. But Kelli already knew that. It had already been swirling around the bowl when Kelli had left. "I'll try to come and see you after school tomorrow, okay? Will you be there? You don't have any doctor's appointments?"

"How would I know if I have any appointments? They're supposed to call me to remind me."

"Okay. What about Axel? Has he got a job yet?"

"He can't get a job any more than I can. He's an ex-con with brain damage. Who wants an ex-con with brain damage doing work for them? Even if it's just carrying lumber around, he could kill someone. They don't know."

Kelli considered. If she went by right after school, then hopefully Axel would not be too drunk. She couldn't leave it until later in hopes that he would be passed out. She couldn't take the chance of being stuck in the neighborhood after it started to get dark. Especially not with her new car. She'd have to find somewhere decent to park it and walk in. She rubbed her forehead. Things were getting complicated.

Patricia was still going on about how awful her life was. Like she hadn't noticed how bad it was before Kelli had left. Kelli hadn't made it any better, she had just lived there and suffered through it like everyone else.

———

When she awoke the next morning, she was still lying with her face on the phone, in the same position she had been talking to Patricia in. She wondered which one of them had fallen asleep or ended the call first. The phone was damp with sweat and saliva. Kelli mopped it off with her pajamas and then stumbled to the bathroom to start getting ready for her day.

Once her teeth were brushed and her hair combed, she sat down in front of the computer. She knew she didn't have long before she had to go down to breakfast. She looked at the clock, told herself only fifteen minutes, and logged into her social networks.

At first, she didn't notice anything unusual. Then Kelli stared, looking at a list of messages that had been posted with her picture and name, that she had never posted. Had someone hacked her account? She clicked on one of the posts, and it went not to her account, but to a new one someone had set up. Same name, same picture, but it wasn't her account.

Kelli tried to log in, but it wouldn't accept her password. Because it wasn't her account. She knew that, but she was panicking. She didn't want anyone thinking that those posts were actually hers. Her cyber friends would know that she wasn't like that, wouldn't they? She wouldn't be blamed for someone else's posts.

She clicked on the site's 'contact us' button, and the only option given was to search the knowledge base. Kelli searched a few different terms, not landing on any article that specified 'someone has set up an account that looks just like mine.' But having performed a few searches, she was given the option to open a trouble ticket. Kelli muttered under her breath and typed up a complaint, linking to both her real account and the fake account.

She could hear voices downstairs, which meant that the judge was already down for breakfast and Kelli was late. She sent the trouble ticket, which then gave her a pop-up saying that she had to confirm it by going to her email and pressing the activation link. Kelli looked at the clock again, and clicked through to her email. There was no confirmation email yet. Sometimes these things were not instantaneous.

Kelli returned to the social network web page. She couldn't get the new account shut down yet, but she could still post on her real account. She posted with a sad face and the explanation that someone was posting comments that weren't hers, so please not to unfriend her for something someone else was doing. She didn't notice until then that her direct message inbox was bursting with new messages. Kelli scanned the subject lines with dismay. It was a combination of people who were outraged over what she had supposedly posted, and nasty, name-calling messages from her favorite school enemies.

Kelli swore. She couldn't respond to all of them before school. She really couldn't respond to any of them, because she was already late. She went back to the tab that her email was loaded on and tried again to refresh the inbox. The email she was waiting for had finally shown up, and she clicked it and then clicked the confirmation link to finish opening her trouble ticket. She closed the computer and hurried downstairs for breakfast.

"There she is," the judge said with a smile. "Running a little behind this morning, sweetie?"

Kelli bent over to give him a kiss on the cheek, and then sat down in her usual chair. "Sorry. Homework and computers, and I'm tired this morning because my mom decided to call last night."

"Your mom?" The judge looked baffled for an instant, then nodded. "Oh, of course. Your mom. What did she want?"

"Just to tell me how awful her life is. Which I already knew. She was drunk."

"Ah."

"That's her normal state of affairs."

"I see."

"I'm going to go over there after school. Just for a few minutes. To make sure that everything is okay."

"Is that safe?"

"I won't stay long. I'll hit it right after school so that it's still light out."

Kelli shrugged. "I'm sure everything is fine. But she hasn't called me or asked me to come over before, so I think I should do it."

He nodded slowly, and concentrated on his eggs and toast.

"Does it bug you that I'm going to go see her?" Kelli asked.

"No. No, not at all. She is your mother. Not biologically, maybe, but she is the one who raised you, and if she ever sued for custody, she'd have a good chance of getting it. I don't want to keep the two of you apart."

"She's not going to ask for custody."

"It was just a comment. That she still has a legal claim over you."

Kelli shook her head. "That seems bizarre… considering that I'm not her child and she never actually wanted me. It's like… it would be like squatting on a property that you didn't actually want. Why would anyone do that?"

He was silent for a while. Kelli didn't really expect an answer. She was just venting. She was more worried about the computer stuff than she was about her mother and going back to visit her.

"I gather from what you have said before that she is not really stable," the judge said eventually.

"Yeah, but wouldn't that be all the more reason to just get rid of me? I mean… leave me at the hospital and just take off? Or adopt me out? Or find you? Why did she bother to keep me?"

He nibbled the corner of his toast. "I think that's a question you need to ask her."

He was right, of course. Patricia was the only person who could answer that question. But she wouldn't. Even sober, she wouldn't answer it. Kelli would just have to assume it was the money. It had to be a part of the settlement with the hospital. She would keep quiet and just raise Kelli, and not ever tell anyone the secret. Patricia must have really resented that. She had never liked to be told what to do.

Kelli inhaled her eggs, hardly even tasting them. The judge had to go, bending over to give her a kiss before leaving. "Don't choke!" he warned, eyes twinkling.

Kelli put down her fork as she watched him walk out of the room. She looked down at the half-meal remaining on her plate. She wasn't even enjoying it, so why was she eating it? And not just eating it, but wolfing it down. Kelli pushed the plate away from her and got up. Pushing her chair back from the table was the exercise that she needed to work on.

Felicia came into the room. She picked up the plates, and Kelli expected her to leave as usual, without a comment. But her eyes went to Kelli.

"Aren't you feeling well this morning? Or was there something wrong with the eggs?"

"No, everything was fine. Just… a bit queasy today."

"Can I get you anything? Some tea? Ginger? A Tylenol?"

"No, I'm okay. It'll pass when I get to school. Thanks."

———

But it didn't go away when Kelli got to school. Her bag with her computer in it felt heavier and heavier as she trudged to her locker. People were turning to look at her as she walked in. And they weren't happy. Kelli gritted her teeth and resisted walking with her eyes on the floor. She hadn't sent those messages, she had no reason to feel guilty about them. And if people didn't know her well enough to know she wouldn't do such a thing, that was their fault for not bothering to get to know her.

Without a doubt, this kind of thing had happened before. People had to know her account could have been hacked or copied. Whoever did it had had a knowledge of the inner workings of the school. Whoever did it was someone she went to school with. And they had probably done it before.

Whispers and muttered comments followed her all the way to her locker, complete with pointing fingers and people deliberately turning their backs on her. Could they get any sillier and more dramatic? Kelli rolled her eyes and opened her locker to sort out what books she would need for her morning classes.

"Well, look who's here. If it isn't—"

"I didn't post that stuff," Kelli interrupted, before Daffodil could finish her sentence. "It's not even my account."

Daffodil stopped. Kelli turned and looked at her.

"It's not me, okay? I wouldn't post stuff like that."

Daffodil turned to her own locker, saying nothing. Kelli rolled her eyes. What would make Daffodil believe that she would go and do something like that? They weren't friends, exactly, but Kelli had never done anything that would make Daffodil believe that she would post nasty things about everyone.

The eggs had been sitting like lead in her stomach since breakfast. Kelli put her hand over her stomach as it gurgled and complained. Because she hadn't had enough to eat? Or because she had gobbled it down? Or because she was letting herself get worked up about the duplicate account? Kelli took a few deep breaths and continued to get ready. But before the bell rang, she knew she wasn't going to be able to ignore the nausea all morning. In fact, not even a few more minutes. She dumped her books back into her locker, slammed and locked the door, and bolted for the nearest restroom.

She just barely made it in time, and hung heaving over the toilet, gasping and choking.

She must be coming down with a bug. She'd never let bullying affect her like that before. She would get angry, she would defend herself, but she wouldn't let it affect her. She was too strong for that.

Maybe she should go home and just rest for the day. She was sick. She could just hide in her room and not have to think about anything.

Kelli spat and blew her nose and tried to just ignore her tight, sick stomach and go on as if nothing were wrong. When she walked into her first period class late, Mrs. Henry glared at her, but then something in her face changed.

"Are you feeling okay, Miss Munroe?"

"Well, no… not really."

"Do you have your assignment ready to hand in?"

Kelli nodded. She saw the stack of papers on Mrs. Henry's desk, and teased the essay out of her notebook to add to the pile. Mrs. Henry took it from her and added it to the pile.

"Why don't you go home? Have one of your classmates email you today's assignment."

There was a lot of whispering going on in the class. Kelli tried to ignore it. Of course they were whispering. They were always whispering. It didn't mean they were talking about her or the fraudulent social media posts.

"I'm okay…"

"You don't look okay. You're not going to get anything out of today's class if you're sick. You need to go home and get some rest."

Kelli hesitated. Her stomach was now empty, so she wasn't really worried about throwing up again. But she did feel wrung out and exhausted. And she was getting tired of the whispering and pointing. If she just went home early one day, and the duplicate account could be deleted, everything would be fine and she could start fresh again the next day with everything resolved and back to normal.

"Go home," Mrs. Henry repeated.

"Umm… okay. Thanks." Kelli turned and walked back out of the room.

———

Kelli had told Patricia that she would visit her after school, but that wasn't going to happen if Kelli went straight home. She considered several different scenarios, and decided the best course of action would be to just drive over before going home to Forester Cottage. She could get in her visit, Axel would probably still be asleep, and then Kelly could just go home and pull the covers over her face and rest.

She parked at the library, figuring that should be a safe enough place for her car so early in the day, and walked to the house.

Kelli stood on the sidewalk outside looking at the yard and the exterior of the house for a few minutes before going in. It looked just the same as ever. But for some reason, the brown grass seemed extra sad, and the house seemed smaller than it used to be. Kelli shook her head and forced her feet to advance up the sidewalk. The door was unlocked, so she walked right in. She could hear the noise of the TV as soon as she opened the house. A comforting, familiar sound. The smell of the place had changed, though. Or maybe Kelli was more sensitive after living with the judge in the pristine cottage for so long. She gagged and tried to breathe through her mouth. It smelled like a sewer. A sewer full of rats and rotting food. Kelli went into the living room. Patricia was slumped over in the chair. Her skin was pale and pasty. She didn't stir when Kelli walked up to her.

Kelli placed her fingers over Patricia's pulse to make sure she was still alive and well. Patricia stirred at her touch and tried to bat her hands away.

"Go away," she protested.

"Mom. Mom, wake up. It's Kelli."

Patricia's eyes opened into slits. "Kelli?" she repeated.

"Yes. Your daughter. You asked me to come over, remember?"

Patricia shifted her weight. "It's not Kelli… What are you doing here?" She squinted in the dim light the curtains allowed into the room. "Isn't it still school?"

"They told me to go home. How are you doing, Mom?"

"Not good," Patricia whined. She rubbed the back of her neck. "I'm old and sick and I need you here with me. Why did you go away? You're not old enough to live on your own yet. That's what the social worker said. You're still only sixteen."

"I know. I'm not living on my own. I'm living with my biological father. Have you been sick?"

Kelli tried to avoid looking around at the piles of trash, bottles, and half-eaten meals. She continued to breathe through her mouth.

"I'm sick," Patricia agreed. She coughed, and Kelli could hear it. Her breathing was labored and raspy. "I had pneumonia, you know."

Kelli stroked Patricia's white hair. "I'm sorry. I didn't know. You didn't tell me about that."

"How am I supposed to reach you, when you're so far away?"

"Well, you can phone, like you did last night."

Patricia grumbled at that. She swung her hand beside her chair, grasping for a bottle that wasn't already empty. Kelli nudged one of them farther away, so Patricia found nothing. Patricia lifted herself using the arms of the chair in order to readjust her bulk again.

Kelli looked around for anything that was out of place. As if she'd be able to see it in the layers of trash. "Did you want me for something, Mom? Is there a reason you called me?"

Patricia patted at Kelli's arm. "You'll stay here now. You won't leave me again."

Kelli cleared her throat. The sick feeling was back full-force. Not because of some stupid internet troll this time, but facing her mother's pleas. "I'm going to go back to the cottage. I'm not staying here."

"The *cottage*," Patricia repeated, her tone scathing.

"That's where I live now. I'll come and see you if you want me to, but I'm not coming back here to live."

Patricia started to cry. Kelli rolled her eyes toward the ceiling. Kelli was going to be a great mom, with all the practice she had in resisting crocodile tears and sniveling. Kelli patted Patricia's shoulder, waiting for the sobbing to peter out.

"You're living so far away, in that posh palace, going to a posh, mucky-muck school, getting everything you want. And I can't even afford to buy my prescription!" She sniffled. "What kind of daughter behaves that way?"

"You need money?" Kelli asked, feeling relieved that they had finally reached the crux of the issue.

Patricia nodded, still blubbering.

Kelli pulled her wallet out of her bag and thumbed out several bills. She put them in front of Patricia's face.

"How about that?"

Patricia took the money from Kelli, her mouth working as she either counted it or tried to form an answer. Kelli left her to think about it while she went into the kitchen, parched and needing a glass of water.

The sink was piled high with dishes. The counters were spread with dirty dishes, and she heard skittering movements as she entered. Kelli looked for a relatively clean glass and washed it carefully, then filled it with cold tap water.

Her parched mouth appreciated it, but her stomach didn't, sloshing around like she had swallowed a gallon of gasoline. Kelli put a hand over her mouth to cover a nasty-tasting burp, and took another swallow.

She went back into the living room. Patricia was staring slack-jawed at the TV, no longer crying. Kelli went over to the wall calendar and flipped to find the right month.

"When is your next doctor's appointment?" Nothing had been filled in.

"I don't know. When they call me to tell me to come in."

Kelli went over to the phone and scanned the phone numbers jotted every-which-way on the free scratch pad with a dental office's logo on it. She found one that looked like the doctor's office, and gave it a call.

The perky-sounding receptionist rattled off the doctors' names and asked how she could help.

"Hi. This is Kelli Munroe. I'm Patricia Munroe's daughter. Can you tell me when her next appointment is?"

There was the sound of keys tapping.

"Mrs. Munroe doesn't have any appointments in the system right now."

Kelli turned and looked at her mother. "Has she switched doctors? Would she be seeing someone else?"

"Hmm… she was referred to a neurologist. Dr. Baker. Do you want his number?"

"Yeah. I mean, yes, please."

The perky receptionist gave her the number and asked if there were anything else she could do to help.

"No, thanks. I'll give him a call."

Kelli put both numbers into her phone contacts list before calling Dr. Baker. Who knew what she'd be able to find the next time she came over, if the trash kept accumulating at the same rate.

The neurologist's office confirmed that Patricia did have an upcoming appointment, so Kelli wrote it in on the calendar. And put it on her phone calendar as well. She wasn't going to drive Patricia there, but she could at least call and remind her, in case the doctor's office did not.

"And... I don't know if he sees my dad as well? Axel Ivanovich?"

There was a pause, but Kelli couldn't hear the computer keys clicking and wondered if they had been disconnected.

"Hello?"

"Uh... Mr. Ivanovich did see Dr. Baker. But he is no longer being seen here."

"Oh, that's kind of weird. It would make more sense having them both go the same place. Doesn't Dr. Baker do cases like Axel?"

The girl's voice was tentative. "Actually... the last time Mr. Ivanovich was here, he was violent and abusive." She gulped audibly. "We had to call the police to have him removed."

Kelli swore. "Oh, man. I'm so sorry. Was he charged?"

"Dr. Baker understands that Mr. Ivanovich has a brain injury that makes him easily confused and it is difficult for him to control his impulses. We asked the police not to lay charges. I think they sent him to Whitestone to have him evaluated."

"Oh. Do you know what they found?"

"No, they didn't tell us anything. You'd have to talk to the police or the staff at Whitestone."

"Okay. Thanks."

"One more thing," the receptionist stopped Kelli from hanging up.

"What?" Kelli fumbled her phone, just about dropping it because she stopped mid-hang-up.

"If Mr. Ivanovich is still living with her, please make sure your mother remembers that he is not allowed to bring her in to her appointment. He has to wait for her in the parking lot. There is a restraining order."

"I'll tell her."

Kelli hung up the phone and turned to look at Patricia, who hadn't moved a muscle in the time that Kelli had been on the phone.

"Mom." She nudged Patricia's shoulder. "Mom, forget about the TV for a minute. I want to talk to you."

It took a few minutes to pry Patricia away from the show. She looked at Kelli impatiently. All pretense over caring that Kelli wasn't living at home anymore was gone. She had her money.

"Mom. Your doctor's appointment is this Thursday. Today is Tuesday. Okay? Two days. I'll call to remind you, in case the doctor's office doesn't."

Patricia grunted her understanding.

"But you have to remember something else," Kelli went on. "Axel isn't allowed to take you in. Do you understand that? Only you can go into the office."

"Why?" Patricia demanded.

"I guess something happened at his last appointment. What was it?"

"What?"

"What happened at Axel's last appointment with Dr. Baker? Did he get in a fight?"

Patricia nodded and smacked her lips at a commercial for orange juice. As if she ever had orange juice without vodka.

"He got in a fight with the doctor?" Kelli persisted.

"With me," Patricia explained. "And then with the doctor and his staff when they tried to interfere." She shook her head. "They don't know what he's like. What good is a brain doctor who can't figure out what's going on in someone's head?"

Kelli nodded her head in agreement. She would have thought that a doctor's office that dealt with people with brain injuries and dementia would have a better plan for dealing with fractious patients than just calling the police on them and taking out restraining orders. Maybe there was some kind of medication that they could give Axel to keep him calm? Some therapy that would help to make those brain connections that were fried by the infection? Or else admit that he was too dangerous to be out in public, and commit him to some kind of residential care.

"So he can't go in with you to your doctor's appointment. He has to wait outside."

"He won't want to do that."

"Then maybe you should go by yourself. Take the bus…"

"I can drive."

"Not with your license suspended."

"I can still drive to the doctor's office, that's not far."

"You could take the bus. It's not that far," Kelli parroted back.

Patricia made a movement toward her and Kelli darted back, putting her hands up to protect herself. Patricia laughed.

"That's right, little girl. You know I can still whip you."

Drunk maybe, but Kelli didn't think she could do it sober. And Kelli wouldn't be trying to beat her up. She'd be trying to get away without either of them getting too badly hurt.

There was a noise upstairs. The squeak of bedsprings as someone moved around restlessly. Kelli looked toward the ceiling. "He's here?"

Obviously, he was there, Kelli had just heard him. But she had hoped when she heard that the police had sent Axel away for evaluation that it meant he wouldn't be back. Why did he have to come back all the time?

"He lives here," Patricia said, as if that should have been obvious. For her, it was that simple. Axel lived there and he would keep coming back. Until something stopped him from returning, and that wasn't too likely. Even if Patricia got it into her head to kick him out, he'd still come back again. And it wouldn't even be his fault, because he simply wouldn't remember that he had been kicked out in the first place.

"He hits you. Call the police and get him put back behind bars."

"He's your father!" Patricia said. "You shouldn't talk about him that way. No one is sending him back to prison. They still have to pay for the last time they did that, and he wasn't guilty."

Kelli glanced at Patricia. She wanted vengeance on the prosecutor and the police? She'd better not try anything. It would take intelligence to get even with the people who had put Axel in prison. Someone with intelligence, like Kelli. Only it wouldn't be Kelli, because she didn't think they had done anything wrong by putting him behind bars. She figured the mistake was when they let him back out.

Patricia looked smug. She sat there grinning at Kelli. The cat that swallowed the canary.

"What did you do, Mom? You didn't do something to get back at the police, did you? You know they were just doing what they thought was right. Axel confessed."

"He never would have confessed if they hadn't made him. They need to pay for that."

"Pay how?"

Patricia's eyes slitted almost closed, just like a happy, purring cat. She didn't answer the question. Kelli looked around the room once more for anything out of place.

Kelli sighed. "I'm going to head out, if you don't need anything else."

Patricia made no effort to talk her into staying. She was already gone again, watching her TV show, lost in a world of talk shows, soaps, and people screaming over big prizes.

CHAPTER 22

Kelli was glad to be back to the cottage where she was safe. Going back to the house had left her feeling jumpy and anxious. She was on edge all the way home, until she walked in the door and closed it behind her. She let out a long sigh of relief and headed up to her bedroom. For once she didn't stop in the kitchen for a snack. She still felt queasy and unsettled from earlier.

At first, she just dumped her school bag on the floor, slid onto the bed, and hugged her pillows tightly, soothing herself. She was sick, so she would probably fall asleep, and then when she woke up later, rested and relaxed, she would feel one hundred percent better.

But as she lay there, she started to get more anxious instead of less. Sleep was the furthest thing from her brain. As she lay on the bed, smothering herself in the soft pillows, her brain was ticking away.

The judge said that intelligent people had a harder time getting to sleep. They had so much to think about, such busy brains, that they often had trouble settling for the night. It wasn't even nighttime, and her brain wasn't going to slow down and let her relax. She thought about the computer in her bag. She hadn't checked yet to see if she had an email regarding the trouble ticket she had lodged with the social networking company. If they had already sorted it out and sent her an update, then she would be able to relax again.

The kids at Central would see that it hadn't really been her posting all of that terrible stuff. Would they even care that it hadn't been her? They should probably have known that already without anyone having to tell them. Kelli had hobnobbed with them all summer and had spent several weeks with them now at school. They knew what kind of a person she was, that she didn't go around saying things about people or bullying them.

Kelli got up off the bed and retrieved her laptop. She sat at her desk and logged in.

There was an update to the support ticket. Kelli tried to relax her shoulders and her breathing. It was going to be all right. She opened up the email and read quickly through it. It wasn't a notice that they had sorted everything out. It was just an auto-reply stating that they had received her trouble ticket and they would get back to her once they had had a chance to investigate. The timeframe specified was five to ten business days.

Kelli swore angrily and got up from her desk. Five to ten business days? Two weeks before they would sort it out? She had already seen she had an inbox full of emails from people who had seen 'her' online posts and had something to say about it. Not nice things. So much for anti-bullying rules. Once she was branded a bully, it was open season, and people felt free to say whatever they liked.

She paced back and forth, nowhere to vent her anger. That was the trouble with a place like the cottage. She couldn't throw things around. She couldn't hit the wall. She couldn't yell at anyone for being drunk and messy. Kelli wondered if she should call Justice Emerson Forester to tell him about the account. Maybe he could make some phone calls and get the social media company to sit up and pay attention. He wrote demand letters and made phone calls all the time to get what he wanted. She knew he would do it for her, if she asked.

But that seemed like cheating. She wanted her case to be handled on an equitable basis, just like everyone else's, not because there was outside pressure being applied. She wanted them to see that she had been wronged, and reverse it.

If they didn't handle it quickly, then she would talk to the judge about it and see what he could do. She had faith that he would be able to do something about it. She hadn't yet run into a situation that he couldn't have some kind of influence over.

———

The day had passed at a snail's pace. Kelli wandered through the house with nothing to do. Not because she didn't have schoolwork and studying to do, but because she couldn't focus on it. Her brain felt completely seized up. She did keep going back to her computer every hour or two, checking to see if there was an update on the support ticket, which there wasn't. It wasn't a complicated situation. Why should it take them more than a few minutes to see what had happened and fix it for her?

She read or deleted the emails from the other kids at Central or people who had seen the fake posts in small batches. She could only manage a few of them at a time. She didn't bother trying to answer them to explain that it was a dummy account and someone at the school was fooling them all. It had to be someone else at the school; who else would know the students well enough to make fun of them and bully them?

Eventually, Justice Emerson Forester got home and it was supper time. Kelli slid into her seat, but didn't know whether she was going to be able to eat anything. Her stomach was still upset. She kept telling herself that it was just a bug, but she knew better. She should have called Les. Gone to meet him after school for a while. He was the best person to help her to relax.

"So… what happened at school today?" the judge asked, studying Kelli.

"What do you mean?"

"I got a call that you missed classes today."

"Do they do that? I didn't know."

"They do. So…?"

"I wasn't feeling well. My first period teacher told me to go home."

"Oh…" His eyes went to her plate, still untouched. "Are you okay? Anything to be concerned about?"

"I'm fine… just a bug, I guess. It's not that bad, but I don't know…" Kelli looked at the pork chops, mashed potatoes, and green beans. "I want to eat, but I'm not sure if I can keep anything down."

"Well, don't force it. If you're still feeling that bad, you should be in bed. Get the rest you need for your body to heal."

"I tried to sleep, but I couldn't. Too restless."

He nodded. "Sit and visit with me for a while, and then maybe you'll be able to relax. Head to bed early. You'll probably be fine in the morning."

"Yeah."

She sat there and poked at her beans and mashed potatoes, trying to decide whether to take the chance and eat anything. Eventually, she pushed the plate away from her. Although she did, as an afterthought, swipe one finger through the mashed potatoes and gravy and licked off her finger. She glanced up at the judge. He had seen her.

Kelli rolled her eyes, trying to suppress the guilty grin at being caught. "I couldn't help it. It looks and smells so good. I just don't think I can eat."

"You can make up for it tomorrow. Do you want to read in the library for a while, or head up to bed?"

"Read. My brain isn't ready for sleep."

Before settling in to read, however, she pulled out her phone and checked her email. More angry, vindictive emails, but no update from the social media company.

––––––––

Kelli was resting, in bed but still miles from sleep, when a ruckus broke out downstairs. She heard a car drive down the lane, but was too lazy to go see who it was. Probably just someone who was lost and needed to turn around, or maybe a colleague that the judge had asked to come over for a nightcap. Then the front door slammed. There had been no doorbell or knock that Kelli had heard. Just a slammed door.

A home invasion? She had always feared them in the old neighborhood, but it had never occurred to her to worry about them at the cottage. It made sense that someone would be more likely to steal from the rich houses than from the poor ones. But home invasions were usually drug-related, and she didn't think there was anyone living close by who was dealing drugs. You never could tell, but Kelli hadn't seen any of the signs.

She slipped out of bed and crept over to her door. Opening it just a crack, she put her ear to it and listened.

She could hear the judge's voice, but he didn't sound angry or upset. The other voice took a few minutes to identify, but eventually she pinned it down. Lisa. What would Lisa be doing there so late in the evening, with no warning?

No longer concerned about armed invaders, Kelli walked to the end of the hall to be in a better position to eavesdrop. She didn't have to listen too hard; Lisa's voice was loud and angry.

"I can't stay with her for another minute! And I don't want to talk to her about it, and I don't want to talk to you about it. I'm going to my room and I'm staying here. No one can force me to live there anymore!"

The judge's voice was low and calm. Kelli couldn't make out his words. The words weren't really what mattered, he was just trying to calm her down.

"Go ahead and call her. Tell her this is where I'm staying. But she'd better not come over here tonight! I'm not talking to her. I'm going to bed!"

Kelli could hear Lisa moving to the bottom of the stairs, so she retreated to her own room. No point in aggravating Lisa more when she was already upset with something. She must have had a fight with Preston, so she was ditching her mom in favor of her dad. Kelli didn't imagine that Preston was going to be too happy about that.

She shut her door quietly, but could still hear Lisa storm down the hallway and slam her bedroom door behind her. Kelli waited to see if the judge would come after her. If it had been Axel or one of the boyfriends, she would have had to barricade the door if she didn't want to suffer the consequences.

But no one came after Lisa. Kelli cracked her door open again and listened. She could still hear Justice Emerson Forester's voice. He must be talking on the phone. Kelli again crept out of her room and again stood at the top of the stairs to listen in. He was at the bottom of the stairs, so she could now hear him fairly well.

"She's here. She's safe tonight, so why don't you just get a good rest? I'm sure you will both feel better in the morning."

A pause while he listened to Preston's response.

"I'm not taking sides. You two will have to work things out between you. But this isn't going to be solved tonight. You should just be happy that she had a place to go and you know she's safe tonight."

Another pause. The judge's voice was even more slow and deliberate than usual, which Kelli knew meant he was getting impatient with her.

"I'm sure it can all be worked out. We'll talk tomorrow."

She couldn't hear him hang up the phone, but he said no more, so Kelli knew that he had. He gave an irritated grunt and then walked away.

———

Kelli didn't remember the scene immediately on waking up. When her alarm went off, her brain was still foggy from sleep and she was just going through the motions of showering and getting herself ready for school.

The computer sat on her desk waiting for her. Kelli had a feeling that she still wasn't going to get an email resolving the dummy account situation. Five to ten business days. They obviously didn't turn things around in a day. They had to do their own investigating, though what that would involve, she wasn't sure. Wouldn't the fact that she had opened her account months before the dummy account prove that between the two accounts, hers was the legitimate account? How hard could it be?

As she dressed, she was trying to talk herself out of opening up the computer and logging on. She would just get upset before school and be late for breakfast again. It was better if she just left it alone. What could she solve by getting upset?

There was a knock on Kelli's door, making her jump. Her heart immediately started racing. It was time she stopped reacting so violently every time some little thing startled her. She closed her eyes and breathed slowly for a few breaths. She looked at the clock as she headed over to answer the door. It was still too early for Felicia to be knocking and telling her that she was late for breakfast. Unless she'd decided to get Kelli moving earlier so that she would get down in time for breakfast.

Kelli opened the door. It was Lisa. Kelli's heart sped even faster. She did not want a confrontation first thing in the morning. She didn't want any kind of confrontation with Lisa. How would the judge handle a fight between his daughters? How could he stand up for Kelli over the child he had raised for sixteen years? How could he choose either side? Or get out of it? He might be a judge, but she wasn't sure even he could make the right ruling in a fight between his two daughters.

"Uh… hi."

Lisa stood impatiently with her arms folded over her chest. "I heard you up." Her voice was challenging. Like Kelli wasn't supposed to be up. Not like she was trying to make inroads into a pleasant conversation.

"Yeah. Just getting ready for school," Kelli agreed.

Lisa made a motion like she wanted to enter the bedroom. Kelli stood there, not sure what to do. Her bedroom was her safe place. She didn't want to let anyone else in, but especially not her enemy. Her rival. Whatever they were.

"Me too. I guess life doesn't stop because you're having family problems," Lisa agreed. She shifted and again nodded toward the room like she would enter.

Kelli put her hand on the doorframe. Like it was just a natural gesture and she was leaning against the wall to think.

"So… what happened between you and Preston? What were you so upset about?"

Lisa swore. "I can't live with it anymore! I can't live with her and hear her complaining all the time about how you came back, and planted yourself here, and turned Dad against us. It never ends! It's not like I bring it up. Believe me, I know what subjects to avoid when I'm talking to her, and I've never said one word about you. Well, okay, maybe one, but that's it. Why would I want to get her all wound up?"

"You wouldn't," Kelli said.

"That's right. I wouldn't. The last thing I need is her staying awake all night, pacing and freaking out over what's going to happen next. She's not going to change what happened. Why not just accept it and get on with her life?"

Good advice. Kelli thought about her own day pacing and freaking out over the dummy account. And what difference did it make? It wasn't like she was friends with all the kids at school who were upset about the nasty posts in the first place. She was there to learn, to try to get the marks that she would need for college. To make her father happy. Not to socialize. Why didn't she just let it go?

But the thought just made her want to rush over to her computer and check to see what new emails had arrived in spite of her own logic. Maybe she was like Preston in some way after all.

"Can I come in?" Lisa demanded impatiently. "I'm not going to touch your stuff. I just need to vent."

Kelli stepped slowly back from the doorway.

"I'm not going to wreck your stuff," Lisa repeated. "What good would that do me? I'd just get thrown out of here! And I've got nowhere else to go!"

Kelli didn't exactly feel sorry for her. She didn't think there was a chance in the world that Justice Emerson Forester was going to kick Lisa out onto the street to fend for herself. He would look after her even if she did destroy Kelli's room. Kelli didn't think she actually would. But that didn't stop the pounding anxiety she felt over letting Lisa into her sanctum.

Lisa walked by her and looked around the room. "You've hardly touched it," she said, sounding a little disappointed. "Where's the stuff that says it's your room? It could be a hotel room. Or a museum."

Kelli shrugged. "I don't know… I like it how it is."

"You should make it yours. Dad wouldn't mind you putting up posters, changing the bedding, stuff like that. It doesn't say 'Kelli' to me."

Kelli took a deep breath and let it out. She wasn't going to argue over interior decorating. Lisa was just looking for something to fight about.

Lisa sat down on the end of the bed and looked at Kelli expectantly. Kelli chewed on her lip. "So… what did you and Preston fight about?"

"I think it started as school… but that wasn't what it was about. It was going to happen no matter what. About something. The subject didn't really matter."

"And you think that's my fault?"

"Your fault?" Lisa's eyebrows went up. "I didn't say it was your fault. Maybe it was about you, but that's not the same as it being your fault. You didn't do anything."

"I came here," Kelli pointed out. She wasn't quite sure what the point was of trying to prove that it was her fault. Did she want it to be her fault? "I could have just stayed away. Lived the life I already had. Then maybe you and Preston would… be on better terms with him." Kelli paced across the room, too anxious to stand still. "I didn't come here to supplant you… or to get something from him. I just wanted… I don't know…"

"A real father," Lisa provided. "One who wasn't a deadbeat."

"My other dad isn't a deadbeat," Kelli protested. Was she really defending Axel now? The world was turned upside down. "He's sick. He has a brain injury."

"Whatever," Lisa seemed unfazed by this. Kelli wondered how much of the story Lisa knew. Preston had surely done her research. Sent a private investigator over to sift through their garbage. As if they ever threw anything out on their own. Bribed someone to get a look at Axel's medical records. Ordered transcripts of the court trial. It wouldn't be hard for a person to find out everything of consequence about Axel. And then to tell Lisa all the gory details, because there was no one else she could share it with. She couldn't exactly tell her socialite friends about it. She didn't want them to know that Kelli was her legitimate daughter. "But you couldn't keep living like that, could you? Not when you knew that you had another family out there."

Kelli perched against her computer desk, studying Lisa.

"I saw a video of my mom, from when I was just a baby. A talk show when she found out that the guy she had been with wasn't my father."

Lisa nodded, as if she already knew this. Had she seen the video herself? It was freely available online. It wouldn't have been hard to find. "The queen bee knows everything."

The comment threw Kelli at first. The queen bee would be Preston, then. It was an apt description. Preston at the center of her little social group. Buzzing around and bossing everyone else.

"You don't know what it's like living with someone who is obsessed like that," Lisa complained. "Everything is about you. And Dad. She's nuts."

Kelli just looked at her. Lisa had every right to complain about anything she wanted, but she was seriously going to tell Kelli how awful it was to live with someone like Preston? Kelli didn't see any sign that Preston was physically abusive. So what if she was obsessed with the new daughter that had come into the judge's life. It was only natural that she would be thrown by a wrench in the works. She hadn't had long enough to get used to the idea yet. Kelli was still trying to find a way to fit in. She didn't expect that Preston had had enough time to adjust to the new situation yet.

"Okay," Lisa held up her hands in surrender. "I know. I'm being a drama diva." She made a face. "It's a habit. I'm a teenager, what do you expect?"

Kelli raised her brows.

"I've always had everything I wanted," Lisa said. "Not like you. Mom has always been super focused on me and whatever I'm working on, whether it's cheer or yearbook committee, or whatever. She's always been there cheering me on. Then you come along, and suddenly it's all about Kelli. Kelli is a gold digger. Kelli is getting your dad to change his will. Kelli is going to be at that party, so we have to find an excuse not to be there. Kelli is getting better grades in English language arts than you are. Seriously. It's all the time and I can't stand it anymore. She wants me to get back into Dad's good books. Well, here I am. She can't complain about me living here if she wants me to work on getting my inheritance."

"You don't think she'll mind that you're here?"

"Oh, she'll mind all right. But she can't argue with me being here. Not when she wants me to 'rebuild my relationship with my father.'" Lisa adopted a lofty tone for the last few words. Kelli smiled and shook her head. Parents all seemed to come with their own set of problems. If it wasn't one thing, it was another. Were there any normal parents left in the world? Or were they all crazy in their own ways?

Kelli had been able to smell the breakfast cooking for a while. There was a tap at the door, and Felicia stood there, looking at the two of them with wide eyes.

"Breakfast?" Kelli asked.

"Breakfast is served," Felicia agreed. She gave them both a little smile, and withdrew again.

Kelli looked at Lisa. "Breakfast. You want some?"

"Do you think he'll have grapefruit? I like a grapefruit for breakfast. Nothing too filling."

Kelli's face flushed, becoming conscious of her weight gain over the summer once again. Lisa knew how to eat properly to maintain her weight. A grapefruit for breakfast. Not a whole plateful of toast, eggs, and maybe bacon or sausages. Just because they had the money to eat three meals a day didn't mean she had to stuff herself like a pig.

"If he knows that's what you like for breakfast, that's what he'll have, won't he?"

"Except that he didn't know ahead of time that I was coming. He wouldn't keep grapefruit in the fridge all the time on the off chance that I happened to show up for breakfast! I don't suppose you eat a lot of grapefruit."

Kelli flushed again at the jab. Lisa's hand flew to her mouth.

"I mean—you wouldn't have gotten a taste for them. Not…" She cut off her explanation, probably realizing how it would sound to Kelli. Kelli ignored Lisa, putting her computer into her schoolbag and getting herself ready to go. "I'm sorry," Lisa apologized, sounding anxious. "I know I'm a… harpy… but I really didn't mean to say anything hurtful. It just came out that way."

Kelli looked at Lisa. Her eyes were wide and innocent, her mouth open in a little 'O' of dismay. She was, again, overacting. That was the trouble with being raised by Preston. She hadn't developed any sense of subtlety. Lying convincingly required practice and a light touch.

Kelli finished packing her bag and led the way down the stairs and to the dining room. The judge was already seated with his plate, but at their entrance he quickly stood, wiping his mouth on the cloth serviette.

"Ladies," he greeted pleasantly. "Good morning."

Kelli had the feeling that he would have held their chairs for them, but since there were two of them instead of just the usual one, he was concerned that he wouldn't be able to seat both of them, and one of them would end up miffed. So he just stood formally at their entrance, and sat down again to continue eating after they had seated themselves.

It was obvious which place was for whom. Kelli's place held a plate full of her usual greasy breakfast. Lisa's small luncheon plate was empty, but a bowl of fragrant, glistening grapefruit was in the middle of the table before her. Kelli looked at Lisa's grapefruit.

"I think... I'll have the same as Lisa today," she said.

The judge's eyebrows went up, but all credit to him, he didn't express surprise or try to dissuade her. He got up again and went over to the sideboard where the china was stored, pulling out a luncheon plate for Kelli. She accepted it politely, and moved her eggs, toast, and bacon over to the side. She didn't need a big breakfast like that. She could get by on just a grapefruit, like Lisa. How many years had she gone most mornings without any breakfast at all?

Somehow it had been easier when she didn't have a steaming plate of eggs beside her.

"You should call your mother this morning," Justice Emerson Forester advised Lisa. "Let her know you're all right."

"I'm sure you already called her and she knows I'm all right," Lisa said evenly, not looking up from her grapefruit.

"She'd like to hear it from you."

"My mother and I are not speaking right now. She needs to get a life and quit obsessing. I'm not going back there. I've had enough."

"That's a little drastic, don't you think? I realize mothers and daughters don't always get along together. But I think you'll find living out here at the cottage tedious. It's not close to your school or your friends..."

"That's crap. I've got a car. I can get myself to school. Maybe it takes ten minutes longer." She took a dainty bit of grapefruit. "But I don't have to make my own breakfast, so it all balances out."

"I don't like to see you and your mother fighting..."

"Uh-huh. Well, if I was at home, I'd be fighting with her a lot more. You just wouldn't see it."

A small smile twitched the corner of the judge's mouth. He appreciated her attack on his semantics. Kelli shook her head, amazed that the mother and daughter who had seemed so united and close when they had come to dinner that first day could be at such odds. She had no doubt that Lisa was being overdramatic for the judge's sake, but they still must have had some blow-up for Lisa to end up at the cottage, refusing to go back to Preston.

"You always said that I could come stay with you any time," Lisa reminded her father. "You never said that Mom had to agree to it."

"She is your custodial parent. She really does have to give her permission if you're going to stay here permanently."

"She'll agree if you promise not to drop the support payments," Lisa advised. "And if she doesn't, let her take it to court. I'm old enough to have a say in which parent I stay with."

The judge inclined his head in agreement. They all sat in silence for a while, eating their breakfasts. Kelli was hating her grapefruit. How Lisa could just dig into it like it was dessert, she didn't know. It was so bitter and sour, Kelli needed something to take the taste out of her mouth. She eyed her cooling eggs. If she just had the eggs, and not the toast or bacon, that wouldn't be so bad, would it? It was carbs that made her fat. The eggs were protein. And she had her fiber and vitamin C already in the grapefruit.

"Did you both sleep well?"

Kelli looked up at the judge. "I was pretty restless," she said. "Couldn't get to sleep for a long time."

Lisa cast a sidelong glance at her. "Was that my fault? Making so much noise last night?"

"I wasn't trying to go to sleep yet when you got here," Kelli said, not quite answering the question. "And I already had a pretty anxious day."

Kelli could see the judge chewing on this. She realized that as far as he was concerned, she'd been sick the previous day, not upset. Lisa's gaze went from Kelli to her father and back again.

"What were you anxious about?"

Kelli shrugged. She pulled her breakfast plate over and took one forkful of eggs. One forkful wasn't going to make her fat.

"I went by to see my mom… she's not doing so well."

"I thought you missed school because you were sick," Justice Emerson Forester said.

"I did. But I'd told my mom I would go see her after school, so I went over there before I came home. To see if she needed anything."

The judge already knew that Patricia had called Kelli. Kelli had a little more of her eggs. They were starting to cool and tasted too greasy. She added a bit more salt and ground some pepper over them.

"How was she?" he asked eventually.

"Not great." Kelli wasn't sure how much to say. She didn't really know how much Justice Emerson Forester knew about the situation. Or how much Lisa did. "She's... I worry about her, with no one there to look after things. And with my dad... well, Axel... things can get pretty bad."

Lisa's eyes were going back and forth between Kelli and her father.

"If she needs assistance, maybe we should talk to someone," the judge suggested.

"I don't know. She already has a doctor. And Axel's lawyer. The police know them both. It's just that... there's no one to make sure she's okay."

"What could you do if you were there?" Lisa asked, making herself a part of the conversation. "You're just a kid."

Kelli forced down more of the greasy, salty eggs. "I could help. Make sure she got to her appointments, that she had something to eat. Call the cops if Axel..."

"It sounds like a job for a social worker or caregiver," the judge said. "Not for a teenager."

"I was doing it before. She doesn't need a social worker. Just a helper."

"If she's not competent to live on her own..."

Kelli could see what direction the discussion was going. And she couldn't let him institutionalize her mother. Not yet.

"Never mind. The doctor says she can still manage daily living skills. I don't want her being sent to some... institution or rest home."

"What would be so bad about that?" Lisa challenged her. "I remember when Grandma was in Good Hope. It was a nice place. They looked after her, and she was happy there."

"She's only sixty. She's too young to be stuck in a place like that."

"It doesn't matter how old she is, if she can't take care of herself—"

Kelli sent her plate spinning away from her on the table.

"I've got to get to school. I'll see you tonight." She gave the judge a quick kiss, waved at Lisa because she didn't know what else to do, and headed out to her car.

What made them think they could dictate what was right for Kelli's mother? They'd never even met her! They didn't care about her or about what happened to her. They didn't know anything about the situation.

Patricia was still capable of taking care of herself. And so was Axel. So the two of them didn't get along together so well sometimes. That was nothing new. They cared about each other, and that was more than she could say about most of the families in the neighborhood. Not too many couples stayed together for more than a decade, especially when one of them spent ten years of that in prison.

Kelli slammed her car door and headed out of the property and down the highway. She could hear the judge's calm voice in her head, telling her to settle down and drive safely. Being ticked off at people who didn't understand her family's situation was no excuse for ending up in a wreck because she was driving mad.

She put her foot on the brake and deliberately slowed down to just under the speed limit. She turned the radio on loud, and tried to lose herself in the music and forget about all of the issues that were drowning her.

———

The eggs were sitting heavily in Kelli's stomach. Something about them, or maybe the grapefruit or how upset she was, made her nauseated beyond what she could handle. Like the day before, she made a hurried trip to the bathroom, and promptly lost her breakfast. It was more than twenty-four hours since she'd had a meal that she'd been able to keep down.

Kelli wiped her mouth and blew her nose before leaving the stall. She needed to rinse her mouth out. Maybe find someone who would share some gum with her to get the taste out of her mouth and the smell off of her breath. She didn't want to walk around all day smelling like a sick person.

She washed her hands at the sink. Anabelle, one of the girls in her math class, was carefully putting on her makeup, her face an inch from the mirror.

"You pregnant?" she asked, not looking away from the task at hand. Kelli looked behind her to see if Anabelle was talking to someone else.

"No, I'm not pregnant!"

"You could be, even if you thought you were protected. Stuff happens, sometimes."

"Not when you're not even… in the vicinity of a boy."

Anabelle snickered. "Well, no. Vicinity is required," she agreed. "What then? Are you bulimic?"

"No!" This question irritated Kelli even more. "I'm just not feeling okay. Is that all right with you? What are you, the bathroom police?"

"No. Just looking out for you. If you're sick, why don't you stay home? We don't want to catch your flu or plague or whatever it is."

"I'm fine. I missed yesterday, I can't miss again today. I just… shouldn't have had such a heavy breakfast after being sick." Kelli shut off the faucet. "Why don't you just mind your own business?"

"Whatever." Anabelle gave a little shrug. "If you were pregnant, wouldn't you want someone to talk to about it? Or if you were bulimic? Don't get your panties in a bunch because I wanted to help."

"I've got enough people trying to help me out," Kelli grumbled, even though she knew she was being unfair. "Just leave me alone."

She exited the bathroom, leaving Anabelle and her questions behind.

It wasn't until she settled into her first period class that she realized she hadn't had a chance to check her emails. She slid her phone out surreptitiously to check it while the teacher was writing on the board. Normally she would follow the rules and not get out her phone during class, but it was an emergency.

CHAPTER 23

What's this about?" Justice Emerson Forester questioned, when Kelli handed him the folded blue paper.

Kelli gritted her teeth. "I got in trouble at school. You're supposed to sign that form."

If she had still been living at home, she would have forged one of her parents' names. It wouldn't matter which one, because if the school called to discuss it with them, either one would bluff their way through it, thinking that they had just forgotten signing the form. But the judge was a little different. Probably the school would never call him to follow up, because it was such a minor infraction. But if there was a phone call or email to follow up on it, she didn't want to be in hot water with him. Better to report a minor violation than to risk him not trusting her in the future. She didn't want to end up out on her butt, fending for herself.

"In trouble for what?" He unfolded the page and glanced over it. She caught his eye-roll before he schooled his face into a properly grave expression. "You were using your phone during class?"

"Yes."

"They don't let you make phone calls in the middle of classes, do they?"

Kelli restrained a grin. "No. I wasn't making a call. I was just checking my email, because I didn't have time this morning. With Lisa being there and all…"

"Checking your email can wait until lunch, then, or in between classes.

Not during lessons." He pulled out a pen and scribbled an unreadable signature with a flourish. Kelli looked at it as she took the paper back. That wasn't going to be an easy one to forge. The judge's eyes narrowed and she wondered if he had read her thoughts. "Why was it so important that you check your email?" he asked, not willing to let the matter drop yet. "Are you expecting something important?"

Kelli tried to think it through quickly. She didn't want to tell him about the duplicate account. She didn't want to show him the things that the other account had been posting and to have him blow up and get the school or the police involved. She just wanted to handle it herself. Quietly.

"I…"

The judge's eyebrows drew down. "What's going on? Do you have a boyfriend I don't know about? Or were you hoping for something from your mother?"

Either of those would be good stories. Kelli could come up with a good backstory for either one. And the judge would believe them, because it had been his own idea in the first place. She loved it when a mark unwittingly helped with his own con job.

Looking at the judge, though, her heart sank. She didn't want to lie to him. She didn't want him involved, but she didn't want to con him. He had opened up his home and everything he had to her; lying to him would be a betrayal.

"It's sort of some trouble with school," she said, staring at the pattern in the carpet until her eyes nearly went crossed.

"You got in trouble for looking at your phone in class… looking for an email from…?"

"This social network that a bunch of the kids are on… I opened an account, so I could keep up, you know, on what people are doing and the news and all… but someone opened a dummy account, with my name and picture, and whoever made it is saying things about the other kids at school, and people think it's me."

He stared at her like she was speaking Egyptian.

"This is like Facebook."

Kelli nodded. "But most kids aren't on Facebook, because that's where their parents are. We have other networks instead, so that it's more… private."

"And someone is pretending to be you."

"Yeah. And being nasty to people."

"What do you do, in a case like that?"

"You tell support, and they take five to ten business days to sort it out, and hopefully shut down the fake account."

"When did this start? Why didn't you tell me?"

"It's just been a couple of days. I didn't think I needed to tell you… I can take care of it myself. It's just routine, it happens all the time."

"But the kids at Central think it's you. How are they reacting?"

"Some of them… retaliate. Or sent me private messages. At school… I don't know what everyone is saying, they mostly don't say anything to my face. But I can tell people are whispering and talking about me."

"A few weeks into a new school… talk about trial by fire. You don't think I need to do anything? You think the administrator will just shut down the account?"

"Yeah. That's all it is. It happens all the time. And then everyone will forget about it."

"You're not afraid that people will resort to physical violence?"

Kelli shook her head. "Just let them try. I could use some exercise." She fell back into a Jujitsu starting position to demonstrate her intent.

"Well, I wouldn't recommend violence in response… but I admit I do feel a bit better knowing that you're capable of defending yourself. I worry about Lisa… she's so delicate, such a girly girl, it makes her more vulnerable."

"She's tougher than you think. But yeah, I'd recommend she at least take some self-defense classes. You never know when you're going to have to protect yourself. They teach some dirty moves in some of those self-defense classes."

"That's what she needs. Maybe you could suggest it to her. I don't think she'd do it on my suggestion."

Kelli shrugged uncomfortably. "I dunno. Maybe if it comes up."

The judge motioned to the paper that he had just signed. "You've had an unsettling few days, then. This social network stuff, going to see your parents, Lisa descending upon us…"

"Yeah. It's been kind of tense. I just want to get an email back from the support guys saying that it's all been taken care of."

"You know, I have a friend I'd like you to talk to. He might be able to help you with some relaxation—"

"This friend wouldn't happen to be a psychologist, would he?"

Her father grimaced and prevaricated. "He does happen to be a family therapist, but he's done some really good work with teens that have come into my courtroom…"

"I'm not some juvie in your courtroom. And I've got this. Thanks."

She knew she was being rude by cutting him of so tersely, but she couldn't afford to let him turn her life upside down. She'd dealt with enough psychologists, psychiatrists, and therapists of all sorts. Right up there with social workers, cops, and judges. She was in charge of her own life and didn't need anyone else getting in her way.

She looked at her watch. "I need to go do homework. Since I wasn't feeling well yesterday…"

He held his hand out to her in a mute plea. "You can come to me when you're having problems, Kelli. Even if you don't want me to do anything about it. I'd like to know what's going on in your life. I'd like to help you to get through it, even if it's just by being someone you can vent to. Can you trust me to do that?"

"I don't know," Kelli said in full honesty. "Trust isn't something I have much of. Give me time." She turned away from him. "Would you have Felicia bring my dinner up? I don't know how I'm going to get all my work done otherwise."

He didn't answer. Kelli didn't look back to see if he were nodding. He would send Felicia with her dinner. He wasn't going to let her go hungry. And he had another child to keep him company, so Kelli didn't have to feel bad about abandoning him for one night.

"Don't spend all your time on social media," he advised. "Make sure you get your work done first."

Kelli ignored the advice and went up to her room.

———

Kelli took a break from her homework after a couple of hours, feeling mentally exhausted and wrung out. A full day of school, a couple of hours' worth of homework, and knowing that she still had more to go, weighed her down. Who said kids didn't do enough homework anymore? She had been busy at PS2, but she'd still been able to fit in time at the library with Les or working cons to get some money. She didn't know how she would fit those extras in with the work load from Central. It was crushing. All to be able to get into a good college in a couple of years.

She went to the bathroom, and for a few minutes, just sat with her hands over her eyes, trying to wash away the fatigue that weighed her eyelids down. Eventually, she stood up and she looked at herself in the mirror while she washed her hands. What was she doing? She barely even recognized the reflection in the mirror anymore. She'd become a completely different person. And she didn't like what she saw.

She'd always dreamed of getting the birthmark removed. And she knew that when that happened, life would be different for her. There would be more opportunities. People would look at her and really see her, instead of immediately looking away in disgust.

But that wasn't how it was. People were no longer distracted by the birthmark. Somehow, her new hair and face and the way that her cheeks and body had filled out were just another kind of mask. People still didn't look past her outward appearance to see the person underneath. And she was changing inside too, she wasn't sure she even liked the person underneath anymore. Was she as shallow as Lisa and the other girls? Or was she pulling the greatest con of her life, pretending to fit in with them?

She didn't like the person she had become. She was no longer helping anyone else. She wasn't cooking, cleaning, or earning money for her family or to split with Les. Instead, she let others serve her and give her things she didn't deserve. Her mother was getting worse. Axel probably was too, if she were to judge by his fighting with Patricia at the doctor's office. Les didn't have enough money to keep his phone anymore.

Instead, she was going to parties, trying to fit in with the socialites at the upper crust school. Trying to act like she had a future, when clearly, she didn't. She might have been a con before, but at least she had been herself at the core. She knew who she was and acted on that knowledge.

The pretty, wavy-haired, pink-complected girl that looked back at her from the mirror... she had no idea who that was. She was somebody who thought that if she got everything she wanted, life would be different.

Different, yes. Better... not so much.

———

Kelli awoke to Felicia's knock the next morning, having slept right through her wake-up alarm.

"It's breakfast, Miss Kelli. Aren't you up yet? Are you sick?"

Kelli closed her eyes again. "I don't know… Would you bring my breakfast up?"

"Of course."

She lay in bed, trying to force herself to get up. But she didn't really want to get up. If she could just sleep all day… every day… then she wouldn't have to think about anything. Wouldn't have to deal with anyone at school. Wouldn't have to worry about schoolwork or social networks or bullying. She could just lie in bed for the rest of her life.

She drifted in and out of sleep until Felicia returned with a breakfast tray. Felicia stood by patiently as Kelli repositioned herself, sitting up in the bed so that she could put the tray over her lap.

"I brought you some tea," Felicia pointed out. "And toast… I didn't know for sure what you wanted. If you're not feeling well…"

"Thanks. This looks good."

"Should I tell Judge Forester that you're sick? He'll want to know if you're not feeling well."

"No… I don't know if I'm sick… I just need some time to myself."

If she were going to make it to school, she knew she needed to get up and quickly get ready. Not sit around in bed having a leisurely breakfast. She would already be late. Felicia stood there a moment longer, looking concerned and confused, then she left Kelli alone to go take care of breakfast in the dining room, if it hadn't already been served.

Kelli stared at the tea and toast. But her thoughts were far away.

She remembered talking about wishes with Les. What would her three wishes be, if they found a genie in a lamp?

As much money as she needed, to buy anything she wanted. She had wealth now. Everything she could want. Her father wanted to give her everything, even things she didn't think she needed. He was only too happy to oblige if she asked for anything. He tried to anticipate what she might need, and provide it. A car. A computer. Whatever she needed.

A parent who cared about her. She couldn't deny that he loved her. He had sworn to stick by her even when it was possible that he was not her biological father. He stood firm in the face of gossip, Preston's fury, and Kelli's own uncertainty. She'd never had a parent who wanted to take care of her before. It was a foreign feeling. She didn't know how to deal with it. But she did have a parent who cared.

And most importantly of all, the birthmark wiped away. The disfigurement that had drawn stares for as long as she could remember was gone. Invisible. It was still there, but no one could see it. She had always thought it would change her life if she didn't have a birthmark. But nothing had changed. She might not get stared at anymore, but she was still the same person.

She might have changed her outer appearance. She might have a parent who cared about her. She might have all that she could ever want in material goods. But nothing had changed. She was still as uncertain and anxious as ever.

Kelli had never had such trouble getting out of bed. There had always been so much to do. And she had looked forward to seeing Les before school started.

Kelli put the breakfast tray on the floor and lay back down again, putting her head on the pillow. She closed her eyes and pretended that she was asleep again and she didn't have anything to worry about.

CHAPTER 24

Lisa checked in on Kelli when she got home from school. She knocked, but didn't wait outside the room for an answer. Instead she barged right in and went up to Kelli's bed.

"Hey, lazybones. Aren't you up yet?"

Kelli groaned and turned her face away from Lisa. She didn't want to have to deal with people. Lisa didn't take the hint, and sat down on the edge of the bed.

"Are you sick? For real?"

"No… just… tired."

"Tired? You don't get to skip school for tired. If Daddy finds out, you'll be in hot water."

"He already knows," Kelli pointed out. He couldn't very well have missed the fact that she hadn't gone down for breakfast or gotten in her car to go to school. He already knew what was going on. Kelli hoped that he understood how hard it was for her to go to school with everything that was going on. Once life settled down again, and the dummy account was deleted, she'd go back to school again. It would only be a few days. She'd be able to catch up again. And if she needed a tutor to help get her back on track, the judge would provide that without question.

"You can't just stay in bed all day. You should get up and shower. Come down for dinner."

Kelli pulled her pillow over her face. "Don't want to go down for dinner."

"You have to eat!" Lisa stretched her neck for a look at the breakfast tray beside the bed. "Have you eaten anything today?"

Kelli grunted, hoping that Lisa would interpret the answer as she pleased and just let it go.

"Kelli?" Lisa persisted. "Have you had anything to eat today?"

"Yes, I had breakfast and Felicia brought up some soup for lunch, too."

She didn't fill Lisa in on the fact that she hadn't been able to keep either meal down, but she didn't need to know that part. In fact, she didn't need to know anything. She was just being nosy.

"Well, that's good. Now get up and go get showered. I'll see you at dinner."

Kelli didn't move or acknowledge the command. Eyes cracked open just a hair, she watched through her lashes as Lisa left the room. Lisa was different from that first day they had met, when Preston and Lisa came to dinner. Was she different because she wasn't acting out in front of her mother anymore? She seemed more like a normal person. More herself instead of drama queen. She was different when there wasn't someone watching.

Kelli wondered what she herself was like when no one was watching. Around other people, was she always conning? Was she ever just herself? What did that person look like, act like?

She closed her eyes and buried her head under the pillow again and blocked it all out.

———

"Kelli. Kelli. Wake up and talk to me."

Kelli opened her eyes reluctantly to look at the judge. She groaned to indicate that she was still tired and didn't want to talk. But he didn't back off. He sat down on the edge of the bed, leaning over her.

"Kelli."

"Just let me be," Kelli begged. "I don't feel well."

"What's going on? And don't tell me it's nothing, because you've barely gotten out of bed for three days."

Kelli rubbed her eyes.

"I'll be fine. Just give me…"

"I've given you plenty of time to rest, if that was what you needed. I think this is something more. So, talk to me."

"I just don't feel up to it."

"I expect you to get out of bed and rejoin the family, or I will be taking you to the doctor."

"I'm not sick."

"Is this because of Lisa? You're going to have to get used to her being here, because I'm not sure that she and Preston are going to reconcile."

"No. It's okay about Lisa. I don't mind her being here. She's been okay."

He looked relieved to hear that. "Good. Get yourself out of bed, because I will cancel my cases tomorrow to take you to the doctor."

Kelli groaned. "Why can't I just stay here?"

"For how long? Until you've got bedsores?"

"Just until…" Kelli trailed off. Until everything was sorted out with her online accounts? Until she made some friends? Until she felt better about the person she was? Until everything was normal again?

"You can talk to me, Kelli. Tell me what you're thinking."

Kelli sighed. "I'll try."

He waited, not moving from where he sat.

"I said I'll try," Kelli repeated, raising her voice.

"You'll try what? I'm waiting for you to tell me what's wrong."

"No… I'll try to get up."

He waited.

"In a minute," Kelli clarified. "You can go."

He sighed in exasperation and stood up. "I'll make an appointment for you to see someone. This has obviously just been too much for you."

Kelli tried to protest, but didn't know what to say. She wanted to tell him how wrong he was? That she was stronger than that? That all the changes had been positive, so why should any of it bother her?

"I'm up, I'm up!"

She forced herself out of the bed, onto shaky legs. How long had it been since she had stood? She had still been making trips to the bathroom, especially after her meals, so it wasn't like it was the first time in three days that she had stood. But it felt like it.

The judge grasped her arm gently to make sure that she was stable. Kelli pulled away. "I told you, I'm fine."

"Get yourself fixed up and come down for dinner. I need to know that you really are okay."

Kelli nodded. "I know, I know."

He looked at her for a moment longer, then nodded and left her alone. Kelli rolled her eyes and headed for the shower. She hadn't showered or even combed her hair in three days. It was going to take some time to get herself properly 'fixed up.' Especially well enough to convince the judge that she was okay and didn't need to see a doctor.

She was feeling better when she got downstairs to the dining room. Better than she had felt in a long time. She felt lighter, like a burden had been lifted from her shoulders. She had been fighting for a long time.

But now… she had fought the good fight. She was done.

The decision to stop fighting against the misfortunes that fate slung at her brought her a sense of calm. She felt like a loud clamor had been silenced, and that for the first time, all was peace and quiet.

Which was funny, because at the moment she walked into the dining room, Lisa and the judge were head-to-head in a loud argument.

"I'm old enough to make my own decisions!" Lisa screeched.

"You're not yet an adult. I know you think you're qualified to make all the decisions that affect your life, but your brain isn't yet fully developed and there are deficits that teenagers have—"

"Quit reading Scientific America and listen to me! I'm not some experiment, I'm a person!"

"I'm aware that you're a person," Justice Emerson Forester said in his usual calm way. "And I am treating you like one. I'm telling you that it's not in your best interest to—" He cut off suddenly, as both of them noticed that Kelli was there.

Kelli raised her eyebrows, then laughed. "Hiya. Is this dinner or a show?"

"Your sister and I were just having a discussion—"

"We are not sisters!" Lisa shouted. "We're not related in any way! Don't you dare call us sisters!"

Her father looked slightly startled at this new outburst. "You are both my daughters," he pointed out. "That would make you sisters."

"No, it wouldn't," Lisa insisted. "We're not related by blood and we're not related legally. We're not related in any way!"

"Okay. I'm sorry. I didn't say it to offend you. Kelli," he turned back to her. "I'm sorry for the disturbance. Lisa and I were just having an… involved discussion… about some family issues. We are done for now. We can sit down and have a civilized dinner."

Kelli laughed. "Whatever you want. I don't care if you keep discussing it. Doesn't make any difference to me."

The judge held Kelli's chair for her, and then sat down in his seat. They had a salad course in relative silence.

"You look like you're feeling better," Lisa observed.

Kelli looked up from her plate. "Yes," she agreed. "I'm doing much better now."

"I guess you just needed a rest… one can get run down, spreading themselves too thin…"

Kelli could hear Preston in Lisa's diction. "Yes, one can," she agreed. "And I think one did."

"You need to make sure that you're getting to bed in good time," Justice Emerson Forester suggested. "You know you have to be up early in the morning, and teenagers need up to ten hours of sleep a night. If your homework and studies are taking too long, we might need to make adjustments, or get a tutor to help you out a bit. Nothing wrong with that. I'm sure you don't want your schoolwork to take all night."

"No," Kelli agreed in a light tone. She didn't get upset over the suggestion that she might need some tutoring. What difference did it make? She wouldn't need any tutoring now.

He looked at her for a moment as if surprised by her acquiescence, then nodded. "You are looking a lot better. I'm glad. I was getting pretty worried about you."

"I told you I'd be fine."

"Good."

The main course was served. Kelli dug into the vegetarian lasagna. She didn't even worry about how much she was eating.

———

The last thing that she did before bed was to take the sleeping pills. Her father didn't need to worry about her not getting enough sleep. That wasn't going to be an issue.

She smoothed her blankets down, making them all neat around her with no wrinkles. It was a beautiful bedspread. A comfortable bed in a room all her own. The judge really had given her everything she needed. She couldn't have asked for anything more. He was a good guy. Generous. He didn't give her things to make up for hitting her. He didn't try to guilt her with all he had done for her. He just gave because he was a nice guy who wanted to do something nice for his daughter who had been raised by someone else and gone through some difficult times.

Kelli reached over and shut off the lamp on the bedside table. She was starting to get sleepy. The sleeping pills were taking effect, and before long, she'd be peacefully off to dreamland. She mentally said goodnight to the judge. To Patricia and Axel. To Les. To Lisa. Before she could think of anyone else she might have missed, she was asleep.

CHAPTER 25

She did not wake up to angels singing or to bare nothingness. Instead, there was a cacophony of sound that she couldn't separate out into separate, identifiable noises. There was pain and movement and being sick. The indignities didn't seem to end. Her face slapped and pinched. Tubes running into her mouth and nose. Being handled like a doll or a bag of trash, tossed from one table to another, rolled over, undressed, thrown around like a sack of potatoes.

Her head hurt. Her throat hurt, all the way from her chest to her mouth and her nasal passages. Her stomach hurt. Her whole body felt bruised, like she'd been in a fight or through a difficult training session at the Dragon.

When she tried to talk, the words wouldn't come out. She gagged and choked and coughed.

Lights shone in her eyes. So bright and penetrating it hurt her brain.

They wouldn't leave her alone. Every time she hoped to drift off into nothingness, they were there again. Shaking her, jabbing her with a needle, putting in or taking out another tube.

Kelli coughed again. Her throat felt raw. The tickle felt like it was ripping her all up. "Water?"

There was a straw held to her lips, and Kelli sucked the room temperature water down, irrigating her throat. The coughing finally settled and she lay back on her pillows, breathing hard.

"Are you awake, Kelli?"

Kelli tried to wave him away. She didn't want to talk. She just wanted to sleep. A deep sleep that she would never wake up from.

"Kelli?" He grabbed her hand and squeezed it. "Wake up. Time to talk."

"No. Just let me… sleep…"

"Come on. Wake up. They said they wouldn't know whether there was brain damage until you were talking. Talk to me. Prove that you're still there."

Kelli put her free hand up to her eyes. They were swollen and sensitive to the light, even with her lids closed. She couldn't possibly pry them open. She laid her hand over them. There was a tugging on the back of her hand. Something taped there. It hurt. Everything hurt.

"Too bright," she told him.

He stood up. She heard him pull a cord and the light behind her eyelids dimmed. "There. How's that?"

Kelli tried to coax her eyes open, but the assault on her eyes was still too bright.

"It hurts."

"What hurts? Your eyes?"

Kelli sniffled. Her nose was dry and felt scraped raw. Even changing her expression pulled at the scabby, sore membranes. "Everything hurts."

"I'm sorry to hear that…" She had finally identified his voice as Justice Emerson Forester's. She didn't know who she thought he was before that. A doctor maybe? She hadn't really had a cogent thought. "But at the same time, I'm glad. At least it means you're alive."

Kelli breathed, thinking about that. Breathing hurt too. Her chest and ribs hurt. Her stomach and the valve she couldn't think of the name for, the one that gave her heartburn, it hurt too. It felt both burned and bruised. Like someone had jammed a lit book of matches in there. She groaned.

"Do you want me to get a nurse?" the judge asked. "They might be willing to give you something for the pain." Something about his voice said that he doubted it.

Kelli doubted it too. They would be very careful about what they gave her or allowed her to have. They would be watching every movement she made for a good long while.

"I'm sorry."

She felt crushed under the weight of the guilt. She had felt so good about her decision. She had been happy, after a lifetime of struggles and fighting against the constant flow of discouragement, to just let go, and let herself drift away forever.

He gave her hand a squeeze. "Talk to me. Why? It doesn't make any sense."

"I don't know… I just… I was just so tired of being… tired and scared and anxious. I just… I just don't want to do it anymore."

"Why didn't you tell me you were feeling that way? I told you that I would get you an appointment with a therapist. I offered to take you to the doctor. We could have gotten you some help without going through all this."

"I didn't want to talk about it."

"Kelli. Please. You think I want to lose you?"

Kelli shook her head slightly. "You could go back to it just being you and Lisa."

"And Preston?" he reminded her.

"No… tell her to go jump in a lake."

The judge was so surprised, he laughed aloud. "I never had any intention of cutting Preston and Lisa off. They're not going to inherit the bulk of my estate, but I never meant to cut them out of my life. Lisa, anyway, and she and Preston are a package deal."

"Still?"

"Hard to say right now. She and Preston have had fights before. This isn't the first time this kind of drama has played out in our lives. They're both high-strung."

"Not like you and me."

He let go of her hand for a moment to brush his fingertips down her cheek. Then he took her hand again. "You and I maybe go too far the other direction," he admitted. "We repress things. Lock them up. Pretend that we don't feel them. We decide we don't want to talk to others about our troubles. Don't want to bring them down."

Kelli nodded agreement.

"But we need to, Kelli. We need to admit that we don't have all the answers. That we're not strong enough to bear it all on our own. We need to be willing to ask for help when we need it."

"Mmm."

"I wish you had come to me, sweetheart. We could have avoided this. We could have found some way to help you."

"More water?"

He held the straw to her lips again. Kelli didn't try to take it from him and hold the glass herself. She was too tired and sore to do even that.

"The doctor said you would have a sore throat."

"Yeah."

She waited for more recriminations, but there was nothing more. They stayed in silence for a long time. Kelli wanted to go to sleep, but the pain now kept her awake and her brain worked feverishly, trying to find another way to escape.

"How... what happened...?"

"You had a seizure. Your movements made the headboard hit the wall repeatedly. Woke Lisa up, and she went to see what was going on."

"Oh."

"Otherwise... I suppose we would have found your body in the morning. It would have been too late to save you at that point."

"Uh-huh." That had been the plan. Go in her sleep. Nothing messy or painful. They would find her in the morning, resting peacefully at last. Gone on to her final reward, whatever that might be. She didn't suppose she could con God into giving her a mansion. But maybe she could talk the devil into something.

"This has been so hard to go through, Kelli. I want you to know... This was really hard on everyone. The whole household. Poor Lisa... walking into your room figuring that you were trying to bug her or were up to no good, and finding you like that... That girl has a set of lungs on her."

That she did. Kelli hadn't heard the scream. Not consciously, anyhow. But she'd heard Lisa's voice raised enough times before to be able to guess at it. Who needed a fire alarm when they had Lisa?

"I'm sorry about that."

"Please promise me you'll never do anything like this again. I couldn't lose you like that, Kelli. I would blame myself for the rest of my life. Tell me what I can do to make you happy."

Kelli sighed, and lightly massaged her sore eyeballs beneath her closed lids. "I don't think... there isn't anything you can do. You've already given me whatever I wanted..."

"I'm not talking about buying you things," he said quietly.

She gave his hand a squeeze, sorry for not being able to give him any answers.

"Have you been depressed before?"

"I don't know."

"You haven't been treated for depression before?"

Kelli thought back. "I don't know. I've seen therapists before. You act out at school too much, and they call in the shrinks. I don't know if I was depressed... or just messed up."

"I wish you'd told me." He went back to the same line again.

"I guess."

There was another period of silence. Kelli listened to the machine beeping beside her, and almost managed to open her eyes to look around. But the world was still too bright and harsh for her.

"I suppose I knew," Justice Emerson Forester admitted.

"What?"

"That you were depressed. It was sort of obvious with refusing to get out of bed for days on end... but I thought it was just the emails... that you'd be fine once they got it straightened out. I was going to take you to the doctor. But then... you seemed like you'd bounced back. You seemed so much happier, like you'd gotten through the valley and were climbing the other side..."

"No," Kelli said. "Just... decided it wasn't worth going any further. I did feel better, once I decided. It felt good."

"And I pushed you into that decision."

"No. It wasn't anything you did. It was just... I didn't have the strength anymore. To keep fighting. It was just too hard."

"It all happened so fast!" He patted her hair with his other hand. "You were doing so well... and then you were depressed for a few days... and then you did this! I didn't know it could happen so fast. I thought you had to be down for months before they would diagnose depression... that it would be a long time before... this..."

"It *has* been a long time. I just couldn't fight it anymore."

"It has?"

Kelli nodded.

"How long?"

"I don't know. It's just been so long, I don't know when it started." She considered. "Months... years..."

"Since before you came here?"

Kelli nodded. "Yeah."

"I never would have guessed. You always seemed so cheerful and easygoing. I didn't know anything was wrong."

"Preston told you… I'm a con artist. It's what I do."

She felt him stiffen. "What do you mean, Preston told me?"

"That day they came over to dinner. She told you I was just a con, that I would just con you out of everything you had. She told you that's why I was there."

"How could you know that? You heard that?"

"Uh-huh."

Justice Emerson Forester groaned. "Why didn't you tell me you heard? What a thing for a child to overhear about herself!"

Kelli tried to laugh, but it hurt her throat and made her start coughing again. He put the straw to her lips. Kelli drank a few sips, calming her throat down again.

"It's not like I didn't already know. She's right. I *am* a con artist. And proud of it. That wasn't really why I went to find you… but it wasn't the furthest thing from my mind. Not after seeing the cottage."

"Anything I have…"

"I know. There wasn't any point in stealing from you or trying to talk you into giving me something, when you were so free with everything. Takes all the fun out of it."

"Then you know about what she did. That she hired a private investigator. That she went through your room. All of her accusations."

"Maybe not all of it. But I figured the rest. Figured you probably investigated me too. I would have, if I was you."

He didn't answer.

"You had to send someone to check me out," Kelli insisted, sensing his guilt. "You couldn't just assume that you knew who I was, the kind of person I was. I could be anyone. I *could* murder you in your sleep."

The judge snorted. "That was never a concern."

"Well, good… but it should have been."

"After all you've been through, Kelli… I wasn't going to treat you like a criminal."

"You're too trusting. I don't think you're like that in court, or your business dealings. But you've got a bit of a blind spot."

"My family. I know it. I'm a judge, I know I didn't have to give Preston any kind of support. We had a prenup and I still gave her money and property when she left. But she was my wife. I've supported her because it was the right thing to do. The gentlemanly thing. And I might have owed Lisa support, but it would have been a lot less than the payments I have made over the years."

"You're too nice."

"I haven't been. I've been hard to live with. The instigator of fights. I have never been physically abusive, but mentally…? Emotionally…? I wasn't there for Preston. I was barely around when Lisa was a baby and in those early years before we broke up. I figured I had to make my millions, and my family would have to wait until things were quieter. The guy you see now… the easygoing, laid-back judge who has time to stop and enjoy the roses…? That guy didn't exist when Lisa was little. I realized too late that I had wasted my time making money and didn't have anyone left to share it with."

Kelli tried to picture it. On one hand, it was hard to believe that the loving, doting father she had come to know hadn't always been that way. But on the other hand, she had seen his steel at times. His determination. His stubbornness. And she knew it in herself, too. Sure, she helped at home with cooking and cleaning. So that she could live in something other than a house full of trash. And she spent time with Les and gave him a generous cut of her winnings to help him support his family. Because it was fun, and taking people's money was addictive, and she didn't want to have to go home and deal with her parents. She had a nice side, making cereal for Patricia or mac and cheese for Axel. But she also had a mean, selfish streak. Dumping Patricia's booze down the drain. Pushing her out of the way or leaving her lying in the middle of the floor where she had passed out. Telling her teachers and strangers sob stories to make them feel bad for her and give her a break on assignments or money or bus tickets or something else of value.

The judge was human too. He had also wanted nice things. A big house and car. A prestigious job. A high position in society. He wanted to make his millions, and so he had. Maybe he'd shouted at Lisa when she was little, for getting in his way or for crying when he was trying to deal with business or to rest before bed. Maybe he had fought with Preston and neglected her so that she had sought comfort elsewhere. Only the three of them knew what had gone on within the walls of the cottage, or wherever they had lived at the time.

"Are you asleep?" the judge whispered.

Kelli startled slightly. She had been starting to drift off, lost in her imaginings.

"Tell me… about your family."

"What's to tell? You know them."

"I mean… your parents. Brothers. Sisters. Where did you come from?"

"Oh…" He readjusted his position and shifted his grip on her hand. "That was a long time ago."

"Where did you come from? Are you an 'old money' millionaire or a 'new money' millionaire?" Kelli had learned this distinction over the summer, as she had circulated at parties and found that even amongst the very rich, there was a hierarchy. A snobbishness.

"New money," Justice Emerson Forester admitted. "My parents weren't poor. Middle class. Working class. Not the type of people who had the money to send their son to law school. I had to work and take out loans. Nobody ever encouraged me to become a lawyer. I don't think they thought I could actually accomplish it. Certainly no one thought I would make it as a judge. But I was one of the youngest ever appointed. I made friends who helped me make good investments. Got lucky a few times. I was already well-to-do when I met Preston. She never had to struggle like I did those first years. But that wasn't enough, and I needed all my time to make more."

"Did you have siblings?"

"I have a brother and a sister. Both blue collar. They have families and children. We don't really have anything to do with each other. We all went our own way, and didn't keep in touch very closely. A card at Christmas. Send flowers on Mother's Day. I could do a lot more."

"That's sad. I always wanted brothers and sisters, like Les… but I'm glad that my mom never had any other kids. It's probably best."

"You're probably right. My mother went through episodes of depression… I guess that's why I thought… I figured you'd bounce back from it…"

"Is she… still alive?"

"No, she died when Lisa was—when you were young."

"Was it because of…"

"It wasn't suicide." He squeezed Kelli's hand. "It was her heart. Which I guess can be related to depression."

He was quiet for a while.

"I'm glad it wasn't suicide. That would have made it a lot harder."

———

The doctor was happy to find that Kelli was awake and carrying on a conversation with her father.

But waking up was just the beginning. They had medications to try out, had her in therapy, had Justice Emerson Forester compiling a family history and giving them all the details he knew of his mother's fight against depression. Kelli wasn't given any time to be bored, moved from one appointment or therapy to another, exhausted any time they left her alone.

The pain gradually went away. She learned details about what had happened between the time she took the pills and when she woke up. Her stomach had been pumped. Her heart had stopped and she'd been given CPR. The seizure had left her with bruises, a lacerated tongue, and muscle and joint pain. All in all, overdosing on sleeping pills had not turned out to be the blissful, peaceful departure she had imagined.

Lisa visited her at the hospital when she was allowed on a family visiting day. Preston did not. And Patricia and Axel were not in evidence. Kelli assumed that they didn't know she was there, but Justice Emerson Forester let it slip one day that he had informed them as to what had happened.

"You called Patricia?" Kelli repeated.

The judge looked at her, pursing his lips, and she watched his eyes as he weighed whether it was better for Kelli if he told her what she wanted to know, or withheld information.

"She is your mother," he said flatly. "She did raise you. Just because I'm your biological father, that doesn't give me the right to exclude her. I thought she would want to know."

Kelli turned away from him. "But she didn't, did she?"

He frowned. "I'm not sure… that she really understood… The woman that I sent said she wasn't very coherent. She didn't react emotionally, she just got angry. I guess that is an emotion and she was just reacting in a different way than we expected… They always talk about anger being one of the stages of grief…"

"Who did you send?" Kelli's heart pounded hard. Had they sent a policewoman or a social worker over there? Someone who was going to make trouble for Patricia? "Why didn't you just call her on the phone?"

"I thought she deserved a little more sensitivity than to be told over the phone. Notifications like that should always be done through face-to-face contact."

"Who did you send?" Kelli repeated.

Justice Emerson Forester looked at her, uncertain. There was a crease between his eyebrows. "Does it matter who I sent? I couldn't leave you alone to do it myself."

"Yes!"

"I asked Cassia to do it." He watched Kelli's face for her reaction.

Kelli breathed out. Cassia. On the plus side, he hadn't sent a police officer or social worker. On the negative… Cassia knew everybody in Kelli's social circle, and while Kelli didn't think she would gossip about all the details, she was in a position to damage Kelli's reputation by revealing the kind of life she had come from.

"I'm sorry. She was the best person I could think of. And she knows you. She wanted to do whatever she could to help."

"Yeah. It's okay. I just… I wish you hadn't contacted Patricia. She isn't very well."

If he had done his background on Kelli, and if Cassia had reported back, then the judge knew very well what kind of condition Patricia was in, and Kelli didn't need to couch it in such socially acceptable terms.

"We didn't know if you were going to survive. Or if there would be permanent damage. She had to be told."

"I guess."

There was silence between them for a while. Kelli picked up the remote for the TV and flipped through channels restlessly. The judge went back to his book. But the silence was uncomfortable. Not like when they read together in the library. Something hung between them.

"How long has she been like that?" the judge asked, closing his book again.

"Like that? I don't know. I don't know what she was like when Cassia was there. She's had… a drinking problem for a long time. Then she's been developing dementia… so it's getting worse…"

"Is somebody… monitoring things?"

Kelli shrugged. "She has a doctor. She's been seeing him."

"But nobody on the home front? It sounds like she might need some assistance…"

"I'll check back in on her," Kelli said. "Once I'm out of here."

"It shouldn't fall to you. You can't be responsible for her."

"Well, I am." Kelli dismissed him.

"Maybe that's part of the problem. Yours and hers."

"You don't think I'm mature enough to handle it?"

"I don't think you're qualified. I think it's too big a burden for you. I don't think you need to be dealing with this at the same time as your mental health issues."

Kelli looked for a comeback. He didn't know how these things worked. Maybe he knew the way they worked in his world, where there was plenty of money to throw at any problem, but it wasn't the same where Kelli came from.

"Have you talked to your psychologist about this?"

"Why would I? It's not any of his business."

"It has an effect on you, don't you think? Anything that has an effect on your mental health should be provided to him."

Kelli shook her head. "This is family business. I don't talk to anyone about family business."

Justice Emerson Forester's mouth formed a straight, thin line.

Kelli looked at him. "What?" she demanded.

"Do you know where I hear that line? The only time I ever hear that is in abusive families. Not talking to outsiders. Not talking about family business. Keeping their lives private. That's a line that parents use on their kids to keep them from talking about abuse."

"We're talking about my mom's brain, not about abuse. What are you talking about?"

"What are you afraid of? Why are you afraid to talk about your mom's problems with a therapist? Your psychologist should know the whole picture. What things are making you stressed and causing issues. You disagree?"

"It's none of his business," Kelli maintained.

"How has that worked for you so far? Has that made things better for you?"

Kelli shook her head. "You don't know how it works," she said. "You haven't had to live with this. I have."

"Then tell me." The judge's expression was stubborn.

Kelli folded her arms across her chest. She didn't like being backed into a corner. "It's private, family information. I don't want to talk about it."

———

When she got out of the hospital, Kelli went up to her room, relieved to be able to get some privacy. To finally get away from all of the prying eyes. All the observers. All the questions. She was a private person, and it irked her to have to be around doctors, nurses, therapists, and other patients all the time.

She put down her small bag and looked around the room. Something was wrong. It felt cold and oppressive. Kelli waited for the warm, comforting feeling of home to blanket her. But it didn't come.

She opened her computer and logged into her email. Most of them she just dragged them into the garbage after looking at the subject line. There was one referencing her ticket number, the official complaint about the fake account that had caused her so much trouble. There was a brief, clinical line saying that the offending account had been deleted. Kelli stared at it for a few minutes, and then deleted it and closed the lid of the computer.

She sat down on the bed. Instead of feeling happy to be home, her anxiety was rocketing through the roof. She wanted to stretch out on her bed to read a book or have a nap, but the bedroom was where she had hoped to die. It was where she had gone into seizures, her head whacking the headboard and the headboard whacking the wall, alerting Lisa.

Even though the bed was neatly made, as it always was, Kelli still saw the scene play out before her. Maybe she had been aware of what was going on, even through the effects of the sleeping pills. Or maybe it was just like with Axel, her brain making up a story to fill in the blanks. She saw herself lying there, convulsing in seizures, and everybody gathered around her. Lisa, her father, the paramedics, the household staff, all hanging over her, aware that she had tried to end her life and that they had to stop it. To save her life against her own wishes.

She saw Lisa's tears and heard her shrieks of horror when she found Kelli convulsing. She saw the way her father looked at her. The horror and deep sadness. The desperation of the paramedic to identify all of the factors and try to save her life.

There was no sign of the scene that had played out there. No discarded syringes or wrappers. No sign of vomit from trying to throw up enough of the poison to save her life. Nor the bodily fluids released during the seizure. Dr. David had told her everything that had happened in great detail, making sure that she'd never be able to forget what she had done to her body. To her family. Kelli saw it all vividly enacted before her, but the cleaning staff had done their job. They had removed every sign. It all looked neat, clean, and innocuous.

Kelli got up off of the bed. She couldn't lie down and rest. She couldn't sleep there. She couldn't fit in there anymore. Not that she had ever really belonged. She was the outsider. The imposter. She'd done a good job of convincing everyone that she belonged there, but she really didn't. She had never convinced herself. The room had never belonged to her.

She paced around, trying to sort things out in her mind.

It had all started when she moved there. When she tried to make herself into something that she wasn't. That hadn't been her goal to start with. She had started out just trying to find her roots. To find the man who was really her father. To find the woman who was really her mother. Her biological heritage. But she'd gone too far. She'd tried to assume that life. The life that had been denied her. It wasn't hers to take. A different family, friends, and school didn't make her a different person. All the nice clothes and hair in the world couldn't change her from a street urchin into a society lady. The erasure of the birthmark didn't unmark her. She was still the same marred person under the ink.

There was a knock on the door, and Justice Emerson Forester was there, looking in on her, making sure that she was settled in and everything was fine. He seemed surprised to find her pacing. He raised his brows at her behavior.

"Everything okay?"

"No." Kelli tried to think of what to say. How to explain the conclusion she had come to. "I need... I need you to understand something."

He nodded slowly. "Yes... what is it?"

"I can't stay here." Kelli rushed through it, trying to get all of the words out before he could interrupt. "I don't belong here. I never did. I need to go back where I belong. Back home."

"Back home?"

"Yes."

"I don't understand." He shook his head. "What did I do?"

"Nothing. It's not about you. It's me. I just... it's not right. I can't live here. There's too much that's different. I thought it didn't matter, as long as I acted like I belonged. But that's not true. It does matter. I wasn't raised to this life and I can't pretend anymore."

"Kelli. You can be whatever person you are. You don't have to pretend to be anyone or anything that you're not. I want you to be yourself. To be genuine and tell the truth. Don't hide it all behind a mask. I want to find out who you really are."

"Who I really am… is a girl who belongs in the old neighborhood. Not here. I can't be genuine here. It's like that old show you were laughing at the other day. That Beverly Hillbillies. They could never be comfortable or belong there, because it wasn't who they were."

"But they did. They found ways to adapt. Ways that didn't mean giving up their identity."

"That's because it's a show. It's just a story. Not real life. In real life…" Kelli shook her head. "You can't just jump into someone else's world."

"That's not true. I did. I told you I didn't grow up in this society. I had to learn to fit in. You can too. You were doing just fine. Really."

"Outside," Kelli said. "Inside I was dying."

"Kelli…"

"Don't try to talk me into anything. I need to go home. I can't stay here."

"I don't understand," he protested. "You were doing just fine. You were happy to be coming back here, to get out of the hospital and be back again. What happened?"

Kelli looked around the bedroom. She would have said that it was haunted. Except that the ghost was her.

"I can't," she repeated. "I just can't do it."

CHAPTER 26

The judge had to drop Kelli off. She knew she couldn't keep her own car in the neighborhood, it would be stolen or vandalized. She left it back at the cottage. Justice Emerson Forester could sell it. She wouldn't be needing it anymore.

"You'll still come back for visits, won't you?" the judge asked. "You're not going to drop out of sight completely? You'll need a vehicle to come back."

"I don't know. I'll find a junker."

She was anxious about him being the one to drive her home, but there was no other solution. She couldn't sleep at the cottage for even one night. Either her father or one of the staff had to drive her home. And he wanted to do it himself. He didn't want one of the staff members doing it. Kelli would have been happier had he allowed Felicia to do it. But it wasn't a safe neighborhood for Felicia to be driving in at night.

His knowing where she used to live and actually being there and seeing it were two very different things. She was sure the private investigator had laid it all out in his reports. But that couldn't compare with driving up in front of the house in the twilight.

Justice Emerson Forester's face was a tight, unreadable mask as he drove through the neighborhood streets getting closer and closer to the house. He glanced a couple of times at Kelli, but didn't make any comment on how rough the area was getting. She quietly gave him directions until they pulled in front of the house.

Kelli saw the judge take in the unkempt yard and long grass. The lopsided blinds covering the windows. The dented, peeling siding. It wasn't a pretty picture. Kelli leaned over to kiss him on the cheek.

"This is it. Thanks for dropping me off. I'll… call you."

"Will you? I feel like…" He shook his head. "I feel like I did something wrong. And you're… running away from me. Like Lisa with Preston. I don't understand what I did, but I don't want to lose you, Kelli."

"You're not losing me. I'm just… living somewhere else."

"Will you call me tomorrow? Let me know if everything is okay? Tell me… if you change your mind?"

"I'll try to call you. But I'm not going to change my mind."

She opened the door and forced her feet to swing over to the sidewalk and for the rest of her body to follow them out. It was what she wanted. To go back home again. To go back to where she started from, back to where she belonged. It was hard to say goodbye to the judge, with him being so sad about the separation. But she was sure they would talk and see each other again. It wasn't a permanent goodbye.

She walked up to the front door without looking back at the car and waving. No long, drawn-out goodbyes. Keep it short and cut it off. She opened the front door without knocking or ringing the bell, and stepped in.

Back into the world she belonged in. The smell and the closeness of the too-warm, dark room. She could see the glow of the TV and hear a canned laugh track. She couldn't yet see Patricia. It hadn't been that long since Kelli had been in the house, but it was already significantly worse than it had been the day she responded to Patricia's distress call. As if someone had brought a truckload of garbage home from the dump instead of taking it out. Kelli picked her way through the garbage, pushing aside what she could to make a path for herself. She called out as she got closer to her mother, so Patricia wouldn't be startled.

"Mom? Hey, what's been going on here? You have a big party or something?"

Patricia made no answer. Kelli paused beside a pile of moving boxes, and listened. She could hear Patricia breathing heavily. It was too early for her to be passed out already, but maybe she had fallen asleep after her afternoon shows. Kelli frowned at the moving boxes, wondering where they had come from, and gave them a little tap to see if they were full. The top ones seemed empty, but the bottom ones were more full.

"Hey, Mom. Are you moving?"

She got up to the easy chair and shook Patricia's shoulder.

"Mom. Wake up. I came back. What's going on here?"

Patricia woke slowly and looked at Kelli with bleary eyes. "What... what are you doing here?"

"I came back."

"What are you doing in my house?" Patricia's voice rose. "Help! There's somebody in my house! Help me!"

Kelli patted her arm. "Mom, calm down. You wanted me to come back, remember?"

Kelli stared into Patricia's panicky eyes, and saw no recognition there.

"Mom. It's Kelli."

Patricia stared at her. Neither of them moved for a long time. Kelli waited for the recognition to come. For Patricia to last a nasty laugh and say of course she remembered Kelli, and what was she doing just standing around picking her nose?

"Mom," Kelli repeated.

"You're not Kelli," Patricia said finally.

Kelli laughed. But she wasn't amused. "Mom, it *is* Kelli," she said. "I'm your daughter. Don't you recognize me?"

Patricia's head shook back and forth. No. She cleared her throat, a long, wet-sounding noise. "You aren't my daughter. My daughter... had a mark on her face. You don't have a mark on your face."

Kelli flashed back to her last visit with Patricia. That had been the first time that Patricia had seen her without her birthmark. She hadn't pointed out the lack of a birthmark, but the room had been dim, and Patricia had been confused. Maybe she didn't really look at Kelli's face. Or maybe she had been too confused to notice the lack of a birthmark. She had still seemed to know who Kelli was. Was it better that she didn't notice the lack of a birthmark? Or was it better when she did?

"Mom, I got the birthmark removed. It is Kelli, Mom. I promise. Don't you recognize me?"

Patricia touched her own face. "It's so dark in here. Why doesn't someone turn on the lights? I don't know where I put down my glasses."

"Give me a second and I'll turn some lights on," Kelli agreed. She pushed her way through the garbage, trying to reach the wall where the light switch was. She reached around a towering pile of laundry and gave it a flick. There was a flash of light and a *pop*, and they remained in the same dimness as before.

Patricia gave a little shriek. "What was that? What did you do?"

"I just tried to turn on the light, Mom. It's okay. The bulb burned out." Kelli tried another switch. This time, a lamp rewarded her with a weak, sixty-watt pool of light. "There, see? Is that better?"

Patricia looked around, and then back at Kelli. "Who are you? What are you doing in my house? You can't just walk into people's houses!"

"I'm Kelli. Your daughter. Remember? I look a little different now. Because I've been away for a while. But it's still me."

"My daughter is dead," Patricia snapped. "Who do you think you're trying to fool here? You are not my daughter."

Kelli swallowed. There was a particularly large lump in her throat. What was she getting so choked up about? She had wanted to die. That was the message that Patricia would have received, if Kelli's attempt had been successful. *We're sorry, ma'am. Your daughter is dead. She took a bottle of sleeping pills and killed herself. So sorry.* Wasn't that what would have happened? Some cop or social worker would have shown up and told Patricia that Kelli was dead. And Patricia would sit there in her chair and feel... what? Would she be sad? Relieved? What would it mean to her?

"I'm not dead," Kelli said. "If someone told you that... they were wrong. I was... sick in hospital. But I'm okay now. And I came home. To help you."

"I don't need any help. My daughter is dead. I don't know who you are; you can just leave."

Kelli stood there for a minute, trying to decide how to handle the situation. Then she shrugged. She went into the kitchen and turned on the kitchen light. The room was a disaster area. She couldn't even find the coffee maker. She pushed things around on the counter, looking for it, with no luck. The smell of mold and rotting food was powerfully strong. Kelli opened the fridge, and the stench in there was even worse. She walked back into the living room, trying to keep from gagging.

"Mom, what's with the moving boxes? Are you moving out?"

Maybe they had a place ready for her at a nursing home. That would certainly throw a wrench into Kelli's plans. But maybe it would be the best thing for Patricia.

"They brought me the boxes," Patricia said, swiveling her head around to look at the piles of boxes. "They said I have to move out. That it's not safe."

Kelli looked at the rotting trash on the floor. Health inspectors must have been called in. She hadn't seen a condemnation notice on the door, but it was getting dark and she had been focused on getting away from Justice Emerson Forester and not looking back. She could have missed a billboard with how distracted she was.

"When are they coming? When did they say you had to move out?"

"I don't know. They're coming tomorrow."

"Do they have somewhere for you to go? Do you have someone to stay with?"

"They left those boxes. Do they think everything is going to fit in those boxes? The whole house?"

No, they probably didn't expect her to take much with her. Just whatever she needed to survive. Did she have anywhere to go? They couldn't just turn her out into the street.

"Where are you going to move to? Do you have somewhere?"

Patricia shook her head.

"What about Axel? What did he say? Is he going to arrange something?"

Patricia's face crumpled. She grabbed at Kelli's arm. "He's gone! Axel is gone!"

"Gone?" Kelli repeated. "Gone where?" Was this another misunderstanding? Something else that Patricia didn't understand?

"Gone away. He said he couldn't stay here anymore. He packed his bags and left."

Kelli glanced toward the staircase, wondering if she dared go see. "Where did he go?"

"I don't know."

Kelli listened. She couldn't hear Axel's TV or hear him moving around. But that didn't mean that Patricia was right and Axel was gone away. Kelli shuffled closer to the stairs, still straining her ears to hear. It was easier to make her way through the room with the lamp on, but it was still treacherous. Several times, she thought that she had put her foot down somewhere stable, only to have it slide unexpectedly. She got to the bottom of the stairs and looked up.

"Kelli?"

Kelli startled violently at the man's voice. She whirled around to face the direction of the front door, raising her hands defensively against the dark figure looming there. It took her a few seconds to realize that it wasn't Axel returning to the house and finding her sneaking around, but Justice Emerson Forester, who hadn't been able to leave her there alone without making sure that everything was okay.

"You scared the hell out of me! What do you think you're doing, sneaking in here like that?" Kelli shouted. "You're not supposed to be in here! You were supposed to go home!"

"I'm sorry. I just… I couldn't leave you here by yourself."

"I'm not by myself. My mom's here. And I was just going to see…" She looked up the stairs again, "whether my dad is here or not."

"I'll come with you."

"Don't walk in here," Kelli insisted. Looking around, she was horrified that he should see her home in such a state. "Just stay there. Go out. Go back to the car. Someone will steal it."

"I'm not going until I'm sure that you are safe." He was surveying the room, eyes wide and white in the dimness. "I can't just leave you…"

"This is my home. This is where I live. Of course you can leave me here."

"No. Not like this."

Kelli started up the stairs resolutely. "I can clean it up," she insisted. "It's just gotten bad because I wasn't here to look after things. In a few days, you'd be amazed, I'll have it in tip-top shape again."

"No, you won't," he said quietly. He hadn't moved from where he stood, and Kelli had only gone up a couple of stairs, so she could still hear him. "There's a notice beside the door. The house has been condemned and slated for destruction."

Kelli's skin tingled. She turned on the stairs and looked back at him. "They can't do that. I can clean it up again. Why would they knock down the whole house?"

"If they think that it's unsafe, that it couldn't be rehabilitated…"

"It's just a little garbage," Kelli said. "I've fixed it up before." With a hand on the rail, she looked up. There was still no sound from Axel's room.

If he had been there and heard her shouting on the stairs, then for sure he would have come out of his room within seconds. And if he was gone... if he had left Patricia all alone... Kelli felt sick. But she didn't have time to feel sorry for herself. She didn't have time to throw up or to send some bureaucrat an email. She had things to do. She had to take action.

She went the rest of the way up the flight of stairs. She stopped outside Axel's door and pressed her ear to it. There were boxes upstairs too. Lining the hallway. With mounds of trash shoveled to the side to make room to get down the hall to the bathroom. Kelli put her hand on the door handle, and sweating, pushed it open. The room was dark. No lights on. No TV. Kelli swallowed hard, trying to swallow the lump in her throat. She was terrified that Axel would not be there, and Patricia would be solely Kelly's responsibility. And terrified that he would be there, and she would have to defend herself, Patricia, and Justice Emerson Forester. There was no body sprawled asleep on the bed. She looked around carefully, just to be sure. The bedroom was worse than the living room. It was obvious that nothing had been cleaned up since Kelli had left. All the dishes that had been used were still there. Many of them with food still remaining on them. How many bowls of macaroni could one man eat? Other piles, unidentifiable in the dimness of the room, took up almost all of the floor space, leaving only a narrow aisle from the bed to the door.

Kelli closed the door again. She looked down the hall toward the bathroom. There was no one in the bathroom. The door stood open, the lights were off. Kelli made her way down the hall, trying not to run into anything or knock anything down.

"Kelli? Is everything okay up there?"

"Yeah. It's okay. Just stay there. There's no one else home. Just Patricia."

She wondered whether the judge would try to talk to Patricia. He was always friendly. Always trying to draw people out when he went to social events. But he'd never faced anyone like her mother.

Kelli pushed open the door to her bedroom and reached for the light switch. Even before she touched it, she knew. There were black shapes in the darkness. Shapes that hadn't been there before.

The room was almost entirely filled with garbage bags. The stench was horrendous.

Kelli was sure of it; not only had Patricia refused to pick anything up or to clean up after herself. She had been actively bringing garbage into the house. Did the neighbors wonder where it was going? Did the trash collectors reach the lane behind her house and wonder why no one had put out any garbage during the week? Kelli didn't know how long Patricia had been accumulating the garbage, but she suspected it had been ever since Kelli left for the cottage. There was just no logical explanation otherwise. Either she had started hoarding or collecting garbage then, or she had every bag of trash from the entire neighborhood stuffed into her house. Kelli's room was wall-to-wall garbage. She couldn't see any of her possessions. She couldn't even see her bed.

The world spun around her. She had no more home. No place to go. No place to sleep. She couldn't sleep at home, and she couldn't sleep at the cottage. There was nowhere else to go. Holding onto the wall, Kelli staggered back down the hall toward the stairs. She tripped over things, crashing along the way.

"Kelli? Are you okay?" the judge's voice carried up from the living room.

She coughed and tried to answer him. "I'm fine. It's okay. Just… tripped."

She found the stairs and held onto the rail as she went down.

"Kelli…?" He started toward her across the room.

Kelli motioned him to stay back. "I told you to stay there. It's not… just stay there, you'll trip." She wasn't doing such a great job herself, but she didn't want him wading through the trash. She didn't want him to see any more of the house. He should have stayed out to start with. Like they had agreed. Or like she had ordered him to. He never had actually agreed to her terms. He was a stubborn man.

"You're obviously upset," he said. "What happened?"

"Axel is gone," Kelli said, starting with the easy part. "Mom said… he moved out. When, Mom? She said he packed his bags and left…"

Patricia looked at Kelli, her eyes glazed. "He said he couldn't live here and he left. Who are you? What are you doing in my house?"

Kelli breathed out, a little squeak of a whine escaping her throat. "I'm Kelli. Your daughter."

"My daughter is dead!" Patricia insisted. "You don't even look like her."

Kelli looked helplessly at the judge.

"She's not dead, Mrs. Munroe," he tried. "She had a close call and she just got out of hospital, but she's not dead. I sent someone over to tell you that she… was sick… you must have misunderstood."

Patricia twisted and bent her neck to study him. "Who are you?"

"I'm Justice Emerson Forester. I'm… Kelli's biological father."

"I don't know you!"

"No."

"How can you be her father if I never met you?" Patricia demanded, with a sudden show of lucidity.

"Because she was switched at the hospital. She's not your biological child. She is mine."

This obviously went right over Patricia's head. She looked at Kelli and grabbed her arm. Her nails were talons, cutting into the flesh of Kelli's arm.

"Show me your face. Turn some lights on."

Kelli bent down so that Patricia could see her more easily. When Justice Emerson Forester looked around for a light switch, she shook his head at him not to bother. Patricia transferred her grip to Kelli's chin, and moved her head back and forth, looking at her face from either side.

"You're Kelli?" she asked finally. Her eyes glistened with tears. "Did you come back for me?"

"Yes." Kelli swallowed hard. "I did."

"What am I going to do?" Patricia bawled, the floodgates opening. She released Kelli. "They say they're going to knock down my house! I have nowhere to go!" She looked around the living room at the stacks of boxes and piles of debris. "I can't take any of my things."

Kelli thought of her own room, everything she owned buried by a mountain of rotting garbage.

"Where did all the garbage come from, Mom? What did you do?"

"I couldn't find it anywhere. I thought maybe someone threw it out. I looked everywhere. Everywhere!"

"Couldn't find what? What were you looking for?" Kelli looked around the room for some clue. For some kind of order to the chaos.

"Your birth certificate. The pictures. My paperwork."

"From when I was born?" Kelli asked. "All the stuff about the switch? Why were you looking for that?"

Patricia stared at the TV screen, tears still running down her cheeks. "There was another little girl," she said. "Born at the hospital the same day you were. Did you know that?"

"Yes. Lisa Forester. I know."

"No," Patricia shook her head. "That's not right. That doesn't sound right."

"Elisa Eleanor Brooks Forester," the judge said quietly.

Patricia's eyes lit up. "Yes! Yes, that was it."

"Your mother had records?" Justice Emerson Forester asked Kelli.

"Yes. That's why I started looking for you and Preston. The first family I went to was black. I knew they weren't the right ones!"

"You weren't a black baby," Patricia said scornfully.

"The papers were in the spare room. I'll… I'll go see if they're still there."

"Do you want me to come with you? I think your mom is safe here, if we're just going upstairs."

"No. Don't come up. Just stay here with her."

His eyes went to the kitchen doorway. "Maybe I could make everyone some coffee. Do you think that would help?"

"No. I already looked… I couldn't find the coffee maker. Just stay here. Please. Don't go through the rest of the house."

He nodded, and Kelli thought he would keep his word. He was a gentleman, and gentlemen didn't snoop through other people's things. Not when you told them to mind their own business.

"I'll just be a minute… if it's all where I left it."

Kelli again made her way up the stairs. Down the crowded hallway, to the spare room instead of her bedroom. She opened it, expecting to see the same wall-to-wall garbage as was in her own room. The room was not quite as bad as Kelli's. It was only half full. The smell choked Kelli, and she breathed through her mouth, trying to get in and out without gagging. Luckily, the side of the room the closet was on was the one that was less littered with garbage bags. She had just started collecting garbage without ever searching through the closet to find the papers where she had stored them away. It was like her brain was turning to soup. Kelli had not had any idea that her mental decline would be so fast. Or maybe, being there every day, she just hadn't realized how quickly it was already happening.

The location of the papers that proved her parentage—or her non-parentage—was burned into her brain. She had no trouble going back to the corner of the shelf she had left the bag on. Breathing shallowly, she pulled the bundle down. She retreated from the room and closed the door. The smell in the hallway was still bad, but not nearly as rank as inside the room. Kelli took a few deep breaths before carrying on down the hall, back downstairs to the living room. She lifted the bag slightly for the judge. Patricia was watching TV, her mouth slack, hanging open.

Kelli looked for somewhere to put down the papers. She swept off the top of a side table without regard to anything piled on top. She took out the papers she had previously seen and laid them out for her father to see. He took out his phone and put it into flashlight mode to examine the documents.

His face looked pinched and more deeply lined than usual in the poor lighting of the room. He was older than Patricia, but had never looked it. Now the shadows cast by the dim lamp and the reflected light of his phone threw the wrinkles into deep relief and he looked ancient.

The judge shook his head as he paged through the settlement agreements and other paperwork Patricia had kept. Kelli dug into the bag again. Patricia had said she was looking for pictures too. Kelli found a few loose photographs mixed in with the remaining detritus in the bag, and she took them out gingerly. She put them down on the table under Justice Emerson Forester's light. Pictures of Patricia holding a baby at the hospital. Looking at them, Kelli's chest hurt, bringing back her recent memories of waking up in the hospital.

"Which baby...?" the judge asked, leaning closer to study the pictures. They both studied the baby, looking for the identifying features.

Kelli gasped. Her father's gaze flicked to her face.

"What is it?"

Kelli pointed to the background of the picture. There were two bassinets in the semi-private room. And in the corner of the picture, mostly cut off, Preston was in the other hospital bed. A younger, happier-looking version of Preston, but still recognizable.

Kelli felt dangerously sick. She stumbled away from the judge. There wasn't anywhere to go. She pushed her way to the door and barely made it to the front steps before being sick into the weeds. She hadn't had much to eat since awaking at the hospital, or before that, so there was little but sour bile to bring up.

She didn't know why it should bother her so much to see Preston in those pictures. It wasn't like she hadn't known that Patricia and Preston had both been there at the same time. Obviously, for the girls to be born the same day and to be switched, they had to be there at the same time, and had been pretty close together. The babies at least had to have been in the same room at some point.

Kelli wiped her mouth and headed back into the living room. The judge looked at her, his eyes hollows in the dimness of the room. He didn't even ask this time if she were okay.

Kelli looked at the pictures again. Mostly, it was impossible to tell which girl was which. The pictures showed only the top of the baby's downy head, or one cheek, not the one with the birthmark. But in one picture, the baby was turned just the right way, and Kelli could see the pink splotch on the right cheek. Patricia was holding Kelli. Which meant that the baby in the other bassinet was Lisa. The switch had already happened. Patricia's face was tired. She didn't smile as she looked down at the baby in her arms. It would be another two years before she discovered what had happened.

"How do you think it happened?" Kelli asked the judge. "How could we get switched? We had bracelets. Anklets."

"I don't know," he admitted. "Maybe they were removed for baths or some kind of testing. I don't know how this kind of thing usually happens. It seems like they would have all kinds of safeguards in place."

"It doesn't make sense to me."

They looked at the pictures and at the documents on the table for a few more minutes in silence.

"I can't believe that any attorney would consider this arrangement ethical. At the very least, they should have insisted that the hospital had to inform the biological parents—us—of the mix-up. For everyone to agree to put a gag on it and keep it all quiet… I just can't believe it."

Kelli nodded. "Yeah. That's kind of how I felt too. How could anyone agree to keep it quiet? For any amount of money?"

"I guess they thought that the damage was already done… anything they did to rectify the situation would just complicate things… not solve anything. And your mother…" The judge looked over at Patricia, slumped in the chair, watching a sitcom rerun. "Your mother desperately needed the money."

"Her boyfriend left and she had a two-year-old," Kelli agreed. "She needed help… but you would have helped her. She didn't have to agree to hide it."

"She didn't know that. She never talked to us. As far as she knew, she was totally on her own."

"That woman took my baby," Patricia said. "She didn't even care."

Kelli and the judge looked at each other. Kelli shook her head slightly at Patricia's paranoia.

"She didn't know, Mom," Kelli told her. "Neither of you knew that you had taken home the wrong baby. She thought Lisa was her baby, just like you thought I was yours."

"She knew," Patricia insisted. "It was her fault."

"Do you know what happened?" Justice Emerson Forester asked. "Do you know how the mix-up happened?"

Patricia slumped back in her chair. She felt beside her for a bottle and found one. She nursed it morosely. Kelli sighed and gathered the paperwork back together.

"It's just paranoia. It's part of the dementia. I don't know if she even remembers when I was born."

"Sometimes the more they lose of the present, the better they remember the past."

Kelli nodded.

"We need to figure out what to do with your mother tonight," the judge said. "She can't stay here. If she's still here tomorrow, they will turn her out into the street or take her to some homeless shelter. And that's not going to help her."

"I don't know what to do," Kelli said. "I don't know where to go."

"We could bring her back to the cottage. I can put her into a guest room. She'd be comfortable there."

"No. She doesn't belong there. She either won't like it, or she'll decide she's staying there. And she can't stay there. She'd just be miserable when she had to leave again."

"We don't have the resources to keep her there permanently, but she could stay for a few days, until we sorted things out."

Kelli shook her head again. "No. Not the cottage." She couldn't go back there. And she certainly couldn't take Patricia there.

"Does she have any family? Brothers or sisters?"

"No."

"And you don't know where your… your other dad went?"

"No. No sign of him. And… I wouldn't want her to go with him anyway. They aren't good for each other."

"Where do you want her to go, then? A shelter? A hotel? The emergency room?"

"Not the hospital!" Kelli objected. "She's not sick. Not *that* way. I guess… a hotel would be the best. She can't afford one, but…"

"But you can," the judge said firmly. "Just put it on your credit card."

"That's your money. You don't have to pay for her…"

"Put it on your credit card," he insisted. "Wherever you want her to go. Just take care of it. Don't worry about anything. I know what it's like to have a mother who can no longer take care of herself. It's devastating to see them like this." He hesitated. "Especially like this." He indicated the interior of the room with a motion.

Kelli nodded, trying to swallow the lump in her throat. He couldn't understand what it was like, but he did the best he could.

"Is there anything she would want to take with her? Besides the papers and pictures?"

Kelli looked down at the bag of documents. "No. I don't think so. She's going to need new things. Nothing here is going to be… sanitary."

"I imagine you're right. No jewelry or special keepsakes?"

Kelli looked at him, wondering if he'd lost his mind. Did he really think that Patricia had anything of value? Or that there was anything of sentimental value in the house that hadn't been completely ruined?

But she didn't challenge him on it. She just went up to Patricia's chair and rubbed her shoulder. "Time to go now, Mom. Do you have your shoes on?"

They both looked. Patricia did have shoes on. Kelli didn't think they matched, but she didn't care. She would get Patricia a new pair of shoes. If she were somewhere she was going to need them. She didn't want anything to slow them down or make the process more painful than it already was.

"Okay. Let's get you on your feet, then." Kelli hauled on the lever on the side of the easy chair, vaulting Patricia into an upright position. Patricia let out a squawk of alarm, grabbing the sides of the chair to steady herself. "Come on," Kelli encouraged, giving her a little push and then tugging on her arm. "We're going out, Mom. Time to get ready. Is your car here?"

"They said I can't drive anymore," Patricia groused. She was on her feet more easily than Kelli would have expected.

"I'll drive. Is it still here or did they take it away?"

"I don't know. Maybe Axel took it. He left. He packed his bags and went away."

"I know. But that means he can't hit you anymore."

Patricia looked across at the judge and gave Kelli a fierce look. "Why would you talk that way in front of company? We don't talk about family business!"

Kelli remembered what the judge had said about this and looked down at her feet, avoiding his eyes.

"Let's see if your car is here. If it is, we may as well take it. If not, the judge will drop us off at the hotel."

"The judge?" Patricia repeated, startled. She looked around. "What judge? What did you do?"

"No, no. I mean… Mr. Forester. He'll drive us if we need a ride. He's here to help us out."

This seemed to go over well with Patricia. She looked at Justice Emerson Forester and went along with Kelli without a protest. Kelli couldn't understand why Patricia had repeatedly demanded to know who Kelli was and ordered her out of the house, and yet didn't seem to have any problem with someone who was a total stranger hanging around. The judge offered silently to give Kelli a hand with Patricia, but there wasn't room for the three of them to get across the room together without falling over anything, so Kelli waved him off. She started Patricia on the pathway to the door and followed behind her single-file, her hands out to redirect Patricia or to grab her if she lost her balance.

On the doorstep, she took Patricia's arm and guided her down the steps. The judge followed closely behind them.

"Here, you take her for a minute," Kelli said. "I'm just going to pop around back and see if her car is here."

He obligingly took Patricia's arm and smiled down at her as they stood in the dim light of the sickly streetlight. Kelli hurried out the side of the house, moving carefully between more mounds of trash bags. How wide an area had Patricia ranged over to pick up all the garbage bags? And how long had she been collecting them? Had they already been filling the back yard the last time that Kelli had come by, just out of sight?

She got to the back lane, and scanned in both directions. No car. And unsurprisingly, no garbage bags in the bins. Kelli shook her head. "Crazy old woman!"

Kelli returned to the front yard, and shook her head at Justice Emerson Forester.

"No car. Axel must have taken it. Or it got impounded."

"That's fine, I'll take you wherever you need to go."

Patricia patted the judge's arm as they walked down the sidewalk to the car. He looked back at Kelli when he got to the car. "Do you want…"

"Put her in the front," Kelli said quickly. "It will be easier for her to get in and out. I'm young and flexible."

He nodded and helped Patricia into the seat. "Here you go, Patricia."

Patricia made happy noises. Kelli went around the other side and got into the back seat.

CHAPTER 27

Dealing with Patricia had not been easy. When they got her out of the house, Kelli discovered that she stank to high heaven. She and the judge rolled down windows to get enough fresh air to breathe, and Kelli tackled the issue when they got checked into the hotel, insisting that Patricia bathe, and taking her clothes to scrub in the sink. The hotel had bathrobes for patron use, so that was what Patricia got when she finally emerged from the bathroom, clean and smelling of soap and the hotel's floral shampoo.

Patricia was used to just passing out in her chair watching TV, so she had no real desire to get into bed. Kelli coaxed her into the bed, where she could lie down and still see the TV.

"Get me something to drink," Patricia insisted, looking around. "I'm thirsty!"

Kelli brought her a five-dollar water bottle from the mini fridge, even though she knew that wouldn't work. Patricia wasn't as much thirsty as she was on the edge of sober, and that wouldn't do.

"What's this?"

"You said you were thirsty."

"What am I, a bird? I don't want water, I want a drink."

"Water is the best thing to quench your thirst," Kelli told her. But she was half-teasing, knowing that there was no way Patricia was going to drink a bottle of water when there was a fridge full of whatever kind of alcohol she wanted.

"Get me a real drink!"

Kelli went back to the fridge. "Okay, but you have to drink the water too. You'll get dehydrated, and that will make you feel worse in the morning. What do you want?"

Patricia looked across the room at the open fridge. "Vodka. Beer. Bring them both over."

"One or the other. It's expensive."

"I can't have just one drink."

"Hotel drinks are expensive." It was an excuse, since all Kelli had to do was put it on her credit card and the judge would take care of it. He didn't care if she charged three hundred dollars in alcohol.

He had insisted that they not book a fleabag motel. "Not for my daughter. You get something nice, and they'll take care of anything your mom needs. She's going to need toiletries, essentials. They'll take care of her." So Kelli had acquiesced. He was right, they wouldn't be able to get Patricia those things at a cheap motel. Kelli would have to go out to a store to pick things up, either taking stinking Patricia with her, or leaving her to fend for herself at the hotel. And Kelli wasn't sure that she'd find Patricia there on her return.

"If they're too expensive, then go across the street and get me something at the liquor mart," Patricia said.

Kelli supposed she shouldn't have been surprised that was the landmark her mother had spotted on their arrival. She brought Patricia the vodka from the minibar and handed it to her. At that point, Patricia was happy to lie there in her fluffy robe, drinking from small bottles and flipping through TV channels with the remote. It was a nice place; the remote wasn't affixed to the side table to prevent theft.

"Where did that man go?" Patricia asked after a while, restlessly flipping channels. She had not cracked her water bottle open, and was eyeing the refrigerator again, having downed the vodka.

"Mr. Forester went back home," Kelli said. "It's just you and me here. And tomorrow… we have to figure out where you can go."

"Is he coming back?"

"No."

"Oh." Patricia sucked on her empty bottle. "Have I met him before?"

"No. Well, I don't think so," Kelli amended. "You might have met him when I was a baby. But that was a long time ago."

"Yes, that was it," Patricia agreed.

Kelli glanced over at her. Did Patricia really remember meeting the judge sixteen years before? She supposed it was possible. Short term memory went first, long term hanging on or even becoming more clear as the present was swept away.

"Why were you looking for my birth certificate, Mom?"

Patricia didn't answer. Kelli got up to shut off most of the lights, hoping to be able to sleep soon.

"Get me another drink," Patricia said. "I wanted a beer."

"You should get some sleep. Maybe you can have something tomorrow."

"I want a beer!" Patricia raised her voice.

Kelli froze and listened for a moment for any noise from the neighboring rooms. She did not want to get kicked out because Patricia got unruly about not getting her booze.

"Okay, okay," she whispered. "Just keep your voice down. We don't want to disturb the neighbors."

"I don't care what the neighbors think. They keep stealing things from the garbage!"

Kelli laughed, leaning over to get a beer from the fridge. "I think you're the one whose been stealing from the garbage! Did any of them see you?"

Of course they had. With the number of garbage bags she had pilfered, someone was bound to have seen her taking at least some of them.

"They stole it from me first," Patricia said petulantly.

Kelli handed her the beer, hoping that once she had finished her drink, Patricia would fall asleep. But of course, it wasn't to be. Kelli kept herself awake, not wanting to fall asleep before Patricia, and have Patricia leave the hotel room and be off wandering around somewhere while Kelli slept. Patricia continued to watch TV and demand more alcohol, showing no signs of slowing. Normally, she would have been passed out by one o'clock, but apparently being taken out of her house and having a bath and all the new experiences of the hotel had hyped her up and, like a recalcitrant child, she refused to be put to bed or show any sign of fatigue. Kelli drifted off a few times and had to move to a wooden chair in order to force herself to stay awake to supervise her mother.

The hours blurred together and it was four or five in the morning before

Patricia started to snore. With a groan of relief, Kelli climbed into bed. She didn't turn off the TV or any more of the lights. Nothing that might wake Patricia back up.

———

Morning came way too soon. While Patricia continued to sleep like a log, snoring away, Kelli was awake again at eight, tossing and turning, too awake to convince her body to go back to sleep. She finally got out of bed and had a long shower, hoping the hot water would melt away her sore muscles. When she was done, she looked in the mini-fridge for anything suitable for breakfast, then picked up her phone.

Justice Emerson Forester had texted her earlier to call him when she got up. She sat on the bed looking at the phone for a long time. She was used to dealing with problems on her own and was still a little irritated that he had followed her into the house and inserted himself into the situation the previous night. She couldn't blame him too much, when they really had needed his help, but he could have waited until she asked for help instead of going into the house. She hated that he had seen it like that.

With a sigh, she pressed his speed dial and walked to the other side of the hotel room so that she wouldn't be talking right next to Patricia.

"Kelli! I wasn't expecting you to be up already. How is your mother? Did everything go okay?"

"She tried to drink the minibar all by herself, so there's going to be a big charge on the credit card. Didn't get to sleep until five this morning."

"You should still be in bed."

"I've been up for a while. Couldn't get back to sleep. I feel like a hamster running on a wheel, trying to figure out what to do."

"About your mom?"

"Yeah. Of course, what else?"

"If you won't bring her here, you will have to take her to some kind of doctor for evaluation. You can go to the emergency room if you want. They will be able to find someone to see her."

"I have her doctor's number."

"Try him, then. May as well be someone who already knows her case. And she'll probably be more comfortable seeing someone she knows." He cleared his throat. "I had someone drive your car to the hotel. It's in the parking lot, so you can take her where you need to."

Kelli felt a warm flush at his words. He really was doing everything he could to be a loving father to her. Even when she was trying her best to run away from him.

"Then what will I need to do?"

"We won't know until after she's been seen. They will let you know what the options are. But from what I saw… she can't live on her own. She's going to have to be put into some kind of care or supervised living situation."

"She's gotten so much worse since I left. Do you think that's because I wasn't there to help? Do you think I could have helped her to hold things together for longer?"

"No, I don't think it has anything to do with you not being there. She still had Axel. She still had her doctor and whatever other support system she has. I don't think you not being there hastened her dementia. I don't think that's the way it works."

"I feel really bad about it. I knew I should have stayed with her. I was selfish to leave."

"You need to have your own life, Kelli. There's nothing wrong with following your heart and pursuing your own path. It won't always work out the way that you expect, but what would you feel like if you had stayed home? Better? You're on antidepressants now. I don't think you would be if you had stayed there. You would have just gotten more and more depressed. And there would have been no Lisa to come and see what was wrong."

"I suppose. But that doesn't make things any better for her. If I hadn't gotten her out last night, someone would have gotten her out today. It doesn't make any difference to her that I came."

He was silent for a few moments, considering. "I think it made a difference to her that you went back for her, Kelli. I think that when she realized who you were, and that you weren't dead and had gone home, it meant something to her. Even if it was just for a few minutes."

Kelli swallowed. "Yeah."

"After you've taken care of her today… what are your plans? Obviously, you cannot go back there to live."

There was a hard knot in Kelli's stomach and chest. "I don't know. I can't think about that yet. I can only do one thing at a time."

"I don't want to overwhelm you. I'm here if you need any more help. And when you need a place to come home to. Your room is still here. Nothing has changed. You belong here."

But Kelli remembered the way she had felt when she went back to her room. She didn't belong there. She had only been kidding herself.

———

Kelli woke Patricia up after noon and got her to change back into her own clothes, which Kelli had hand-washed and hung to dry in the bathroom. Kelli did her best to make Patricia presentable. Then they were on their way to the doctor's office.

"I don't have a doctor's appointment today," Patricia insisted, covering her eyes to shield them from the sun.

"We're going to see him anyway. He'll see you on an emergency basis. We need to get his help."

"Why do I have to see the doctor today? Why can't we just go home?"

Kelli didn't want to mention the scheduled destruction of the house in case it upset Patricia too much. "We just can't do that right now. It was fun to stay at the hotel, wasn't it? I've never stayed at such a nice one before."

"It's because of that man."

"Mr. Forester? Yes, he paid for the hotel room."

"Will we be seeing him again?"

"I will," Kelli said. "Probably. But I don't think you will."

"Won't he come to see us at the house? Where would you see him?"

"He won't come to the house. He just came the one time."

"Was it the garbage?"

Kelli looked over at her mother. Patricia's brow was furrowed deeply and Kelli thought there was a tear on her face.

"What?"

"Is that why he won't come back? Because of the garbage?"

"He doesn't care about the garbage."

"Are you sure?"

"I'm sure. Do you know… why you were collecting the garbage? Do you remember what you were thinking?"

"No… Not right now."

Kelli reached over and gave her hand a squeeze. "Don't worry about it. It doesn't matter."

"Where are we going?"

"Just to see the doctor."

"I don't have an appointment."

"I know."

Kelli didn't initiate any more conversation on the way. When they got to the doctor's office, dull and dingy with a handful of sad seniors sitting reading magazines or looking vacantly at the wall, she had Patricia sit down and went up to speak to the receptionist.

"I brought Patricia Munroe," she said. "I know she doesn't have an appointment, but it's an emergency."

The tired receptionist opened her mouth to argue.

"Her house was declared a public health risk and is being destroyed today," Kelli said. "I got her out of the house with nothing but the clothes on her back, and I had to wash those. She doesn't have anywhere to go. She doesn't have anyone to take care of her."

The receptionist considered this. "You're her daughter."

"Yeah… sort of. But I can't take care of her. I don't have anywhere to live either."

She felt a little guilty saying it. Was she so out of practice from being a con artist that she was feeling guilty over a little lie? She *didn't* have anywhere to live, because she was supposed to be living in Patricia's house. She knew she had other options, if she wanted them, but at that moment, she didn't have a home.

"I'll pull her file and squeeze her in to see Dr. Baker. He's really booked up today, but I guess Mrs. Munroe can't wait. You'll stay and sit with her?"

"Yeah, sure. I'll keep her from wandering off."

———

Kelli had been resigned to sitting there waiting for most of the day. But it was less than an hour before a nurse called Patricia's name, and Kelli walked with her to the office in the back. Patricia seemed comfortable with the familiar surroundings. It was an office rather than an examining room like Kelli had been expecting. She slid into a seat beside Patricia, looking around with wide eyes. In a minute, the door opened and a balding, oval-headed doctor walked in, looking at a file. He sat on the other side of the desk and looked at Patricia and Kelli.

"Patricia, it's nice to see you again. How are you feeling?"

"My head hurts and I feel sick," Patricia complained. "I need a drink."

He seemed unfazed by the answer. Then again, if he'd been Patricia's doctor for any length of time, he probably realized that was the usual state of affairs.

"And you didn't have Axel bring you today. Are you going to introduce me to your…"

He trailed off, waiting for Patricia to pick up the thought, but Patricia didn't.

"Who is this with you?" Dr. Baker asked bluntly.

Patricia turned her head to look at Kelli. She frowned. "I don't remember. This is…"

"Kelli," Kelli supplied. "Your daughter."

"You're not my daughter. My daughter is dead."

She had known who Kelli was all day, and the relapse into the previous day's behavior struck Kelli to the heart. She didn't argue, but looked at Dr. Baker. He wrote something in the file. He looked at Kelli.

"You said it was an emergency. Have there been changes?"

"I went to her house yesterday. It's full of garbage. Like, floor to ceiling. She's been taking bags of garbage from around the neighborhood and bringing them into the house. The house has been condemned and it's being destroyed today. And she doesn't remember who I am." Kelli's throat was too hot to continue. She stopped and tried to clear it and go on.

"Patricia. What's going on with the garbage?" Dr. Baker addressed his patient.

"What garbage?"

Kelli opened her mouth to explain what Patricia had told her so far, then closed it again. The doctor needed to listen to Patricia and to hear how she reacted to his questions.

"The garbage in your house. Have you been taking garbage from the neighbors?"

"They took it from me."

"Why would they take it from you?"

"They are stealing things from my house and hiding them in the garbage."

"What kind of things?"

"Important papers. Photographs. Money."

"Have you been taking your medications?"

Patricia just stared at him. Dr. Baker looked at Kelli.

Kelli shrugged. "I doubt it. I don't think she's taking anything."

"Her partner was helping make sure she took them."

"Axel? I doubt he could remember them himself. And he's apparently taken off."

"He packed his bags and went away," Patricia whined.

"She no longer has anyone else in the household? Are you living with her?"

"I was going to go back to live with her," Kelli said, "but the house is being flattened. We don't have anywhere to go."

"She can't live on the street. She needs a stable, regulated environment. She doesn't have the ability to take care of herself right now."

"I noticed."

"Okay. I'm going to get a social worker involved, and we'll try to track down an emergency care situation for her. It may just be an Emergency Room bed today, but we'll find something for her."

Kelli breathed a sigh of relief. "Thank you. I didn't know what I was going to do."

———

Kelli left Patricia at the hospital and went back to the house, at a loss as to what to do. She went to the place where her home used to stand and sat in the car looking at the mass of rubble and the workers moving around it with hard hats on and masks over their faces. Some of the neighbors stood around watching the carnage. Nobody paid any attention to Kelli.

It was a good symbol for what had happened in her life. First it had been full of crap, and then it had been destroyed, razed to the ground. Then everybody stood around gawking at the ruin.

Eventually, she drove away and left it all behind for good. She didn't know where to go, but found herself where she had always gone when at a loss. Les's house.

He, at least, would commiserate with her. He'd always been there before and gotten her through the worst life had to offer. Kelli left the car at the curb, hoping it would be safe there for the short time she planned to stay, and went up to the door.

It was awkward knocking on the front door. In former days, she had always just walked in and out of the Broke home as if she belonged there. But it had been too long, and walking in didn't feel right.

It was Desi who came to the door. She looked through the screen at Kelli, face expressionless.

"Hi, Desi," Kelli greeted with forced cheer. "Just wondering if Les is around."

Desi said nothing.

"It's Kelli. Is he home? Or is he out somewhere?"

"Is that really you?" Desi asked finally, staring at Kelli.

"Yes."

Desi put her hand on the door knob as if to open the door, but she didn't, keeping the screen between them.

"He's still at school."

Kelli flashed a glance at her watch. He never stayed that late at school. Not ever.

"At the school… or somewhere else?" she teased.

Desi shrugged and turned away from the door. Kelli watched her retreat, then reluctantly went back to her car. She was quite sure that Les wouldn't actually be at the school so late, but Desi had seemed pretty certain. Kelli parked in the school lot and went in. School had let out some time ago, so the halls were eerily empty. There were after-school activities in the gym and several classrooms, but she and Les had never gone out for any of the clubs or sports. The only place she could think to go to was the library. They had always gone to the public library together rather than the school library, but maybe the school had finally replaced their stone-age computers with something useful, or the public library was doing renovations or there was another reason to avoid it.

Kelli looked around at the individuals and little knots of students at the computers and study tables. Not very many people hung out at the school library.

Les was toward the back of the library, sitting at the same table as a boy whose name Kelli tried to remember. Something that started with a C. Chad? Cory? Clinton? She thought that was it. Clinton. Kelli took a couple of steps into the library to talk to Les. Clinton leaned over toward Les, and showed him a notepad, stabbing his pencil into it as he spoke animatedly with Les. Les took it from him, grinning and leaning slightly toward him. Les's face lit up like it used to do when he and Kelli discussed a promising new con.

Kelli went cold.

She had always thought that Les needed her. More than she needed him. He needed his cut of their take for his family. He didn't have any other friends, so there was only Kelli and without her, he would be isolated and alone. She protected him from the bullies and any other physical threats. He needed her.

But there he was, sitting with Clinton, looking like he was having the time of his life. He was happy and relaxed and laughing over whatever Clinton had written in the notebook. It obviously wasn't homework. They were making plans. Plans that didn't include her.

Kelli whirled around and crashed out through the door.

CHAPTER 28

Kelli went back to the hotel, but she didn't want to stay there by herself, running up the judge's credit card account and doing nothing to support herself. A shelter? The street? She didn't know what was left for her.

The pain was enveloping. Her family was gone. Her best friend was gone. There wasn't anywhere she belonged and fit in. The idea of taking pills again filled her with revulsion, but she could think of no other way to escape.

The phone buzzed in her pocket. Kelli slid her phone out, but she knew before she looked at it what the words on the face would be. Justice Emerson Forester calling.

She swiped to answer. "Hello?"

"Kelly?" His voice sounded relieved. "Are you okay?"

Had he sensed somehow the crisis point that Kelli was at? How had he picked that moment to call?

"Hi," Kelli said, not answering the question.

"Where are you?" he asked. "Can I come get you?"

"I've got my car," Kelli reminded him. She didn't need him to drive her anywhere.

"I know… but I could still pick you up. We could get your car later or have someone else pick it up later."

"No. You don't need to do that."

"Will you come home? Please, Kelli?"

"I don't know what to do." There was a lump in her throat again. Was she ever going to stop crying? "I can't sleep there…"

"Did you get any sleep last night?"

"Not much."

"I suspected you wouldn't. Come on, Kelli. Please come home. I need you here."

Kelli snorted. "You don't need me."

"I do. I need you here. Safe. Can't we figure something out? Talk to me about why you don't want to live here anymore. Talk to a therapist. Don't just shut me out and run away."

"I can't."

"Then just come home for supper."

Kelli sat in her car, looking at the phone, thinking about it. She could go back for supper, couldn't she? She couldn't remember the last time she ate. She didn't want greasy fast food. She could go back to eat and to update the judge on what had happened. After that… maybe they could find someone she could stay with for a few days while they tried to formulate a more permanent solution.

"Okay."

"You will?" The judge sounded both surprised and pleased. "Thank you, Kelli. I'm sure we can figure something out, if you just give me a chance. I don't want to lose you again."

When Kelli pulled into the drive, her route to the garage was blocked by a white convertible. Preston's car. Kelli considered turning around and leaving again. But she didn't have the energy and she had promised the judge that she would come to dinner. She couldn't just leave without talking to him first. He probably hadn't known that Preston was coming by. Preston would be there to talk to Lisa, not to Kelli. Kelli would just stay out of the way until they were done.

She parked her car to the side so Preston would still be able to get back out, and went in through the kitchen door. Felicia and the cook were busy in the kitchen and looked up at Kelli's entrance. Felicia's eyes went wide.

"Oh… Miss Kelli. Mrs. Brooks is here…"

"I know. I saw her car."

"She won't be staying for dinner, I don't think, but she might hold things up for a few minutes…"

"I'll just go up to my room until she's done," Kelli said, not stopping. "You can get me when the judge is ready to eat."

Felicia nodded in relief. "Yes, Miss Kelli."

Kelli retreated upstairs to her room. She could hear Preston's and Lisa's strident voices coming from the direction of the annex, with Justice Emerson Forester's low voice occasionally breaking in, trying to mediate between the two. Good thing she didn't have to be part of that discussion.

She sat at her desk with nothing to do. She'd left her computer in the car with all the rest of her things and she didn't want to have to go down again to get it. She didn't want to deal with her email and whatever had been happening on her social networks.

With nothing else to do, she took out her phone and played the solitaire game it had come preloaded with.

Lisa pounded up the stairs—so loud for such a slim, delicate-looking thing. She stopped at the top of the stairs, right in front of Kelli's door and shouted back down.

"You don't want me! I'm not even your biological daughter! You're going to obsess over Kelli constantly anyway, so why don't you take *her* in? Because I… am not… coming… back!"

She stomped the rest of the way to her bedroom and slammed the door.

Kelli sat at her desk, frozen, not sure how to react. There was nothing to do but remain quiet and still. Lisa obviously didn't know that she was there, and Kelli had no desire to step into the middle of the argument.

She didn't hear Preston until the woman was in the hall outside Kelli's door. Unlike Lisa, Preston wasn't stomping around and giving notice of her location.

"Of course I want you!" she shouted at Lisa. "You're my daughter! I chose you! Please come home!"

Kelli put her hand over her mouth to hold back an exclamation. Had she heard right? What did Preston mean by that?

"Leave me alone!" Lisa screamed back. "I'm not your daughter!"

"You *are* my daughter." Preston rattled Lisa's door handle, but it was locked. "Open this door. I understand why you are upset, but please talk to me. I thought we were best friends. You can't just abandon me like this!"

Kelli heard the judge's slow, deliberate approach. He wasn't loud, but his step was heavier than Preston's. Kelli kept her head cocked toward Preston, trying to make sense of what she said.

"Preston…?"

"What is it?" Preston snapped through gritted teeth.

"What did you mean… you chose Lisa?"

There was a long pause. Kelli waited for the answer.

"When Kelli came and found you," Preston said. "Of course I would choose Lisa, the child I raised for sixteen years, over a stranger."

"I don't think that's what you meant."

Lisa's door squeaked open. "What did you mean?" Lisa's voice quavered.

"What are you all talking about? I told you what I meant."

"You used to say that when I was little," Lisa said. "You said that out of all the pretty blond baby girls, you chose me. I thought it was just… silly nonsense. Like a fairy tale. Something you say to make your child feel good about herself. Pretending that you had a choice. Because you don't get a choice when you give birth. It's not like adoptive parents picking out what baby at the orphanage they want…"

Kelli slumped over her desk, putting her hands over her face in disbelief.

Preston.

It *hadn't* been an accident.

It hadn't been a clueless nurse putting the bracelets back on the wrong baby after bath time. They had shared a room. The bassinets had been side-by-side. Kelli had seen them in the picture. And Preston picked out which baby she wanted.

The judge was swearing. Lisa was crying. Kelli could hear nothing from Preston.

"Tell me you didn't," Justice Emerson Forester said. "Tell me you didn't intentionally take someone else's baby."

"I took my daughter," Preston said stolidly. "I took Lisa."

"Why didn't you take Kelli?"

"She was disfigured. Why would I take a baby who I knew would grow up to look like that?"

"But you didn't know. You couldn't have known. The doctors said it was just a bruise."

"The doctors thought I was an idiot and that they could lie to me about it. I would just believe them and when it became obvious it would be too late to do anything about it. But I knew what it was. I knew how disfigured she would be."

"How could you know that?"

"My cousin had a baby like that. It started out all pink and blotchy, like a bruise. And within a year, it was that horrible purple mark. I could not have a child like that."

Lisa was still sobbing.

"Will you stop your blubbering? Big girls don't cry. You know better."

"You knew I wasn't your baby? You just took me away from my birth-mom because you didn't want an ugly baby with a birthmark?"

"You are the baby I chose," Preston told her firmly. "I never wanted any other baby."

"What you did was criminal," Justice Emerson Forester said in disbelief. "Kidnapping. It wasn't just an accident, you intentionally stole someone else's infant!"

"You may be big enough to accept a child with disabilities. But I'm not. I could not raise a child like that. Those other parents didn't care. They weren't in the social spotlight. They didn't need a child who could be on the front page of the social section. She was just going to be mired in some city slum where nobody would care what she looked like. That's the kind of people they were."

The judge said nothing.

"Quit looking at me like that. You know I'm right. You saw how those people lived. She was garbage. A throwaway. That woman had no morals. No motherly feelings. I rescued Lisa from that fate. Your daughter grew up like she did because of me. Beautiful and happy with a home where she was loved and cherished, a society where she belonged. All of that would have been wasted on the other one."

"You need to leave," the judge said.

"You can't tell me to leave, I'm here to talk to Lisa, you can't kick me out—"

"You need to leave *now*." There was steel in his voice. Kelli could only imagine the coldness in his eyes as he ordered Preston to get out of there before he lost control. Because there were no more protests from Preston. She didn't even say goodbye to Lisa; she just left.

In the distance, a door slammed. A car engine roared to life.

And Preston was gone.

"Lisa…" Justice Emerson Forester said, his voice totally different. Full of compassion and love. Lisa had grown up in a home where she was loved and cherished. Kelli couldn't remember a single time one of her parents had spoken that way to her.

"Leave me alone," Lisa sobbed. "I need space. I just want to think."

"Nothing that your mother said or did changes the way I feel about you."

There was another voice in the hall. Felicia's. "If you and the girls would like your dinner now…"

"We'll wait until Kelli gets here. We're going to need some time…"

"But Miss Kelli is already here. She came up to her room…"

There was a long, silent pause. Then a soft knock and the door swung open. Justice Emerson Forester looked in at Kelli, his eyes wide, his face pale and old-looking again.

"Kelli… you heard…? Everything…?"

Kelli nodded.

He groaned. "I can't think of a worse way for you to have learned…"

"At least it was fast," Kelli said, choking back the hot tears that again threatened. "Like pulling off a bandage."

"This is horrible. This is shocking news for all of us. I'm so sorry, Kelli. I'm just so sorry!"

"You didn't know. No one knew."

"No. Only Preston, and she…" He shook his head. "There's something wrong with her, Kelli. No normal person could have abandoned her own child that way."

"People leave babies in the department store toilet," Kelli pointed out. "Abandon them in trash bins. People kill their own children. They don't even call it murder, they call it infanticide. Like a baby isn't really even a person. She's not the first one to be so… cold."

"I just can't believe it. I can't believe she could do it, and then to stand there and justify it to me!"

Kelli felt empty. Not sad or angry, just hollow. So full of nothingness she would just blow away in the wind.

Her father came over to her, and put his arms around her. Kelli sniffled. "I'm okay."

"Kelli. Let it out. You don't have to be so brave. You've been through too much lately. Your whole world is spinning."

Kelli melted into his warm, comforting embrace. She tried to put all images of Axel and the men of the past out of her head and just accept comfort from the judge. He didn't want anything from her. He wasn't going to hurt or molest her. It was okay to just be present and take what he offered.

The tears came faster. She had already cried so much, she didn't understand where they were coming from. She should have been too dehydrated to cry any more. Lisa joined them, putting an arm around each of them. The judge murmured to them both.

The words didn't matter, just that he was there, holding them, and it was a safe place to be.

———

In the end, sleeping wasn't a problem. Not having anywhere else to go wasn't an issue. Justice Emerson Forester told Felicia to bring all the food up. They lined up the serving dishes on Kelli's desk and they camped out and ate it right there on the bed. Mostly in silence, all of them sharing the fresh, raw wound. There wasn't anything to discuss. Nothing that any of them could say that would make the others feel any better. And it didn't matter.

After they had eaten, sitting, lounging, or lying wherever they were comfortable, the judge suggested a movie. They went down to the family room and put on silly old movies, laughing and escaping reality. Kelli fell asleep in front of the TV. Later, the judge roused her.

"Let's get you up to your bed," he whispered. "You'll get a better rest there."

She wanted to just stay in the comfy couch, but he kept encouraging her, and she figured the only way to shut him up was to do what he wanted. He helped her up the stairs to make sure that she wouldn't fall and hurt herself.

When Kelli walked into her room, it wasn't cold and foreboding. It was no longer the place she had tried to commit suicide, but the place they had hugged and cried and eaten together; where she had at last started to heal.

Her father pulled the covers back for her and then stretched them up over her once she slipped into bed.

"There. Sleep well, sweetheart. I'll see you in the morning."

"Night, Dad."

"Goodnight."

———

Kelli never would have imagined that she and Lisa, the stuck-up snob, would ever be able to get along with each other, let alone enjoy each other's company. Lisa was a huge brat. And a drama queen. And a pain in Kelli's butt.

But she was also the only one who could even come close to understanding what Kelli had been through in finding out about the switch and then about Preston's criminal behavior in the matter.

They exchanged their stories a bit at a time. Not too much all at once. Lisa's privileged upbringing was just as unbelievable to Kelli as Kelli's slum background was to Lisa.

Kelli told Lisa about the day she had gone home and the judge had followed her in and seen the condition of the house. How off-the-rails Patricia had gone during Kelli's absence.

"Look at this." Kelli showed Lisa the hospital pictures. Both mothers. Both babies. The bassinets side-by-side in the room when the divider curtain was pulled back.

"That's your mom? I mean… my biological mother?" Lisa studied the picture. "I've never seen this before."

"Patricia had it. With the DNA tests and hospital settlement papers."

"All this time… just waiting to be discovered."

"She said she remembered Preston. I doubt if she really did, but… who knows? Her memory is all messed up, so maybe it is easier to remember what happened sixteen years ago than a day ago."

The doorbell rang, and Kelli knew it would be Cassia. She ran down the stairs to get it, but Felicia beat her there.

"Come on up," Kelli invited. "We're just gabbing."

Cassia followed her up to the bedroom and joined them, looking through the pictures and listening to their stories.

"So… you guys are like sisters now," Cassia observed.

Kelli looked at Lisa, remembering how Lisa had freaked out when their father had called them sisters. Lisa gave a little eye roll, obviously remembering the incident as well, but she smiled at Cassia.

"Not sisters," she said. "Twins."

"Well… I guess you were born the same day and have the same two sets of parents… so that *would* make you twins."

Lisa gave Kelli's hair a little tug. "But I'm older. So I get to tell you what to do."

"Watch it," Kelli warned, pushing Lisa's hand away and assuming a defensive posture. "I know Jujitsu."

EPILOGUE

K elli? Is that you?"

Kelli turned around to face the speaker. People hurried past on the busy city sidewalk. It was a young man. His curly hair and twinkling eyes were familiar, but his face was a chiseled man's face now instead of a boy's.

"Les?"

"Wow, look at you!"

Les stared openly at her face, his eyes wide. Kelli was used to that, of course.

For a while, she had considered having the birthmark re-tattooed across her cheek. It was a part of her identity, part of who she was and why her life had gone down the path that it had. Without the birthmark, Preston would have kept her and raised her. She wouldn't have been toughened up by the bullying and stares that she got, not just from kids, but from adults too. She would have been a different person

In the end, she had chosen to transform herself. In every way. But the thing that everyone noticed right from the start was her face.

The tattoo on her face was similar in size and color to the birthmark that had disfigured her for her first sixteen years. But it was the delicate shape of a gorgeous purple butterfly. When Kelli saw herself in the mirror, she felt like it was her, only better. She'd long since gotten rid of the long, wavy locks she had used to camouflage her face, choosing instead a short, easy-care do that better fit her lifestyle.

Les gave her an impulsive hug. "You look so good. You look… happy. Are you? Really?"

Kelli nodded. She sighed. "I try to be. It's tough sometimes. I fight depression. And my new therapist says I have PTSD. But… I like who I am and what I'm doing. I do the best I can."

He linked his arm through hers and they walked comfortably down the sidewalk, as if no time had passed since they had been sixteen and the best of friends.

"What is it you're doing?" Les asked. "What is it you like?"

"Teaching Jujitsu." Kelli laughed. "Only part-time, because I have other responsibilities to keep up with. But that's when I really feel… complete. I run some classes for kids who are… like we were. They're subsidized, so they don't have to scam for the fees like I did. I don't tell them much about my background, but… they know. They can tell. It's amazing to be able to teach these kids self-confidence; how to stand up and defend themselves. The light that comes into their eyes…" She blinked at Les, trying to resist the tears that suddenly threatened. "Well… it's just cool. Seeing them come alive."

"Yeah," Les agreed, studying her face. He touched the tattoo on her cheek. "I know exactly what you mean."

Did you enjoy this book? Reviews and recommendations are vital to making a book successful.

Please leave a review at your favorite book store or review site and share it with your friends.

Don't miss the following bonus material:
Sign up for mailing list to get a free ebook
Read a sneak preview chapter
Other books by P.D. Workman
Learn more about the author

Sign up for my mailing list at pdworkman.com and get Gluten-Free Murder for free!

PREVIEW OF TATTOOED TEARDROPS

BOOK #1 OF THE TAMARA'S TEARDROPS SERIES

Winner of Top Fiction Award, In the Margins Committee, 2016.

CHAPTER 1

(i)

T*AMARA FRENCH HAS BEEN a model inmate throughout her incarceration.*

Great reference. You could go far on that one. Tamara sat on an uncomfortable bench in the brightly-lit lobby waiting for her ride. It was strange being on the other side of the guard booth. She stared at the too-white sneakers that stuck out below her dark pant cuffs, wondering what kind of life she had to look forward to with that ringing endorsement. She jiggled her legs up and down, trying to resist picking her nails. Eventually, a tall, middle-aged woman with a bun came in and stood before her. Tamara stared at her boxy black shoes for a moment before reluctantly looking up at her.

"Tamara?" the woman said.

"Yeah."

"Ready to get out of here?"

"I guess."

"I expected a bit more enthusiasm," the social worker said with a hint of a smile in the corners of her lipsticked mouth.

"I'm sorta nervous," Tamara said.

"I guess that's understandable. Come on, let's go."

Tamara sat there for another moment, then finally stood and followed

331

the woman out of the juvenile facility. She got in the car and buckled up, holding her bag tightly on her lap.

The social worker introduced herself, but Tamara paid no attention, completely forgetting her name the next minute. The woman attempted small talk a few times, but Tamara turned on the radio and stared out the window, freezing the social worker out. Eventually the woman got the message, and stopped trying to engage her.

(ii)

They pulled up in front of a brick house that was at least a hundred years old and needed some work. There had been an attempt made at land-scaping, with some flowers and bushes bunched around the concrete steps leading up to the porch and the front door. There was peeling paint on the fence and mailbox post.

"Here we are," the social worker announced. "Let's go in."

Tamara unbuckled and got out slowly. The social worker took her in, knocking on the front door and entering without waiting for an answer.

"Hello, Marion, come on in," a woman's voice called from up above. "I'll be right down."

Tamara stood beside the social worker, waiting. She held her paper bag awkwardly at her side, wishing that she didn't have anything to hold onto. She made a show of examining the front hall and living room of the house, but in all honesty, she didn't care what it looked like. It wasn't prison. Her concern was not with the house, but what the foster parents were going to be like. The front room was fairly neat and presentable. No children's toys scattered about. A load of laundry neatly folded in the basket sitting on the couch. The TV shut behind the doors of an entertainment center so it would not be the central focus of the room. The furnishings were nice, not thrift store or destroyed. There were footsteps on the stairs, and Tamara looked up for her first glimpse of her foster mother.

Mrs. Henson had a pleasant, round face. Blond hair that had been lightly styled in an attempt to hide that it was starting to thin. She didn't look more than forty. She was overweight, but not grossly. She just looked soft and comfortable. She was wearing a sweater and pants, and inconse-quential gold jewelry. She didn't look anything like Mrs. Baker, but that was no guarantee.

332

"Hello!" her voice rang out cheerfully.

"Gerry, this is Tamara," Marion introduced as Mrs. Henson reached the bottom of the stairs. "Tamara, Mrs. Henson."

"Hey," Tamara muttered, without meeting her eyes. "Where do you want me?"

"Your bedroom is at the top of the stairs. First door on the right," Mrs. Henson offered. Tamara made the trek up the stairs. There was a dark wooden bannister, ornately carved. Not too scarred for being in a foster home. Tamara turned at the top of the stairs and opened the door to her right.

There was a bed and a crib, and Tamara stood there, her heart speeding up, wondering if she'd been sent to the wrong room. Surely they wouldn't have given her a room with a crib in it? She could almost see Julie's still form lying on the high mattress… Mrs. Henson was there a moment later, having said a quick good-bye to Marion. She breathed a little heavily after her trip back up the stairs.

"Go on in," Mrs. Henson encouraged. "We sometimes take teen moms, to help teach them how to take care of their babies. We don't have any right now, so you get this room. That way you don't have to share."

Tamara walked into the room. The walls were a light green, freshly painted, with a white board wainscoting all the way around it. There was a pull-down blind with gauzy green curtains around the window. Tamara tossed her bag onto the bed, where it sat looking pitiful and inadequate.

"The others will be getting home soon," Mrs. Henson offered. "I'll introduce you then."

"Yes, ma'am."

"I'm happy to have you join us, Tamara. I was very impressed with your file."

Sure. It was certain to be the last place she went that anyone was impressed with her prison record. She'd wowed them all at her parole hearing. There had been tears, and not all of them hers. So many of the inmates protested their innocence and refused to take responsibility or express remorse at their parole hearings. Tamara had been working on her performance for three years, and it was good. The board's vote was unanimous. Now she was free. But to what kind of life?

Mrs. Henson stirred, making Tamara jump, startled. They both looked at each other, not knowing what to say. Mrs. Henson smiled and nodded.

"Make yourself at home," she encouraged, motioning around the room.

Tamara nodded. Mrs. Henson backed off, and left her alone. Tamara stretched out on the freshly-made bed to wait. If there was one thing she was used to doing, it was waiting.

(iii)

There were no bells that rang to mark the passage of time and the transition from one activity to another. Instead, disconcertingly, it flowed along with small shifts and gradual transitions. Tamara heard the front door open and close several times, with voices reaching her ears even through the closed bedroom door. Mrs. Henson did most of the talking and others answered her questions or made comments during the pauses. Tamara couldn't tell what any of them were saying, just the tone of voice. They all seemed to be casual and relaxed.

There was a knock on Tamara's bedroom door, and before she could get up to answer it, Mrs. Henson poked her head in.

"We're going to get dinner going," she said. "Why don't you come down and help? Then you can meet everyone."

Tamara studied her for a moment, assessing her options. Was it a choice? Was there a consequence for not complying? She was so unused to making her own decisions that she wasn't sure what to do when faced with one.

"Come on," Mrs. Henson encouraged, motioning for Tamara to come.

Tamara got up slowly and followed her foster mother down the stairs and to the kitchen. She was suddenly confronted with a whole pack of new people to meet. All bigger and older than her. Tamara made an effort to unclench her fists and not look confrontational. This wasn't juvie. She didn't have to prove herself physically here.

It hadn't occurred to Tamara when she had met Mrs. Henson that the foster children would not all be white like her. But of course, she already knew the statistics. There were more non-white children in foster care, and very few non-white parents. So they couldn't pair black children with black parents. Tamara was intimidated by all of the dark faces looking back at her. She wasn't prejudiced, but juvie had taught her to be acutely aware of race relations, and how her white-faced, blond-haired presence could be aggravating to others. They would immediately judge her as stuck-up, privileged, and ignorant.

Tamara was fifteen, and not tall. There were only four other children, Tamara realized, not the mob that she had originally perceived them as. They were all bigger than her. Most of them taller than Mrs. Henson. Studying their faces, Tamara figured that they were seventeen or eighteen. One boy seemed even too old to be eighteen.

"Everyone," Mrs. Henson said, "this is Tamara, our new foster child. I know you'll all make her feel comfortable and help her get settled in."

They all nodded, smiled, and waved. Tamara nodded back.

"Hey."

Her voice was hoarse, the greeting barely audible. Tamara wasn't sure any of them had heard her. She nodded again and didn't repeat the greeting.

"Okay, are you ready?" Mrs. Henson asked with a wide smile. "This is Nita," a Hispanic girl with long hair and perfectly plucked eyebrows, "Deshawn," the darkest face, a girl with cornrows and a brilliant white smile, "Jason," black skin, close cropped black hair, probably eighteen, "and Harry." Harry seemed a particularly non-ethnic name for a boy who appeared to be some mixture of black, Hispanic, and native. He smiled nicely for her, but his resting face was serious, contemplative. He was the one that Tamara was sure must be older than eighteen. He should have already aged out of the system.

Tamara nodded again and swallowed. Now what? Was she supposed to repeat them back? Greet each one separately? Shake hands? Tamara just stood there, lost, then looked at Mrs. Henson for direction.

"Okay, let's get started on dinner," Mrs. Henson suggested. "Nita, why don't you show Tamara where the dishes are, and she can help you set the table…" She went on, but Tamara didn't hear the rest of the instructions she gave to the remaining kids. She had her instructions. Go with Nita and set the table. She made her way across the room to Nita, and Nita smiled at her.

"Welcome," she said in a low voice that was almost a whisper. "I hope you like it here."

Tamara nodded. "Yeah. Thanks."

"Well, come on. The dishes are in this cupboard here, and the glasses, and the cutlery." Nita indicated each location.

"How many...?" Tamara asked. She cleared her throat. "Is there a Mr. Henson? Or anyone else?"

"Yeah, Jesse will be home for dinner. That's Mr. Henson. So seven altogether."

Tamara counted out the plates and trucked them over to the table, where she put them down carefully. Her hands shook slightly as she set them down, and it was an effort not to let them clatter. There was a baby's high chair, pushed against the wall. Tamara looked away from it and continued with her work, breathing shallowly. Setting the table only took a couple of minutes, and then Mrs. Henson gave them various other small tasks until everything started coming together for the dinner. She looked at her watch.

"Thanks guys. Take a break for about twenty minutes. Then everything should be done cooking, Jesse will be home, and we'll eat."

The kids dispersed. Tamara headed back up to her bedroom. Deshawn stopped ahead of Tamara, blocking her way into her bedroom.

"Do you need anything?" she asked Tamara.

Tamara shook her head.

"Sometimes... people don't come here with very much," Deshawn said. "Missus buys up extra toothbrushes and all, and we all share clothes..." She glanced over Tamara's figure. "My pants won't do you much good, but if you want a shirt, some accessories..."

Tamara stood there and contemplated the idea. For three years, she had worn nothing but an orange prison jumpsuit. Social Services had provided her with two very basic changes of clothing for her release. T-shirt, pants, socks, underthings. One pair of white tennis shoes. It was more fashion than Tamara had access to in all her time in juvie, but she was aware that it was sorely inadequate for a teenager on the outside.

Deshawn made an encouraging motion.

"Come on. Let's see if there's anything you want to borrow," she said.

Tamara followed her to one of the other bedrooms.

"Nita and I share the room," Deshawn commented. Nita was not there; maybe she had gone to watch TV or something. The room was painted sky blue. There was a utilitarian set of bunk beds, a couple of dressers cluttered with scarves, jewelry, and books, and a closet that was jammed full. The knobs on either side of the open closet door had been pressed into use to hold more hangers full of clothes. "It's mostly thrift store," Deshawn said, "but you can find some pretty good stuff if you look hard enough. Sorry, it's sort of a mess. Come on. See what you like."

Tamara went to the closet and looked over the hangers full of brightly-colored clothing. It didn't appear that either Deshawn or Nita went for anything understated.

"If you want t-shirts, they're in the dresser," Deshawn pointed, "and just grab whatever you see that you like. Just bring it back or throw it in the laundry when you're done with it."

Tamara saw herself in the mirror mounted on the back of the closet door. There hadn't been any full-length mirrors at juvie. And the only mirrors that had been there were polished metal or plastic, and you could never really see your reflection very well. Tamara had grown up a lot in juvie. She wasn't the soft, shy little farm girl she had been when she went to the Bakers. They had changed her. And juvie had changed her. The years had not been particularly kind ones. But she had developed a figure now, and was going to have to learn how to dress it up, instead of simply shrouding it in a jumpsuit. She had tattoos and piercings that she hadn't had before her incarceration. Her hair was dull and lank, like everybody else's in juvie. Tamara wound one lock around her finger, staring at the stranger reflected in the mirror.

"Why don't we do something with your hair?" Deshawn suggested. "There's not much time, but if we blow-dry, we could be done before supper."

Tamara raked her fingers through her limp blonde hair, disgusted with it.

"Yeah. Could we?"

"Mmm-hmm," Deshawn agreed with emphasis. "We'll shampoo it in the bathroom, and use leave-in conditioner…" she led the way out into the hallway, still chattering away to herself what they would do. Tamara just followed.

Tamara knelt by the tub while Deshawn used the hand-held shower attachment to quickly wet her hair down. The warm water felt so good on Tamara's scalp, she wished she could get in for a full shower, and just luxuriate in it for hours. Three years of quick, cold showers. But Deshawn turned off the water way too soon, and applied a fruity shampoo with strong, capable fingers; working it in and then rinsing it back out. She handed Tamara a towel and while Tamara rubbed her hair,

Deshawn rifled through the myriad toiletries lining the back of the counter, the medicine cabinet, and a couple of deep wicker baskets under the sink.

(iv)

"Girls! Dinner!" the impatient call came again from downstairs.

Deshawn poked her head out the door.

"Just one more minute," she called back. "We'll be right down!"

She returned her attention to Tamara.

"Okay, just sit still for one more minute, girl," she instructed.

Tamara sat frozen, while Deshawn wound sections of her hair around the fat curling iron, holding it and then releasing. There was no way that she was going to be done the whole thing in another minute. But Deshawn worked quickly, sure of herself.

"That will do it for now," she announced.

She laid the curling iron down on the counter and unplugged it from the wall. Standing Tamara up, Deshawn shuffled her over and turned her to face the mirror.

"Ta-da!"

Tamara looked with astonishment at the face in the mirror. She was amazed at what a big difference a hairstyle could make. She still didn't have on any make-up, hadn't changed her clothes or accessories, all she had done was let Deshawn clean and style her hair. Her image in the mirror was no longer so harsh and plain.

"You're gorgeous," Deshawn gushed. "You've got really good color and proportions. We can have a lot of fun glamming you up. For now, this will do."

Standing behind Tamara, Deshawn used her fingers to wind and read-just a couple of curls. She lowered her head so that it was on the same level as Tamara's, and gave her a smile.

"What do you think?"

"It's… it's really pretty. Thanks," Tamara said. She cleared her throat, realizing that she was whispering. She had learned in juvie to use a strong, confident voice, not to be soft or timid. The Henson's home was so different in atmosphere, she felt like she was in a library or something. That she needed to be quiet to avoid upsetting the peace of the place.

"Come on, we've got to get down to dinner, or Missus will not be happy!"

Tamara followed Deshawn back downstairs and to the dining room table that she and Nita had set. It was now covered with serving dishes, and everyone was seated, waiting for them. All eyes turned to Tamara as she looked at the three empty chairs, trying to decide which one she should take.

"Tamara, doesn't that look lovely," Mrs. Henson complimented. "Here, sit down. These boys will eat everything before we even get a bite, if they have to wait much longer."

She gestured toward the empty chair nearest to her, and Tamara went over and sat down. Deshawn took what appeared to be her usual seat, beside Nita, which left one empty chair at the table of eight. Tamara looked for the first time at Mr. Henson. Slim, on the tall side. Handsome boyish face. Short-cropped curly red hair. He smiled at Tamara.

"Welcome, Tamara. I'm Jesse."

Tamara nodded, looking down at her empty plate. Her stomach tightened and it was suddenly hard to breathe. The only men that she had been around for three years had been guards, doctors, and administrators. The last man she had lived with before that… her foster father, Mr. Baker… that had been a bad scene. A very bad scene. Tamara swallowed. She tried to slow her breathing, but it just made her breath louder in her own ears. She was sure everyone would be hear how loudly and quickly she was breathing.

"Dig in," Mrs. Henson said, and Harry and Jason acted like two Rottweilers just told to attack, diving into the serving dishes immediately. Conversation started up around the table, and rather than trying to follow any of it, Tamara just let it wash over her like white noise. She served up small portions of each of the dishes that passed her, and dutifully passed them on.

"So tell us about your last home, Tamara," Nita said. "Where did you come here from?"

Tamara looked at Mrs. Henson. The woman just smiled and gave her a small nod, and didn't jump in to help her out. If Tamara didn't want to answer questions, she was going to have to be assertive and speak up. The conversations around the table quieted as the others paused to listen for her answer. Tamara swallowed a very dry mouthful of potatoes. They stuck right in the middle of her chest.

"I wasn't at a home," she said finally, careful to keep her voice up, not to duck her head down. She was not vulnerable and had nothing to be ashamed of. She was strong and knew how to take care of herself. She had just as much right to be here as any of them. "I was in juvie."

There was an initial silence, and then conversations started back up again without further comment on Tamara's answer.

"Sorry," Nita said. "I didn't know."

"It's okay," Tamara said, shaking her head. "It's not a secret. That's where I was."

Nita nodded.

"Most of us have been in trouble at one time or another."

Tamara glanced around at their faces. None of them looked particularly troubled. They seemed happy and relaxed. At peace with themselves. Maybe they had been in trouble before, and maybe they hadn't. You couldn't always tell by looking at someone.

"Harry's probably spent the most time in juvie," Deshawn contributed, nodding to her brother. "How much time, Harry?"

"All together?" Harry questioned, laughing. "I don't know. Longest stint was two years. But I had plenty of shorter stays before that."

Tamara studied him more closely. He met her eyes and nodded.

"Harry's twenty," Mrs. Henson said without being asked. "So he's not officially a foster child anymore. But we told him he could stay on here while he does some more schooling and gets on his feet."

Tamara nodded, looking back down at her plate.

"That's really nice of you."

"It's to our benefit too. Harry contributes a lot to the family, and since he's working part-time, he's also paying a bit of rent to help keep us afloat. So it works both ways."

Tamara bit into some sort of casserole.

"I guess you'll learn about everyone's backgrounds gradually," Mrs. Henson said. "We try to be open with each other. Everybody's been through some pretty tough stuff. We don't judge. We just try to help."

"That's cool," Tamara said, pushing her dinner around on her plate. She wasn't hungry.

She watched everyone else chow down, and conversations flowed back away from her again. Tamara watched for the appropriate time to leave the table. There was no end-of-dinner bell anymore. She had to relearn all the social graces. How to judge the end of a conversation. When one could politely leave the dinner table. How long she could look at someone before they decided she was being too aggressive. It was like living in a foreign country. A dangerous foreign country.

"Not very hungry?" Mrs. Henson observed, as dinner conversation started to peter out.

Tamara looked down at her plate, still nearly full.

"No. I'm sorry… it's good… I just feel kind of… my stomach hurts."

"It's all right. It takes time to adjust. You can scrape it into the garbage. Nita can show you where. Everyone rinses their own plates and puts them in the dishwasher."

"Sure," Tamara agreed. She stood up, grabbing her plate, and Nita got up and led the way back into the kitchen, where they took care of their dishes. Tamara looked back at the dining table. "Do you want help with clean-up?" she asked Mrs. Henson. "Or would I be in the way?"

"Of course you can help. Usually, I'd probably tell you to go do your homework while I cleared, but you don't have any today, so why don't you and I clean up together?"

Tamara nodded, and she and Mrs. Henson bussed the serving dishes back to the kitchen, found lids for things, and put them into the fridge. Mrs. Henson turned the dishwasher on and wiped down the dining room table.

"You can watch some TV or take some 'down' time. In bed at nine, and lights out at ten."

"Okay," Tamara agreed.

She wandered around the house a bit, but wasn't comfortable sitting down with anybody else, and so she made her way back to her bedroom. As she approached, the door to the other girls' bedroom opened. Nita peeked out.

"Hey," she said. "You need anything? Do you have pajamas?"

Tamara shook her head.

"No," she admitted. "If I could borrow a t-shirt or something…"

"You bet. Come in."

Nita opened the door the rest of the way for her, and Tamara went in. Tamara looked down at Nita's feet, nails freshly painted and toes spread apart while they dried. Nita giggled and hobbled on her heels over to the dresser.

"You want to do yours?" she asked. She pulled out a handful of shirts and tossed them at Tamara.

"No. Thanks," Tamara said, fumbling with the shirts to see what her options were. "I'm going to hit the sack."

She found herself strangely unable to choose one of the shirts. There were three of them. They were all cute. Any one of them would work. All she had to do was decide which of the three she liked best. Nita was watching her, head cocked slightly.

"The blue one is a really good color for you," she suggested.

Not the blue one. Tamara looked at the other two. She didn't know which she wanted, but she had to decide before Nita made another suggestion. She had to make her own choice. Tamara tossed the blue one back to Nita, and with a knot in her stomach, tossed Nita the pink one too. Tamara looked down at the purple and blue patterned shirt in her hands.

"This one is good," she said.

She felt a little sick. Worried that she had made the wrong choice. How silly was that, to be worried that she had picked the wrong t-shirt to wear in the privacy of her own bedroom? But she was. She had an overwhelming feeling of dread.

"Have a good sleep," Nita said with a smile.

"Thanks."

Tamara went back to her room. She changed into the t-shirt, long enough to reach her mid-thighs. She lay down on the bed and stared at the ceiling. There would be no bell ringing to tell her when to go to sleep. Would her body know when it was time, without the bell? Would she be able to adjust to a new schedule? Not feeling the least bit tired, Tamara lay staring at the ceiling, twitching her foot and waiting for sleep.

———

Tattooed Teardrops, Book #1 of the *Tamara's Teardrops* series by P.D. Workman can be purchased at pdworkman.com

ABOUT THE AUTHOR

Award-winning and USA Today bestselling author P.D. (Pamela) Workman writes riveting mystery/suspense and young adult books dealing with mental illness, addiction, abuse, and other real-life issues. For as long as she can remember, the blank page has held an incredible allure and from a very young age she was trying to write her own books.

Workman wrote her first complete novel at the age of twelve and continued to write as a hobby for many years. She started publishing in 2013. She has won several literary awards from Library Services for Youth in Custody for her young adult fiction. She currently has over 70 published titles and can be found at pdworkman.com.

Born and raised in Alberta, Workman has been married for over 25 years and has one son.

————

Please visit P.D. Workman at pdworkman.com to see what else she is working on, to join her mailing list, and to link to her social networks.

————

If you enjoyed this book, please take the time to recommend it to other purchasers with a review or star rating and share it with your friends!